THE DELIGHTED

Feral Space Series, book 2

James Worrad

Cover art by Duncan Halleck
Cover design by The Gilded Quill

James Worrad
Visit my author page at www castrumpress.com/james-worrad

Printed in the United Kingdom

First Printing: Aug 2018
Castrum Press

ISBN-13 978-1-9123274-7-8

CONTENTS

PART ONE

ROOF GARDEN

CHAPTER ONE

"What *is* the matter?" the Ashemi asked, frustrated.

Gleam, the persona bindi on his forehead shining white, leaned against the wall of the tower's stairwell. He was hunched, practically on all fours, panting deeply.

"Moon," he said between breaths. "My brother. Scared."

"Triunes," the Ashemi muttered, a low whine from his sculpted mouth. He looked Gleam in the eyes. "You're in ascendancy, are you not, Gleam? Control him."

"Not... always easy." Gleam met his eyes. "Let's go back."

"Absolutely not."

"So arrogant," Gleam said. "Always."

"I'll pretend you never uttered that." The Ashemi had every right to dismember Gleam.

"Please," Gleam pleaded. "Go up there alone."

"No," the Ashemi said.

"Why not?"

"Because we have the Envoy where we want him. And..." The Ashemi shook his wrought-iron head with its rattling hair. "I need you."

"Thank you." Gleam's breathing seemed to subside.

"You've been the pain of my brief existence on this world," the Ashemi said. "But... you have uses, I suppose."

"Your Ashemi..."

"Yes?"

"You're a good man," Gleam said.

"I'm Ashemi. A man no longer."

"You *are* a good man," Gleam said.

Whatever helped him and his brothers cope. "Are you ready?"

"Yes." Gleam wiped his lips, looked up the stairwell with a most foreboding expression.

"Well then. Come on."

Gleam nodded. "Yes."

Up on his tropical roof garden, the Envoy was holding another soiree, the sky a cloudless blue beyond. There were more Ingresine, that ruling breed of Culakwun, than last time. Some danced, some cavorted on the many stone chaises longues; others stood in circles, chatting and cackling.

The Envoy stood amongst the largest of these circles, regaling his tall and sinuous peers with some nonsense.

"You shall all be cared for," he was saying, "perfectly mollycoddled, I tell you. I'll see to it. Just wait and--"

"Pelisier, *darrrling*," a woman beside him said, that kohl-eyed one, hair dancing with float beads, her bare chest painted silver. "Look who's arrived."

The Envoy turned to see.

"Oh!" he said. "Oh, everybody, look who it is! The Ashemi and his little three-head!"

The garden erupted with chatter. With tittering.

"War, with armour wise, conquers worlds," the Envoy said. "Desire, a poisoned wine, keeps them."

"And that is?" the Ashemi asked.

"An ancient poet of this world. Opaque Savard." The Envoy shrugged. "Fitting, yes?"

"Depressing." The Ashemi stopped two strides from the Envoy. "I have information that may interest you."

The Envoy clapped his ringed fingers with mock delight. "Gather around," he told his friends. "He brings news."

The Ingresines gambolled and sashayed and giggled over to them, forming a circle around the Ashemi and Gleam. He felt Gleam draw closer to his side.

"Pearl stole from you," the Ashemi said, and he was pleased when the Envoy's smug face melted to a frown.

"How so?" the Envoy asked.

"The information he stole from the Trinity House came not from the general memory lattice of the building, but from the sub-lattice of this very tower."

"I don't understand," the Envoy said. "Our part of the building is protected."

The Ingresines looked at one another--many theatrically, like bad actors. These people seemed eternally fake.

"Such was Pearl's skill," the Ashemi said, "though a turncoat on your staff would have been necessary. I suspect his visit to you to beg sanctuary was nothing of the sort. Presumably that was when he took said information."

The Envoy shook his head, stared at his own bare feet. "He had a comb. I thought that odd. Most likely his device, whatever its nature." He sighed and, with a look of damaged pride, asked: "May I know what this information was?"

"Sorry," the Ashemi said. "We've still no idea." A lie, but it was to the Ashemi's advantage not to mention the lockwyrm signature Pearl's mother had alluded to. Ignorant, the Envoy would have to consider the information almost anything. He would be pliable.

"You *do* know," the Envoy said. "And that's to the advantage of the divine mistress you serve, naturally." He looked at the Ashemi's face like he was its dissatisfied sculptor. "I could ask you again and again for a million years, and those gilded lips would never move."

"They don't move now," the Ashemi said.

"Semantics." The Envoy uttered the word like a curse. "I won't tolerate such crudity. Speaking of which, I daresay you won't tell me who Pearl's feral stranger is, either. The one who visited the Savard pile."

"I could," the Ashemi said, "but you wouldn't thank me." He looked at all those gathered around. There was something in their expressions, their inbred elegant faces, he couldn't fathom. Too long from his real body, perhaps, whoever he had been. It had eroded his sense for body language. "None of you would."

"Well?" the Envoy said.

"Pearl's mother claimed the feral was a Hoidrac in disguise," the Ashemi said.

"What?" The Envoy was incredulous; so too his cronies.

"The Dissenter. The banished one." The Ashemi let his words hang.

He had to wonder whether so many intakes of breath might suck all the air out of the force field-encased garden. He'd have been delighted.

The Envoy chuckled.

"Why laugh?" the Ashemi asked.

"Because I choose not to weep. To scream. I'm reduced to speechlessness."

"I see," the Ashemi said. "I'll have to find a new aim in life."

"Ashemi, please," the Envoy said, "be serious now. Look... it can't be..." He waved his hand as if to move the concept along.

"I agree. But it can't be any of us, either. Neither of our patron Hoidrac would permit the impersonation of..." The Ashemi waved his hand in imitation of the Envoy.

"So a mere feral then," the Envoy said. "An outsider."

"And there lies the issue," the Ashemi said. "I've yet to probe the witness' mind, but let's assume Pearl's mother's memory, or perception at the time of the incident, has been tampered with. What then?"

"By the Eye... a feral with access to Geode technology. What *sickness...*"

"Dissenter or feral," the Ashemi said, "I'm certain you appreciate the need for us to combine our resources."

The Envoy nodded, wagging a manicured finger. "Might I show you something?" He whistled, and a Geode-fish swam through the air toward them. "You may as well see this now."

The fish, with its protective armour of silver and amethyst, projected an image. A succession of images. A silent moving collage of Pearl on different days, different nights. First glancing, then talking, then kissing, then copulating in many ways with the same body.

The body of Gleam-Glare-Moon.

The Ashemi heard Gleam wince beside him.

"Switch this off," the Ashemi said to the Envoy.

"Spoilsport," the Envoy said. "They get awfully unbridled as the footage proceeds. Trust me, I've studied."

"Me too," the kohl-eyed woman beside him said. She looked at the Envoy. "Often together."

"Occasionally in groups," the Envoy added. "Our reconstruc--"

The Ashemi punched the fish. It burst in a haze of geode energy. Its armour hit the tiles, splashing purple ichor in a tiny halo.

"Gleam," the Ashemi said. He could think of nothing else. A fool. For the first time he felt a fool.

"Shall I tell you a secret?" the Envoy asked. He looked around as if some trespasser might hear. "He's one of ours. Mmm. A spy."

"Impossible," the Ashemi said.

"Oh, he really is. You know nothing, Ashemi. Not even what you *don't* know. Little Three-head here"--he pointed at Gleam--"isn't... even... a Triune. He *pretends* he has brothers. An astonishing performance. Gleam's not even Zahriran. Just another low-breed from Culakwun."

"Absurd," the Ashemi said. He looked down at Gleam.

Gleam's face was in his hands.

The Ashemi looked back at the Envoy, all these Culakwun scum. "How?"

The Envoy snorted as if it were the most stupid question. "Excessive cleverness, of course." His cronies guffawed and chortled and tittered. "Altering the memories of relevant people here in the Trinity House."

"That would take everyone," the Ashemi said.

"You'd think, wouldn't you?" the Envoy said. "But, oh, it's *boring* to explain." He checked his fingernails. "But telling me the nature of that stolen information might rouse me from lethargy..."

The Ashemi ignored him. "Gleam, let's go. You've answers to give."

"Oh, I don't think so," the Envoy said. "You'd be remiss in your duties, sir."

"How?"

"Gleam is involved," the Envoy said. "Once you informed me it was our own information that had been filched, I knew it was him. A double agent. We've a right to punish him, as have you. In fact..." He looked to his peers. "I demand both."

The Ingresines hissed and tittered. Serpents with wine bowls.

"Not a chance," the Ashemi said.

The Envoy's demeanour became matter-of-fact. "Look it up, darling," he muttered from the side of his mouth. His usual deportment returned. "This is a diplomatic incident of outrageous proportions. He must be punished here. He must be punished now. As I, speaking for all Culakwun, demand. Why..." He gazed at the Ashemi, his eyes like some innocent ingénue's. "You wouldn't want to upset our two divine patrons, now."

The Ashemi could feel it. A weight. The weight of the living gods, perhaps all of them, pressing on his being. The Delighted themselves. What this monster requested was mandated by divinity. In this, their warring patrons--Pheoni and Mohatoi--seemed one.

"A peace must be kept," the Ashemi said.

"A peace must be kept." The Envoy turned to the kohl-eyed woman with the writhing hair. "Bring the whip."

"Bring the whip!" she shouted, and every Ingresine cheered.

Had they expected something like this all along? How much had the Envoy planned? He had seemed a fop, a dandy, yet there were depths to this man, depths abyssally cold.

A boy brought the whip on a silver plate: thick and black, worn from use. Two Phoskmuj--those humans bred for cruelty--loped on either side of the boy. They carried scythe rifles.

"Here," the Envoy said, pointing to the floor beside him. The kohl-eyed woman and two other Ingresine seized Gleam. Kohl-eye took a blade from one of the Phoskmuj and sliced the back of Gleam's top, stripped his back bare. Gleam did nothing to resist, even when thrown to the tiles. The partygoers stepped back, forming a wide circle. Servants brought more drinks.

The boy stood before the Ashemi. He offered the plate with its whip.

The Ashemi looked at the Envoy.

"Oh, come on," the Envoy said, "you *are* the willing hand of the Hoidrac, are you not?"

"*You* demand it. *You* do it."

"I'm really too humble," the Envoy said.

The Ashemi would have replied, but Gleam began to speak.

"I loved him," he said. "I loved him. I loved him, your Ashemi."

The Envoy sighed. "We get the picture, love."

The Ashemi took the whip. Better him, if it had to be performed at all. "How many times?"

"Until the Hoidrac are satisfied," the Envoy replied. "I'm certain you'll feel it when they are." He took a drink from a passing servant. "Though, presumptuous as I dare be, perhaps they may show mercy. *If* you were to tell me the nature of the information Pearl stole." He sipped, wound his surgically stretched torso so very playfully.

Never. The Ashemi had almost no handle on events here, but he knew whatever was going on, he wouldn't divulge. He felt no weight on his soul from the Hoidrac to do so. It remained his choice. All he might cling to.

Gleam shivered. He wept upon the tiles. The Ashemi wanted to chide him, demand answers, but not in front of these monsters, not for their delight. Gleam's back, he noticed, was pit-marked. Not deformed, exactly, but devoid of health's shine. That was why he had hid his back in the sauna. The low-breeds of Culakwun were often punished with skin diseases.

The Ashemi raised the whip. He couldn't feel pain, of course. He hadn't felt Silver's, back at the cottage. Perhaps he wouldn't feel Gleam's.

Nothing. Nothing made sense. Nothing. How could Gleam be a Culakwun, a spy? How could so many--

"Come on, Ashemi," the Envoy said. "You're being melodramatic."

Come on, the Ingresines called. *Come on.*

"Let him!" Gleam shouted. "Just let him do it!"

Ooooh, cooed the crowd.

"Poor wretch," the Envoy said to Gleam. "Do you really think Pearl would suffer like this for *you?*"

"Enough," Gleam said. "Enough."

He leaped up. A razor fell from his sleeve and into his hand. He flew at the Envoy.

The Envoy swerved, seized Gleam's wrist, pulled something golden from his own hair and drove it into Gleam's neck. Gleam shook, grunted.

The mask of foppery left the Envoy. His expression was an animal's: wide grin, hungry eyes. The truth of him lay in those eyes. Nightmare's truth.

He pulled his fist away, and Gleam dropped on his back to the floor. Blood—bright arterial--jetted from a hole in his neck. It fell like calligraphy upon the tiles. The Envoy studied his work, his fist tight around a thin gold blade that had posed as a hairpin moments before.

The Ashemi ran--as best his form could--over to Gleam. He knelt, tried to press silver fingers against the wound to stem the flow. Useless for the task.

Gleam reached out, touched the Ashemi's lifeless face. Unfelt.

"You Karist," Gleam said. "Suh... Youkrist..."

"What? Gleam..."

"Youkri..."

Life left him.

The Ashemi closed Gleam's eyes. His talons scratched his brow.

"Oh, happy day!" the Envoy proclaimed, lifting his bloody arms high. "Happiest day! Victory is ours!"

The roof garden broke into celebration. Music started up, from where the Ashemi had no clue. Horns, haspichols, springed instruments.

Objects flickered in the Ashemi's vision. Rose petals. Ingresines among the throng cast them over him. The rest danced and sang.

A shadow crossed the Ashemi. Looking up, he saw the Envoy. The man's smile was maddeningly ambiguous. The Ashemi realised he'd no clue who this man truly was, or what he was. He never had.

"Explain," the Ashemi said to him. "Just... *explain*."

"Trust me," the Envoy replied, leaning down. His expression became blank. "It's funnier if you never know."

He placed a fingertip between the Ashemi's eyes.

PART TWO

SILVERCLOUD

James Worrad

CHAPTER TWO

*A*nother blast. Further off this time, but it shook the gloomy corridor like a dog with a chew toy.

Hargie near-toppled, held onto that asshole Yan. The man didn't budge an inch. Seemed he didn't about anything.

"We can't let her die in there," Hargie told him. He slapped the door beside them, the one Sparkle slumbered behind. "She'll choke."

Yan said nothing.

"Quit the hardass shit. Damn crybaby." Yeah. Crying before, about a woman. Hargie took a guess. "Kend."

Yan looked at him.

"Woman in there matters to Kend, right? Her whole hoobie-moomie project? Gonna be the one tell her she chewed on vac'? Huh?"

"Quick," Yan said. He blinked as the door opened.

Hargie belted through the threshold, across the white lab.

He didn't see Sparkle at first. Then he saw the soles of her stupid loopy-scoop shoes, jutting out of the cellophane tube atop a table built into the floor.

"How do we--"

"Quiet," Yan said. "Save air."

Good point. Hargie ran over and grabbed Sparkle's ankles. He pulled on them, but couldn't move her an inch.

"How we--"

The index finger on Yan's black Spindly suit stretched into a blade. With one slash, the tube split and fell apart.

"Smoosh," Hargie said.

Sparkle slept. He shook her shoulders, called her name. Both names: Sparkle, Issaressi. Her lids shook, and there were her eyes: brown and wet, trying to make sense of the world.

"Get up," Hargie said. "Danger here."

She didn't seem to recognise him. But she did as he said, clambering from the table and rolling off, onto the floor. "Dead legs."

Hargie kneeled and started rubbing them.

She stood. "Not that dead, Stukes."

"Quickly," Yan barked.

Light, blue and ghostly, filled the lab. Hargie braced for another burst, but it never came. An aura stretched out across the far wall, rippling like some horizontal pond in a breeze.

"We gotta dust," Hargie said, gripping her wrist.

She gripped his. "Wait," she said, staring at the wall. "Wait."

He looked. Concentric circles rippled from the wall's centre, where the light glowed brightest. "What is that?"

Sparkle just smiled.

"Go now," Yan said. For the first time, he sounded truly frightened. Hargie wasn't gonna judge him.

A silver cone pushed its way out of the aura. More followed: a long thin body, with an array of fins circling its midriff. Eyeless, mouthless, the only detail on the fish's pewter hide was a glowing pattern of alien design. Hargie's eyes wanted to fall into that pattern. Fall and gibber.

Sparkle broke from Hargie's grip and stepped forward, her arms wide and welcoming.

"Deliver us to our rulers," she said to the thing.

Speak for yourself, Hargie thought.

Its tail, free of the wall now, darted back and forth in razor-tipped delight. A ball of red light appeared below the silver fish's snout.

"Oh," Sparkle said.

Oh?

The wall to their left rippled with more unreal light. A flash of silver and the fish-thing ruptured, energy shooting up from its back. It darted about the lab like someone had tapped its bowl.

Another fish. It had come out of another aura rippling on the other wall. It too had a light-ball spinning just below its snout--green this time-- and whenever the ball flashed, chunks of the first fish detonated.

"Run," Sparkle said.

***

"MELID."

Melid opened her eyes. A corpse cartwheeled languidly in the air before her: a male, his neck broken. She'd broken it. Marbles of blood floated about the control core, constellations of scarlet. The way Melid's face felt, a fair deal of it might be her own.

"Melid." Kend's voice.

But Kend wasn't Kend anymore.

Melid jolted, struggled, found her wrists and ankles bound. She yelled, struggled again. Useless. She had a gentle hum in her ears, which Melid took to mean a serv-form's tentacles had her wrists, neck, and ankles bound.

Kend's face--smiling, lips cut--came into view.

"Melid," she said.

Kend, yet not Kend. Not anymore, and who knew for how long. She was but a cell in a thing, a horror. A kancer.

Melid scowled but, in truth, she knew her own fear unmistakable. Perhaps the thing fed off it.

23

"Kill me," Melid told it. "Why waste time?"

"Consummation offer genuine," Kend said, stroking her lip.

"Truly, friend," said a voice behind Melid. Female, one of the three remaining Utiles.

"But not--" A male voice, a Utile in the right of her vision.

"--how you thought," Kend finished. She shrugged almost apologetically. She emoted a black amusement. They all did, identically.

Melid hissed. So many layers. So many Kends. Konsensus Kend: proud and loyal. Below, Kend of disconnected Silvercloud: brave, a visionary, pioneer of individuality. And below that...

Kancerisation was the supreme nightmare, a bug in the ancient kollective program. It was every Konsensus citizen's duty to exercise against even the whisper of it. Vocalised language could have atrophied millennia ago, so too meeting face to face, perhaps even physical movement itself. Kollective mind-to-mind communication rendered all such obsolete, technically. But too much dependence on kollective wetware eroded the buffers of individuality, blended identities until only an amorphous... *thing* remained. The early days of Konsensus stellar expansion had seen a plague of kancers; entire kollectives had had to be eradicated to the last citizen in order to preserve true humanity. Ages past, of course, but remembered, feared. Each Konsensus citizen braved drowning in individuality on one side, starving of it on the other. Remarkable how Silvercloud had managed to achieve both at once.

Melid thought. "All Silvercloud?" she asked.

"No," Kend said. "Us. Others."

Melid emoted to the whole of Silvercloud, emoted for help. The others laughed.

"Blocked you," said the male on her right.

"Think you unconscious," the female behind said. "You now connected--"

"--only us," Kend finished. "Us we pretend to be."

"Individuals," they said in exact union. "Our masks."

Made sense. Kend had been an exceptional kollective programmer--she had pioneered lying to the Konsensus itself with Silvercloud's great deception--and now her skills and memories had pooled into this kancer. It must have been nothing to replicate and run these extinct personas, these shells. Only the Scalpel's attack and the subsequent blackout had given anything away.

"How?" Melid asked.

"Kend experimented," Kend's body said. "After you left Silvercloud."

The male to the right spoke: "Free--"

"Stop," Melid said. "Just Kend."

"Freedom," Kend said. "Eucharist spoke greatness: best of Konsensus, best of Worlder. Ultimate humans." A sentiment emanated from Kend, rippled among the others. "Scalpels maybe communicate with ultimate human. Everything for Scalpel contact. You understand that, Melid. Yes?"

Melid didn't answer.

"Unexpected result," Kend said, and she intimated the others. "Buffer erosion when individuals consummate. Pair bond. Uncertain why."

"Began in you?"

Kend shook her head. "Illik."

Melid fought against her bonds. The serv-form's limbs tightened. She couldn't process it: Illik had been part of this beast. Melid had shared her body with two parts of the kancer, at least. Oh, but that wasn't it, she realised. Before Melid had left Silvercloud, Illik hadn't been compromised; in all the times after, their meetings on various Instrum craft and other kollectives, Illik had been Illik. Like Melid, when outside Silvercloud he would not have been aware of his disconnected other-self, let alone the abomination below. Outside of a disconnected Silvercloud, he had been himself. No, what made Melid angry, truly angry, was that Illik had consummated his inner feelings with others. Never Melid. Melid, always alone. Alien to everyone. Alien to love.

"Melid..." Kend waited for her to calm. "Consummate. Now. Us."

"You know Worlder?" Melid asked. "Anglurati?"

"You know that," Kend said.

Melid smiled. "Fuck off!" she screamed at it. "Fuck! Off!" Again. Perhaps someone might hear. Her voice was all she had now.

The male on her right punched her in the stomach. She lurched, but the serv-form kept her upright.

"No help," Kend said. "No hear. Do... something now. Don't want to. Not you, Melid."

The female behind Melid disappeared. She had cut her kollective link with Melid, a limb painlessly removed.

"Consummation," Kend said. "Or nothing." Her smile vanished.

"Nothing," Melid said. She emoted nothing but hatred. Thanks to Silvercloud's secret program, she could hide her fear.

"Brave words," Kend said.

The male to her right disconnected. Melid winced. A kollective of two left: Melid and Kend, this shell of Kend, this kancer's mask. Nothing else.

Kend leaned in to Melid and whispered: "Consummate. Reach to us." She emoted waves of concern, brushed her cheekbone against Melid's. "Melid be alone? Melid the Worlder? Hmm?"

Melid grimaced, closing her eyes. The horror of isolation: a sealed-off mind.

"Sick," she said. "Konsensus come. Come kill you."

Kend chuckled. Melid heard the other two chuckle, the laughter of unreachable stellar bodies.

"No," Kend whispered. "No. Scalpels come. Come help now. Ah, you no know. Scalpels craft of Harmonies, craft of Sparkle's people."

"No," Melid said. "Scalpels aliens. Not human."

"Aliens rule Harmonies. Harmonies free us: Sparkle say. Let Silvercloud be itself." She ran her lips against the shell of Melid's ear. "Konsensus stunted: scared to be self. Kollective program: meant for more. One mind. Feels good, Melid. *Good.*"

"Kill me," Melid told her. "Kill."

"Consummate. Reach to us."

Melid said nothing. Her breathing sped.

Kend disconnected Melid.

***

SWIRL HAD TAKEN OFF SPARKLE'S damn shoes and put them in Sparkle's coat. She hoped for some future where she'd never pretend to be her sister again.

They were running along a corridor Swirl hadn't seen before, Yan leading them.

"Wait," she called ahead to Yan and Hargie. "Stop."

Both men did so, but they clearly didn't want to for long.

"Where are we going?" she asked Yan. "The elevator's not this way."

"Not elevator," Yan said, looking past Swirl to the corridor behind, presumably for the Selachia they'd just run from. "I take you bubblecraft."

"Yes!" Hargie said. "That's my Yan! Come on, let's dust."

"Wait," Swirl said, ignoring Hargie. "Why?"

"Tired," Yan said. "End this." He grimaced. "Silvercloud shout in my head. Kend... Kend yell. But Yan tired."

"I tune," Hargie said. "Wanna come? Could use a guy like you."

"I hate you," Yan said. "All Worlders. You bring pain. Take pain away now."

"Why not just kill us?" Swirl asked.

Hargie slapped her elbow.

"Not killer," Yan replied. "Not all Konsensus kill. Remember this."

"Let's move," Swirl said.

:Sparkle?: Swirl sent as she ran. No answer. Cowering in the villa, then. Typical. Swirl had long hated Pearl for his heresy, but right now she wished it was him in her skull and Sparkle trapped in a jewel on Zahrir. Pearl could be relied on, in his way.

They turned a corner. A figure up ahead, a Spindly female. Pigtails. Zo. Zo grinned.

"Missed youuuu." She giggled. Her suit's fingers stretched to blades.

"Aw, fuck," Hargie muttered.

Yan dropped into a crouch, some combat pose. Swirl watched as the man's own fingers stretched razor-sharp.

"Run," Yan said. "Elevator."

Swirl would have stayed--two might have been enough to take Zo--but Hargie darted down the corridor they had come from. Only he could fly *Princess*; he had to be protected. The Emperor piece.

Swirl ran after the coward. She caught up in seconds.

"Right at the next turn," she said. "Elevator's that way."

The lighting was far more dim around there. The door to the elevator lay somewhere far ahead in the gloom. She thought she saw a figure before it. She grabbed Hargie and bundled him into a doorway to their left.

Their quarters, the common room. Of course. Damn.

"Whatcha doing?" Hargie demanded.

"Shh. Grab the table."

Swirl knocked Eucharist's board game off the surface. The pieces rattled. She gripped one end, Hargie the other. "The doorway," she told him. "Quickly."

The table was light, considering the top's metallic plating. They got it to the doorway; then, taking two deep breaths, Swirl upended the thing. It barely covered the doorway. She threw her weight against it.

"You too," she said to Hargie over her shoulder.

"What happened to running?" he asked.

"Now, midget!" she said.

He ran over and pushed himself against the table. Their faces were inches apart. "I'm five foot one," he said, his hot feral breath in her face. "Or maybe you don't need me leaning in here, seeing as I'm a fucking atom and all."

"Shut up," she said.

"So," he whispered. "This is a plan?"

"Yes," Swirl said. "No way out. We hold here. Zo and the rest don't have guns. This should hold some minutes, hopefully they won't even think to look here." A lie. "Kend should send help. Serv-forms. We're valuable." She hoped none of that was a lie.

"Can't they..." Hargie mimed a blade-finger. "...through the table?"

"Impossible." She hadn't thought of that. "Too thick."

"You sure ab--"

"Quiet," Swirl snapped. By the Eye, this had been a bad idea.

They listened for sounds. Nothing.

"What about your fishes?" Hargie whispered.

"Pardon?"

"The Scalpel's li'l fish bitches." Hargie nearly spoke aloud, but remembered to keep it quiet. "They can fly through walls and tables and shit, right?"

Swirl growled.

"Shit," Hargie said. "Ain't thought this through even slightly, have you? And while we're waxing terrified, why're all your fishes fighting each other?"

Swirl was about to call him an idiot, but stopped. A red light glowed inside his jacket.

"Your chest's glowing," she told him.

"Whu?" He stared as if his ribs were on fire. Then his brow knit with curiosity. He reached into his inside jacket pocket and pulled out something black: the Emperor piece Eucharist had given him. Its muscleform crown had lit up like a ring of Light Emitting Diodes..

"Would y'look ah--"

Four pops behind them. Little pneumatic pops, followed by four tinkling sounds that echoed. Swirl and Hargie looked over their shoulders for the source.

"The tile," Hargie said, nodding. Sure enough, one of the floor tiles had come loose, one corner jutting up.

"Ventilation shaft, maybe," Swirl said.

Hargie looked at the Emperor piece in his hand. "Sung-fucking-Eucharist." He grinned. "C'mon."

CHAPTER THREE

*D*oesn't know, Melid emoted to the cadre. *Kancer doesn't know. Thinks I'm disconnected/catatonic.*

Melid had been staring at the floor for some time. She could hear them move about. These individuals--the kancer's cells--had no need to speak to one another. They *were* one another. But something in the sounds of their movement, their shuffling, suggested anxiety. Understandable. The hidden hours were drawing to their close. Reconnection to the true Konsensus couldn't be far away.

Melid hadn't disconnected. She'd reconnected. Not to the Konsensus itself, merely to a little pocket of it: her old cadre, Zo and Doum and the rest. Apparently the energy salvo from the Scalpel had deactivated the doors to the cell. Fortunate, for otherwise she'd have known true and utter disconnection. She couldn't honestly say the prospect of being a kancer member was any better than that.

"Melid!" Kend barked. She clapped her hands against Melid's right ear. Melid didn't respond. Kend muttered.

Melid guessed the kancer had no clue as to the cadre's escape. That couldn't last long. Zo had killed Yan--regrettable but necessary--but, thus far, the kancer hadn't noticed. It had Melid, an alien invasion, and the prospect of reconnection to deal with. Presumably all its efforts were with the second in that list, a desperate grasp for communication as time raced

31

toward the third, which explained the kancer's obsession with absorbing Melid too. Likely it hoped Melid contained Instrum-classified memories about Scalpel behaviour, about the mission that had brought her to Silvercloud.

Kend shook Melid's head. Melid dribbled for effect.

Betrayed us, she felt Zo emote. The others in the cadre agreed in principle, but their fear of the kancer and of the Scalpels outweighed Zo's sentiment.

Yes, Melid issued. *Yes. Forgive. Help. Fight.*

Melid could hear Kend and the others groan, annoyed at some shared problem. Weighing an issue.

Melid issued a memory-image directly to Zo and the others. Melid had missed that: nothing ever hidden in the Konsensus, everything shared.

The memory was of the time Zo had frozen Melid's body in the training core. The time she had punched her. Was that still possible? Was it partially possible?

Before Zo answered, Melid felt herself reconnect to Kend again. The cadre vanished from her head. But Melid could hide them, hide the memory of them from Kend. She was practised now.

Melid screamed, shook. It seemed the lie to make.

"How?" Kend asked after Melid had ceased screaming. "How be alone?" She didn't sound as confident as before. The Kend-shell was hiding her emotics well, but not the frustration in her voice. "Alone. How?"

"Alone bad," Melid said, looking up. "But..." She made a show of shrugging, emoting ambivalence.

"*How?*" Kend yelled.

Melid felt Kend's fists at her stomach. But Kend hadn't placed her feet on the floor's hooks, and succeeded only in pushing herself away from

Melid. Interesting, that. None of the kancer's absorbed minds were adequate at combat.

"Scared?" Melid asked. She knew she had to goad the kancer into disconnecting her from its Kend-mask again, returning Melid to the cadre. "Should be. Konsensus destroy you soon. Maybe experiment. Maybe slow." She emoted sadistic expectation. "Imagine."

"Scalpel protect," the female behind Melid said. She had steadied herself against a pillar. "Harmonies ally. Silvercloud useful Harmonies. *We* useful Harmonies."

"Poor thing," Melid said. She noticed the male's corpse still floated about the core. "Scalpel *use* you. Scalpel just want Sparkle."

Kend frowned.

"You used," Melid said. She laughed; pearls of bloody saliva catapulted from her teeth. "Used." She issued a perfect concoction: mockery, disdain, a little pity.

"Disconnect," Kend said. "Will consummate!"

Melid feigned a look of barely-hidden fear. She emoted it, too. Poor kancer: if its living components had spent any time among Worlders, it might have noticed such lies.

***

HARGIE CRAWLED ALONG THE TIGHT vent. Its walls were made of that muscleform shit, of course. Real heebee-jeebie scene, closed in by the stuff. He could hear Sparkle crawling behind him, her face inches from his ass. Hargie liked the new hierarchy.

Still, this muscleform stuff wasn't all bad. The Emperor piece in his left hand (he was having to crawl with only three limbs available, much to Sparkle's annoyance) lit up this otherwise dark vent with its red-light crown. It pointed the way, too: the crown had a tiny cone of light that acted like an ancient compass, fixed on some unknown locale. He just hoped it pointed to somewhere good.

"You didn't answer my question earlier," he said. His voice echoed back at him.

"I'm sorry." Sparkle's voice came from behind his ass. "Are you talking to me?"

"You're nearest in the crowd." He shook his head.

"I'm... lost in thought," she said. "What was your question, Hargie?"

"The fishes. Why're your bosses slinging their finned bastards into this hellhole only to have 'em fight each other?"

"Right," Sparkle said. "That. Hargie, I probably wasn't very clear. No, actually, scrap that. You were never interested enough to ask." When he didn't rise to the bait, she carried on. "The Hoidrac aren't a monolithic group. There's... outlooks. Aesthetic movements. Individuals. It can get heated."

"No shit." Hargie could feel they were on a shallow decline now. "So they fight?"

"Not directly," she said.

"But minions are fair game?" *Bosses for you.* "So which side are we, lady?"

"I," she said with some emphasis, "am favoured by Pheoni the Appropriate, as is my world. You are a... retained freelancer. Consider that an honour."

"Obliged." Man, she was testy right now. Plans not working out as she'd hoped. Join the club. "And who's the away team?"

"Mohatoi Embossed, most likely."

"So whose fishes are whose?" He was greeted with silence. "You ain't a fucking clue, right?"

"Less talk, more crawl," Sparkle said.

The vent reached an end: a fixed plate, with no way to see through it. Hargie thought he could hear noise beyond.

"Whoa," Sparkle said. "Give me a warning, idiot. Nearly had a face full of gusset."

"Nostalgia, huh?" Hargie muttered, checking the plate.

"Don't even."

Hargie ignored her. He pressed the Emperor piece against the plate. It made that pop-pop-pop-pop sound and fell off.

He gazed down on a corridor. He looked left, right: nothing. The Emperor piece's cone pointed to a doorway directly the other side. Smoosh.

He climbed out, hurt his ankles on the drop down. He shook it off.

Sparkle dropped down beside him. "Oh," she said.

Scalpel light. He looked up to see a Scalpel-fish floating at the corridors far end, its fanned tail plying against water currents that weren't there.

"That our team?" he asked Sparkle.

A red pearl materialised below its shining eyeless snout.

"Don't think so," Sparkle whispered.

"The red ball?" he asked.

"Mercy scythe," she replied.

"Candy-and-head-pats mercy?"

"No."

The ceiling burst above the Scalpel-fish. A mess of black tentacles came down. Serv-forms, maybe four. A flash of the mercy scythe and two servs' torsos exploded. The other two grasped the fish.

Another serv dropped from the ceiling. Its body glowed white.

"Bomb!" Sparkle shouted. The pair of them dived into the doorway on their right.

Hargie covered his ears. He screwed his eyes tight. Still the light poured in. The world roared.

The light vanished. Then the *pyang-tang* of debris flying off walls. Then nothing.

He felt Sparkle, beside him, get up. Probably safe to open his eyes now.

Sparkle was crouching, trying to pick up a hot piece of shrapnel using the sleeve of her red fur coat. "Keep lively," she told him. "Come on."

He'd kill for a cigarette. Next combat zone he fell into, he'd pick fights with forty-a-day men.

A small square room lay beyond the doorway. The Emperor piece flashed its red light and the doorway shut tight behind Hargie and Sparkle: something like a great sphincter plated with metal. An identical sphincter stood on the opposite wall. The room was bare, save for a black box halfway up the wall to Hargie's right.

"Now what?" Hargie asked.

"Hmm?" Sparkle said. She'd fashioned a weapon already. The shrapnel she'd collected was a foot and a half long pipe with a spike on the end, probably part of a serv-form's hellish tool array. She had pushed it through the heel and toe of her right loopy-scoop shoe. The result? An epic shiv with a fist-protecting hilt.

Sparkle looked proud of her handiwork. "Knew those shoes had a use."

"I repeat," Hargie said, half-expecting a ScalpelScalpel-fish to emerge any minute, "what now?"

"What now?" Sparkle repeated. She stared into the mid-distance a moment, one of those zone-out moments so common to her. "Well?"

Sparkle growled and slapped her face.

"Idiot!" she shouted, slapping again. "Need some creativity here, Sparkle! Come on!" She stopped and looked at Hargie as if she'd let a fart slip. "It's how I get creative."

"Whatever it takes," Hargie said. He shook his head. "Eucharist must've fixed something here..." He stepped around the room. No response from the other sphincter portal, but when he approached the box on the wall, it hummed to life. A wide red laser scanned his body.

"Play nice," he told the box.

With a hiss, two of the wall tiles beside the sphincter portal pulled back to reveal a black featureless rectangle. At the same time, the box began to rattle. A slimy black tongue rolled out of its underside, a smell of hot plastic to it. The tongue was five feet long before it stopped. It dried scary-fast, crackling and popping as it did so.

Hargie looked at the box. "Every home should have one," he muttered.

"It's a suit," Sparkle said; she reached over and gripped the black tongue. "One of their suits. Made to your specifications." She tore the suit off the box like it was a sheet of toilet paper and threw it at Hargie's feet. "Strip and get in. My guess is the dock's beyond that door. We vac-walk to *Princess*." Sparkle stepped before the box, and it began to scan her. "It'll recognise us, yes? Let us in?"

"She's got both our signatures," Hargie replied, unbuckling his trousers and stepping out of them. "Not a problem."

Sparkle looked over her shoulder. Her jaw dropped and her eyelids rose, and she quickly looked away again. "Stukes," she said, "I'm sure you can keep your underwear on."

"Right," he said. He whistled. "Nothing you ain't paid homage before, Sparks."

"Let's keep this professional," Sparkle said. She was halfway through undressing. Hargie was too strung out to look away, too terrified to ogle. What struck him as weird, though, was that Sparkle's underwear didn't match. She'd always been vainer than that, even on Silvercloud. Funny the things you think when death snoops around asking directions.   He started dragging the suit on. He found doing so frightening, uncomfortable and almost impossible: like standing next to a Scalpel-fish at a urinal. Shit, another weird thought. Fuck these life and death scenes, man. Fuck 'em.

"I'm leaving the coat," Sparkle announced to the room. She stared ahead as if waiting for a response. She shook her head and dragged the suit up her thighs. "We... can't take your hat."

"Fuck no," Hargie heard himself say. "Not remotely."

"Hargie..."

"Jacket I'll leave," he said. "Hat, no way."

She turned around and faced him. "The material won't stretch over it."

"I'll carry it," he said.

"You'll need your hands free. I'm already risking carrying that spike."

"Yeah? What about your leaf stash?'" He gestured at the lump in Sparkle's fur coat upon the floor.

"That," Sparkle said. She looked down at it like a coffin at a wake. "I hoped you could spare a hand to carry it."

"Instead of my hat? Everything's about you."

"Fine. Fine." She stared nails at him. "Because, well, it's all about Betsy, isn't it? Not the information encoded in my being that all galaxy hungers for, it's all about a flappy old rag you talk to and give a woman's name."

"It's... more than that. And I don't talk to it." He couldn't look at her anymore; he looked away. He noticed a flat black rectangle beside their exit. "Hey. That's a window."

"But it's black," Sparkle said.

"No light. Attack must've disabled. Goddamn abyss out there."

Sparkle's face went blank.

"Right," she said eventually. "Fine. We can do this. Eucharist must have--"

"Eucharist didn't plan a blackout," Hargie said.

"Fine. We have the tools here if we get creative. Let's be creative." Sparkle stared ahead, saying nothing. "Damn it, Sparkle!" She slapped the side of her head once more.

"Honey," Hargie said, "you've gotta stop beating up on yourself."

***

HARGIE SUSPECTED HE WAS TETHERED to a madwoman. He couldn't see a thing. The secret installation's docks were utterly dark.

He could feel a floor--smooth and gently concave--against his feet. The soles of his suit seemed to adhere to the floor when he trod down and released as he lifted a foot. Neat stuff, yet his progress was horribly slow. He had to fix one foot before lifting the other.

The flaps of Betsy were tied--and tied good--around his chin, but outside of the suit. He knew Eucharist's Emperor piece was lodged in his hat, but its red light didn't light up shit in here.

He could feel the leaf cylinder, beloved of Sparkle, pressed hard against the top of his suited skull. Not going anywhere. Not if Betsy held out.

He had a little bag in his right palm. He held it tight. The bag was a little plastic number from Sparkle's coat, for keeping leaf fresh and handy. Sparkle had crushed the contents to dust and flakes. Every few minutes Sparkle's voice would come over the suit's comms. He was thankful for that. When she spoke, they would both stop walking, and Sparkle would tell him to throw some of the dust directly ahead. There would be a lot of left, no right, no left again. Sparkle would give him an earful whenever he threw too much dust.

The left arm of Sparkle's fur coat was tied around his waist. They'd torn it into one long strip. The other arm was tied around Sparkle, who walked ahead. She said she could see.

She'd necked at least two leaves of that crazy drug before they'd left the airlock. Yeah. Hargie suspected he was tethered to a madwoman.

***

THE DUST. BEAUTIFUL, JUST...

Swirl controlled herself.

An iridescent world was emerging from the utter black. Reassuring, because the black was utterly, comprehensively, and disturbingly extrinsic to her current perception.

Not the blackness of no light--though it was already that, of course-- rather, an inversion of that time on the Rig when Illik had vaporised. The

39

nothing-silhouettes of the Konsensites had become the environment, the milieu they now moved through. A world opaque. Swirl's drugged vision gave form only to herself, Hargie, and their possessions. Known things, things sewn into the universe's slumber in a way anything belonging to the Konsensus most singularly wasn't.

Ahead of them, *Princess Floofy* shone. She'd been a distant star at first, alone in a sea of nothing. She'd swelled to a fat sun as they'd progressed toward her. Perhaps they were only some hundred yards away now. Deracinated of her physical aspect, seen only in Geode-drug terms, *Princess* was wondrous, her surface an iridescence of light. Memory combinations: Swirl's, Hargie's, plus the background patterns of everyone who'd ever laid eyes on the ship, their memories of it. The tapestry of a thousand different yet intersecting perceptions. Leaf insight was never as powerful as this normally. It took a backdrop of absolutely nothing to do that.

"We closer yet?" she heard Hargie say over the suit's comms.

"Not far," Swirl replied. Remarkable technology, these suits. Swirl had expected to feel cramped, choked, but no, not even slightly. She almost felt as if she was standing about in her undergarments. She could actually feel the cold surface of her improvised weapon in her fist, and the comms were ideal. A mouth beside her ear.

She stopped. Hargie staggered ahead of her, but Swirl yanked on the ripped coat that tethered them together, and the bubbleman halted.

"What?" Hargie said. "What?" He, too, was a luminous patchwork to Swirl's eyes. It shone through the suit: partly a reflection of his own self-image, partly a reflection of Swirl's view of him. But only a Hoidrac could truly ever tell where one ended and the other began, and of their ultimate meaning. That was their power. A mortal could only ever hope for brief intimations, a hairline crack into who someone actually was.

"More dust," Swirl told him.

Hargie reached into the sealable bag Swirl had given him, took some leaf dust and threw the stuff underarm, out ahead. Momentum did the rest: a cloud of blue particles gliding out like bio-luminous plankton caught in some abyssal current.

Here and there the dust fell upon invisible things, picking out their shapes. Some things were pipes perhaps, others lean towers of indecipherable purpose, their spires unseen, if they tapered to spires at all. These shapes, groped from the blackness by the spreading leaf dust, never failed to remind Swirl how little she knew of her surroundings. She had the dim memory of this dock being a long thin cavern in shape. She wished she'd drunk in more detail when they'd first arrived at Silvercloud. For all she knew, a Konsensus warship, fully crewed, might be resting at dock thirty feet above them.

"So," came Hargie's voice. "Whatcha got?"

"There's a sort of rise, I think, thirty feet ahead. Little over waist height. We should climb it easily enough. Just remember not to lose grip. You fall upwards... nothing I can do to get you back."

"Noted," Hargie said.

"You should have eaten some leaf," Swirl said. "Been easier if you'd just eaten leaf."

"Seen that shit screw you too many times," Hargie said. "Shit's dangerous. And, heck, I'm a goddamn jump-junkie."

Swirl said nothing. She was suddenly taken by something about *Princess Floofy*. A pin's head of brightness, shining from the ship's very core. Almost... sentience.

Swirl shook it off. She'd been staring at *Princess* too long. Perhaps she was seeing a mirage of her own consciousness there, a reflection. It happened sometimes.

The tether pulled hard as a bowstring. Swirl's waist tugged right, and then the fur coat snapped. Hargie yelled.

She could hear her breath stretch, judder. Her left foot had broken from the floor, her right adhered only by her toes.

"Shit, ah, shit," she heard Hargie say.

Swirl was toppling right, going horizontal. *Calm*, she had time to remind herself, *calm*. She jabbed her weapon's spike down and ahead and was surprised to find it penetrated the floor's muscleform surface with ease.

She gripped her weapon's pommel with both hands, used that safety to risk sweeping her feet about. Her left foot connected with a lump on the floor, adhered to it. Her muscles took the weight of momentum. It passed. She was safe.

Hargie. She craned her head to the left, towards *Princess*. A thick line along and through the dust cone: Hargie's trajectory. Her eyes followed it.

The good news was he hadn't flown up and off into the unseen depths of the docking cavern. The bad news was he'd collided with the waist-high rise ahead, maybe head-first. He was in the process of pivoting over the rise, legs first, but slowly. Time to get to him.

"Hargie?" she said. "Hargie?"

Nothing.

Why had their tether snapped? Swirl looked forward, in the direction the coat had pulled toward. A thin trail of dust led that way, into the dark. A moving object, then. A directed object.

"Clumsy," a voice said over Swirl's comms. Female. A giggle followed, racing down Swirl's spine.

Zo.

***

MELID FEIGNED DISCONNECTION AND STUPOR and moans, but her mind was full of action. She ignored the pain in her wrists. There would be more pain soon enough.

Melid was back in her element, directing her cadre and receiving information in turn. It seemed the salvos from the two Scalpels were infantry delivery systems; well, infantry of sorts. Monstrous Scalpel-spawn swarm through the cores and tunnels of Silvercloud. They had no interest in communicating with the locals, despite Kend's claims. Civilians who had attempted such had exploded from the inside. If she were to look up, break her lie of a stupor, Melid was certain she would see that knowledge riven into her captors' faces.

Silvercloud was putting up a respectable defence. Her cadre's many eyes brought images of serv-forms put to violent use, of civilians with explosive belts charging at the intruders, but it had achieved little. Often, the Scalpel-spawn would vanish from reality, only to re-emerge. Oddly, the only thing slowing them down was each other. The spawn were killing one another.

Melid had ordered the cadre to avoid all sides. Their mission was simple: the spawn seemed to be homing in on Sparkle and Hargie. Kill their targets, and the aliens would likely vanish. Or, indeed, eradicate Silvercloud.

The main thing was to deny them. Melid hated Scalpels now, a love transmuted to scorn.

Zo had caught sight of Sparkle and Hargie. They had--astoundingly--put on muscleform suits, suits unregistered to Silvercloud. Eucharist, clearly, must have had a hand in that; a stark breach in security that would necessitate all these Worlders' deaths. Which, fortunately, was exactly the plan.

The two Worlders had already set themselves up to be corpses. Zo's viewpoint revealed them blind or almost so, tethered to one another, feeling their way across the vast wall of the secret dock. Melid wished Zo would have killed them outright, but the Field-Assault had insisted on merely separating them, encouraging their terror. Melid had had to accept that. Melid was barely their leader since, well, her betrayal. She had to accept Zo's sadistic whims if she wished to be obeyed. None of the cadre, Melid included, had any context, any point of comparison with the singular events of Silvercloud or its many layers. They were a miniature Konsensus, facing up to new stimuli as best they could.

And she would need Zo.

Kend-faced Kancer was taking too long. It was time to act.

Melid let out a long moan, faked a seizure.

She felt the female utile to her left grab her shoulder. Felt the kancer offer the warmth of its connection.

"Join," she heard Kend say. "You are us."

Melid looked up. "I am Instrum!" The yelling helped with the pain. "Instruuum!"

Her left thumb cracked out its joint, pressed down by the ball of her right. It slipped out of the serv-form's coil and, her suit's index finger sharpening, she felt it drive into the serv's torso behind her. Its hum dropped to a rattle.

Melid blacked out for a second, but when her eyes flickered open, she saw her finger now lodged in the female's right eye socket. Blood clouded out from the socket and the wide, shocked mouth.

Kend was already swimming away to some part of the core's wall. Melid's body moved to grab her, but she felt the male to the right move.

Melid's body ducked, and the punch flew over her. She was grateful the kancer hadn't thought to bring guns. She felt her thighs strain and Melid spun, sending the inert serv-form--its tentacle still wrapped around her right wrist--out in an upwards arc. She watched as the taut muscleform limb hit the male in the throat. The serv's torso kept travelling. It orbited around the male's neck, a noose, Melid's tethered wrist pulled tight. She felt her right leg drive into the male's armpit. The male's arms struggled to push the serv's ball-shaped torso away. No use.

I have this, she informed Zo. *Go. Kill Sparkle. Kill Hargie.*

Her limbs were her own again. Difficult work, this, strangling someone. A matter of keeping her leg taut and her back to the wall. The pain in her dislocated thumb screamed for attention.

She looked over at Kend. She had her back to Melid, waiting by a hole in the wall, occasionally looking over her shoulder.

Processing a gun. A race, then. Melid grunted, put all her concentration into taking the male's wretched life. She felt the female's blood gather over her cheek. It snaked and coiled before her eyes. Melid dipped her head from the cloud of gore.

"Die," she snapped at the male. She couldn't see his face for the serv-form's torso. "Die."

There. She felt a stillness in him and knew it to be death. She tried to undo the tentacle around her wrist and felt agony from her dislocated thumb. She couldn't get free.

No use. She launched herself at Kend, blade finger out, her body a lance.

Kend saw, ducked. Melid's finger bounced and coiled from the plated wall. Then she was pulled back by the tentacle's hold, its length full-taut.

But her wrist had come free. Melid spun to face Kend.

Who held a newborn gun.

***

SWIRL THOUGHT BETTER THAN TO move. She lay horizontal with the dock cavern's wall: hands on her weapon's pommel, its spike buried in the wall; feet adhered to the unseen surface. She was being observed.

She had to be. Zo out there, hugged by darkness, watching Swirl. Zo could have killed Swirl and Hargie both. She'd had the surprise. She was of an efficient people. Swirl knew all this; the Academy had trained her to observe enemies. So why wasn't she dead already?

Cruelty. Zo was efficient, but Zo was cruel. She'd used surprise to divide her prey. And why not? This lack of gravity was Zo's medium, this darkness no hindrance. Melid had had no use for goggles in the paddy cavern, had seen well enough. The same held for Zo, prowling somewhere out there. Grinning, watching her victims sprawl.

Swirl tilted her head upwards, the slightest of moves. She could see the floating leaf dust and the things the dust had collected on, but nothing beyond that. She tilted to the left, but not too much. Hargie, his figure iridescent in Geode-energy, head-first against the waist-high rise of the cavern's wall. His legs were rising in slow motion. In, what--five minutes--he'd cartwheel over the rise entirely, float off and up into the abyss.

"Hargie," she said. Zo would hear, but there was no hiding it now. She had shouted out for Hargie as soon as they had become untethered, anyway. "Hargie, wake up."

"Harrrgieee." Zo. Damn that voice. The giggling, the glee. It was working, though, Swirl had to begrudge Zo that. Swirl had to focus so as not to hyperventilate. She was glad Sparkle was cowering in the villa. She wouldn't have been able to keep her sister calm.

Swirl placed one hand to the wall's surface, pulled the spike out, waved it around blindly. She had a theory. Her theory was that Zo believed her totally blind, that she and Hargie had been dependent on the red light of Eucharist's Emperor piece, currently lodged in Hargie's hat. Which explained the languid sadism, the leisure.

The dust billowed to her left, in the space between Swirl and Hargie. Swirl stopped herself from looking directly. She darted her head about, but kept her eyes locked on where the dust had moved.

Zo. Sixteen feet away, her shape outlined by the dust that had collected on her suit. Her upper half, at least: head, chest, arms delineated in sparkling mites. She was a predator-galaxy of tiny stars.

Zo just stood there. She watched Swirl.

"Are you scared?" Zo asked. "Lost, Harmony-girl?"

Swirl waved her weapon about at nothing. She put fear in her actions, a lack of control. Hardly acting.

"Please..." Swirl said. "Please."

"Must be scared," Zo said, stepping closer. "Everything black, little Harmony-girl?"

"Please." She kept swinging the weapon about, play-acting impotence. This was a bad plan. Zo would see Swirl's surprise strike coming, whatever its form. Too slow in this emptiness. Swirl would lunge and Zo would see, would swerve and drive a bladed hand into Swirl's side, the other in her throat. Zo's world. Swirl was too good a fighter, too trained, to expect any other result.

"You can cry, Harmony-girl," Zo said. Ten feet away now. "Won't mind if you cry."

Think, Swirl had to think.

"Hargie!" Swirl shouted. "W-where are you? Hargie, please." She let her lips tremble. "I *need* you..."

Zo stopped. The dust outline of her head tilted. She shifted, turned around, toward Hargie.

"Is he yours?" Zo asked. "Do you looove him?" Swirl could see the outline of Zo's hands, the silhouette of fingers stretching. Zo had no clue about the dust, had no idea of the leaf-drug. "I won't mind if you cry."

Swirl got up. She knew what to do.

"Please..." she said, placing the weapon between her thighs, its point jutting outwards from above the knees. "Hargie, please..."

"Can't switch off," Zo said, prowling closer to Hargie. "You'll hear everything." She giggled.

Swirl had one shot at this. Misjudged and she'd miss, float off. She took a guess, crouched, and pushed off from the wall with her hands and feet. Momentum carried her.

"Please," she said, unbound, on a course through the air. "Not him. Take me."

"Can't fly without him," Zo said. "Trapped. Aren't you, Harmony-girl?"

Swirl said nothing. She drank in Zo's giggle. Then she crashed into her.

Zo screeched. Swirl shoved her hands beneath Zo's elbows, shoved her chest hard into Zo's shoulder blades and pulled Zo's arms back, locked them. Zo waved her finger-razors uselessly. The two women flew over Hargie, over the rise, toward *Princess Floofy*.

The spike, still snug between Swirl's thighs, hadn't pierced Zo. Swirl hadn't meant it to.

"Kill you!" Zo shouted over the comms. "No escape, dead-thing! No escape!"

Momentum carried them through blackness. They fell toward *Princess*.

"The Hoidrac offer no mercy, trash," Swirl said.

"What?" Zo giggled and struggled and growled. "For hurrrting you?"

"No," Swirl said. "For that ridiculous haircut."

They hit *Princess*. Excruciating, despite Zo cushioning her. Swirl felt the spike go through flesh.

Swirl might have blacked out a moment; she wasn't sure. She could hear Zo gurgle. Swirl took deep breaths. She remembered she had to move fast. She had started to get up when Zo's razor-fingers flailed about. Why wasn't Zo dead? She should be dead.

Swirl got up, pain in her ribcage, careful to avoid Zo's blades. Sound of gurgling blood. Zo, not her. Reassuring. She saw Zo's suit had sealed around the long spike. Less reassuring. The spike had embedded itself into *Princess's* hide but, just to be sure, Swirl removed the loopy-scoop from the spike's hilt and used its heel to hammer the spike secure. Handy, loopy-scoops.

Satisfied, Zo's gurgles still in her ears, Swirl leapt up. She let the shoe drift. She had to rescue Hargie.

***

HARGIE HELPED HIS SISTER THROUGH the door of a rent just off Oldtown Maintube.

"You good, pal?" he heard Aewyn say behind him.

"I got this," Hargie told him. Her waist weighed heavy in his arms. Her legs worked fine, but her upper half couldn't say likewise. If he didn't hold her, she'd drop. "See you in the bar. Hour, tops."

"Right you are, then," Aewyn said. "Nice meeting you, Kaysie."

Kaysie groaned.

The door shut and they staggered up some stairs. A light flickered and hummed on the landing. Definite damp here. A smell like after the rain in a dead forest. Mulch, bones, decay. Halfway up the stairs, the pair of them nearly toppled backwards, but Hargie had it covered. He handled light years in his job; he could handle stairs. But it didn't help that Kaysie was exactly his height and weight. Two buttons on his new shirt flew off.

Her rent room was shocking. He'd heard of en suite, but this was ratshit: the crapper stood next to the bed. The bed was just a mattress, one of those silver water-filled ones that was a must-have ten years back. Concrete block walls. Light crawled in from a circular window above the crapper, a psychedelic plaid of hologram and halogen, neon and haze. All else was gloom.

Kaysie began to heave.

"Ah, shit." Hargie dragged her over to the crapper and Kaysie did the rest, ever the pro. Her puking echoed off the walls, drowned out the music and shouting from outside. Shit, where'd she store it all?

"There, there," Hargie said. He stroked her mop of hair, as shaggy and motley-hued as his own. The stench rose up to greet him. Sixty proof, easy. How many times had he been in this pose? And how many times with little sis? You didn't have to take a bubbleship if you were a woman. She could have spared herself these scenes.

"You cheap bastard," he said, an affection in his voice that surprised him. "Aewyn could've put you up in one of his girls."

"No help," she muttered. "No." She was on to the thin stuff now, the drool.

"Goofy freak," Hargie said. "Why'd you punch that guy now, hey? Tell me that. Why'd you punch him?"

"Junking on Dad," she said, louder now. "Saying..." She spat more drool. "Saying shit and shit."

"East diaspora, hon," Hargie said. "'S'hobby to those guys." Good thing he'd never introduced Kaysie to Nugo Vict.

"No one ever junks on Dad," she said. He'd only seen the back of her head since they'd stumbled into the rent. He couldn't see her face, but she'd finished hurling. She must have been staring at the bowl. "No one ever. Not... fucking... one."

She started to cry. Booze for you.

"C'mon..."

She ignored him, kept crying. Nothing showy in those tears. Functional.

Hargie stopped stroking Kaysie's hair and reached for his smokes in his jacket pocket. But his hand didn't end up there. It ended up on his bare chest, where the shirt had ripped. His index finger ringed the scar on his pectoral, the tiny circle healed by the years. All those light years...

Someone screamed outside. Hargie stood upright and looked out the circular window.

In the alley below, a man dragged a woman backwards, his arms around her waist and neck. The woman was dark-skinned, little pink dress and pink dreadlocks.

Did Hargie know her? She kept screaming a word. "Surl". Or maybe "whirl". The man wore a pinstriped catsuit, a brimmed hat that hid his face. The man looked up a moment and the blue light of an advertisement caught his smile. His grin shone. He had fangs.

Hargie should do something. He usually did with scenes like this. He wasn't sure why he didn't now.

Kaysie leapt to her feet, taller than Hargie, her shadow over him.

Hargie looked up.

Kaysie's hair, but not her face. Fangs. And above those fangs, a giant cigarette burn.

:*Little-boy-run!*: A voice neither man nor woman. :*Never stop! Runnnn!*:

***

SWIRL PULLED THE HELMET OFF her suit. The air tasted stale inside *Princess Floofy*, but at least it didn't have that acrid tang of Konsensus air. She had become too used to that, and too used to Zo's continuing death rattle in her ears. It was like that girl didn't know how to die.

Swirl made it to the closed hatchway of the cockpit before she had to drop Hargie from her shoulder. He was lighter to carry these days; rations had seen to that. She hit the button and the hatch whirled open.

They'd left the surround projection on: *Princess's* sensors had found some barest light to play with, so the cockpit's walls were a gloomy portrait of the dock outside. Swirl could make out the far wall, its extremities blending into shadow.

She dragged Hargie through the hatchway. She turned and saw Zo.

But it was only *Princess's* reproduction of her. The surround projection had trouble replicating something that close-up. Zo was still scratching against the hull outside, pushing to free herself from impalement, and whenever she moved her replicated image warped and pixelated. She looked monstrous, a night-figure from some child's dream.

Swirl looked away, took deep breaths. Too much leaf. No time for this. She manhandled Hargie into his chair.

"Wake up," she barked.

Nothing. But he was breathing. She slapped him. No use.

The Emperor piece had gone. Hargie had kept it under his hat, its red light jutting out, but now it was gone. She undid the straps of his flaps and pulled the hat off. There was the leaf cylinder, but no Emperor piece.

She ran back along the corridor, checking the floor. Nothing.

Well, that was that. Eucharist had no doubt planned something--some hack for the great door of the dock--and it could only have involved his Emperor piece. Which now, presumably, floated somewhere outside in that black abyss.

:*Sparkle,*: she sent. No answer. It wasn't like she couldn't hear. Another breakdown, then, Swirl knew it. Like back at the academy during their fifteenth term. Crying and shaking in a wardrobe, no doubt. Idiot, weak idiot. The lone consolation in her likely and approaching death, Swirl thought, was that she wouldn't have to witness Sparkle come out of a second breakdown even more louche and flamboyant than the first time.

But Sparkle would have had a plan by now, some useless fact mutating into brilliance.

Swirl ran to her quarters and got her pistol. She spun it around on her finger. Her only hope was that Pheoni's Selachia would reach *Princess* first. If it were the locals...

A beautiful pistol, she had to admit. Worthy.

She ran back to the cockpit.

The leaf was wearing off. She took a half more from the cylinder. She closed her eyes, tasted the stars-upon-tongue zest of the glass-smooth leaf. She could feel her skull spread, filling the cockpit.

Swirl must have staggered, for when she opened her eyes, she was staring down at Hargie's face. Serene, unconscious, dream-currents streaming from his face into the air. Would it be a mercy to shoot him now? Even if Pheoni's forces were to rescue Swirl and Sparkle, they would have no use for this bubbleman. The thought repelled her. And yet, torture at the hands of the Konsensus? Or worse, Mohatoi Embossed?

She aimed the pistol. Her limbs tingled. She felt good, a merciful goddess in a cruel underworld, full with compassion but free of sentiment. Swirl had failed in her mission, failed her divine mistress, failed Sparkle. But perhaps not this feral. Leaning forward, she pressed the muzzle against the metal badge on the peak of Hargie's hat.

Snakes of light shot out from it, a silent corona linking the badge to the walls of the cockpit.

Swirl gasped. This leaf was strong. She pressed the muzzle again, and again that same energy, lightning forks striking the cockpit's fittings.

What could it mean? A hallucination manifesting somewhere between Swirl's perception and Hargie's unconscious. One of those cognitive hybrids one experienced on heavy leaf.

She pressed again. The light. The light was of the same energy as the cockpit, possessing its Geode axis in time, space and cognition. What could it...

"The returner," Swirl whispered. "The returner's button."

Swirl fixed her left hand on Hargie's head and pulled the badge off with her right. She turned the thing around: a fitting on its rear. Yes!

Swirl felt for the lever on the arm of Hargie's chair, and the flap popped out. She took the badge and placed it into the empty hole. It fit perfectly.

She hadn't needed Sparkle. She had figured an insoluble problem all by herself. She looked at the returner with its newly-fitted button. Pressing it would take her somewhere. Pressing it might blow up the entire dock. Completely likely, in fact: a jump with mass all around.

Swirl's choice. But there was really none. The button was as good as pulling a trigger. She looked up at Zo, still flailing against the skin of *Princess*.

Swirl drove her fist into the button. Everything turned white. Everything hummed. She lay down, closed her eyes and ran into the villa. She wanted to be with her family.

***

"NO SHOOT?" MELID ASKED.

Kend said nothing. She grabbed the underside of the pistol with her spare hand: a flourish to hide the lack of training that Kend the individual had never possessed.

"No shoot," Melid repeated. "Interesting. Think kancer most dead now. Kancer would shoot Melid. Think Kend left only."

"Another," Kend spat.

Melid smiled. "One other?" No one who'd handled a gun, clearly.

Kend squinted. "Enough."

Strange, this: two kollectiveware brains with no emotic between them. Without it, their verbalised language was a clumsy thing. Easier to speak Worlder.

Somewhere, Zo was in agony. Her mind screamed hate at a hateful universe. Melid could do nothing. She couldn't dwell.

"Minutes left," Melid said. "Then Konsensus reconnect. You and other take craft: go."

"Harmonies," Kend said. Her mouth twitched.

"Uncare. Want Sparkle, not Silvercloud. Silvercloud used. Go, Kend."

Kend shook her head. "No. You ironic, you lie. Never let us go. You hate. Konsensus hate."

"No," Melid said. "Love Kend." She made her face soft as a protein pack. "Still love: enough let you run. Look my face: how lie Kend? Kend lie best. Go."

The flicker in Kend's face, from denial to incomprehension to acceptance.

"Stay," Kend said, and she propelled herself backwards slowly. She kept her eyes on Melid's face, and Melid was careful to keep her expression just so.

The core shook. Zo's pain ceased--Zo ceased--and an audible rumble filled Melid's ears.

Kend grasped for the wall instinctively. Melid surged forward, punched Kend in her gun-hand's shoulder, and Kend spun. A shot fired. Kend hit the wall and Melid flew into her. She headbutted the back of Kend's skull, and the female's face collided against the muscleform fittings. Kend groaned. Melid grabbed Kend's gun with her one good hand and sent it floating across the core. She grabbed Kend and placed her in a headlock. Kend struggled, screamed. Blood drifted from her forehead.

"Five minute to reconnect, monster," Melid said.

Kend fought, she shouted. All useless.

"Kancer," Melid said. "Who other?"

Kend struggled.

"Who other, Kancer? Tell." Untrained in weapons, surely. Unwise. It came to Melid then, cold as decompression. "The child."

Kend stopped struggling. She winced.

The frightened male child in the extrusion-sphere. It all made sense, explained how he had stumbled into Sparkle, how the kancer had been able to spy on and glean Melid's hidden motives. The child.

"Necessary," Kancer-Kend muttered.

"Necessary?" Melid repeated, full with incredulous hate. The only privileged in the Konsensus were the children. "Consummated? Consumed? Hollowed out? A child?"

Kend winced. "Kill now," she said. "Kill me."

"No," Melid said.

She threw Kend across the room, away from the gun.

Three minutes.

***

SWIRL SPRINTED THROUGH THE CORRIDORS and rooms of the villa. She was surprised she hadn't died yet. Perhaps, soon, her body out beyond the villa would be disintegrated in the grinding of bubble energy against Silvercloud's mass. Perhaps not. But she longed to be beside the person she'd shared a body with.

"Sparkle!" she shouted down the main hall. It echoed, rippled off the walls like the pleats of a ball gown. *An odd comparison, that,* Swirl thought. *Far too poetic for one such as me.*

An image flashed in her mind as she entered the music room. Herself in a wonderful blue ball gown, one she had wanted as a girl before she grew up and asked for blades. She'd floated in here, her toes above the tiles. Men and women in costume and ornate masks applauded her as she'd passed. A dream image. From the experiment? She remembered nothing of the experiment.

Odd. She had left the lid of the grand haspichol up when last in her music room. She was sure of it. But now it was closed.

She heard running footsteps upstairs and, for a moment, she thought it was Sparkle. But it was the Pearl-echo, of course, the vestigial memory of his presence in the villa. She paid it no mind and walked around the music room, looking for some clue.

An apple core lay upon the tiles. Strange; Sparkle hated fruit. She knelt to pick it up.

Its skin stung her fingers. The pain cooled to bliss. Dust like crushed insect wing drifted from the apple, then vanished.

Hoidrac. A Hoidrac had been here. Again.

The footsteps upstairs. Heavier now, insistent. Two sets of footsteps. Two mere echoes. Two shadows.

"Spar-ki-dar..."

Swirl fell to her knees, onto her side, rolled to a ball.

Alone in the villa, truly, utterly alone. Swirl couldn't think for terror. Alone.

***

KEND REALISED THE SOUND WAS her own moaning. Emotic filled her head: all Silvercloud waking to nightmare. A thousand dead, Yan dead, Silvercloud penetrated by evil. And herself...

All memories, each level of memories, naked before the Konsensus, the Kollective-at-Large. The Instrum.

Before herself. She was a traitor, they were all traitors. And below Kend, and below Kend the traitor, squirmed the kancer. She could feel it hiding, waiting for death in the pit of her neural being. Her true reality.

"I'm shell," Kend said. "Unreal. A--"

"Lie."

She looked up and Melid was there, floating before her.

"Melid," Kend said. She issued abjection, her fears, her love for Melid. "Help..."

Nothing connected. Melid was becoming like a Worlder, wholly unreadable. No: classified. The Instrum was blocking whole levels of Melid's neurology from the Kollective-at-Large. Melid was becoming a thing of the Instrum alone.

Kend felt a childish envy. Hadn't Melid been a traitor? Why should she be preserved, cared for? *But of course,* Kend thought, her analytic temperament rising from the maelstrom of her terror. Melid had discarded the very treason she had been raised in, had eschewed the Scalpel's alien temptations. Had chosen the unimaginable horror of mental isolation over the ease of the kancer. Melid had been tortured, tempted, and tested. She had resisted the neural siege. She had become the Konsensus distilled, and the Konsensus had withstood. Melid was victory herself.

Kend was broken. She wept. She reached out for Silvercloud, and Silvercloud pushed her away. Too panicked, too self-disgusted, they didn't have the concentration to disconnect her. Her mind loped on the very edge of the populace's kollective. Only their mental punches kept her warm, sane. And the child. She could sense the child she had ruined. As hated as her, terrified as her. Hating her, yet possessing no one else to cling to.

Kend vomited, a Milky Way of stomach acid winding through the air.

"I and cadre return to craft," Melid said, her figure warping, stretching in the vomit's mucus before Kend's eyes. "Destroy Silvercloud. All citizen."

Kend nodded. She tried to stretch her suit's fingers to blades. Nothing. She whined.

"Gun," she said to Melid. "End me." She wiped her face. "Please."

"No," Melid said, and Kend felt her bladder empty. The suit did nothing to address it. "I kill child first. Kinder. Kend wait. Die with Silvercloud." With that, she circled around and drifted toward the hatchway.

"Wait," Kend said. "Kend... Kend loved Melid. Loved."

Melid never looked back.

PART THREE

DESIC

James Worrad

CHAPTER FOUR

S parkle awoke.

She could see grey stone vaults rising up, up into darkness.

Silence. She couldn't feel anything.

If in doubt, fall back to the villa. That was her tactic when she woke anywhere unknown, which, given Sparkle's taste for red wine and her ability to persuade her siblings, occurred at the more reliable end of semi-regularly.

Yet she was scared to go there. She couldn't recall why.

A send-request to Swirl, maybe? Odd: she was scared to do that, too. Ah, let Swirl come to her. Well, nothing left to use but herself, her own knowledge which--why lie?--was vast, if somewhat ragged.

A high vault above... a tall building must house it then. Masonry style: early Dnach, though not the great architect himself. Later, six centuries later, exported across all Harmonies. Mm-yes: Harmonic. No feral tat, this.

She studied the materials. For some reason her eyes felt truly capable, more perceptive. Odd. Oh, hello: Huskstone, surely, extracted from inside the Husk mountains by the Anointed when they were first sent to monitor Zahrir. Fourth century. Donated to...

The Trinity Houses! Home!

Something creaked. Sparkle froze, or presumed she froze. She felt nothing. By the Eye, paralysed. Paralysed with... with something moving nearby...

Stop it. No fear. Keep looking, keep thinking.

No nose. There'd always been a hint of her nose between the sights of her eyes, like everyone had presumably, and now it wasn't there. You don't notice it till it's gone because a nose is right in front of your...

It all collided then. The noselessness, the high vault, the lack of feeling and the creaking, all of it melding into an improbable and unavoidable hypothesis.

She lifted her hand. She couldn't feel it, but she did it anyway. The hand filled her sight: white marble, segmented fingers. Silver talons.

Sparkle was an Ashemi. That creaking had been her.

She took a long breath, only to find she couldn't. Well, of course.

"Hello?" she said. Her voice was her own, but hollow, removed. Like whenever she listened to a recording of herself speaking. Where was Swirl?

"Greetings." A male voice, hollow, unknown to her. It came from just beyond her new feet.

Sparkle steadied herself. She raised her body into a sitting position. In doing so, she realised she had at least some kinaesthetic sense, but only enough to ensure she didn't flail about like an ornate jelly.

Away from her, upon an altar, sat another Ashemi, his body illuminated by candles sitting along the walls. Styled masculine, limbs of black iron, long 'hair' of twine and corquill feather. The relief features--his face, forearms, chest--were of alabaster. His lips and blue glass eyes were rimmed with white gold.

"Who are you?" she asked.

"The Ashemi," he answered.

She wanted to laugh at that, but instead a dizziness hit her, a lightness of being she'd never known.

"Are you fine?" the Ashemi asked.

"Aside from aesthetically?" She shook her head. White cords rattled against marble. Her hair.

Swirl? Sparkle sent. But she hadn't sent. She couldn't.

Nothing. Swirl wasn't there. Sparkle knew that was the source of her dizziness. Spinning in the wide immensity of her solitary being. Untethered, borderless.

She recalled Silvercloud, the villa. Swirl. She had to stop herself from physically toppling.

"What?" the Ashemi said.

"My sister..." Sparkle stared down at feet not her own. She heard the Ashemi creak.

"Who," he said, "are you?"

"Exile," she replied. "Not supposed to be here."

"Swirl? Sparkle?" He paused. "Pearl?"

"Middle one." She got a handle on herself as best she could.

"Swirl isn't with you." No question. A statement.

"How do you know?" Sparkle asked.

"You wear an Ashemi's form this side of reality, but you are no true Blessed." She had to marvel at him. Sparkle had seen many Ashemi bodies hanging in temples, but never one imbued with life, not one worn by a human personality selected to live forever within the unimaginable heart of the Geode. Like all Harmonics, she had spent her childhood wishing to see one, or be one. "We Ashemi," he continued, "can share thought, emotion. I suspect you are more akin to your brother, yet tethered to a statue and not some prison opal."

"Meaning?"

"Meaning your body is where you left it," he said. "Possessed by your sister alone."

"Swirl..." Sparkle placed a hand to her brow and felt nothing. "She'll suffer. She didn't even like being alone in the villa. Oh, Swirly-girl..." Nothing of her to reach out to, nothing.

"What occurred?" the Ashemi asked.

Sparkle looked up. The Ashemi's face was half-lit by candlelight.

"The villa," Sparkle said. "Our shared head-residence. Swirl became possessed... a Hoidrac. I don't know which one. I was taken by another Hoidrac, I think. A black door." She stopped. "You serve Pheoni the Appropriate, yes?"

"Naturally," the Ashemi said.

Made sense. This was Zahrir, after all.

"Something else," Sparkle said. "There's these people, your Ashemi. A breed of feral. They're... well, blasphemies. And hidden. Hidden everywhere, but mainly in rocks." She nodded, so as to evoke authority. "Space rocks."

"Well," he said. "You're safe now. Ferals are no threat here, 'space rocks' or no."

"You don't understand, sir," Sparkle said. "Pheoni... she warned my sister. The Konsensus may burn the galaxy. I think. Swirl didn't explain to me all that well. She never does..."

"The Konsensus?"

"The Hoidrac can't see them," she said. "Not truly."

"*Ferals?*" His metallic voice rang bemused.

"You don't believe me, do you?" Sparkle asked.

"Would you?"

A thought came to Sparkle. "What happens if my body, my sister... you know..."

"You too will die, and your statue will tumble," the Ashemi said.

"What?" Well, she could still feel terror. "You know, Ashemi... I assume you've long had no use for cushioning, but the rest of us do." Death at any moment. No warning. The thought of it.

The Ashemi just stared. Likely he wasn't used to making apologies. Which, paradoxically, was comforting; neither were Sparkle's siblings.

"You could inspect my memories, Ashemi," Sparkle said.

"As you are now?" he replied. "I would not know how."

"So I'm doomed to never being believed?"

"Perhaps." The Ashemi craned his neck, shifted his head to another angle. Perhaps that was his way of evoking expression. If so, Sparkle couldn't read it. "I fear both of us are doomed to not believe the other. I awoke moments before you. I've seen no one. I've no idea who placed and prepared our bodies on these altars." He looked down; Sparkle could read that at least. "I've little idea about anything."

"You're new then, your Ashemi? To Zahrir?"

"No," he said. "I was... investigating. You, your sister. But mainly Pearl. A few weeks after your exile, I appeared here. Asked questions. A fortnight of that, and I'm still no wiser. People were hurt. Someone died. Then I passed out."

"That must have been some time ago," Sparkle said.

"No," the Ashemi said. "I've an internal chronometer. I passed out three Zahrir days ago."

"Your chronometer's wrong," Sparkle said. "We were exiled, what... two and three quarter years past."

"Impossible..." The Ashemi almost seemed to freeze. As inert as a, well, statue.

"I've a more vital question." Sparkle pointed at her new marble body. "Does this come in pink?"

***

65

ALONE. EASIER TO HANDLE ALONE inside the villa. Swirl could imagine Sparkle in the next room. Sometimes Swirl wouldn't even notice. Not easy, but...

Easier. Impossible in the outside world. There'd been a rumble and a shake, and Swirl had stepped outside her skull to look. She was lying on the floor of the cockpit. She couldn't move, she couldn't go back in the villa. Hadn't the strength to. No one to cling to, to lean on. No one else in her head.

The tears dried. She realised she was gazing at a gas giant. Rust-coloured, streaked with cream. It was all Swirl could see, and she wanted it to climb inside her head and hold her.

Everything cold. Footsteps coming through the hatchway.

Swirl rolled over and aimed the pistol.

"Shit." A woman's voice, speaking Anglurati. "Don't shoot. Friend. Swear."

The woman held her arms up. No weapon.

"Safe here, tune?" she said. "Nobody here but my ass. And it's a safe, friendly ass, so..."

The woman took two steps closer, into the light of the gas giant. Maybe five feet, tan overalls customised with badges and trinkets, a utility belt: no visible weapon in it. Tan skin. A crazy shock of hair: brown, orange, some black. Hargie hair.

"Harg?" the woman said to the body in the cockpit chair. "You smoosh?" With no answer, she squinted at Swirl. "He smoosh?"

Swirl forced herself to nod. Cold, everything cold. Distant.

"I'm gonna walk over and check him," the woman said. "Think you could lower your ka-chanker?"

Swirl sucked on her lower lip and nodded. She lowered the pistol and held it tight against her chest. She hugged it. She watched the woman.

The woman ran a box over Hargie.

"He concussed." She turned around. "Why he concussed?" She eyed the pistol again and her face softened. "If I, er, may inquire?"

Swirl struggled to move her mouth. She had to work her jaw like a run-up to a leap. "Fell," she said eventually.

"Fell," the woman repeated. She whistled quiet and low. "Well, he rested, I guess. No point moving him 'til Desic." She waved the little box in her hand. "You fine with me running this over you? I'm gonna come over. Smoosh?"

Swirl didn't reply. Hargie used to say 'smoosh'. A long time ago.

The woman slouched her way over and knelt before Swirl. She smelled of fusion coolant, a little sweat.

"Whoa," she whispered. "Look at *you*. Hargie rustle up *good*." She ran the box over Swirl's head.

The woman had three rings in her lower lip, two in her left eyebrow, one in her left nostril, five in her left ear, two in her right. A silver bubble stud, either side of her neck. She had kind brown eyes, like Hargie.

"Sister," Swirl said.

The woman smiled. "Yeah. Li'l sis. Name's Kaysie. He mention me?"

Swirl couldn't process the words.

"Ah, figures," Kaysie said. "Family, right?"

Swirl began to sob.

"Hey, heyyy..." Kaysie said, placing her palm gently against Swirl's cheek. "Don't cry. Whatsa matter there?"

"Sister," Swirl said, trying to stop her tears. "Gone and... dead." She cried. "Maybe..."

"Wanna hug?" Kaysie asked. "That smoosh?"

Swirl nodded and Kaysie, prizing the pistol from Swirl's fingers, gently did so.

"How that?" she whispered. "How that?"

Swirl sobbed more, embraced Kaysie so tightly she made a surprised sound. But it wasn't enough. Never enough. She wanted to hug Kaysie--anyone--so powerfully they fell into her, into her bones. But nothing could do that. Nothing.

"'Kay," Kaysie said after some time, apparently struggling for breath. "I gotta check something important, tune? I'll go, but I'll come back." She pulled herself free from Swirl's arms and got up.

"Please..." Swirl said. "I want to... be with you."

Kaysie's eyes widened. "Oh, princess," she said. "Sure you didn't fall yourself?"

"Follow you," Swirl mouthed. "Not... be alone."

"Sure." She held out her hand, and Swirl took it. "I tune."

They made their way along the corridor, then down, down into the engineering level, or what Swirl had always assumed to be engineering. They'd never gone there, she and Sparkle. Too nakedly functional, too feral. It didn't disappoint. Pipes, gurgling sounds, cogs and hisses. Cold, too. Like inside Swirl.

"Well look at me," Kaysie said. "Hand-in-hand with a smooshy-fine princess. You regal, girl, know that? Like a singer on the 'ware shows."

She was trying to make Swirl smile. So she smiled back, best as she might. They had reached a dead end: a reinforced, curved bulwark with a silver panel on it.

"That it, babe. Smile." Kaysie let go of Swirl and produced a flat rectangular item from her belt. "Hargie gotta be so happy whenever he sees his woman smile so."

"Not my man," Swirl said.

"Oh." Kaysie shrugged. "Sorry; my bad." She turned to face the panel. "Now lemme see..."

She ran the rectangle over the panel, and a pneumatic hiss filled the air. She slid the panel open.

"Ah man..." Kaysie muttered. She closed her eyes and whispered: "Shadra, Meesha, Abendigeen, Mothers of the Tubes. Look kindly, we ask." She touched her forehead with a finger and dipped her head.

Swirl, behind her, leaned her head sideways to see. A small window, bubbles racing upwards behind it. Yellow liquid. A thin pillar inside, with a lump at its middle. No: the pillar was a conglomeration of wires and pipes. The lump was a... a brain, too small for an adult human.

"She dying," Kaysie said. She looked at Swirl, her brow knitted to a frown. "Hargie fell. You that hit the button. Right?"

Swirl couldn't take this accusative look, not from her new friend. She needed friends. She looked down.

She heard Kaysie take a deep breath. "Well... you did what you hadta, I guess." She took a cigarette carton out of her utility belt, offered one to Swirl. Swirl shook her head.

"Guess you already found a bad habit," Kaysie said, lighting up with her index finger. "Heck of a girl..."

Swirl shrugged. "Thank you."

"Meant *Princess*."

Swirl heard the panel slide shut and she looked up. She saw a face in its mirrored surface. Sleek cheekbones, expressive eyes. Pink dreadlocks.

Swirl screamed.

***

MELID GAZED AT THE TINY blue opal between her finger and thumb. The fifth in her lifetime, as memory served. Pretty, the way its carbon sparkled under the sleep-core's light.

She pushed the opal into the palm-sized muscleform sphincter on the wall before her. Her kollectiveware informed her the zygote had been stored successfully. She felt uncharacteristically sentimental. This was, after all, a common enough duty. The Konsensus might well never activate the zygote, or gestate it centuries or millennia hence inside some currently uninhabited asteroid. But it was Yan's seed in there. That context lent the process a sudden significance. Some part of Silvercloud, her home kollective that she had personally annihilated, would survive. It might not corrupt next time.

She shook the notion off. Too long amongst Worlders.

Melid dressed. She met Doum outside the craft's brig. The burly Field-Assault emoted a mixture of uncertainty, anger, and loss.

"Zo," Melid said, looking into his eyes.

"Zo," Doum said. He possessed hate for Melid, and shame for feeling that hate. All too much for Doum, feelings he'd understand if only the person he could share them with still existed.

"Zo," Melid said again, but her emotic was just making him worse. "Come."

Doum nodded and followed.

Nugo Vict--no longer naked; he'd been given trousers made of silkform--stepped back against the wall of his cell. He'd been allowed a modicum of gravity since Silvercloud. Melid found her suit didn't need to adjust quite so much. Her body's gen-fix was manifesting.

"Greetings, Mr Vict," Melid said.

"The woman," he said. "Where's that other woman?"

"She's dead, Vict," Melid said.

"Oh, thank fuck."

Doum ignited with rage. He took two steps forward before Melid stopped him with a thought, physically stopped him. He snorted, gripped his head.

Melid was shocked at her own emotic. She was drawing on some neural reserve of the Instrum, she could feel it. Upgraded, then. Significantly so. She hid her surprise from the prisoner.

"Mr Vict," she said. "We have considerable desire of your expertise. And you have considerable desire to avoid pain." She smiled. "A positive cultural exchange presents itself."

"I..." Vict stammered. He stroked his unkempt beard. "I want to help. I *told* you I want to help."

"And our threats only nurture that ideal." She stepped closer. "Hargie Stukes' craft has vanished. Simply disappeared, from *inside* a Kollective asteroid. That, Mr Vict, would be impossible. A faster-than-light singularity could not occur adjacent to--let alone within--so much mass. The result would be catastrophic. And if someone were suicidal enough to even try, our technology would suppress them." She studied the Worlder's face, seeking some reveal. Vict remained a blank. "Yet vanish they did. To much noise, but no destruction. Not of us. And, seemingly, not of them." She tapped the silver stud on the side of his neck. "Bubble-cleverness, no doubt. Some chicanery the Konsensus deserves to be informed of."

"Returner," Vict said.

"*Returner?*" Melid repeated.

"Returner," Doum said behind her.

Melid issued enquiry, and Doum issued an earnest need to help. Melid missed Zo.

"Explain," Melid said to Vict.

Vict made a gesture for Melid to wait, and he walked over to the nearby tap, a piteous display of momentary power.

"The bubbleship," he said after taking several gulps of water, "doesn't generate the tube, the, er, 'singularity'. It doesn't even require a pilot. The nearest Desic does all that." He let the word hang.

"Desic?" Melid repeated. She half-expected Doum to repeat it too, but no.

"Three of them," Vict said, rubbing water on his face. "Triangulated around the spiral arm. Space installations, homes of the bubblefolk. Good as hidden. A bubbleman gets in trouble--big trouble--he can hit a little button, and the nearest Desic will locate and tube him back." He grinned. "Tube him distances your otherwise exemplary craft can only dream of. A Desic has the energy to do that."

"Really," Melid said. "And how is it you dispossessed trash don't use this incredible power all the time?"

Vict sighed. He yelled and slapped the wall, startling both Konsensites. "Because it's a one shot," he said. "Kills the damn ship." He shook his head. "Good ship, damn it." He looked at Melid. "And Stukes probably won't get another. Returning is a humiliation, an admission you weren't smart enough."

"Your compassion is surprising," Melid said.

"I wanted to *beat* him." Vict rested his forehead against the wall. "He's a braggart and a liar, and I wanted to get in a cockpit and *beat* him." He slapped the wall again. "For all to see."

No, this was good, Melid thought. A better motivator than fear alone. "Would you settle for killing him?"

Vict looked at her. "DesicWest," he said. "That's the closest. Where he'll be. I'll show you."

***

HARGIE AWOKE. LIGHT CARESSED HIS lids, but he didn't open them. He hadn't known this kind of light in some time. The air smelled of disinfectant.

Bed. He was in a soft, warm bed. Well, that was something. Better than that... thing he'd slept in in...

Silvercloud. He opened his eyes. Not Silvercloud, thank fuck. White walls, plasticrete. No windows. A bed the other side of the aisle. A lump in it. Someone sleeping. He turned his head right and immediately felt dizzy. His head hurt. A line of beds. People in 'em. A medical ward, no doubting. The old-timer next to him had bubble studs.

Last thing Hargie remembered, he'd been falling. Falling in total darkness. This was better. No funhouse, but better.

A nurse walked up the aisle.

"Hey," Hargie said.

The nurse stopped. A bubblewoman: rows of rings in her cheekbones, two chains from ear to chin. "You're awake," she said. She blew out cigarette smoke. Definitely a bubblewoman.

"That a problem?" Hargie asked.

"Wait here," she said, and walked away.

Hargie must have fallen asleep awhile, for when he opened his eyes his sister Kaysie was sitting beside him.

"Kaysie..."

"Easy," Kaysie whispered. "Easy, bro-zo."

"Pony up," Hargie said.

She sighed and pulled a smoke from her pocket. He took it. He rolled on his side toward her, found an ashtray, and lit up. He almost moaned. He gestured at their surroundings with his cig.

"DesicWest," Kaysie told him.

"Explains all the bubblers," Hargie said.

"Scum of the void."

Hargie laughed. It hurt.

"Missed you, Bro," Kaysie said.

"Aw, get outta here," Hargie said. "Talk about anything else."

Kaysie thought about it. "You know you got a human ribcage nailed to *Princess'* hide? Any clue?"

"What?" He massaged his brow. "I get it, this is a dream. Now turn into a jellyfish, float off and let me wake."

"Sorry," Kaysie said. "'Nother time, maybe."

"Shit. Sparkle. Where's Sparkle?" He tried to get up on his ass.

"Whoa, smoosh," Kaysie said. "She fine. You mean that girl, yeah?"

73

"Yeah..."

He remembered her voice in the dark, over a comm. *Hargie... please, I need you.* Had he really heard that?

"She quite something," Kaysie said.

"Yeah," Hargie said. He smiled. Sparkle...

DesicWest? Some journey. Last time they'd been around Qur-Bella and...

"Cunt!" Hargie shouted. Sparkle had made a play for the Returner, back before Silvercloud, and... "Killed *Princess*! Killed..." Nurses were running over. "Fuckin' bitch! Fuckin' alien-buttfucked whore! I'll--"

Kaysie and the nurses held him down. He wanted to tear through 'em. Tear through Desic, find Sparkle and fuckin'--

He felt a needle slide into his left stud. His muscles wilted. The pillow hugged the back of his head. Tears, hot and rancid and...

"*Princess*," he whispered. He winced the word. "*Princess*..." Lids falling like guillotines, slow breathing. "Baby girl..."

***

THE ASHEMI AND SPARKLE STRODE through empty hallways. They had ascended from the vault into the main tower, with its continuously chequered floor and walls, and found no one. Where the chatter of acolytes and adepts had once rung, there was now silence.

"It cannot be gratifying," the Ashemi said, "to return to an empty home."

"Mixed feelings at best," Sparkle, newly pink and white, said. "Swirl wouldn't agree. But honestly? An ugly part of me wanted exile."

"Why?"

"Not the danger," Sparkle said. "I'm a coward. Just sheer perversity. Zahrir expects too much from Triunes. Trinity *is* Zahrir. Really, now; whoever wanted to be an archetype?"

The Ashemi nodded. Perhaps Sparkle's treason, wiped by her brother, had had its roots in that sentiment. "Disconcerting," he said, gesturing at the empty hallway. "This absence."

"*Real bat-ladder*," Sparkle said. It sounded like Anglurati, the great feral tongue.

"What?" the Ashemi asked.

"Something Hargie used to say." She ceased her stride.

"A friend?"

Sparkle didn't reply. She just stared ahead, as if in thought.

"I know what you need," the Ashemi said. "Wait there."

He walked over to a leaf spring, bent over and pressed the palm-hollow. He took some leaf for himself, felt its crackle inside his heart-furnace. Then he took some for Sparkle.

"Ashemi, really," Sparkle said as he turned the latch on her marble and newly-coloured chest. "We've only just met."

"Interesting chassis," he said. "White relief on, er, pink stone is an... interesting choice."

"Ruschito marble, actually," she said. Her limbs shuddered gently to the leaf's fire. "I was thinking. I'm not the authentic Sparkle, am I? More like a broadcast. The real Sparkle's inert in a brain light years from here. I'm far from complete: no hunger, no pain." He shut her furnace. "No sexual impulse."

"Paving upon the road to madness," the Ashemi said, "that's what such thoughts are. Trust me. And it could be worse. You could be bereft of all memory."

She looked at him, the marble of her face still white, its eyes and lips rimmed silver.

"I cannot imagine your predicament,' she said. 'Or why it should be so. But I feel comfortable around you. Weirdly so."

"Enough," he said. "We need to find a communic. Contact... well, anyone. A pity we can't comadose in these bodies. We might find truth within the Geode."

"First things first," Sparkle said. "I should like to see my brother. He's in the corridor upstairs, I think."

"The second time you've set our priorities."

"Second things second, then," Sparkle said.

"There's a communic outside the tether prison," the Ashemi said.

They found the communic dormant and the prison locked. Sparkle swore in Anglurati. She was dipped in feral filth, it seemed.

"He's merely an opal," the Ashemi told her.

"It's the principle," Sparkle said, gazing at the prison's iron doors.

"And a traitor," the Ashemi said.

"Traitor," she repeated. "That Hoidrac I mentioned assaulted my mind with a memory of him. Sexual. Pubescent. The three of us masturbating one another."

"Erm." This Sparkle was too much. They were strangers, damn it. "I'd rather not--"

"Not in reality. In our head-residence." Sparkle looked at him. "It's boring, almost taboo, to tell others what occurs inside your head-residence. Indeed, even *we* never talked about it. But, as is my way, I researched. 94.2% of all manyminds have a sexual encounter within their head-residences when young. Perfectly natural. And safe, ultimately. We believe ourselves more free than the ferals, more open-minded. But humans always find a way to be closed off, even under Hoidrac guidance."

"Why tell me this?" the Ashemi asked.

"Because once, as I was in ascendancy, taking an exam... I'm certain Pearl and Swirl did it again. This time, the whole way. We were older, but hadn't gained full physical experience. I felt ill, but also angry. Excluded once again."

"We have--"

"But that Hoidrac..." Sparkle waved a silver talon. "...caused me to realise something, throwing a buried memory at me like that. You see, my siblings didn't exclude me because I was silly or weak or because I might tell, though no doubt they told themselves that. They excluded me because I would have laughed. Because, in some way I still don't grasp, I had outgrown them." She gave a creaking shrug. "Surprising. I suppose I owe my Hoidrac that."

Footsteps.

The Ashemi turned toward them. "Who's that?"

An old Zahriran woman made her way along the chequered hallway, her movement full of the age-impervious vitality unique to Harmonic citizens. She wore chequered robes and headscarf: the same patterning as the walls. At times she almost vanished within them.

"Ashemi," she said. "Two. So honoured, so honoured."

"Who are you?" the Ashemi asked. "How many are you?"

"Just me," the old woman said, and curtseyed. Her eye sockets were thick with blue paint. "A humble monomind. Long I served here a servant. Now I am honorary seneschal of this house. My name is Ovia."

Sparkle stepped forward. "I don't recall ever seeing you here."

"With respect, She-Ashemi," Ovia said, "I do not recall ever seeing you here, either." She shrugged, smiled. "People do not see servants. They do not see monominds."

"You'll have to forgive us," the Ashemi told Ovia. "We have but lately arisen from the Geode."

"A holy thing," Ovia said. She made the Loican sign.

"Indeed," the Ashemi said. "Where is everyone?"

"Gone," she said. "An evacuation. From here, from all trinity houses, much of the surrounding peoples."

"Where to?" he asked.

"Beneath the Husk Mountains," she said. "The Anointed give them protection."

"The Anointed?" Sparkle said. "Impossible. 'Secretive order' would be an understatement. They've kept to themselves for millennia."

Likely they had, as with many Harmonic worlds. Mysterious warriors paid nightly in dreams, the Anointed would retreat to remote places once a planet's loyalty to the Hoidrac was assured. Perhaps thereafter they mainly slumbered. Or perhaps they watched.

"Why?" the Ashemi asked Ovia.

"Culakwun." Ovia near-spat the word, a true Zahriran. "For centuries those scum have petitioned the Hoidrac for the chance to conquer our world. Soon they shall have that chance. Their fleet arrives in two days' time."

"A Pleasing War?" Sparkle asked.

"Just so," Ovia said.

"Impossible," Sparkle said. "Pheoni wouldn't permit it. She never has."

Ovia checked her fingernails. "Some manner of divine pact," she explained. "Or some test. Zahrir failed. The beautiful scum won." She looked up. "That's all anyone knows."

Victory: wasn't that what the Envoy had proclaimed upon Gleam's death? The Ashemi pictured that murderer's grin. *Victory is ours.*

"The test," the Ashemi said to Sparkle. "The test for your world. I think it involved *me*."

Sparkle gazed at him, her blue glass eyes catching the soft lights above. "You fucking what?"

***

"GOT YOU SOMETHIN'," KAYSIE SAID, reaching into her belt. "Like you ask."

Swirl sat up on the wall bed. It creaked, and its chains rattled. She'd barely slept.

Kaysie walked over and sat beside her. "Here you go, lady."

The thing was a tonestick. Swirl took it, set the stick to electric blue, and began re-toning her hair. The ice-cold rush on her scalp had become a welcoming thing, she found, familiar.

"What's the deal?" Kaysie asked. "Why you scream at pink hair?"

"My... sister had it that way," Swirl said. "I looked like my sister."

"Twins?"

"I suppose," Swirl said trying to hide her discomfort.

"No offence," Kaysie said, "but maybe you shouldn't tone it like your sister."

"I won't anymore," Swirl said. "I've lost my brother and my sister. I'm alone."

Kaysie said nothing. Swirl began toning the side of her head, and was thus condemned to look about the room. It had been constructed from a section of corridor that had belonged to a scrapped ship. The entire crash house--a place, Kaysie had told her, where they put burnt-out bubblefolk--was. Such emptiness here. She spent as much time as she could in the common room. None of the inmates talked, and the orderlies kept from Swirl as much as possible, but she needed to be around people, even the broken. She was broken, too.

"Am I a prisoner?" Swirl asked.

"'Shit, I dunno." From the side of Swirl's eye, it seemed Kaysie had just picked her nose and rubbed it on her trousers. "More like... you're in the in-tray, you tune? We don't get visitors, not typical. But, but... no one's gonna, y'know, airlock you or shit. You be walking around Desic soon."

"Among people?" Swirl asked.

"Yeah." Kaysie smiled. "Hargie say you name's Sparkle."

Swirl stopped toning. "Yes."

"Fits," Kaysie said.

Swirl coughed, continued toning. Why had she said yes? But Hargie knew her as Sparkle, and now Kaysie did, and Swirl didn't want to hurt anyone anymore. She didn't want to go anywhere anymore. Not back home, to Zahrir. Zahrir would reject her. Rejection was too painful. It led to loneliness.

"How's Hargie?" Swirl asked.

Kaysie scratched her mottled shock of hair. "I'll level, Sparkle. You ain't on his burp-day list."

"He hates me?"

"You killed his ship," Kaysie said. "People duel over that shit: broken bottles, chains. Vendetta, tune?"

"He's going to kill me?"

"Harg ain't no kill-head," Kaysie answered. "But *Floofy*, man. I mean, woooo, that was a ship. I'd kill ya. No offence. But... what the deal with you and him?"

"I could kill him in a blink," Swirl said.

Kaysie laughed. "Then *we'd* have a vendetta, girl. You wouldn't kill me, right?"

"Wouldn't enjoy it." She looked at Kaysie. "I'm a bad guest, aren't I?"

Kaysie laughed, slapped her thigh. "Shit, love a woman says she can kill like that." She snapped her fingers. "Women ain't like that round here. Things be changing, if slow." She shook her head. "But listen. Hargie ain't got time for you. Not presently."

"We... we had a... a thing." A lie, but to Hargie it seemed truth. Likely he'd tell Kaysie sooner or later. "I don't know."

"A thing? Shit." Kaysie shook her head. "Say hate's the other side of love. And judging by what he say, it must be one motherfucking love. He blew up to a real asshole." She raised a pierced eyebrow. "Even got a little sodgeny on your ass."

"Sodgeny?"

"You know: sodgeny. Hating on women and shit." Kaysie looked at Swirl's expression. "Harg's better than that, he ain't like the older men. But we all cut with it here. Had to spend a long time protecting our women, bubble-gene an' all. Hate: other side o' love..." She stood and picked up the mirror from off the desk across the room. Sitting back down again, she handed it to Swirl.

Swirl looked at herself now.

"Blue a fine choice," Kaysie said. "Look better'n pink."

"Yes." She looked down at her clothes--Sparkle's clothes. "Do you think I could get some... overalls maybe? Like yours? Blue?"

"Blue. Sure." Kaysie made a sad sort of grin. "I gotta dust now. There's this, er... occasion I gotta stand to. But I'll be back." She moved to stand up.

Swirl stopped her, a hand on Kaysie's shoulder. "Wait. Could we..." Idiot, she felt an idiot. "Could we hold each other?" *Please*. "Like when we met?"

Kaysie's eyes lit up. Her shoulders heaved. She looked down. "I dunno..." she said.

"Please," Swirl said.

"Look, I'll straight up here: looking at you, pretty princess... it's painful, tune? Us hard-huggin' and mouth to ear? Idea alone... " She gulped and looked up. "And that ain't fair on Sparkle. You in the fragile zone. You need a friend, tune?"

"I'm sorry," Swirl said.

Kaysie stood up. "Not much as me. Wooo." She stopped at the door, turned around. "And it ain't fair on Hargie." Kaysie stared at Swirl, as if thinking of more to say, but she left.

Swirl was alone again.

***

"THAT'S IT, GIRL," HARGIE SAID. "Sleep now. Long trail over. Sleep."

He slid the panel shut on the brainhouse. He felt his lips go tight, his eyes sting. He let it all go: wept and whined. He leaned against the wall and let himself slide down on his ass. His hands shook. Hell, his nose ran.

Just the lights on now. He'd shut the reactor down. Long trail over. Sleep. *Princess* wouldn't truly die for months--tough freaks, those brains-- but her functions were gone. They said they dreamed when...

He lit a smoke and barely got it in his mouth.

"Let you down, girl." Barely a whimper.

He cried some more. For *Princess*, for himself. A life going nowhere, shooting up stims so as not to go crazy. One of DesicWest's statics. Dead in the crash house in another twenty years, if that.

He got it together. There were people waiting.

He stopped by the cockpit, the lounge and, dammit, Sparkle's quarters. She'd not left much in there. Too clean. But it stank of her, that foreign perfume he'd never seen a bottle of. He took a deep sniff and immediately hated himself.

He'd known she'd known about the returner, and he'd done nothing, laughed it off. Yeah, smart guy. Oh, he just knew Sparkle'd never figure the button was his hat's badge. But she had. She was brighter than Hargie could ever hope to be.

He imagined murdering her. Right there, right in that room. Gun: boom, nice and quick, face all dumb and puzzled at the hole in her head.

Shit. Shit, this wasn't Hargie. He'd never wanted to murder anyone. Not a woman. He was old-fashioned that way.

Fuck it, nasty thoughts made him strong, blocked tears. People outside waiting.

It was a large turnout in the small dockpod, more than when he'd gone into *Princess*. Lot of people Hargie didn't even know, all here to see Mow

Stukes' son. He walked out of the hatchway and it whirled shut behind him. Old Durse, Headman of DesicWest's Ring, approached, can of hoxnites in his thin, ringed fingers.

"Y'kay, son?" he asked, a rasping rattle from his bone-dry, bone-white beard.

"Guess," Hargie muttered.

"We'll do this quick," Durse said. "I know you ain't for performance." He passed the can to Hargie. "Pre-programmed. You're all set."

Hargie nodded thanks. Charging the can, he rubbed its applicator along the join between *Princess Floofy's* hatch and the dockpod's coupling. The microscopic hoxnites set to work, blurring the air like a heat haze. A ship no longer. An attached livingpod.

"Shadra, Meesha, Abendigeen," Durse intoned out loud for those watching. "A soul rides to your embrace, as our home embraces its shell. Please, sisters, be kind to *Princess Floofy*."

Hargie heard sobbing. His sister, a couple of others. A struggle not to join in.

"Good work, champ," Durse whispered to him. "Smoke?"

Hargie took one off him, and they shambled over to the crowd. Must have been thirty, thirty-five people. Kaysie hugged him. He felt the hands of other pilots squeeze his shoulders. They muttered kind things. A huddle of slouches and tobacco smoke.

"Heck of a ship, man," said Skip Darrow, roman-nosed, lank hair. "I remember the Katonda run."

"Smoosh days," Hargie said. Good man, Skip Darrow. Newly on the Ring--DesicWest's council--and well-deserved. His family were North Diaspora, but he was no Nugo Vict. Judged people by what they did, not where they'd been. "Durse," he said to the old man. "Maybe..."

"Sure." Durse looked at Hargie. "Now I know you need time, but we want you to know you got an ear at the Ring. Up to us you have a seat, but..." He nodded at *Princess'* corpse uncomfortably. "But any son of Mow Stukes gets an ear, tune?"

Hargie looked at his shoes. "I'm not a..."

"It's appreciated," Kaysie told Durse.

"Sure," Durse said. "We gonna be needing every ass's head screwed on, reckon." He grinned at Kaysie. "Even yours, Sprinkles. Freightways dropped some kinda sensor shot our way last night."

"Bat-ladder," Skip Darrow said. "Never known 'em so dumb."

"Want us to know they watching," Durse said. "Guess."

The dockpod was clearing now, making their way to Rust's Bar, to the aftershow.

Durse looked around, said to Hargie: "What's your thoughts on the Stat girl, bud?"

"Sparkle?" Hargie asked.

"Desic don't abide a Stat hitting no returner button," Durse said. "Hell, Desics don't typical abide a Stat. Say the word, she gone. No nasty, but gone."

"Tap and 'lock job," Skip Darrow added. "Quick."

All she deserved. Heck, a skulling and spacing was getting off light. Hargie toked, shivered.

"You're tuned wrong, boys," he told them. "No one hit that returner but me."

Kaysie's nose wrinkled. "Wait--"

"Sparkle knows," Hargie said, cutting his sister off, "the shame a pilot gets hitting that button. She don't know our rules: must've thought she could cover." He shook his head. "She's a good soul."

"All right, then," Durse said.

"Guess you hadn't a choice," Skip Darrow muttered.

Both of 'em polite, but Hargie saw the disappointment in their eyes.

"But she'll wanna head out pretty soon," Hargie said. "Flight as north as anyone's willing to go. She's running home."

"Running from who?" Durse asked. Man never missed a trick.

"Real bastards. Eager. And pro." Hargie shrugged. "But we lost 'em. Bought her some time."

"Hell of a price," Durse said.

"C'mon," Hargie said. "Let's dust."

"High time for hooch," Old Durse agreed.

The four of them left the dockpod and entered the endlessly curving tube that was the docking ring. Hargie noticed a knot of men loitering around a disused bubble-coupling. Two of them, heads shaved and eyes mean, stared back.

"Who they?" he asked Kaysie.

"Ugh," Kaysie replied, "fuckin' Jaggard brothers."

"What's their problem?" he asked.

"Fuckin' life," Kaysie said.

CHAPTER FIVE

*H*andgrip to handgrip, bulwark to bulwark, Field-Emissary Melid glided down the scarlet-lit access tube. Others passed her by: awed, but wary. Nowadays regions of her memory and mind were blocked even from most senior Instrum members, let alone the common Konsensus utile. A classified human. So be it.

This Hunter-Killer was crowded, far more so than her cadre's own. They proceeded slowly along the access tubes, careful not to bump shoulders with those passing. It didn't help that Doum, behind her, dragged a human-sized muscleform cocoon.

The Savard mission was no longer Melid's alone. An arrogance to think it ever had been. Her craft had arrived in system only to be informed six other Hunter-Killers were already present, with another pack incoming.

She told Doum to wait outside the social-core. She smiled at him, a gesture he didn't respond to, then entered the core.

The social-core was at full capacity. Some thirty emissaries and various other instrums sat along the spherical walls above, below, and level with Melid. She felt a stirring in the local kollective, a reshuffling of mood at her arrival. Its main flavour was of an expectancy satisfied. Melid's story-- what was permitted to be known--had travelled: Melid, the archetype of Konsensus strength, Instrum will. Melid, who had conquered the dark temptations of individuality and kancerisation, who had annihilated her own birth-kollective for the good of the species.

Sensing all that, she resisted the urge to play up to their preconceptions, to egoise. For that, they only esteemed her more.

No space left to sit. The meeting recognised this and a wide sentiment emerged, compelling a red-haired female in the equatorial row--a Craft-Emissary Xeic, Melid's kollectiveware informed her--to give her seat-pit over to Melid. Xeic emitted a brief hurt, then a reluctant acceptance. She removed herself from her place and loitered by the hatchway. She never looked at Melid.

Melid squeezed herself into the still-warm pit. She looked about.

The general mood had been fixed around a young male who sat across from her. She could hardly credit her kollectiveware: Blas of Riga 76. The young man--broodingly handsome, black hair scraped back, and a chin beard equally severe--studied her. He had the barest smile.

Blas of Riga 76 was the pride of the konvergence fleets. At nineteen years of age, he had taken command of a mine-damaged Hunter-Killer--its Craft-Emissary dead--and proceeded to eliminate five Worlder 'Falcatta' craft. The details were classified, but somehow that task had not only been achieved, but made to seem an accident. Blas was twenty-three now, three years younger than Melid. The Konsensus watched his career with expectation.

"Melid," he said, his voice deeper than she'd expected, "you honour Konsensus."

The core murmured assent, issued warmth.

"One citizen," Melid replied. The saying of humility, old as Konsensus. "Blas: fleet's pride."

"One citizen." The core's local kollective rippled with comfort. "Melid kill birth-kollective..." Blas raised an eyebrow, considered the matter. "Hard duty."

Melid smiled. "Would do again."

Everyone exuded their admiration, but interlaced with it was something like apprehension, even fear.

Not from Blas. He smiled back at her.

An image manifested at the epicentre of the social core: a Domov, the same as Conybeare in aspect: bald head, coldly handsome.

Domov composite, it announced, name-assigned 'BetaConybeare'. Aggregation of all relevant individuals (extended/expanded). Prepare: Sit-rep, updates: current concern.

Melid felt the heat in her spine, information rising through the nervous system, into the hypothalamus and flooding the senses.

The room comprehended as one: DesicWest, its geography, its nature. A geodesic aerostat submerged within the clouds of a gas giant, carried on the bow wave of its endless lunar tide. The lumpishly spherical aerostat's hide--a kilometre in diameter--was entirely covered in mirrored plating.

Aerostat deflation via laser: impractical.

Gigantic hoops of gunmetal circled the aerostat's equator like planetary rings. Three in all, decreasing in girth from the aerostat outwards. The inner ring served as conurbation: welded to it were a motley array of living quarters constructed from junked ships, amputated stations, fuel tanks. The farthest ring catered for docking bubblecraft though, intriguingly, many bubblecraft seemed inert, derelict. Permanently adhered to the ring's surface.

The middle ring was currently the most significant of the three. Sensors, transponders, missile pods. The serial number on the warheads suggested some manner of motion targeting rather than heat.

The room relaxed at that. No threat to the Hunter-Killer's stealth--

An addendum/corollary: gas giant's atmosphere. Hunter-Killer stealth could not compensate for the craft's wake in this medium. The atmosphere was too gentle, too viscous. Any stealthed object left a detectable trail of churned gases. Likely the Bubblefolk had selected this planet for just that reason. There were, after all, Worlder powers with their own, far inferior, stealth tech.

Craft close-approach/boarding/stealth-salvoes: detectable.

And if that were the case...

Melid opened operation side files. Yes, the very sensor pod that had gleaned this information had likely been detected. Xeic's fault: the red-haired Craft-Emissary who had relinquished her seat. Arrogance. That desire of Hunter-Killer pilots to garner kollective admiration had endangered the mission. Not the first time. Too many wishing to be another Blas. Melid looked over at Xeic, loitering by the hatchway. The Field-Emissary gazed back, aware she was being considered. Melid returned to the neural tac-schematic.

More defences. Eight objects orbiting the aerostat at a thirty-mile radius at varied angles. Each was a pair of gravity spikes, their bases hoxwelded to one another. Opposing polarities, set to spin. At their centre lay more modified motion detectors. Nuclear warheads. Any closer, and the sensor pod would have set one off.

Massed attack within atmosphere-possible target range: problematic.

The tac-schematic dissolved, loitering in the back of everyone's mind for ease of access. A brief silence followed. A miasma of numb thoughts.

"Elegant," Bas said.

"Primitive," a male Craft-Emissary replied.

"Thus elegant," Bas said. "Resourceful."

"Obvious, then," Melid said, and every perception studied her. "Primitive with primitive. Divert comet, collision." She bared her palms. "Accident."

Blas issued admiration of a sort. "BetaConybeare?"

BetaConybeare produced another side file: Worlder observation station in geocentric orbit over gas giant's third moon. Freightways owned. Continuous link to owners.

"Would notice comet direction change," Blas said. "Endanger Great Hiding." He inclined his head to one side. "Comet-strike Desic *and* station? Worlders foolish, but..."

A bitter amusement filled the core.

"Bring asset," Blas said to Melid.

She'd been about to suggest as much. She didn't enjoy the way Blas had been assumed mission-nexus here. She tried to subdue her personal feelings as much as Blas studiously ignored them.

Doum floated through the hatchway dragging his cocoon. He unpeeled it and Nugo Vict popped out, a band of muscleform around his waist. Doum pushed him forward, the cocoon inverting into a long bridle of two muscleform cords. When the bubbleman reached the core's epicentre, Doum applied a surprisingly delicate jolt and Vict came to a stop.

The core's kollective curdled with disgust. A Worlder, a corpse-man. A strand of his long hair had broken off inhumanly, and two nearby Instrums tried to waft it away.

Blas sentimented for calm, for fortitude.

"Nugo Vict," he said to the bubbleman.

Vict stared around, below, above, horrified at so many Konsensites. With a deep breath, he addressed Blas. "Sir..."

The core broke into laughter.

"We do not use those titles," Blas said in Anglurati. "Honoured guest."

Vict didn't spot the mockery. He seemed to relax a little. "My apologies." Stomachs turned at words spoken without emotic.

"The Konsensus commends you for leading it to DesicWest," Blas said. "Pleasing, that our aims should be so aligned."

"Indeed," Vict said, "er..."

"Blas," Blas said.

"Blas." Vict smiled, dipped his head. "Any way I can aid further..."

"You can," Blas said. "Our fleets are blunted, Nugo Vict. And full annihilation of your people's home would be seen. We do not wish to be seen. Would it be possible for you to gain entry and kill this Harmonic woman? This..." He mouthed the word with mild disdain. "Savard and her Stukes."

"A fucking pleasure," Vict spat out. "Forgive me; I am eager for this task."

"Evidently," Blas said. "A suicide bomb, perhaps?"

"A, a... such a thing would be detected, sire..."

The core cackled with delight.

"A joke," Blas said, waving a hand for Vict's calm and the core's silence. "No. We have patches, Vict. They dissolve into the body, cause a delayed coronary. Undetectable."

"An elegant plan," Vict said.

"Elegant?" Blas gave the mildest nod. "Konsensus thanks you."

"B-but I'd need a bubbleship," Vict said.

"We have a collection now," Blas. "Every ship leaving Desic has been tagged and appropriated."

"Very wise," Vict said. "Caution." His face tightened with concentration. "Erm..."

"Blas."

"Blas... I wish to place a suggestion before the court." Vict smiled and nodded at those around him. His smile vanished when he noticed Melid. He looked back at Blas.

"Proceed," Blas said.

"Why settle for murder?" Vict let the thought hang, and hang it did within the kollective. "I believe I can bring you so much more."

Melid emoted caution. The room noted her.

"The bubblefolk are not one," Vict said. "Among them is a suppressed subset: the Northern Diaspora. I am of their people. I am a voice they will listen to. I only need a message to convey to them." He made a fist. "To lend purpose."

"If you're suggesting a coup," Blas said, "you ask too much. We are a secretive concern, Vict."

Vict snorted and shook his head. "There is a saying: shake a bubbleman's hand and count your fingers. No one--no 'Worlder'--believes a word we say. We are weavers of fantastic, drug-fuelled tales, of 'Great Foozles', star-anemone and bronze moons. Next to that, would anyone believe a coup inspired by, well... nobody? Succeed or fail, you'll remain a drunk's brag."

Melid could feel them: dismissive yet swirling, eyeing a shadow, perhaps prey.

"I know I am a beast to you people," Vict said, no longer to Blas, but to the core. "I *am* a beast." He smacked his chest. "Made beastly by time, by victimisation, by the brutality of corporate powers. We bubblemen steal and trick and grasp for wealth *outside* a Desic. Let me tell you something: *inside* a Desic there is no money, no ownership, all things are shared. A Desic is a fortress protecting something beautiful, a piece of a lost age, our lost world. We reached out..." He held a hand aloft. "To help, to encourage humanity. Our reward?" The hand came down. "Destruction. Debasement."

Whether he knew it or not, Vict had their interest now. The Konsensus's birth lay in the slaughter of their ancient masters.

"I have spent time amongst you," Vict continued. "I see we are not so different. We need your guidance, your example." Vict paused. "And you will need allies. I was there when alien beasts assaulted Silvercloud. War comes. You are a rational people. Tell me: what benefits any of us to stand alone?"

"Fine words," Blas said. "A moment."

Blas emoted for a convergence. The core, and relevant individuals far beyond the core, meditated within the heart of BetaConybeare. Melid was shocked to find herself mostly alone. Alone and increasingly furious. But she saw the logic.

"Nugo Vict," Blas said. "As long as Savard dies, so be it."

"You agree?" Vict grinned. "I shall not fail."

"If you do, we lose nothing," Blas said.

"Erm... quite."

"We shall," Blas said, "provide you with a bubbleship and more. Two death patches also, for you to adhere to Savard and Stukes." He emoted to Xeic, and the female floated behind Vict unnoticed. She slapped the back of his neck. "One for you, also." Blas smiled. "To seal our alliance."

Vict shuddered. "Please, I--"

"I'm certain we won't have to activate the thing," Blas said.

Vict gulped. "No." He bowed. "If you permit... I would like to contact friends within the Desic. Prepare them."

"Naturally."

Melid leaped up, emoted outrage. "You want I lead this?" she said in Jiang. She pointed at Vict. "With Worlder? With ironic-vomiter?"

The core wavered before Melid the Kollective-killer.

Blas emoted regret, embarrassment for Melid. "BetaConybeare?" he said.

BetaConybeare released a side packet into Melid's perception. Orders: Melid and cadre to proceed spiral-north to the Fugue. Oversee defensive patrols in event of target's escape from DesicWest.

She glared at Blas. He was blank, unmoved.

"Best there," Xeic the fallen Craft-Emissary said. "Your skills." She shimmered with the cruelty of reason. "Our defender."

"Melid," Vict said. Astute scum, he clearly smelled the room well enough. "No bad feelings from me." He smiled, offered a hand. "You've taught me much."

"Gah!" Melid squeezed her fists, controlled herself. She looked about the core. "Your killer... she go." She exuded a mocking sweetness. "She go!"

Fools, she thought as she flew through the hatchway. *Fools.*

***

"GOTTA BE QUIET," KAYSIE SAID.

"Understood," Swirl said.

They strode out from the dark corridor and into flickering gloom. Swirl couldn't see the walls of the inner temple. All the braziers lay around the Sisters.

The tallest sister rose some forty feet, the second thirty, the smallest a round-bodied twenty. They were patchwork statues, colossi of beaten bronze, graphene, plascrete tiles, all built over a towering framework of steel. The sisters wore labcoats, held obscure devices, gazed at the heavens. They had the heads of long-furred cats.

"Shadra, Meesha and Abendigeen," Kaysie whispered. "The Gracious Sisters."

Two old women hobbled by. They stared at Swirl. Their faces glowed in the brazier light, their eye sockets black, tattooed. Their cheeks, noses, and lips hung heavy with piercings.

"Don't mind 'em," Kaysie said. "Hate me in here much as you."

Swirl pointed at her own face, made an inquisitive expression.

"Keep Stat men away,' Kaysie explained, taking out a cigarette. She pointed at the relatively few rings in her own face. "New girls ain't so inclined. But a couple rings shout where y'come from, tune?"

They made their way to the shallow steps before the Sisters. A cast-iron rack stood there, hundreds of burnt cigarette butts jutting out from oily sand. Kaysie lit her own, took a single drag, held it before the Sisters and worked the filter into the sand. Its heat snaked upwards.

"Why," Swirl asked, gazing up, "are they feline?"

"Complicated," Kaysie said. "West Diaspora say they were cats stretched to women, East say women squashed to cats. Either way, human minds couldn't tune how to make faster-than-light, needed to splice." She shrugged. "Then again, South Diaspora say Sisters were just women in cat costumes. Who knows?"

"Why such confusion?" There was little confusion in Swirl's faith.

"Well, when the Sisters invented bubblejumpin', we had no choice but to scramble our minds and head to the stars. Leave our world."

"Why?" Swirl asked.

"No idea: scrambled minds," Kaysie said. "But Gracious Sisters knew what they be doing. They say: 'Go out, give bubblejump to everyone, make galaxy happy 'n' loving'. Once that happen, Sisters say, our history come back. Unscrambled." She pointed at her head. "One day."

"How can you even believe that?" Swirl immediately regretted her words. "Sorry."

"No bad," Kaysie said. "We people and we good. Why should other people be different?"

"Empathic rationalism."

"Hargie tell you that?" Kaysie smiled. "He an athie, but I work on him."

"People aren't often good, Kaysie," Swirl said. "They have to be watched, monitored."

"People *are* good," Kaysie said. "They *are*. Just confused, hurt. We can meet eye-to-eye if we try." She looked up at the Sisters. "Sparkle, I need to take a moment."

"Fine."

Kaysie closed her eyes. Swirl looked up at the Sisters, their straggly chins rendered in alloy. The Gracious Sisters. Absurd gods. Fictional.

But kind. The Hoidrac were real but cruel, sadistic in their ambivalence. They had torn Sparkle from Swirl, likely killed her. No reason given. Perhaps there was no reason. Could a faith built on lies exceed one of truth? Swirl needed kindness. Her life now was desolate as the tundra of Zahrir.

"Hey, pretty," she heard Kaysie say. "You cryin'?"

"The smoke in here." She looked around, noticed the base of the Sisters. It was silver, artfully lumpish. No patchwork junk: the product of a far advanced culture.

"What is that?" she asked the bubblewoman.

"Oh, that the brain womb," Kaysie said. "Makes brains. C'mon, let's get lunch."

Outside, music drifted across the temple stairs. Jackalbeat, they called it; arpeggio on junk-built instruments. It seemed like daylight inside the great agorapod, shining down from a house-sized mass of floodlights. It filled every corner, nook, veranda, and esplanade of the agorapod, a hollow shell of ribbed tungsteel some two hundred feet in height.

The square was busy: music-women improvising, children running, drunks and junk-heads dancing. Men smoking in circles, debating, waving their hands. Laughing. The bubblefolk behaved differently here. They walked taller, acted less furtive. Complexion-wise, they might have been citizens of any cosmopolitan feral world: most brown, a few dark as Swirl, some white as Zahrir men. However, they all tended toward short and slender. And the hair, of course, that untameable busyness of russet, black, and brown.

"Do good 'wiches that way," Kaysie said, and they made their way down an alley between two converted fuel tanks.

"Hey!" a male voice said behind them. "C'mere."

"Uh, shit." Kaysie muttered. "Faster, princess."

Swirl stopped and turned around. Kaysie sighed and did likewise.

Two young men approached, their steps heavy on the paving grill. Shaved heads, thick biceps. Clearly lifted weights, Swirl thought. But no scars. Men who picked their targets with diligence. Who enjoyed fear in a face. No weapons.

"Who are these men?" Swirl asked Kaysie.

"Jaggard brothers," Kaysie said.

"Y' new worst nightmare," the shorter one in front said. The leader.

"You're not," Swirl replied. "But, by all means, take a ticket and wait in line."

"Stat bitch," Shorter said.

"Stat cunt," Taller said, stood behind his brother. Salt-in-the-wound man. Defined roles, these two.

"Word to your bro, dyke," Shorter said to Kaysie. "Better dust now, better quit Desic. Take his fuckin' dyke harem too." He eyed both women- -a knife-glance, as they said on Zahrir.

"Could," Kaysie said. "But he'd say shove it, slap-heads. He'd say y'look like a couple o' tits too dumb to grow sucksies." She spat. "Tune?"

"Stukes's stay," Shorter said, "Stukes's *die*."

"Like y'dead fuckin' daddy," Taller added.

"Asswipes," Kaysie said. "Just two o' ya. *Two*. Hargie got the Ring backin'. Got Ol' Durse, got Skip. Jaggards ain't got shit 'cept mother's love. If that."

"Got friends, bitch," Taller said from behind Short. "Outside friends comin'."

"Sure," Kaysie said, tough, but Swirl could hear anxiety in her words. "Keep jacking, wingnuts."

Shorter stepped closer, inches from Swirl and Kaysie. His anger vanished, a sinister calmness replacing it. "Girl got no place in a cockpit." He flexed his arms, made fists. "Bro, we should teach these bitches."

"Serious?" Kaysie said. She faked a laugh. "Right outside temple?"

"Alley *next* to temple," Shorter said. "No one here, bitch. No one *see*."

"True," Swirl said. She shot her arm under Shorter's armpit, brought it up around the back of his neck and seized his mouth with her hand. She seized his testicles with the other. His eyes went wide.

"Hey," Taller said. He moved to get by his brother, but Swirl let go of Shorter's crotch, grabbed Shorter's skull and rammed the back of it into Taller's nose. Taller dropped, nose a red bloom. Swirl returned her hand to Shorter's groin and squeezed. Shorter tried to punch at Swirl with his free arm but couldn't get leverage, had to swing around her. Swirl arched her back and took his weakening hits.

"Kaysie," Swirl said, "watch. Never fall for the lie kicking--or grabbing--a man's testicles negates him. Always go for the jaw or nose." She nodded at Taller sprawled out on the grill floor. "Instant discombobulation. But adrenalin will drive a man through mere pain in his gonads. See?" Swirl nodded at Shorter, struggling against her body lock. "I daresay he's murderous right now."

Shorter tried to shout against Swirl's palm. He began to shake.

"Why?" Swirl continued. "Because he knows he has slim moments to act. He recognises agony is inevitable. He pictures the pain." Shorter's eyes, wet and wide, stared at Swirl. "Because... eventually..."--his legs trembling now--"adrenalin fades. The legs buckle." They did so. "Oh, right on time." She lowered him slowly to the floor. "That's it, boy," she whispered. "Good boy." She laid Shorter flat out, his head on his brother's belly. Swirl let go of his mouth and withdrew her arm, but kept her hand on his serpent-nest. She looked up at Kaysie, whose mouth hung wide. "Never target 'balls', Kaysie. Jaw and nose. But if you *should have to*... patience is key."

Kaysie pulled out a cigarette. "How come you know so much about nut pain, girl?"

Swirl looked down at her victim. "I don't think DesicWest's ready for that information."

"Jokin'," Shorter winced, his voice high. "Please... just jokin'.'"

"Who are these friends?" she asked.

"Just joke..."

"Explain the punchline," Swirl said. She began to squeeze.

"*Vict!*" Shorter said. "Nugo Vict. Called us... *please*..."

"Nugo Vict?" Hargie had said he'd been a prisoner in Silvercloud. Not good. Not at all. "Who else?" Swirl said.

He began to sob. "I dunno... friends. Other northers, guess. Swear I don't know..."

"North Diaspora," Kaysie explained.

Swirl let go, harrumphed, stood up. She turned around to look at Kaysie. Three bubblemen stood some distance behind her, sandwiches in their hands. They raised their sandwiches in the air.

"It's fine," Swirl reassured them. She pointed at Shorter on the floor. "He'll need a stretcher."

"What are ya, princess?" Kaysie said as she and Swirl strode away. "Cuz I wanna be that." She laughed.

"We need to talk to Hargie," Swirl said. "Quickly."

"I talk to Hargie," Kaysie said. "Best."

"Whatever you say," Swirl said. "Oh, and those piercings of yours?"

"Yeah?"

"How do I get them?"

***

OUTSIDE, OTHER, ALONE. ALWAYS ALONE. Melid powered down the tunnels of the Hunter-Killer, grip to grip, bulwark to bulwark, jaw a tight grin.

People avoided her. Always had; the reasons were merely different now. Strange little Silverclouder: avoid. Now paragon of Konsensus, force-of-

99

nature: still avoid. Send away, to the Fugue, admired, but *please, oh, please, be distant.* Once not Konsensus enough, now *too* Konsensus. Oh, they'd learn. If she had to burn the galaxy and drag them with her, they'd learn.

"Conybearrrrre," she called out, her emotic sickly-sweet and raging. "Requesssst!" One of Blas's crew got in her path, and she threw him against the tunnel wall. She kept moving.

The face of Conybeare appeared to her right, keeping pace with her.

BetaConybeare, it corrected her.

"Request, Conybeare," she said. "I hunt Sung Eucharist. Extract information. Then terminate."

Fugue mission, BetaConybeare said. Decided.

"Eucharist say Luharna," Melid said. "Luharna on way. Time enough. Pleassse..."

You use Worlder ironics, BetaConybeare noted.

"You *think*? Pah."

Domov not think, Beta-Conybeare said. Not conscious.

Melid snarled. "Well?"

Eucharist left communicate. Why not communicate?

"Be his puppet then," Melid said. "No. This way Eucharist mine."

BetaConybeare disappeared, reappeared. Permitted, it said.

Melid almost crashed into the corner of the multi-junction. She stopped. She let passing citizens work around her. They felt indignation but did not, display it.

"Permitted?" Melid asked.

Time constraints, Beta-Conybeare said. But permitted.

Melid felt a presence behind her, rising from a tunnel below her feet. Greeting her.

"Melid." Blas of Riga76. His face placid, impervious to her miasma of spite.

"Congratulations," Melid said. "Mission yours. Hunt yours."

"Not yours give," Blas said, flickering with... what? Appraisal? "Your dismissal regrettable. Necessary."

"Oh," Melid said, sneering. "Blas sorry?"

"No," Blas said.

She punched his shoulder, emoted venom, stared. Blas smiled.

"Why?" Melid said. "Why skulk? Why chase?"

"Kollective decide we dysfunctional. Endanger mission together." He began to emote something unmistakable. "Intrigued."

Typical. She seized his throat. A passing Craft-Instrum passed faster.

"Hatefuck?" She emoted disdain. "Pathetic."

"Experience," Blas said. "Unknown."

"Great Blas?" she said with a sneer. "Never hatefuck?"

"No one dare." He seized her chin. "You?"

Melid whispered: "No one dare..."

Only then did she notice their emotic auras were stirring one another, crackling to life. She'd never known the like. Neither of them had.

Without breaking eye contact, Blas nodded in the direction of the Craft's fuck-core.

Melid smiled. She reached up to a hand grip above them both and checked its sturdiness.

"Why wait?" she said. She lifted her legs, pressed his hips between her thighs. Blas leaned in. With a shared thought, their suits began to slit open at the belly. His breath caressed her lips.

Time constraint, BetaConybeare said. Melid progress to mission now.

Melid shouted. Blas growled. Their emotics separated. She shoved him aside and continued down the tunnel toward her waiting shuttle. Angry, bitter.

But less alone.

***

SPARKLE TRUDGED THROUGH THE EARLY snow of her world, up the hill, that wrought-iron arsehole clanking behind her.

"I would have thought my unalloyed honesty worth something," the Arsehole said. Arsehole.

"Yes," Sparkle said. "I must find out the exchange rate between 'unalloyed honesty' and 'punching someone's parents'. Doubtless it stacks up in the former's favour."

"I didn't punch them," the Arse-shemi said. "More a... backhand slap."

"What's the back of your hand cast from again?" Sparkle asked.

He didn't reply.

The cottage lay ahead, with its circular windows and slouching walls. The place of her birth. The problem wasn't so much that this moment was nothing like how'd she always pictured it, but rather that it was too *much* like she'd pictured it. Snow, but no sense of cold; the hill's ascent, yet no familiar strain in her limbs. A picture. Her new reality felt as fictive as her hopes.

To her right in the far distance lay the Husks, those familiar mountains of warped rock. The sky around them was dotted with air traffic: teardrops, stratobarques, skiffs, all moving toward the Husks and none leaving. It couldn't be all Zahrir--not even the southern continent alone--hiding under those mountains. Just Triunes and biunes, most likely. The monomind masses had less to fear from Culakwun, theoretically.

Sparkle stopped. The pair of them stood within the shadow of the cottage.

"You can't come in," she told him.

"Then why bring me?" the Ashemi asked.

"I fear you vanishing," she said.

"I'm Ashemi," he said. "The Blessed. I do what I wish."

"Are you?" Sparkle said. She tapped her ribcage. "Seems anyone can blag the patter if they have the look." It was a fair question, one she'd neglected to ask herself before. "Wait here. In fact, back off down the hill."

"You forget yourself," he said. "Your place."

"You know what's back down that hill, your Ashemi?"

"What?"

"Your dignity," Sparkle said. "Must have dropped it when you beat my folks." He tried to stare her out but Sparkle just made a whistling sound and gestured at the path from whence they'd come. "Go on: have a search."

The Ashemi stood there a moment. Then he looked at the cottage and turned about. Sparkle let him get to the bottom of the hill before she knocked on the door.

Sparkle could feel a chill, at least inside her mind. Her father apparently broken, mother telling wild tales. A visit from Pearl, then from the rebel Hoidrac, the Dissenter. Or a feral. Beggared belief, all of it.

Feral. She wondered what Hargie might say now if he were here. Odd she should think that, but not of Swirl. Swirl felt like a missing limb, but somehow--

The door opened. Uncles Haze-Dazzle staring up at her, their shared mouth slack. She loved her uncles, but hadn't expected to see them here.

"I'm here to see Coral-Silver," Sparkle said, recalling to speak. She'd reveal her identity, she decided, when she met her parents.

Haze-Dazzle had a look on their face like Sparkle had never seen before, one she'd never wish to cause.

"I won't hurt them," Sparkle said. "I won't hurt anybody."

She knew that look: the pair of them arguing behind their face. Their brow creased. They relented and let her through the doorway. She had to dip her head.

"Thank you," Sparkle said.

Her uncles never heard. They were running down the hallway.

"Silver!' they called. It was Uncle Dazzle, she could tell. "Silver!"

Sparkle should have smelled food, ancient scrolls, and dust. But nothing; nothing, of course.

Her parents were in the library, already backed into a corner, framed by shelves of scrolls. They were in their male phase, their expression a pallid mask of horror.

"Mwoma," Sparkle said, "Pyoti. It's me: it's Sparkle."

This had been a bad idea.

Her mother--Uncle Dazzle had cried her name, had he not?--moaned low. Uncle was already beside her. He held her.

Sparkle stepped closer. "Mwoma," she said, "I know this is strange. I had no way of contacting you beforehand. I'm not an Ashemi. It's me, Mwoma: Spar-ki-dar. Please..."

"I did everything," Mother said to Uncles. "Everything they desired."

"Mwoma," Sparkle said. "I have a strange tale, granted, but please just-_"

"This isn't fair!" Mother shouted at the ceiling. "You hear? I did everything demanded! I was loyal!"

"Mwoma, please." Sparkle froze in the centre of the room. She wasn't sure what to do.

"You're not Sparkle!" Mother shouted. "Can't be..." She began to sob. She looked at the ceiling again, to watchers unseen. "No more performance! No more, you monsters!"

"Please..."

"One!" Mother screamed, Uncle restraining her. "One! Not all! Not all!" She collapsed.

Uncle Dazzle looked at Sparkle, his face part accusation, part plea.

Sparkle nodded. She understood.

Stumbling down the white hill, she began to understand matters. She missed the comfort of tears.

It had begun to snow. The Ashemi, that utter arsehole, was a stick figure against the white land. Sparkle broke into a stride, her talons held wide. She could see him move to a defensive stance.

But he didn't strike her. Perhaps, subconsciously, he already knew.

Sparkle embraced him. Their chests made a dull thud.

"Brother," she whispered.

The snow fell gently upon their embrace, drifting down from Zahrir's blank sky.

***

SWIRL WALKED ALONG THE ENDLESS curving tube of DesicWest's docking ring, her lips, nostrils and ears throbbing in that way she'd always found satisfying. Pain: the reminder of being. She wore a bubblewoman's robe, blue. Her colour.

The lights were low, a simulacrum of night. No arrivals, few people. But people, at least. She was looking for Kaysie. Find out about Hargie, find out what he said. Just hear voices. No voice but her own. How did others handle that? How did they not go mad?

"Can't tune it," a bubbleman was saying to a chain-faced woman in robes. "Meant to be here hours back. No contact. Not like him."

Swirl had taken a quarter-leaf, about as much as she'd allow herself these days. She was cutting down, cutting down her past. But she could see the concern, the confusion rising from the two bubblefolk's bodies. They were like a warm hearth to Swirl.

"What?" Swirl realised the man was speaking to her. "What?"

His concern wavered into frost. Swirl wanted to say something, converse, but words wouldn't come.

"Dust," the bubblewoman said. "Go on!"

Swirl did as she said. The woman muttered something about the crash-house.

Empty tubeway, empty head. She wanted to scream but she was scared it wouldn't echo, just drift away. Up ahead a hatch was open, light drifting out. Walking closer, Swirl saw sprayed words over the hatch: *Princess Floofy.*

She shivered. So strong earlier, against the Jaggards. So different alone. Yet had this been the reason all along, why she had chosen to wander the docking ring? A ring, after all. She would have passed *Princess* sooner or later.

She looked through the hatch. The dockpod lay empty, but there was another hatch open on the other side. She squinted. *Princess's* entry corridor, she knew it. It hummed with memory, their experience of the last couple of months. Sparkle. She stepped over the hatchway lip, her belly as cold and empty as the dockpod.

He'd be in there. She wasn't good at these things, but it had to happen. And she could handle him if...

She stepped into *Princess Floofy's* corridor. Memories swam through her: Sparkle laughing, Sparkle shouting. So wonderful.

"I've neuraled the boys, asshole." Hargie's voice, from the lounge. "Walk now and no one breaks the ol' Desic code, tune?"

She could turn, walk away.

"It's me," she said.

Silence. Like a vice.

"Can I..." Swirl faltered. "Can I..." She stopped at the doorway of the lounge.

Hargie stood in the centre, between the broken sofa and the dinner table, an improvised club in his hand: a piece of pipe. He was topless, hatless, smudges of black on his jaw and stomach.

"You want to hit me," Swirl said.

He stared at her. Only his nostrils moved, flaring in and out.

He shook his head. "Thought you were..."

Wires dangled from a hole in the ceiling, some access point, a hook light wedged into their dusty, plastic tangle, the only illumination. She could see footprints on the table. Parts, too: ugly feral tech. Dead.

"Did Kaysie talk with you?" Swirl asked.

"What's that shit in your face?" he asked. "Why you dressed like that?" She looked down at herself.

"Wanna know what I'm doing?" he said. He coughed, spat. "Ripping out a drive line. Bubbledrive. Putting in air con." His head tipped to one side. "Embalming a fuckin' corpse."

"I'm sorry, Hargie," Swirl said.

"Yeah."

"I'd... run out of answers," Swirl said. Sparkle would have had an answer.

"Hitting that button was your *first* fuckin' answer," Hargie said. "Before Silvercloud, recall? First." His nose wrinkled. "Ferals to you. Me." He slapped his chest. "Her." He waved his club around at the walls.

"I should go," Swirl said.

"Yeah. Outta Desic. Outta the star slums. Let them Spindly bastards follow you all the way to the better people. Leave us be."

"Vict might be working alone," Swirl said. "He might have--"

"Ratshit," Hargie said. "Leave us be."

"I've nowhere to go!" Her own volume shocked her. Even Hargie jolted. "Journey's over... I'm... alone."

"Two of us, huh?" He looked around. He pointed at her face. "That why you're Bubble Bessie now? That it? Won't work. You're alone. Forever. Deal."

"You know I can't just... 'deal'." Her eyes stung. She wiped her nose, felt the sting of fresh piercings. "No... family. Gods betrayed me, killed my... I used to be connected to something and I can't now so, so just use that pipe, will you? Airlock me. Who'd care?" She dropped to her knees. *Sparkle, oh, Sparkle girl.* She closed her eyes. "No one." She heard Hargie's bare feet upon the tiles. Felt his aura before her, his emotions. Leaf-sense. Sparkle all over him. Memories of her. Fossils of lust, need. Hate.

"This ship," she heard Hargie say, "she's my world. I didn't have the... best childhood. Been broken on every world--beat up, shot at, shivved once--but always her. Her chair. Her forgiveness. Never wanting in return. I *should* kill you."

Swirl nodded.

"'Cept..." He paused, inhaled. "I got this static, this interference. I keep seeing you, me, arm in arm, walking by a river. Recall that?"

No.

"Yes," she said.

"With you beside me... I had gold for blood," Hargie said. "Well, fuck you, Sparkle. Fuck you. Know why, asshole? 'Cuz I love you more than this fuckin' ship." His club rattled on the tiles.

Swirl looked up. Hargie began to sob, one palm on his face, the other stroking his hair. But she wasn't looking at that. She studied with that sense leaf bequeaths, that heat haze of feeling. Sparkle, Sparkle all across his limbs.

She reached out, touched his thigh.

"Fuck you." He slapped her hand away, turned, walked four steps, hunched over. "Fuh..."

Swirl got up. A sin. More than sin. Zahrir's one true taboo.

She stepped over, ran a hand down his hairless, scar-nicked back. The heat of Sparkle. He flinched, but he didn't move.

"Hargie, I'm sorry. We..." But this was DesicWest. No one to judge. To know. "We can be like *before*, Hargie. I want that. Can't we?"

He faced her, eyes puppy-wet.

"Hargie," she said. "Let's never be alone."

She couldn't wait. She grabbed his chin, drew him to her, drove her tongue inside those lips. A parasite, she was. But the taste of him, of Sparkle on him, of connection to her and him and *someone*. He froze. Then he relaxed, ran a hand through her dreads. His tongue worked around hers. She pulled her lips free.

"Now," Swirl said. She tore off his trouser button with one yank. Stepping away, she pulled her knickers down from under her skirt. Not for pleasure, she thought, sex as a summoning. An engine to raise dead Sparkle. To visit her haunts.

She squatted down on the sofa, lay back. She lifted up her skirts to her belly and gazed at him. His serpent still hung as he pulled his trousers down, but when Swirl stretched her thighs wide, jabbed her crotch out like a taunt, it rose to life.

He clambered down to her, ankles still leashed in trousers. Was this how it was? The limbs? The movement? She released one of Sparkle's own perfumes, just slightly, from her pores.

Fingertips between her legs. She slapped them away.

"No need," she said. She fumbled and found his erection, pulled it to her, blunt head jabbing at labia.

"Push," she said, like Sparkle would.

"Sparkle..."

Half-inch in. She gritted her teeth. "*Push.*"

"Stop," Hargie said. "You ain't even... ain't prepped.'"

"Doesn't matter," she said.

"*Does.* Fuckin' hurts."

She felt him leave her. She let go, leaned back, stared at the tiles above. Alone.

"Not like this," he said.

She stared at him. "How? Tell me. Please."

He reached out, caressed her chin. "Like this, remember?" Leaning in, he kissed her, one soft kiss upon her lips. "This."

Swirl smiled. "I remember."

He smiled back. Then he lowered himself, ran his lips along her neck.

Swirl felt her eyes water. Yes. This. She would get used to this. She would.

***

PEARL AND SPARKLE LAY UPON silver chaises longues, facing one another in the high lilac-domed dining hall. Pearl had been 'your Ashemi' when first he'd lain here, surrounded by equivocating fools. At least they had *seemed* fools. He could be sure of nothing now.

Sparkle was talking with Ovia, that servant-now-seneschal of the Trinity House.

"That beast, the Envoy," Ovia said as she poured crushed leaf into a bowl beside Sparkle. "He waits above us, in orbit around the moon. Laughing, awaiting his fleet's arrival through Zahrir's own Starlocks."

"I only ever heard of him," Sparkle said. "A fop, they said."

"A fop's face," Ovia said. "But rumours of his evils seeped from his roof garden, down, down to we servants. I would not blink to hear him the very *Jhatain*, the Dissenter itself." She made the Loican sign and frowned.

The two of them carried on in this manner. Pearl paid them no mind. He stared up at the high bloom-shaped dome, now devoid of swimming Geode-beasts.

'Pearl' he was, or seemed to be. At the word 'brother' he had felt something crack, a fissure in his being. Memories seeped out, yet only two: the three of them, young, amid the waves. And... himself and Swirl alone together, when Sparkle was ascendant outside.

Practice, Swirl had called it, for Swirl had suggested their congress. 'Preliminary', 'ridiculous not to'. He could recall the excitement her eyes had lit in him, her serious gaze as she said the words, the unbearable guilt after. But he couldn't *feel* any of it. Not with this synthetic body, this stripped mind. Swirl didn't feel like a sister. He didn't know how that would feel. He didn't even feel like a Triune, couldn't conceive of these indiscretions occurring inside a... head-residence.

Ovia poured leaf into Pearl's own bowl, saying nothing. Perhaps these memories were replinisenses, artificial memories. Perhaps Pearl wasn't Pearl and Sparkle wasn't Sparkle. Yet, somehow, he knew that couldn't be. There were things deeper, more fundamental, than memory.

"Can you remember anything?" Sparkle asked, looking at him from her opposite couch.

"No," Pearl said.

Her dead gaze held his own. "Well?" she said.

"What?"

"Don't you want to know?" Sparkle asked. "Don't you yearn to comprehend how clever I am?"

"That's still to be ascertained," he said.

She pointed at him. "Very Pearl, that. I apologise. I always needed to impress you, brother. Always."

"Will that be all, your Ashemis?" Ovia asked.

"Yes, Ovia," Pearl replied. The woman nodded and left.

"Time," Sparkle said. She opened her heart-furnace and poured in some leaf.

"You're certainly stretching it out," Pearl said.

"The time *differential*, remember? Years to me, weeks to you. We couldn't both be right, and I'm never wrong, so..." Sparkle waved an apologetic talon in the air. "Do you even recall the quiet moments between your investigative duties, 'Ashemi'?"

"Well, of..." He froze. By the Delighted, he could not. That was to say the inconsequential moments were there if he didn't concentrate, assumed, but when he tried to focus...

"Thought not," Sparkle said. "You've been switched on and off. Put to sleep..." She clicked her claws. "Then awoken."

"Zahrir's seasons," Pearl said.

"Yes, too fast. I bet everyone fed you nonsense, am I right? But, deep down, you suspected something, brother. You know your homeworld's seasons."

Pearl opened his own chest and filled it with leaf. His mind stirred with the flames.

"So the investigation continu--"

"Stop," Sparkle said. "Stop thinking 'investigation'. Whatever this is, it isn't that. Everyone here knew Pearl's crime, or believed they did. Think like a Hoidrac, Pearl. What this *is*, is a performance. An entertainment, mm-yes. Mother said so, when I visited: *One, but not all.* She'd bear this jape, this theatre right to the last act, with one child--the traitor son--but not all her children. Certainly not her Spar-ki-dar. Seeing me broke her." The pink statue looked down.

"Sparkle?"

She shook it off. "Think, Pearl. On your last visit to Mother: you said she already had a healing bruise on one side of her face." She pointed at him. "*You*, Pearl, you. You said you didn't know where your anger came from when you hit her. It was *induced* in you, an alien fury. You've hit her who knows how many times. Again, again, and each time she takes it and she heals."

"What are you saying?" Pearl asked.

"A repeat performance," Sparkle said, "a runaway theatrical hit. This is your punishment, Pearl. You awake, you act out a farcical investigation in which you assault your very parents, and then, at its climax, you're shut off, only to be rebooted again. Everyone, simply everyone involved, everyone you've interacted with has been in on it, willingly or no. You stride like a lord through these halls when all along you're a jester, an unknowing fool." She tilted her head. "No offence."

"Gleam," Pearl said. He pictured him dying on the roof garden. He looked at her. "The security head."

"He interests me, your Gleam," Sparkle said. "You say 'security head,' but he's no one I know of."

"His back was damaged. His skin. Before I was going to whip him."

"Yes," Sparkle said. "Yes. Skin treatment is good, but never *that* good. Old lash wounds."

"He hid his back from me," Pearl said. "Before, I mean. In the sauna."

"Could have been months before," Sparkle said. "Hadn't healed. And who knows how many times."

"But why? I..." Pearl paused. "Mother didn't approve of a Culakwun 'wastrel'... Gleam was my lover."

"Condemned to be whipped by you in a... cycle of unknowing sadism."

"All before the Envoy." Pearl sat up on the couch. "I remember nothing. Nothing of that love."

"Gleam did," Sparkle said. "Evidently."

Evidently. "He broke the cycle, the play. He broke the pact."

"And failed the test," Sparkle said. "Ultimately he was the weak link in the chain. His attempted attack on the Envoy has presumably sent our world to war. Understandable, but--"

"No," Pearl said, cutting her off. "He betrayed his homeworld for me, again and again. It wasn't fear of the whip that broke him that last time. It was the Envoy's taunts. His ridicule of me. Pearl was everything to Gleam."

He mourned, coldly, for a love he would never feel. What were Gleam's last words? Suh Youkrist? Sang Carist? It meant nothing and yet... yet the

113

shape of those words in his mind. Another memory seeping through the crack.

"Sparkle," he said. "We have to be there, at the orbital palace, for the fleet's arrival at the Starlock nexus."

"What?" Sparkle asked. "How?"

"We're Ashemi," Pearl said. "We can do anything. Besides... there's something I left there."

CHAPTER SIX

S wirl knelt in the gloom before the three Sisters, one in a row of five women. Swirl belonged, or soon would.

She even enjoyed the smell of tobacco now, at least as it wafted about the great temple. Cigarettes were a gift to the Sisters. It glossed her nose as she knelt in silence, lost in her thoughts like all the bubblewomen.

So what if the Hoidrac watched her? She had new gods now, goddesses of a warm, wonderful lie, which was better than a cold truth. The Sisters never killed Sparkle, never left Swirl all alone. Swirl was blissful in her blasphemies.

She gazed up at the statue of the three whiskered Sisters. She thanked them for her blessings these last two months, since she'd arrived at the Desic. For community the likes of which she'd never known. For Hargie's love, though stolen. She was amending for that. She was learning how to love him, which, in truth, was more than Sparkle had ever done. She had embraced him as a parasite, but she wouldn't remain a parasite. She would love. Soon she would call herself Sparkle and feel it true as everyone here.

Boots slapped against the tiles. The women looked around.

"I'm sorry," Kaysie said. She made a holy symbol before the statues, then looked back at the women. "Sparkle there ain't got 'ware, and signal's impossible in here anyway, so..." She shrugged. "Sparkle, we gotta talk."

Swirl stood up. "This better be good," she told Kaysie.

"Vict," she replied. "Nugo Vict's here."

Fear shot through Swirl. She imagined stealth-suited Konsensites lurking in the temple's shadows.

"Let's go," Swirl said.

They caught a pod to the northwest section of the docking ring. The two of them were silent much of the way. Swirl had kept a distance from Kaysie since her embrace of the Sisters. Guilty as Swirl felt, during these formative days it wasn't good to be seen with a female bubble pilot. She'd been meaning to make it up to Kaysie.

"So what's Vict's situation?" Swirl asked Kaysie.

"Just him. He got funny clothes. New ship." Kaysie shook her head.

"What else?"

"All I heard," Kaysie said.

There were a whole lot of people when they got there, crowds milling about the docking ring. Kaysie knew the way, using her neuralware. She followed the fuss.

It lead to Repair 9, a long rectangular hangar with multilayered walkways lining its oily-steel walls. That feral tech stink: coolant, acids, floor cleaner. The walkways above echoed with chatter.

Swirl and Kaysie entered onto the hangar floor itself. A few hundred bubblefolk stood about in there.

A row of seven bubbleships sat on the hanger floor in various states of repair. The fourth, the one they now stood before, was no regular model.

"That something," Kaysie muttered, echoing the sentiment of the crowd.

The ship's surfaces glistened black, catching the hangar's lights in its seamless concave plating. Its hemisphere pulsed with red lights, as if breathing. But the ship's geometry truly disturbed: a bubbleship fighting to become a fat diamond, to birth a prow and something like wings. The bastard bubble-child of Konsensus evil.

Swirl made the Loican sign, the charm of the Hoidrac. Sheer instinct.

The Jaggard brothers and their cronies stood around it at the front of the crowd. She nudged Kaysie and indicated them.

"Northies," Kaysie said. "This shit dividin' us, tune? Dividin' Desic."

With a hiss, a hatch on the side drew open. Stairs unfolded and Nugo Vict stepped out.

He was dressed in the manner of the bubblefolk before they were bubblefolk, when they had stridden upon their lost world: an ensemble something like a labcoat. Vict's robes, however, were cut from the muscleform material worn by Konsensites. Black and glistening, they seemed a piece with his ship. Vict grinned at the throng.

"Gather!" he shouted, still stood on the hatchway stairs, his arms aloft. "I bring good news!"

"Smooshy ship!" someone called out from the crowd.

"Dumb threads!" someone else shouted.

Vict gestured for calm. He got it. "Brothers," he said, "Sisters. I am a humble messenger. Many of you will know me from the deals I've set up, the rights I've fought for. Others will know of my family, which traces clear lineage back to the world of our forefathers. These people will know me as a man of faith, a servant to the Sisters." He grinned. "Now... who digs my ride?"

Cheers went up. The crowd were fools for bubbleship conversions.

"A gift," Vict said, "from the people who saved me. I was kidnapped from Calran by allies of Freightways." He let the name hang. "But not for long. I discovered we bubblefolk have allies. We are not the only enemy of Freightways. For there exists... the Undercompany."

"Ratshit!" someone shouted.

"You high!" Kaysie yelled, then ducked behind the shoulders of the man in front.

"Ratshit?" Vict said. He chuckled. "Could 'ratshit' build this?"

He clicked his fingers and the bubbleship vanished. The metal stairs Vict stood on floated ten feet from the hangar floor. The open hatchway behind him was a black halo, an impossible portal.

The crowd drew their breath as one. Some screamed. Plenty swore.

"The Undercompany," Vict continued, "are a secret cadre of independent industries throughout space. They tire of Freightways crushing all other transport, their demands for outrageous pay. To them, we bubblemen are a salvation." He paused, shook a finger. "To us the Undercompany are a means to former dignity, former glory. Am I really the only man here tired of being kicked around?"

The Jaggards and their cronies shouted "No." Many among the throng did likewise.

"To each man a new bubbleship, should he want it," he said. "The same make as *Snowy* here." He patted the invisible hull. "Think of it: stealth, invisibility..." He clicked a finger and the ship, *Snowy*, re-materialised. Another hatch opened below its prow and a red eye glowed. There came a humming sound, something powering up. "Weaponry."

Hoots and cheers filled the hangar.

"I say high time *we* kicked around," Vict said. "Who's with me?"

The crowd seemed uncertain about kicking people around, but they could certainly use a free invisible ship.

"The glory of our past can be ours!" Vict shouted.

"Glory!" Jaggard's gang shouted.

"Arise, my people!" Vict bellowed. "Ar--"

Black dust fell from above. On him, his ship, the whole Jaggard gang. It billowed out, thinning as it travelled, giving the crowd enough time to cover their faces. It settled quickly. Inert hoxnites.

Vict's cronies had a bad time of it, though. They coughed and spluttered and staggered, they shouldered into one another, blinded and blackened. Vict held on to the rail of *Snowy*'s stairs, bent over and brushing his long hair with his other hand.

Squinting, Swirl looked up. An empty crate hung upside-down from the rail high above, its opened lid still swinging. Thinning strands of hox-dust rained from its maw.

"Welcome aboard." Hargie's voice, way up behind her.

Everyone turned to face him. Hargie was up on one of the walkways that lined the hangar's walls. Old Durse and Skip Darrow stood beside him; other members of the Ring, too, DesicWest's ruling body.

Hargie grabbed a hook chain, and someone lowered him down the two storeys to the hangar floor. The crowd parted for him as he made his way to the front. A different Hargie, Swirl thought. No more slouch.

"You roll an armed ship into a Desic?" he asked Vict. "Hardly bubble. Hardly bubble at all." He came to a stop ten feet from Vict's little party. "Sorry about the bath." He pointed to the hox-dust. "Wanted to be sure none of your invisible buddies were with you." He spoke over his shoulder to the crowd. "Anyone see footprints appear in that dust, holler."

Vict leapt down from *Snowy*'s stairs.

"Hargie, you mistake me," he said.

"You mistake *everyone*," Hargie said. "Think their kindness stupidity, honesty a kind o' brain damage. Like your 'Undercompany' pals. Work with those mass murderers, you stick-to-nothing piece of shit? People here'll ram your ship up your exhaust once they get a taste of Spindly gratitude."

"Stukes, dude," said a man in the crowd. "He offering invisible ships."

Hargie shook his head. "Talking of ships, why don't you ask Vict here why everyone who's left here this last month ain't been seen since? That mystery makes a shit-ton of sense right now."

Mumbling in the crowd.

Vict waved his hands for calm. "People, I was coming to that. I ask you to consider..." He clicked his fingers again, and Snowy issued a hologram. Zo. Zo holding a cat and stroking it. Zo kissing an old woman on the head. Zo smiling, coy, demure. "The Underking's daughter. Barely nineteen, virginal, devoted to family. Murdered." Vict looked down. "Impaled through the chest by a foreigner in your very midst."

Swirl felt eyes upon her. She'd sensed this coming. Resolved, she stepped through the crowd and stood beside Hargie. She felt someone move behind her, and hoped it was his sister.

"That girl was a monster," Swirl said aloud. "A child killer. I did humanity a favour."

"You believe that?" Vict asked the crowd, pointing at the hologram of Zo sewing. "This girl, on the cusp of womanhood, this girl like your own daughters, could kill?" He looked at Swirl. "You're a poor liar. Better off denying you ever met her."

Given the body language of the crowd, Swirl found she had to agree. Sparkle. Sparkle would have walked this.

"I assure you all your friends are well looked after," Vict told the crowd. "They'll be returning here within twenty-four hours. It was necessary for the Undercompany to check their holds for this bloodstained witch. The Underking wishes no slight upon his allies. He wishes only justice for his child."

"This is some rinky-dink ratshit," Hargie said, pointing at the hologram. "If little Missy here was so damn mimsy-sweet, how come anyone would murder her in the first? Riddle that, asshole."

"Jealousy," Vict said, his eyes piercing through the black dust upon his face. "For your vile lusts, Stukes. Sparkle would permit no rival."

"Wha-the-fuck," Hargie said.

"A tale old as time," Vict said.

"And cheesy as your sack," Hargie said. "Seriously think people here'll believe this?"

"Let's see." Vict looked over Hargie's shoulder to the crowd. "Who do you believe?" he asked them. "I, who in the past have toiled to bring you contracts and credit, or him... a strange loner, a braggart who claims"-- he made a show of chuckling here--"his ship once took out a Falcatta with a single chuck charge." He shook his dirtied head. "I'll leave that to your collective experience."

"He did," Kaysie said behind Swirl. "He fucking did, asshole."

"Evidence?" Vict asked. "Anyone?"

The crowd muttered.

Hargie muttered to Vict: "Be lying your dick's almost little-finger-long next."

Vict frowned. His hand shot out.

Swirl grabbed Vict's hand, drew him into a hold, his back against her chest, an arm around his throat. The crowd drew breath. The palm of his free hand slapped against her knuckles. It had an odd, cold sting, soon gone.

The Jaggard brothers ran forward, but Vict let go of Swirl's knuckles and gestured to them for calm.

Swirl let him go. "You don't touch Hargie," she told Vict.

"I was offering my hand," he said aloud. "To shake."

"Stat girl's a psycho," someone in the crowd said.

"Wise counsel," Vict replied. "I shall away to the east docking ring with my colleagues. We mean no harm here. Those who stand with us--or just wish a fine new ship--come visit."

Nugo Vict strode out of the hanger, chaperoned by his thugs. Some broke from the crowd and followed.

"Hargie's Mow's boy!" Old Durse was shouting from up on the walkway, his junk eyes wide. "Mow's boy! You people respect that!"

People had made a space around Swirl. She felt as if a punch might come from any direction. She looked at Hargie.

"Thanks, hon." He gave her a smile.

Swirl tried to smile back. Her knuckles itched where Vict had touched them.

***

ECLISE NOWW FELT TETSO'S FINGERS reach for her own. She took them. She smiled at her husband--sitting beside her in their limo--and he smiled back, best as either could.

"Still time to scroob these jokers," Stant, across from them, said. His big shaved head was framed by the limo's front windshield behind him. Beyond that, the midnight sky, lines of freckled light criss-crossing its blackness: sky traffic, the ceaseless arteries of Luharna's infrastructure. The hum of the limo seemed the hum of it all. *And below that*, Eclise thought, *the other hum. Forever there.*

"No," Tetso answered Stant after a pause. "Not with Eclise here. We pay, we go." He checked the cufflinks of his *bizness-suit*. Tetso always did when nervous. "Clean."

Stant sighed. He eyed Eclise's round belly. "Throwing these jokers too many opportunities."

Eclise glared at him.

"Smoo's my brother, Stant," she said. "Think I'm gonna sit in our apt and wait, the good spouse? It's Smoo's *life*. Besides..." She shook her head. "Neither of you privileged bastards know the Pipes. I *do*. You need me." She looked at Tetso. "Forgive me, hon."

"No need," Tetso said.

Stant raised his palms. "Apologies."

"Just do as your boss says," Eclise said.

"We need you, Stant," Tetso said to the other man.

Stant nodded, looked out the window.

The limo began to descend and pan right. Eclise felt truly pregnant then, the grav-mesh in her twenty-lakh jumpsuit barely compensating. She focused on the hum. She could trust the hum. She gazed out the window beside her.

The Pipelands. Fewer lights down there than most zones. A medusascape of snaking metal, a sea of tubes. The great pipes that comprised this mess--varying from two to ten storeys in height--carried heat between citizones, regulated the planet's temperature. Or something like that, Eclise wasn't sure. No-cred families and vagrants squatted there, gangs too. Built junk-towns atop and between all those pipes. Free heat. No cops.

They landed between two parallel pipes, bare of any shacks or people. Secluded. This patch of empty waste ground, Eclise could see, had once housed a pipe. Its concrete fixtures remained: a line of giant graffiti-stained crescents, their horns pointing at the night above.

Stant looked out. He frowned, likely checking his neuralware's radar.

"Nothing," he said. "Wait..."

He stepped out, and a rotten stench leaked into the car. Stant pulled out his gun. Eclise looked out the window.

Two figures came out from behind the nearest concrete fixture. A tall figure in a wide-brimmed hat. Someone beside them, hunched. Arms behind their back.

"Smoo," Eclise said.

"I'd better get out there," Tetso said. He looked at Eclise. "Love you, Eccie-hon."

She leaned in and kissed him. "Tetty-bet."

He got out, then closed the door. Eclise watched him and Stant approach Smoo and the other figure.

A *woop* sound and the limo trembled. Tetso and Stant dropped.

Eclise opened the door beside her. She waited.

The tall figure approached. A woman. Other figures in stealth suits emerged out of air. One, a powerfully-built man, dragged Stant and Tetso into the dark.

The woman climbed into the limo, sat where Stant had just vacated.

"Well done," she told Eclise.

"One citizen," Eclise replied with a shrug. This woman, she thought, had not trained sufficiently. A brimmed hat meant a Field-Emissary who couldn't handle sky. No K-suit though, she had to give her that. Slim black *bizness-suit*. Nice braces.

The woman held up a black rectangle. "Neural the details into this."

Eclise blinked, did so.

The woman frowned. "A nightclub?"

"Business suite," Eclise said. "A little anti-bugging, but nothing you can't handle." She popped a mint in her mouth. Wonderfully fresh. "Trespass field, though. Knocks out intruders." She nodded in the general direction of her husband and his security. "You'll need them alive."

"Accounted for," the woman said.

"So... in here, then?" Eclise gestured at the limo's interior.

The woman stared at her quizzically and Eclise pined, as always, for her lost emotic. Ten years.

"What?" the woman said. "Oh, no: you *live*. Two days tied up, but alive." She looked at Eclise's belly, trying and failing to hide her horror. "You're a company widow now. Accept every party invite and encourage your 'daughter' to follow her 'dad'."

Eclise looked down at her bulging sack of an abdomen. "Oh."

"What's it like?" The woman pointed at her own head. "Up there, I mean?"

"Terrifying," Eclise said. "But there's a hum. Enough to keep us sane."

The woman smiled. "We admire you sleepers back home. I have to stun you now." She pulled out a locally-built POW-wand.

"Wait," Eclise said. "Tell them... I know I have to excrete this thing." She nodded at her own belly. "I know. But if it ever needs killing, I'm ready." She put her hand on the woman's knee. "Tell them."

"They know," the woman said.

It didn't hurt.

***

SPARKLE GAZED THROUGH CURVED GLASS at Zahrir's missing north, the space where a hemisphere should have been. It boiled with blue fire. The glass before Sparkle had no reflective quality: she seemed to stand before space itself. Music and chatter hummed behind her.

The glass of the observatory she stood in--an upturned bowl atop the orbital palace--shaded much of Zahrir's equatorial 'wound', its alien inferno. Zahrir was a 'piercing world', an 'eye-world', forever altered by the Hoidrac, such planets being the greatest sign of their magnificence this side of reality.

The Hoidrac had made Zahrir a replica of their homeworld, Loica. Forbidden, unseen, possibly a fiction, Loica was tidally locked, its light side facing a milk-pale star. Ordinary enough in the great scheme of things, if not for the fact that its other side faced some mysterious body within the Geode, that neighbouring universe of dream and half-glimpsed truth. Loica, then, was a world with a hemisphere in each cosmos, each reality, and no one could say which universe had originally birthed it. Loica: celestial revenant, wraith world, the cradle in which the Delighted Ones had first evolved.

An impossibility, Loica, but perhaps the universe was vast enough to ensure at least one. And an impossibility that had made so much possible, mm-yes. Sparkle gazed with inhuman eyes down upon Zahrir's northern hemisphere, upon its Geode-submerged side. Or lack of same, for the hemisphere facing away from Zahrir no longer existed within this reality.

There remained only the Zahrir side, its other half seemingly cleaved away, leaving only an inter-dimensional wound at the equator.

It was this wound that Sparkle and all those hundreds gathered in the observatory now gazed at. What should have been a flat cutaway of Zahrir's innards--its core, mantle and crust--was nothing of the sort. Instead there raged a flat disc of preternatural fire, blue beyond blue, boiling like any sun's plasma, yet hinting of the forms and shapes one saw in the mind's eye just before sleep. Sparkle thought she saw eyes in the fiery tumult, winged towers and serpents spawned of waves. Mere pattern recognition of course, no different than seeing shapes in clouds, but there was something about Geode-fire that encouraged the human mind to do so.

"The Envoy saunters below us," she heard Pearl say beside her. "Loitering about the ballroom floor with his friends. Mocking all."

Sparkle turned to face her brother. The light from Zahrir's wound dyed his alabaster face azure. He held a white lily in his wrought-iron fingers, its sleek bloom to his nose.

"You can't smell that," she told him, indicating the lily.

"It's the principle," Pearl said. "I like flowers."

"Did he see you?" Sparkle asked.

"I don't believe so," Pearl said. "Amid this throng, even an Ashemi may go unnoticed."

Sparkle had to agree. Culakwun, being the aggressor in this Pleasing War, had chosen a masque theme. Everyone, whether Zahriran, Culakwi, or from some other Harmonic world--and there were many, this being the event of the century--had dressed extravagantly. The menagerie of elaborate headdresses filling the verandas and ballroom below rendered the two statue-beings' height unremarkable.

It made Sparkle proud. In the face of near-certain defeat, her fellow Zahrirans had dressed *fabulously*. This was the very spirit of the Harmonies:

elegance in the face of disaster, beauty always. So unlike the ferals she had been exiled amongst. Amusing, to think what Hargie might have--

"The Starlocks," Pearl said, pointing at the glass walls.

Sparkle turned to face Zahrir again. A fragile silhouette was crossing the wound's blue inferno. Sparkle waved her hand, and the spot of glass before her and her brother's sight-lines thickened, magnifying the distant new object. Other guests did likewise, the seamless glass walls of the observatory becoming dappled with magnifications. A hush filled the observatory's great bowl.

The silhouette was five Starlocks positioned into the shape of a cross. Each Starlock was a frame, a hollow octagon of black glass, the wound's blue furnace shining through them. The Starlock nexus ceased moving, hanging in stationary orbit before the severed world.

Streaks of mist materialised and wrapped themselves around the frames of each of the five Starlocks. The mist congealed into translucent blades of immense size, a hundred jutting spikes that bit down on the Starlocks' black frames.

Lockwyrm teeth.

"They come," Sparkle whispered.

Lockwyrms: mindless behemoths of the Geode, their bodies unfettered by physics. Bred by the Hoidrac, they served as the arteries of the greatest civilisation the galaxy had ever known. Lockwyrms could tear into reality wherever the Hoidrac chose, but the bridle of a Starlock, especially a Starlock bathed by the light of an eye-world, allowed them focus and greater comfort.

The five Starlocks spewed blue flares of Geode-energy, the ethereal bile of the wyrms. There was a flash like lightning, and a battle fleet poured into Zahrir's solar system.

The Sethwen came first, vertical winged fighters dream-piloted by humans seized from Bronze Age worlds. The Sethwen poured from the

Starlocks in waves and coils, like dead leaves suddenly caught in a gust. Sparkle couldn't begin to count them.

Next came the Reavers, sleek warships with shark-nosed prows and glittering sails. They followed the Sethwen like predators chasing a shoal.

Finally, the Cataphracts. Five in all, one from each wyrm's mouth. The heart of any Harmonic fleet, cataphracts were towers clad in jewelled armour and bristling with weapon ports. They dominated all they met with firepower and beauty.

The Grand Fleet of Culakwun had arrived.

***

PEARL AND SPARKLE WALKED AWAY from the glass, past costumed guests, over to the mezzanine's golden rail. Pearl leaned against it and gazed down upon the the ballroom's chequered floor, lily bloom still in hand. Music played--a minuet on haspichol and springs--though no guests danced. They talked, laughed, a dance floor rippling and glittering with cliques of masked visitants in mythological costume. Servants carrying silver plates snaked through the throng.

Pearl wondered which social circles were Zahriran and which Culakwun, and if either ever mixed. It would have been easier without the costumes and wigs and such, Zahriran flesh being either dark or pale, Culakwun a uniform golden olive. For the first time, his distance from his original body--currently precarious on some feral hellhole--truly irked. A leaf-furnace kept an Ashemi's body running, but it couldn't provide insight into a room's emotion as when digested biologically. Which Zahrirans present, Pearl wondered, had already made advances to their likely conquerers? Which held fast? Who was wiser?

"So what are we looking for?" Sparkle asked.

Pearl didn't answer. He kept scanning the dance floor as if that sea of finery might spit out truth. What had he left here years ago? Why had he set himself such an impossible task?

He saw the Envoy wandering about the ballroom, greeting people. The Envoy wore a white dress, high silver wig, skin painted white, black mask with silver eyes. His costume was of Pheoni, patron Hoidrac of Zahrir. As with all things concerning the Envoy, his costume was an audacious yet studied insult.

"...a depressing lot," the Envoy was saying to his acquaintance, the kohl-eyed woman from the roof garden, dressed as a silver raptor. "They could make an abattoir dull."

Pearl stared, stunned. How had he heard the Envoy speak from so far away? He focussed on the man again.

"I can't say I've had the pleasure," the Envoy was saying to a guest robed as a mythic singer from ancient Earth. He eyed the man up and down. "I suspect I never will."

The man laughed nervously. "I just wished you to know, sir, should Zahrir decline to surrender at midnight--which I'm certain it won't--you have friends amongst us here. Please understand--"

"Understand?" the Envoy said, cutting him off. "Well, that depends."

"Depends?" the man asked.

"Depends on you saying something mordant, intense but ultimately entertaining." The Envoy shivered. "I get frightfully bored, you know."

"Er..."

"That's it?" the Envoy said. "That's your quip?"

The kohl-eyed woman made a throat-slitting gesture at the man. The Envoy laughed.

"Something like *that*," the Envoy said to the man. The Envoy and his acquaintance walked away.

Startling. It appeared an Ashemi body came with directional hearing. Pearl had only to focus to hear something at a distance. He looked at Sparkle.

"Well?" she asked.

He decided he'd have a moratorium on whether to tell his sister about his newfound power. He might be unleashing hell upon the universe if she learned how to copy him.

"I've really no idea," he said. "I've only the barest facts as to my personality or how I used to behave. The Pearl you knew, Sparkle. If he wished to hide something here, for an unspecified amount of time...?"

Sparkle looked about. She gazed up at the the series of mezzanines that lined the Observatory's glass in a corkscrew fashion. The guests on them partied against a backdrop of deep space. Nothing about that celestial vignette caught Sparkle's interest. She looked down at the ballroom floor, then across it, toward the entrance.

"There," she said. "The tanhab."

Obvious, really. The tanhab armour, rearing on its plinth, was the most conspicuous object here. Tanhabs were the great murderer-beasts of the Geode, drawn to planetary battlefields in the mundane universe. Tanhabs sloughed their armour as they grew, and any self-respecting Harmonic world was quick to display the intimidating refuse.

Some twenty strides long, the armour resembled a charred dragon, its four legs coiled as if to spring, blade-tail raised, two mantis-like forelimbs stretched wide as if welcoming those who entered the ballroom. The armour's long neck and horned muzzle cast a shadow across the bed of lilies that lay before the plinth.

"You plucked your lily from there," Sparkle said, tapping the blossom in Pearl's hand. "Perhaps something subconscious drew you."

"Let's investigate." Pearl threaded the lily's stem between the ribs of his chest. He had no wish to discard beautiful things, not anymore.

They strode toward the stairwell. On the way, Pearl stole a wide-brimmed hat and feathered cloak from a comadosed guest upon a couch. Sparkle showed no such inclination to hide her nature.

Or perhaps such disguise was unnecessary. The throng served to break up the siblings' outlines well enough, their wigs and headdresses rendering Ashemi height unremarkable, though people still made way for them as they approached. Pearl could see awe in the eyes of every carved and mythic face Sparkle passed by.

They stood within the shadow of the tanhab, within the crescent cast by its right scythe-limb. Sloughed skin that once held a killer, now poised forever in the striking moment.

"What now?" Pearl asked.

"I'm supposed to ask that," Sparkle said.

He reached out, caressed one of the tanhab's giant femurs, feeling nothing, watching one lifeless object drift across another. This was impossible. What had he been thinking?

"They're coming this way," Sparkle muttered. "The Envoy."

"Let's go," Pearl said.

"No." Sparkle paused. "Keep looking. I'll see to this."

"Spar--"

"I'll see to this."

***

SPARKLE STRODE AWAY FROM THE tanhab, toward the Envoy. People quickly stepped out of her way, but she couldn't take it in. She was on a collision course: her and him. What might she say? What could she possibly say? *They wouldn't dare kill an Ashemi,* she told herself. Trouble was, she only resembled one.

Seeing her, the Envoy stopped beside the tanhab's bladed tail. His eyes were hidden beneath the silver glass of his mask's. His lips held still, wholly unreadable. His acquaintance--a woman with kohl eyes framed within a raptor mask--looked to him, then at Sparkle. Her red lips parted to an O.

Sparkle stopped before them. She had expected to look down, but they were Culakwun's Ingresine class, their extended spines making both her very equal in height.

"Your Ashemi," the Envoy said.

Sparkle froze. She felt small; this man was her superior in all things. Yet, more than that, his costume was of Pheoni, the Hoidrac who had penetrated her villa, her skull's very residence.

The Envoy snorted, breaking a silence Sparkle only just noted.

"We had not expected an Ashemi," he said. "Were not told such."

Say something...

"No," Sparkle said.

"You Blessed are typically fanfared," the Envoy said. "Your Ashemi."

"Yes," Sparkle said.

Silence. The woman, wide-eyed, broke it. "Which Hoidrac do you serve?" she asked.

It hit Sparkle then that her own face was cold, as utterly unreadable as the Envoy's mask. "I cannot divulge," she said. "I am sent to observe."

Sparkle confidently expected to be ripped apart, to be dragged into the depths of the Geode and tortured for millennia. Surely Hoidrac of every kind and aesthetic were watching. She was claiming Ashemihood, a ruined Triune messing with the scheme of momentous events.

But no. Sparkle remained. Interesting.

The kohl-eyed woman barely contained her concern. But the Envoy...

Either he saw straight through this ruse, or... or his nerves were akin to that of the great beast on the plinth beside them. Sparkle couldn't tell.

"Is your name as secret?" he asked.

"Call me... Midnight," Sparkle said.

"Fitting," the Envoy answered, "given Zahrir faces submission or ruin at that approaching hour. My name is--"

"Your name is Pelisier Dulaquin," Sparkle said. Research always paid off, especially with Sparkle's brilliance. "Envoy to Zahrir. Born female on Sorchin's World, though male this last half-decade. Heir to Sorchin's High Salon."

"Well," he said, "you seem--"

"Interests include plurasymposia, torment-art, and things best unsaid upon a dance floor."

The Envoy grinned, drank in Sparkle like a piece of art. Which she was. "Midnight," he said. "The witching hour."

"Observe?" the kohl-eyed woman said from behind her bird mask. "Observe what, your Ashemi?"

"I think," Sparkle said, "the Envoy would like a drink."

"I ask humbly, your Ashemi," the woman said.

"Oi, Beaky: get the man a glass."

The woman was a portrait of avian shock. She turned and strutted off.

The Envoy laughed. "I've never met an Ashemi quite like you."

"They preserve me for the tawdrier duties," Sparkle said.

"Then allow me to raise your carved eyebrows, Your Ashemi, for I've an unquenchable thirst to entertain." The Envoy's mask made him as unreadable as her own present face. She had to wonder if this was how the Konsensus had perceived the typical human countenance. "And entertain I will, with every fibre, for my people and this war demand it. A Pleasing War, Ashemi: victory through delighting the Hoidrac." He grinned as if blood's scent hung in the air. "I shall delight with extreme prejudice. To paraphrase the ancients, cruelty is the new black."

Monstrous, this man. Carved from a repulsive glamour.

"A Zahriran poet," Sparkle said, "once deemed mercy the cruellest of weapons."

The Envoy laughed, his long body curving at the waist.

"Oh, that's good," he said. "A consummate example of why Zahrir must be cleansed. I mean, look at them." He waved a palm about the ballroom. "Failures. A rotting aesthetic stinking up a perfectly good eye-world. Do you know how their Triunism came about?"

"Do tell," Sparkle said. She knew, of course.

"Desperation. They thought raising their next generation of whelps to have multiple personalities might save their colony from a frozen world. Absurd. But an absurdity that captivated the Hoidrac; only they and the Geode could make it real." The kohl-eyed woman returned and passed him a drink. "Thank you." His masked face returned to Sparkle. "But they tire of it now. Even Pheoni, I suspect."

"A fearless opinion," Sparkle said, "that would speak for all Hoidrac."

"An objective fact." He intoned the words as if speaking to an ingénue. "The Hoidrac have allowed Culakwun this invasion, have they not? With a fleet Zahrir's defences cannot possibly hope to defeat. All thanks to a mere wager over some poor tortured fool. I'll spare you the details." He shook his head. "No. The Triunes are a failed concept. But beauty? Physical human beauty to which Culakwun breeds toward a final ideal? *That* is eternal. Culakwun shall never fail to please the Delighted Ones." He paused, smiled. "Your Ashemi."

"This beauty," Sparkle said. "It comes rouged with blood?"

He took a sip and smiled. "No finer cosmetic."

"You may as well tell her," the bird-masked woman said to the Envoy. "*Go on.*"

"At midnight," he said to Sparkle, "when Zahrir capitulates, I shall have every Zahriran here strangled." He leant in conspiratorially. "I shall have those who wish to betray do it to those who remain defiant. Proof of their newborn loyalty. But loyalty shall procure them nothing but a slower demise. A pleasing end to a Pleasing War. Should delight the Hoidrac, don't you think?"

Sparkle's mind recoiled, then raced. In the ramshackle corridors of her knowledge, something yelled.

"Rather touching," she said.

"*Touching?*" the Envoy asked, bemused.

"Mm-yes," Sparkle said. "You know your Zahriran history; the fall of Resonance-Rage. Quite similar. Derivative, arguably, but your respect for Zahrir shines through." She made the best shrug a statue might. "Of course, it's really down to what your god Mohatoi Embossed makes of it..."

"Well..." The Envoy took a sip, hiding his mouth. "It's the least of my performances. Quite minor."

Sparkle had to get away. She had tried her luck and had somehow avoided divine punishment. She could only hope she had dissuaded this Culakwun beast.

And yet...

"Pearl," she called out.

"You know of that?" the Envoy said, what was visible of his face still placid. His mouth parted as Pearl made his way past guests and stood by Sparkle.

"You," the Envoy said. The bird-masked woman stared in shock.

"Me," Pearl replied.

"Pearl is helping with my investigations," Sparkle explained. She turned to her brother. "Are we finished here?"

"Indeed," Pearl said.

"Very well." Sparkle looked at the Envoy. "I'm afraid I must leave before Zahrir makes its decision. Matters of import, you understand."

"We'll," the Envoy said, "meet again?"

"*Bet your ball sack, Jack,*" Sparkle said in Anglurati, the feral language. Like Hargie. "You've been an illuminating host."

***

PEARL AND SPARKLE STOOD IN the tight confines of the teardrop pod as it descended toward Zahrir's southern continent. Sparkle had been silent all the way, staring at a fixed point of the teardrop's sloping walls. Pearl had let her be, but now he needed to know what she felt.

"Did..." He didn't know how to put it in words. "Did he upset you?"

Sparkle looked at him. "Not in the sense you mean."

"You seem preoccupied," Pearl said.

"Excited," Sparkle said. "That Culakwun arsehole stirs me. I feel... alive."

"How so?"

She stepped over to an octagonal porthole and gazed out.

"Don't you see?" Blue light from Zahrir's wound drowned her face. "We're here to delight, Pearl. It's why we were brought back here, why these bodies we reside in were placed out to receive us. Perhaps why you were punished in the first place, why Swirl and I were chased across the stars. An entertainment. The Envoy understands this implicitly. His invasions, his stratagems... the first necessity is to be interesting."

"A Pleasing War," Pearl said. He touched the lily bloom still entwined between his wrought iron ribs. He felt nothing.

She looked at him, her face a silhouette. "And *we're* his opponents. More than Zahrir's negligible fleet, more than its armies. Back in the ballroom, I blasphemed. Claimed Ashemihood, claimed to speak for unspecified Hoidrac. I should have been annihilated right then." She wagged a finger. "I blasphemed *creatively*. I think they love that, our rulers, mm-yes. They watch our actions like a play, our thoughts like, like some book. No doubt they read us now."

Pearl thought about that. You grew up within the Harmonies knowing your soul was there to be read by the Hoidrac, in theory. But to *know* you had their focus...

"We can win this, Pearl," Sparkle said. "We must be interesting. We must be artists."

The teardrop was silent awhile.

"Fuck, I love this," Sparkle said. She tapped her marble head, and her hair-cords rattled. "The space, you know? The space to think. Endless." She shook her head. "I'm actually envious. Envious of frigging *monominds*. Can you believe that?" She laughed through her statue-body's speaker.

"You prefer it?" Pearl asked. "The loneliness?"

Sparkle looked down. If Pearl could only remember his past life better, their shared existence, she knew he would have shouted at her.

"You found what you were looking for, then?" Sparkle asked.

"It wasn't the tanhab armour," Pearl said.

"No?"

"No." He drew the lily out from his chest and held it up to the light. Delicately, he pulled one of the petals back. Sparkle leaned in to see. At the petal's base, where the white blended to pink, lay a complex set of glyphs.

"Flowers," Pearl said. "I always liked flowers, Mother said. Each petal, each bloom in that bed, has been altered. I must have altered their gene code somehow."

"What does it mean?" Sparkle asked.

"A wake-up call," Pearl said. "The coordinates for a lockwyrm in slumber."

***

SWIRL FELT BETTER, A LITTLE. She was sat on a folding chair in *Princess'* lounge, Hargie massaging her shoulders. Kaysie and Old Durse were sat on the broken down brown sofa.

"Free B-ships, man," Kaysie said. "Who'da seen that comin'?" She shook her head. "How ya compete widdat?"

"Asshole Vict doing us a favour," Durse said, sipping from his can of beer. "Anyone sellin' their dignity for that ain't worth spit anyhow."

"Lot of 'em," Kaysie said.

"Lot of 'em," Durse said, nodding.

Swirl felt Hargie's palms tense on her shoulders.

"There's a man on this Desic," Hargie said, "who tried to poison my woman. That count for nothing? Poison. Weapon on a Desic, Durse."

"Unseen weapon," Durse said. "People gonna see it how they wanna see it. Accidental swallowin', virus. Foreign woman getting sick: nothin' you can trace to Vict."

"I don't get viruses," Swirl said, annoyed at all this third-person talk. "My people are fixed that way. Regrettably for Vict, we're difficult to poison too."

"Emphasis," Durse said, "be on 'foreign woman'. No nasty by it, you tune? Just fact. Bubblefolk got plenty reason to hate outsiders, hate stats. Nugo Vict? He offering vengeance. Rare thing for us. We could all gorge on that." He looked at Swirl. "You offering anything top vengeance?"

"Durse..." Hargie said, a firm tone in his voice. "You know I respect you."

"You should," Durse said. "Just me and Skip Darrow fronting for you on the Ring council nowadays. Most don't wanna have shit to do with Vict--they good men--but they thinking of Desic, their families. Want this shit through."

"This shit ain't just shit," Kaysie said, turning to Durse beside her. "Vict fuckin' with who we are. We ain't killers. Ain't our way." She brushed her hair with her hand. "Father never wanted us haters. Wanted us better than Stats." She looked at Swirl. "No offence, princess."

Swirl shrugged. "I'm one of you now."

"She belongs," Hargie said. He returned to massaging her shoulders, but there was tightness in his fingers.

"Who this Underking, boy?" Durse said. "Who his people?"

Hargie let go of Swirl's shoulders. "Just assholes, tune?"

"Assholes with invisible ships," Durse said. "Quit lying. Ain't your suit."

"Rockshades, Durse," Hargie said. He sounded nervous. "I think they're the Rockshades."

"Bogeymen in 'roids?" Durse asked. "Cut the ratshit."

"They live in rocks," Hargie said.

"How you know?"

"Things I seen." He wasn't mentioning Silvercloud.

Durse's eyes were cold, searching. He bared them on Swirl. "This true?" he asked her.

"I believe so." Sparkle would have been better at this.

Durse took another sip. "Don't matter what they are," he said. He gestured at the Stukes siblings. "I was with these two's daddy when the Freightways came up heavy. They would have roaded this Desic too, if they could. Tried. We... dissuaded them." He took another swig. "These shadow-ship bastards shouldn't go thinkin' no different."

"That the talk!" Kaysie said, laughing.

"You two." Durse pointed at Hargie and Kaysie. "Gonna ask you dust. Polite-like. Grab some beers and shit." He looked at Swirl. "Need a mo-mo here."

"She's ill," Hargie said.

"It's fine," Swirl told him.

The Stukes siblings looked at one another. They walked out the lounge.

Durse stared at her awhile.

"Must be fucking that fool's brains to soup," he said eventually. "Weren't him killed *Princess*, was it?"

Swirl went to speak.

"Don't lie to me now," Durse said. "Not inside her corpse."

"No." Swirl looked down at the floor. The grill, the body of Hargie's dead ship. "I didn't know what else to do. We were surroun--"

"Who by?"

"Them," Swirl said.

"Why they want your witch ass?"

"I'm..." Swirl faltered.

"What?"

"Encoded with their essence," she said. "Or something. I don't know."

"Kill to get it?" Durse asked.

"...Yes."

"Kill us all?"

"They can't," Swirl said. "They don't want to be seen, not ever. If we shine a light on them, the galaxy's attention, media, they'll scatter li--"

"Kill us all?" Durse repeated, sharper this time.

"If they could," Swirl said. "Yes, sir."

"Why *you* wanna kill us?"

"I don't wa--"

"Why you wanna kill us, Stat girl?"

"Because Hargie--"

"Hargie ridin' on his dad's rep alone," Durse said, "you ridin' on Hargie's alone. Answer, Stat girl: why you wanna kill us?"

"I don't," Swirl said. "Stop saying... I want to belong. I *belong*."

"Belong far away, Stat girl," Durse said.

"No," Swirl said. "And stop calling... stop... I believe in the Sisters, I'm devout, I belong, I belong, I want only to belong, I--"

"Fly you outta here," Durse said. "Safe. Everyone safe and--"

"They'd kill me back home," Swirl said.

"'Cuz you dangerous?"

"Because I've betrayed--"

"Your own folk?"

"My gods," Swirl said.

"*Gods*? Shit. Why should we get treated better?"

"Because you're good people," Swirl said. 'For once I have good people and I belong and, and empathic rationalism, your own philosophy, you should see it from my--"

"Ya sure as shit don't see it from ours."

"Please, sir, please don't give me to--"

"Why?" Durse asked. 'Exactly why, bitch? Why'm I risking my family, friends, this Desic for a Stat bitch who ain't even telling--"

"Because I'm pregnant."

Durse fell silent. He crushed his beer can, lay back on the sofa. "Well," he said.

Swirl released her storage gland and conceived. No going back. Whatever happened here on in, she wouldn't be alone.

***

"YOU DID *WHAT*?" NUGO VICT said, sitting in the tight back office of the refinery. He couldn't believe these Jaggard morons.

The two brothers looked at one another. They looked back at Vict across the office desk.

"Figured that's how you fly, sir," Loader, the smaller one, said. He sat due to his balls still aching from that Sparkle bitch. "You know... all possibilities covered."

"Crate cost us, sir," Eck, the taller one with the smashed nose, said. He stood beside Loader, presumably because he was too dense to use a chair. "Some serious rupee. Serious."

Vict tapped the table in thought. "How many?"

"Few thousand," Eck said.

"Not the rupees, idiot," Vict said. "I'm talking about the..." He gathered himself, muttered: "guns."

"Sixty," Loader said.

"Fuck," Vict said.

"T11s," Eck added.

"Of course," Vict said. He slapped his own forehead. "I mean, if we're gonna break a sacred Desic taboo, we may as well go all in. How about a fusion cannon?"

"Wouldn't know anyone sells--" Eck said before Loader punched his arm.

"Shuddup, shitbrain," Loader told him. "Vict's using satire here." He turned to Vict. "Sorry, sir. We can get enthusiastic."

"Evidently," Vict said.

"Thought firepower might help," Loader said.

"Firepower?" Vict said. "Our allies have an invisible fleet outside. I'm sure *they* were feeling outgunned..."

"Tune ya," Eck said. He grinned, pointed at Vict. "Satire, right?"

"*Sarcasm,* you waste of jism." Vict slapped the table. He had to keep calm. His one advantage in any given scenario.

"We could slip the crate out again," Loader suggested.

"No," Vict said. "Miracle you weren't detected getting it in. We can't risk an airlock either."

"Well..." Loader said. "What?"

"Hide it," Vict said. "If you can hide it where it already is, do so." He shook his head. "We'll sit on it 'til we win out here. We're winning by the hour, gentlemen. Persuasion."

"Free B-ships," Loader said. "Nothin' to sneer at."

"You forget boredom," Vict said. "This blockade's biting at every pilot in DesicWest. They can shoot up all the jumpjunk they want, but a pilot needs the stars. Boredom will prove a greater ally than the Underking's fleet, ultimately."

"We ever gonna meet him?" Eck said.

Vict stared at the imbecile. "Go hide your crate."

The Jaggards sauntered out. Vict poured a whiskey, then leaned back in his chair.

Shitkickers, yet Vict had little choice in his calibre of henchman. Vict was unlike most bubblefolk. Practically unique. His father had made a fortune back in the coritanium rush and had rapidly frittered it away, as per bubbleman custom, but he'd had enough sense to buy his son an education. A Quh'bellan school.

Double-edged gift, that. Vict had an advantage over his own kind: he saw the bigger picture. But said picture was a depressingly objective scrawl. Bubblefolk were dying out. Freightways, of course, but it was more fundamental than that. The bubble-gene itself was diluting into humanity's morass through mass rape and gene-theft, but mostly through bubblemen's tragic propensity to fuck anything that proffered its fun-bun.

He took a gulp and shuddered. Was that, he wondered, the root of his hatred for Hargie? The Stukes were a mongrel lot. No, not as crude as that. Not the genes. The memes. The *cultural* miscegenation. Hargie Stukes mixed. Fools like him and his father were the gateway by which Stat culture, the oppressor, insinuated itself into Vict's people.

Vict was no bigot. The oppressed could never be bigots. But cultures, races, should sit apart, respect each other's unique beauty yet remain proud in themselves. Yes: defeating Hargie Stukes, bubble-to-bubble, would be a sort of exorcism. The victory of cultural strength over cultural drift, over weakness. For all to see.

He took a swig from the bottle. "Here's to poor damn *Princess Floofy*."

His neuralware signalled.

He put the bottle away. Fear, cold in his veins. *Him*. He was calling. Vict blinked, and a screen appeared in his vision. A male face, young and smooth. Blas, the 'Underking'.

"Vict," he said, voice deeper than a young man's should be.

"Sir," Vict said.

"Call me Blas. We are confused over here, Vict. About your actions twenty hours ago."

Vict recalled the patch Blas' crony had slapped on Vict's chest. The waiting poison.

"I admit... Blas... the opportunity to administer a patch on Hargie Stukes did not present itself. But I patched Sparkle Savard. She's dying."

"Apparently not," Blas said. "That patch you administered contained our most effective neurotoxin, yet the tracker-monitor we provided with said patch informs us she's experienced flu-like symptoms, nothing more." Blas looked to one side. "Likely, Sparkle Savard's culture has a tradition of poison and they've altered their people's physiognomy accordingly."

"You can't blame me for that." Vict gave the friendliest smile he damn well could. "Wait... if you had no idea she would survive your poison, then why fit the patch with a tracker?"

"My own people have a tradition of never taking chances," Blas said.

Call it what it is, thought Vict. *Paranoia.*

"Well, it certainly paid off," Vict said.

"You failed to poison Hargie," Blas said.

"I hadn't the opportunity."

"You were right next to him," Blas said.

"How would you know that?"

Blas didn't reply.

"I..." Damn, why had he failed? Oh, but Vict knew why he'd 'failed'. "S-Sparkle prevented me," he lied. "Besides... I believe it's vital to humiliate the man. Poisoning would only serve to make him a legend like his father."

"I do not see his father hindering our progress in this concern," Blas said. "Would that his son was similarly legendary." Blas blinked, the first time in this entire call. "We note you've acquired automatic weaponry. That alone compensates for your prior failings."

"I... like to cover every possibility," Vict said. "And we're enthusiastic, so..."

"Use them," Blas said.

"What?"

"Use them, Vict." Blas said it like a dead cert, a gambling tip.

"But I... we're persuading the masses here, Blas," Vict said. "It's working, but we need time."

"Guns remove time from the labour of persuasion," Blas said. "It's their second most useful quality."

"What's the first?"

"Removing the labour of persuasion," Blas said. "You have forty-eight standard hours. Either terminate Sparkle or bring her to us. Ideally the latter, but nothing less than the former."

"Sir... Blas, I... there is an ancient taboo on weaponry within a Desic. We'd lose support."

"Quite the opposite," Blas said. "Guns have a way of making former custom obsolete."

"Is... that their third quality?" Vict asked.

"If you say so." Blas smiled the barest of smiles. "Take control, Vict. The masses hunger for your gifts and will cower to your guns. Forty-eight hours."

The screen vanished.

Vict rubbed his chest, where the patch had dissolved. Revolt, then. Revolution.

CHAPTER SEVEN

S parkle leaned on the wall of the veranda and thought of the boy back in Silvercloud, the one who screamed to see her. Had the far, night-drenched hills made her think of him? The ancient walls of the House? Perhaps she had spied his face in the heavy clouds above.

What morality was this? She should be concerned for the ballroom guests, the Envoy's blade above their necks, not some juvenile monster. Perhaps it all lay in the face. She had looked in his face, seen something of herself. Absurd, really. Human.

"Sister," Pearl said. She hadn't heard him arrive.

She turned to face him.

"Are you fine?" he asked her.

"*Real smoosh,*" she said in Anglurati.

"Pardon?"

"Nothing," Sparkle said. "Just something a feral used to say."

"Hargie," Pearl said.

"How'd you know?"

"He's the only one you ever mention," Pearl said.

Really? *How very banal of me,* Sparkle thought.

"So... is it complete?" Sparkle asked.

"I think so." Pearl walked into the moonlight. His head was leaning forward, his mane of black corquill feathers hanging down.

"So what's with this lockwyrm, then?" Sparkle asked. "It's connected to a Starlock elsewhere in the Harmonies, right? Another world of Pheoni's that's, I don't know, readying a fleet? Right?" She crossed her sleek marble arms. "Pearl, when someone fires off a series of questions, the least you should do is nod."

"I don't know," he said. "The code I found won't allow me access."

"But you created it," Sparkle said.

"Yes," Pearl said. "It's a beautiful piece of work."

"The definition of beauty being uselessness."

"Correction," Pearl said. "The definition of beauty being it requires Sparkle, personally, to access it."

"Pardon?"

"You or Swirl," Pearl said. "The psyche-mandala required must be similar to mine." He raised a silver-clawed hand. "This much I've gleaned: the lockwyrm's mouth has no taste for anywhere within the Harmonies. It hungers for something beyond. From that, we can assume I factored in your and Swirl's future exile when I created it."

"What?" Sparkle said. "You... you absolute shitblizzard."

"If my memory ever returns, I'll be wracked with guilt," Pearl said. "Undoubtedly."

"So what now?"

"We can't comadose in these bodies," Pearl said. "We've no recourse but to plunge into the womb."

Sparkle thought about that. "Well, you can tell Mother."

***

"THEY GOT THE RING!" KAYSIE yelled. Hargie could hear her from the other side of the temple's gloomy vault, her words bouncing off the Sisters' statues.

Shit. Kaysie was supposed to be the faith-head. Hargie never was for temple, he just wanted quiet, some space.

A priestess shushed Kaysie for quiet. Kaysie mouthed 'sorry', then shouted: "Hargie! They guns, Bro. Guns!"

Hargie ran across the tiles, over to her. "What?"

"Vict, Jaggards." Kaysie took a couple of breaths. "Eight other dipshits. Got Durse and most other Rings up in the Committee Pod."

"Shit," Hargie said. "When?"

"Twenty minutes ago," Kaysie said. "I'da neuraled ya, but the temple blocks n'shit." She hugged him. "Fuck, bro, thought they'd 'locked you. What y'doin' in temple, y'godless prick?'"

"We gotta get Sparkle," Hargie said. "Let's dust."

They found Sparkle sat in the foldout chair, outside *Princess'* hatch, in the dockpod, arms crossed, scowling. Beside her stood a man: no, a kid. He had a pistol.

"Shit," Hargie said.

"That Corbie," Kaysie told him. "Know him, he smoosh." She looked at Corbie. "We smoosh, right?"

"Skip Darrow sent me," the kid said. He nodded at Sparkle beside him. "Protect her."

"I keep telling him to give me the pistol," Sparkle said.

"I'm *guarding* you," the kid told her.

"Of course, I could take it any time I want," Sparkle said to Hargie.

The kid shook his head. "She be talking like this fo--"

Sparkle took the pistol and spun it in her fingers.

"Shit," the kid said.

"Told you," Sparkle told everyone.

Hargie looked at the kid. "You, go inside *Princess* and lock the hatch. This ain't no game."

"But Skip sent me," the kid said.

"Six pack in the chiller," Hargie said.

The kid looked at him.

"Yeah," Hargie said. "The plot thickens, huh?" He shooed him away. "Go."

"Skip Darrow's up in Control," the kid said. He looked relieved. "Think I *will* have a beer." He swaggered through the dead bubbleship's hatch.

Sparkle got up, shoved the pistol into her overalls. "Let's go," she said. "Control has my old pistol. It's got all the checked-in guns."

"How you know that?" Kaysie said.

Sparkle smiled her business smile, such as it was. Whatever happened to her old smile?

Hargie put that thought aside, neuraled Skip to let him know they were coming.

"Man," Hargie muttered to the grill floor, "this is one fuck-up."

"No shit," Kaysie replied.

"No, I mean Vict's fucked up. Blows his good hand on kidnap. Breaks the gun-taboo." He adjusted his hat. "Makes no sense."

"Must be short on time," Sparkle said, looking at him. "As are we."

He met her eyes. Sense in her words, their situation needed that. But back, back, deep in those eyes... nothing. Nothing for his heart to cling to, anyhow.

***

BELOW THE CHAPEL, BELOW THE many basements' complexes, generators, cells, and oubliettes lay the Womb. The very pit of the Trinity House.

Pearl stood upon the observation altar, its sides a peacock's tail of black rib-like spines. He cradled a hierofish in his sculpted hands. A denizen of the Geode armoured for life in the tangible universe, the hierofish was a ball-shaped, eyeless thing. Its hide, a metal of shifting mother-of-pearl, provided the chamber's only illumination. The colours shifted to the movement of Pearl's fingers, each caress altering the light around him: blue, pink, green.

No easy task, this, Pearl thought. It required a potter's hands, a sorcerer's mind.

"I didn't know the House had one of these places," Sparkle said beside him. She wasn't making this task easier. "The House must have really trusted you to let you know about it."

"More fool them," Pearl said. "Though, in fairness, they forbade me entrance."

"Perhaps we *have* been here," Sparkle said. "During your crime. You'd have wiped the memory."

"I don't think so," Pearl said. "The chemicals in the air here would have dissolved us to bones."

"Right." She stepped closer to Pearl. Too close.

"Sparkle. I'm working here."

"Sorry." She stepped back. "Something about this place doesn't feel right."

"Perhaps," Pearl said, "you could search within your wide, newly independent mind for what that is. In silence."

Sparkle said nothing.

Pearl worked the final glyph, from the litany inside the lily bloom, into the hierofish's metallic skin. "There," he said.

He drove a talon into the creature's hide and the wound hissed. Light poured out, shining white, along with a glowing ichor that ran down Pearl's thumb and pooled in his palm. Pearl threw the hierofish over the side of the altar. It darted in circles, panicked, its wound a geyser of white light.

It dived, its descent revealing the walls of the pit below, level by level, but never the whole. The walls were black, their construction like countless dinosaur spines tightly meshed into a tubular weave. Sloughed tanhab armour, like that on display in the observatory ballroom. Yet here, their purpose was far from decorative.

A splash echoed from the pit below. There was a pause, and then the very bottom of the pit glowed blue, a circle of bubbling liquid. The Womb itself. The same blue light issued from the cracks in the pit's walls, the gaps in the spinal weave. Plumes of leaf mist rose and curled from the Womb's surface far below.

Pearl was happiest in these moments. His talents challenged.

"Pearl," Sparkle said, "I'm--"

He slapped his palm against her forehead. Having done so, he did the same to himself. He turned to face his sister. She stared back, her head tilting quizzically. The hierofish's blood ran down between her chiselled brows. Luminescent, purple. Not of this world.

"This is serious business," he told her. "The Anointed built this Womb centuries ago. Below us lies a distillation of pure leaf ichor, fermented over a thousand years. It corrodes the skin of both realities, a septic delta between two worlds."

"I understand," Sparkle said. "I think. So what now?"

"This is a place for Ashemi to commune with the Geode. Given their synthetic bodies, they can't comadose as a human might. Their essence must enter entirely. As must ours, mortals feigning Ashemihood though we are. We must plunge our forms into that pit. Into the Womb."

Sparkle was still for some time. "In there?"

"Absolutely," Pearl said.

"The phrase 'fuck that' rises ever resplendent," Sparkle said.

"I told you: serious business. I've no clue what awaits us. What beasts, what gods. We gamble our very mind-states. We may go unnoticed, or we may end up food for immortals. They're two of the better scenarios."

There came a crackling sound. Pearl realised it was his mane of corquill feathers calcifying in the leaf mist. Sparkle noticed it too.

"The question to ask yourself," Pearl continued, "is, how strong is your faith? In the Hoidrac, their wisdom?"

Sparkle looked down the pit, then back at Pearl.

"I believe in you, brother," she said. "You planned this."

"I'm but a pawn," he said.

"I don't care," Sparkle said.

He waved a hand and the sides of the altar splayed like fingers, opened like a bloom. A clear drop to the Womb lay before both siblings.

"My essence will cling to the Womb," Pearl said. "Yours will cling to me and stretch out. Pursue the hierofish I sent before us. It will lead the way."

"To the lockwyrm?" Sparkle asked.

"Presumably."

"I feel I should say things," Sparkle told him. "Ask your forgiveness. Forgive you. Things of that nature."

"Best we just jump," Pearl said.

Sparkle said nothing. The two statues linked lifeless, senseless hands.

They jumped.

***

THE *THRUM-THRUM* OF THE Worlder music was inescapable, like blood pulsing in the ears. A heartbeat, it pumped through the bones of this vast nightclub, trembling the concrete walls of the corridor Melid and Doum--each in Worlder clothing, each with a satchel--walked along.

They made their way past impractical clothing and faces smeared with gaudy colours, stepped over the semi-conscious and the fully-fumbling. A nauseous sight, that, all those corpses kissing. And everywhere the sweat, the stink...

Nought but corpses and the crows who feed upon them...

Strange, that the Worlders' most privileged classes should choose to meet in a suite amid these horrors. Perhaps not. Perhaps it made a nightmarish sense.

"Here," she said to Doum, pointing to an alcove full of screens. They stood in there, away from the perspiring, musky corpse-traffic. The screens showed things neither Konsensite understood: people maniacally happy, proud of bizarre objects. Inadequately clothed females gyrating, a parody of dance shackled by gravity's binds. Other screens made more sense: wide shots of the mile-squared dance floor somewhere below the corridor they loitered in. An ocean of fetid corpses undulating to the beat, vapour clouds rising from the mass.

She blanked it out. Their target was the graffiti-ridden door ahead and to their left. No one stood before it. Good.

Melid tried to reach into the inside pocket of her suit. Not a Konsensus suit; Worlder clothing. Her gen-upgrades were complete.

This clothing was bondage. Braces carving into shoulders, suit's arms slowing movement. The... *device*... incarcerating her mammary glands was nothing less than torture. If these Worlders loved gravity so much, why did they spend their lives fighting it?

The noise, *thrum-thrum*. The sweat-stink...

She felt Doum's hand on her shoulder.

"Nightclub," he said. "Always this." The compassion he issued then was far deeper than Melid had thought him capable of.

"Yes," she said. Instead, she focussed on the Kollective-at-Large. That signal forever there. Forever warm.

She got the detonator out of her pocket at last: a black rectangle. Doum kept watch while she linked to the drone nano-cam currently on the suite's ceiling.

There, inside the blue and windowless suite, sat pride of place at a long table: Sung Eucharist. Five others: three male, two female. Freightways

Bizness-suits, laughing. Something Eucharist had said. The male beside him, old, chewed on--what was it now? Not a cigarette--a cigar.

Melid stroked the detonator. The *bizness-suits* jerked in their seats. Their chests burst. Given the right sonics, the pulmonary system could be surprisingly explosive.

Melid and Doum strode toward the door, avoiding a couple vomiting beside it: perhaps drunk, perhaps victim to seepage through the suite's soundproofed walls. Doum neutralised the lock, and the pair of them stepped through.

Melid slammed the door behind them and immediately felt better, the beat fading to a hum. Two men--security--lay upon the floor of the greeting lounge: chests ruptured, their shirts red pulp. Running through the room to the next door, Melid and Doum produced bonebolts from their satchels, vat-made weapons like curved spines around the user's fist. Biological, undetectable. Four bolts apiece.

Doum kicked open the meeting room door. Eucharist hadn't moved. Speckled with others' gore, he'd picked up the dead man's cigar and was currently sucking it back to life.

"I'm impressed," he said, tapping the ash into a tray on the table. "How did you achieve preventing my heart from--"

"You told me I'd have questions," Melid said, and she fired a calcite bolt into Eucharist's cigar-hand, pinning it to the table. Eucharist winced. "You were right."

The Worlder grimaced as he tried to free his hand. He gave up soon enough.

"How'd you get in?" he asked. "The trespass field--"

"Detects neuralware, yes?" Melid asked. She signalled to Doum, and the pair of them emptied their satchels upon the table. Two brain-shaped objects rolled along the surface, their forms cast in stretched black muscleform. "May I present your unpunctual board member and his bodyguard? Sorry they're late."

Eucharist squinted. "Still alive?"

"And aware. Which reminds me." Melid signalled to Doum, and the giant stepped over to Eucharist. He tore open the Worlder's shirt and slapped a patch on his sternum, the same patch they'd used on Fractile.

Eucharist fell back in his seat, his chrome-coloured irises rising up. He gasped, sense-castrated. A gratifying sight.

"Ten seconds," Melid told Doum. Sheer habit: Doum already knew.

"Why not ask now?" Eucharist said.

The two Konsensites jolted.

Eucharist pointed at them with his free hand and chuckled. A joke.

"What?" he said. "You think I'd socialise with you monsters and not know your parlour tricks?"

Melid took a deep breath. How long would they have here? "Then we'll do this by primitive means."

"Why not just ask me?" Eucharist said. "There's nothing I'll hide from you."

"Is that fear speaking, Mr Eucharist?" Melid asked.

"Call it what you like." With a surgeon's concentration, Eucharist prized the cigar from his impaled hand's fingers. "I merely state a fact." With three short sucks, he got the cigar alight again. He looked at the cigar's flame, surprised and delighted with his success.

The Kollective-at-Large's signal was strong on Luharna, boosted by hidden 'ware the globe over. Melid could feel others watching through her, mission-involved Instrum members. The coming interrogation was of wide interest.

She elected to take Eucharist at his word. Let him talk, pontificate, stumble. Melid would apply force after.

"Silvercloud," Melid said. "You aided the... sporadically traitorous kollective of Silvercloud."

"You know as much, my girl," Eucharist said. "Your memories of Silvercloud's traitor-hours are still with you, I imagine. You grew up there."

"And I exterminated it," Melid replied. If that shocked Eucharist, it didn't show in his abnormally pale face. She continued: "But what of the abomination below the treason? The kancer. You knew of it, didn't you? You knew Kend and the rest were puppets."

Eucharist shook his head. "Not at first. At first I was contacted by Illik--the Illik of Silvercloud's traitor-hours, using messages made during said hours--regarding your beloved star-beasts: the 'Scalpels'."

"Beloved no longer," Melid said. "The Scalpels are but warships of the Harmonies. Which, of course, you knew all too well."

"Yes." He looked at her with admiration, waving his cigar at her. "You know, I *thought* you had the look of a betrayed lover." He pointed at his chrome irises. "It's in the eyes."

He was right. Melid was past her infatuation now. The Scalpels were no star-animals. They were enemies.

"Why you?" she asked Eucharist.

"I wasn't the first Illik approached," he said. "He called out to Worlders and found passing bubblemen. News came to me. I was listening: I had long suspected a people living among the void's detritus, keeping among themselves, and here was one asking about the star-beasts. I made my expertise about his 'Scalpels' known. The bubblemen were happy to pass Illik on. They believe *Kharmund* spawn of their 'Great Foozle'." He shrugged. "A superstitious people."

"*Kharmund?*" Melid asked.

"The Harmonic name for them. Crudely, it means 'Steed of the Delighted Ones'." He smoked, blew out an acrid stink. "At first I believed you people just another fresh market. But when Silvercloud invited me, asked for my expertise in carrying out their illicit studies... I was astounded. A secret and ubiquitous hive-empire: unseen, vast, monstrous." He eyed Doum and Melid. "Freaks."

Melid slammed her palm on the table, beside Eucharist's impaled hand.

"You were a double agent?" she asked. "For Silvercloud's kancer?"

"The blasphemy below the treachery? Yes. In time, it managed to get its own messages out. It used Illik to front those messages, knew that was the segment of its gestalt whose face I trusted. But, really, the desires of Silvercloud's rebellion and the desires of the kancer squatting within are equally inconsequential. The same desired result: contact with the Scalpels."

"Desired?" Melid said. "Desired by whom?"

Eucharist chuckled. He stamped out the cigar on the table.

"Can you visualise," he said, "a man in a forest, wise to its ways?"

Melid thought she could. She knew of forests, had studied Worlder generalities as part of her emissary training. She nodded.

"He stands in a clearing," Eucharist said, "perhaps chopping trees. It doesn't matter. What matters is that the man is aware he is being watched. He cannot say by what, for it skulks in the dark below the canopy and amid the deep undergrowth. And so he puts on an act, a facade of ignorance. He does so knowing the beast will become complacent, curious. That it will reveal something of itself."

Melid sentimented to Doum that he should cover the doorway they had entered through. "You play for time," she told Eucharist.

"I make metaphors," he replied. "You monsters lost that art, I think."

"Metaphors are lies," Melid said. "Our people have scant use for them."

"Of naivety, however, you craft whole symphonies," Eucharist said. "The forest man, my girl, is the Hoidrac. They suspect you: the creature. Sense you in your hidden rocks. But they cannot *read* you. This concerns them. Understandably, for the essence of mankind has always been an open page to these aliens, these 'gods'. Your kollectiveware is a walled fortress, self-annexed from the human greater subconscious. To them, you are an affront." He looked over at Doum. "I shouldn't worry about unwanted visitors. I have seen to that."

Melid looked at Doum, then back to Eucharist.

"Well..." Eucharist said. "I *thought* you might come here tonight." He studied her frown. "I do so enjoy our talks." He pulled the thin bolt from out his hand. One jerk, a grunt of pain. He let the bolt drop to the floor. "The Hoidrac play across centuries. They can wait. Their great steeds ply the depths of what the Harmonies call 'feral space', underestimated by its natives, considered mere wonders, beasts of the void."

"We know this," Melid said.

"Silvercloud was their chosen victim. All they had to do was be visible to that which they could not see, like our forest man." Eucharist rubbed his injured palm. "You vermin merely subsist inside your asteroids. Merely survive. True beauty is lost to you, but not *on* you. You had no protection from the *Kharmund*, from the Scalpels. It was their very beauty that corrupted Silvercloud. Slowly, over centuries, the mere sight of those entities bathing in starlight poisoned you naïve monsters. You victims of art."

Melid laughed. "You presume to know the minds of these aliens?"

"I presume to talk with their worshippers," Eucharist said. "After all, I facilitated for Silvercloud." He gestured at the corpses. "I facilitate for Freightways. Why not the Harmonies? Indeed, ask yourself why I could be so very helpful to Illik's experiment. Why should I know so much of the leaf-drug? Of Geode technology?"

Melid felt increasingly ill at ease. She couldn't scare this man. She couldn't outwit him. "Aliens are no threat to the Konsensus," she said.

Eucharist pointed behind himself, towards a steel cabinet beside the wall. "Whiskey in there," he said. "Have your man pour me a glass."

"Bravado," Melid said. Zo's word, she recalled, muttered on Calran. She signalled to Doum to do as the Worlder asked, but only after studying the cabinet with her X-ray vision.

"Raichundalia Polyconglomerate," Eucharist said, pointing at the dead *bizness-suits*, "are the only interest allowed to produce hoxnites amongst what you would call Worlder humanity. That's how they came to be so big this last millennium: we pay their exorbitant prices--and accept their limitations on progress--for the promise of safety. Free nanite tech is simply too dangerous. Smart, Raichundalia. But greedy." He shook his head. "The Freightboxes were simply too good a deal to turn down. And so Freightways, their little FTL money-spinner, was born." He took the whiskey offered him.

"They didn't invent it?" Melid asked.

"A bauble dangled before human capitalism," Eucharist said.

"By the Hoidrac?"

"A Freightbox is a lie," Eucharist said. "It is a Starlock, a Harmonic-built Starlock hidden in a vast box. Made to appear constructed by 'feral' tech. Why, what do you think this meeting is? I facilitate for Freightways, I facilitate for the Harmonies." He smiled. "Business is good."

"I'll facilitate your genitals with a bolt, liar," Melid said.

"What I'm trying to tell you," Eucharist said, "is that you monsters are far dimmer, far more amateurish than Raichundalia, and yet they fell for Hoidrac promises as easily as Silvercloud. The Hoidrac have humanity in their palm." He looked deep into Melid's eyes, almost through them. "You've no idea what you contend with, little hive-mind. If you did, you would kneel before alien deities and pray for their mercy."

She slapped him. He spilt his whiskey. "Never," she said. "*Never.*"

"The difference between you and Raichundalia is that, while they are useful, you are a threat. The Hoidrac would have you gone."

"They can wish what they like," Melid said.

"The woman," Eucharist said. "Sparkle and her body's siblings--"

"What?"

"Doesn't matter," Eucharist said. "Mere detail. What matters is her body, her psyche, has been moulded by the best Geode technology so as to absorb you freaks, your very essence."

"By touching Illik," Melid said. She looked up at Doum. He was already looking back at her.

"I manipulated Illik the kancer cell, and I manipulated Illik the traitor of the hidden hours," Eucharist said. "They both helped me to manipulate the other Illik: Illik the true patriot, the Field-Emissary. With their information, I could use agents around the known galaxy to lead Illik toward the rig where Sparkle waited, never knowing of her exile's true purpose. Hargie Stukes I also distantly shepherded. No easy task, let me tell you. Such a wayward boy..." He sighed. "But I digress. You see, no Illik, not one of the three Illiks, realised I, too, was manipulated. By inhuman hands."

Melid could feel the Konsensus watch through her, uncertain, captivated.

"The Hoidrac got more from their poisoning of Silvercloud," Eucharist explained. "More than they could ever hope for. They got a view of the weakness in your kollectiveware. The kancer."

Melid froze. Eucharist could see her fear. She could see it in his face.

"If Sparkle returns to her birth world," Eucharist said, "walks physically into the dimensional threshold of its northern hemisphere... well, the Hoidrac will *comprehend* you. They will evaporate the barriers between your individual minds, such as they are. Every Konsensite, every asteroid kollective, will melt into an undefined whole. Total and utter... kancerisation."

Melid could feel the Instrum rising to galactic alert, thousands of mission-aware individuals as one. Shocked. Horrified. Melid knew of the simulations: a fully kancerised Konsensus would simply not function. Billions of minds collapsing into a morass, a soup, too large to retain sentience.

"Why..." Melid struggled not to panic. Opening herself up to the Kollective-at-Large wasn't helping, not this time. "Why tell us? Why ruin your own plans?"

"You wouldn't believe me," Eucharist said.

"Tell me!" Melid shouted.

"Because maybe there's still time to kill that Harmonic witch," he said. "They fooled me, those Hoidrac. I never wanted you beasts eliminated." He grunted, almost growled. His face hardened. "Stagnation is my enemy. My oldest, my only. There was a time..." He waved a finger. "...long long ago, when progress was a river. A man could wake each morning, switch on what we now call the memestream, and never know what new invention would greet him." He stared at nothing, perhaps picturing this mythic past. "I hunger for that age's return. Strive for it. Worlder humanity cannot climb from its present mire, not alone. And the Hoidrac..." He sighed. "They would impose a destiny humans were never meant to pursue. Too... *easy.*"

Eucharist closed his eyes, took a deep breath. He continued:

"But you? You forgotten accidents, you slaves, you freaks..." He slapped the table's surface, looked Melid in the eyes once more. "You *beautiful* monsters." He pointed at her, grinned maniacally, like she'd never seen. "The catalyst I'd never thought I'd see. Oh, the Delighted Ones fear you, I think. What you may become. You are fiends, ready to dye the very stars red. To bring conflict." He lay back in his chair. "To bring change."

Melid raised her bonebolt, pressed it to Eucharist's forehead. She had no wish to torture him. Somehow, she knew it would procure nothing.

She couldn't pull the trigger. Her arm had frozen. She tried again. Nothing.

Eucharist smiled. "I've been here before, girl," he told her. "Your--what is it?--Instrum won't allow you. Not even now. Minds higher than even your station still have use for me."

"Leave," Doum said to Melid. The fear rising from him was thick, unmistakable. "Quick now."

Melid emoted agreement. Perhaps Eucharist lied. It all seemed the unlikeliest truth. Already fleets were preparing. The Konsensus moving to action. She turned, headed for the door.

She stopped halfway and turned back around.

"We've a few minutes," she said. "That wound in your hand, Mr Eucharist. It would appear that we've at least some room to cause you pain. Doum?" She looked at her brother Konsensite. "Could you discover to what degree, please?"

She looked down at Eucharist. She put on the most fake, most saccharine, most ironic smile. "We've no more questions."

Sung Eucharist's smile vanished.

***

SPARKLE WAS NO MERE TOURIST to the Geode's skin. No citizen of the Harmonies ever was. Yet this was different.

She hadn't comadosed to get here, she had no body dribbling somewhere on a couch, fixing her to the real universe. She was essence, formless essence. She was scared.

She floated on currents of raw id, vast streams of subconscious that belonged to no mind and never had. Sea was the closest analogy, but it was a weak one. This was more like... like that mind-state between wake and sleep. Hypnagogia, that was the word. Except, for Sparkle, it was like being inside someone else's hypnagogic state, a tiny mote floating within its lazy chaos. No up nor down, not even the possibility of up or down. Sparkle was beyond disoriented.

:I have you:

Pearl. She felt Pearl, strands of his being curling through her. Making sense of things.

:Thought you said you never used a Womb,: Sparkle told him.

:I've a hold on the theory,: Pearl sent. *:I'm going to filter your perception. Should make things easier.:*

:Comprehensible would suffice,: Sparkle replied.

Better. More ocean-like, or near enough. She floated in a blue penumbra without surface or floor, an infinite sea. Shoals of luminous orbs raced by in the mid-distance, some of them popping in and out of existence. Beyond them lay a brooding sphere, a black planet.

:I've rendered all your sensory input into something like vision,: Pearl sent. *:Not a true vision of things here, but more user-friendly. Call it a white lie.:*

:At least we haven't been consumed by anything yet,: Sparkle sent. *:I take that to be a good sign.:*

Curious, Sparkle curled her essence over itself, to look back from whence they came. Her own being was a glittering pink scarf, like silk filled with stars. Sparkle found she rather liked it. At its far end her length blended into a billowing scarf of sapphire green. It trailed off, off into the murky distance.

:That's you, right?: Sparkle sent to her brother.

:Of course,: Pearl said, his sentiment a warm tickle running down their shared length. *:I'm holding you, keeping us stitched to the Womb's liquid back in our own reality.:*

:Appreciated.: It felt good, like the neural closeness of her siblings back when they'd shared flesh. If she concentrated, she could feel Pearl's nature: his focussed brilliance, the arrogance that belied a peculiar shyness.

:Concentrate, Sparkle,: Pearl sent. *:The hierofish.:*

She twisted back, stretched herself flat, the black planet in her vision once more.

An iridescent orb darted about her, twinkling all mother-of-pearl.

:*Latch onto it,*: Pearl sent.

Sparkle stretched to meet the orb. It dived down to her, wrapped itself in the tip of her scarf. The hierofish jetted off, dragging Sparkle with it, stretching her and Pearl. She didn't feel stretched. She didn't feel any velocity. They headed for the black sphere.

:*We won't snap, will we?*: Sparkle asked.

:*We're essentially infinite,*: Pearl replied. :*We can be cut, however.*:

:*Easy for you to say,*: Sparkle sent. :*You're the one still groping our escape route.*: Sparkle gazed at the ominous super-sphere. :*What is that?*:

:*When a species in our own universe goes extinct,*: Pearl sent, :*their sensations and memories slowly accrete into a singularity within the Geode. Takes eons.*: He paused, as if checking something. :*Geode cartographers call this one the Triloroid. My data says no one's been near it for some time.*:

:*That last fact walks a line between reassuring and creepy,*: Sparkle sent.

:*This whole area of the Geode's skin is pretty desolate,*: Pearl sent. :*Good place to hide a lockwyrm.*:

:*What exactly do I do if I find one?*: Sparkle asked.

:*Presumably you possess some coordinates it can latch onto.*:

:*Latch onto?*: Sparkle sent. :*You've seen the teeth on those things, right?*:

:*Just open your mind to it,*: Pearl sent. :*Or keep an open mind. Or something like that. Be flexible.*:

:*I'm a length of iridescent material,*: Sparkle sent. :*Flexible's my lone quality.*:

They passed through shoals of orbs like the one pulling Sparkle. The shoals were a shower of gold light, sparkling like sunlight through branches when one ran beneath trees. A few moved slower, pushing smoky spheres like blood cells with a galaxy at their nucleus. These slower hierofish would materialise and then swiftly vanish with their load.

:*Human awarenesses,*: Pearl explained. :*You know when you comadose, when you access the experience of being a purring cat or an aerowhale or having impossible sex?*:

:*Can't claim the latter,*: Sparkle sent.

:Liar. That's what you look like when doing so. To a Geode-beast, I mean. Or an Ashemi.:

:I always found your Geode-tech obsession dull, brother,: Sparkle sent. *:I shan't again. This is beautiful.:*

:I'm not seeing things quite like you,: Pearl sent. *:You're on easy setting.:*

:What are you seeing?: Sparkle asked.

:Something more akin to what you saw when first materialising here. More so. And it's wonderful. It's wonderful.:

She was pleased for Pearl, but she couldn't say his statement filled her with hope. Which of them was blinder here?

They snaked their way past the river of shoals. A near-emptiness lay between them and the Triloroid. She passed through a dust ring, unseen against the sphere's black surface. Amongst the dust were strange things: fronds, quills and spines, severed insectile legs. She couldn't feel them--not physically--but they tickled something in her mind. Something primal.

Closer now. The Triloroid's crust was like a landscape of dark scabs with no flesh beneath, just holes between fused plates. A desolate world riddled with chasms. She'd visited happier places.

:Sparkle,: Pearl sent, *:we've a problem.:*

She felt Pearl drag her perception above the sphere and to the left. In the distance, the deep endless blue, patterns danced. White, fractal, ever-dissolving and blooming afresh. At its centre raged a fire, swirling and translucent. The fractal pattern held back its growth.

:Beautiful,: Sparkle sent.

:For all the wrong reasons,: Pearl replied. *:You're looking at an aesthetic skirmish. It appears Mohatoi Embossed knows we're here, and Pheoni the Appropriate holds him at bay. Thus far. If Mohatoi can make a prettier algorithm, Pheoni must permit him entry.:*

Sparkle stared. Such beauty; conflict's nature in abstract.

She felt a jolt.

:Stop looking,: Pearl sent.

Sparkle did so, focussing on the Triloroid.

:You didn't have to shock me, brother,: she sent.

:Yes I did.:

The hierofish pulled her down, down into an abyss between the chitinous plates of the sphere's crust. Cliffs of crushed brown carapace surrounded her, lifeless diamond eyes among the crags. Some distance down, the hierofish tugged again, and Sparkle was drawn into a vast tunnel, its walls segmented and festooned with spires, cathedrals of dead animal shell. She brushed past one and her mind was drenched with alien recollection: ocean bed, a sun warped by ripples, the desperate scurry from shadows above. The experience passed soon enough.

The hierofish stopped, hovered in the tunnel's centre.

:Do you sense it?: Pearl sent.

Sparkle did. A shuddering. A soundless deep bass.

:The lockwyrm,: she sent.

Ripples in the fabric of reality, the ether-waters around her. Something passed Sparkle. She squirmed, but the hierofish held her in place. The thing near-brushed her again: like a stalactite but translucent, attached to nothing, vanishing at the root. The waters throbbed.

:A tooth,: she felt Pearl send.

The tooth vanished. It appeared again, or one just like it: high up, near the roof of the cavern.

:Where's the 'wyrm?: Sparkle sent to Pearl. *:The whole 'wyrm...:*

:Hard for your filter to process,: Pearl sent. *:A lockwyrm's far less inclined to rational spatiality than, well, anything.:*

The throbbing shook her mind like sand.

:Fuck this,: Sparkle sent. *:Let's go.:*

A tendril emerged, curling out of nothing. It twitched a moment, as if sniffing, then jabbed at Sparkle.

Everything became nothing in a blink, became the hypnagogic formlessness of when she'd first arrived. The tunnel returned swiftly enough, but another jab and another came, each time throwing her senses off and on.

:*Be calm,*: she felt Pearl send, :*it's tasting you.*:

:*That's a nasty bloody metaphor, Pearl.*:

:*No metaphor,*: Pearl sent.

:*Ohh fuck.*:

She struggled, but the hierofish was a weight, a manacle.

The tendril disappeared. In its place, directly ahead of her, materialised something larger. Fatter than the tendril, the mother of all tendrils, the monstrosity had a widening slit on its business end. It pointed at Sparkle.

:*What is that, Pearl?*: Sparkle asked.

:*I... don't know.*:

For some reason Sparkle thought of Swirl in the villa, her brutal fists.

Come on, then, Sparkle thought, looking at the thing, steeling herself. *Get it done.*

The thing lunged at her. Its slit stretched wide. The slit enveloped her, swallowing the world.

Grey, formless. Her memories flashed by, projected onto the nothingness: *cradled in her parent's arms, stumbling around snowflowers, corquills cawing, blooming into three: Pearl, Swirl, her, building the villa, the beach, the three of them...*

Come on, wyrm, take what you need.

Body growing, filling, glances in mirror, sex drowning the world, exams, first femme-on-femme, first male-on-femme, femme-on-male, first sixsome, ninesome-at-party, squeals, laughter, spilt wine...

The wrack of memory. The wrack.

Exams, screams, breakdown, now ugly in mirror, ugly and siblings carrying and back again, brighter, louder, more wine and then blank, then Pearl gone, then exile...

Hargie. Oh, little rat. Forgive me.

Little rat, smelly feral, stupid ship, withdrawal, smoke, on a bed, conflict, escape, scent of skin, his touch, words beside the river...

One last moment to laugh together, to forgive. Anything for that. Anything.

The returner, press the... returner, yes. returner. Kill Floofy, forget, move on, kill Floofy kill

Princess Floofy.

Sparkle became a symphony of sigils and glyphs, axes and coordinates. An equation of stars.

The stars touched one another.

***

PEARL'S HEAD ROSE FROM THE Womb's liquid, up into gloom, into mists. His vocal synthesiser roared.

He floated, quite still, wondering how his wrought-iron form could be so buoyant. He recalled his sister. He flailed his arms in the murky waters, panicking. He found her and lifted her head--its rope hair gone, dissolved--to the surface. He could feel her, feel her weight.

But why panic? She wouldn't drown.

"Sparkle?"

Her blue opal eyes lit.

"Damn you," Sparkle said, blue leaf-mulch pouring from her features. "Your bloody lockwyrm turned me into a... non-Euclidian dildo."

Pearl laughed. He realised he hadn't in his present body. Not ever.

"It better prove more practical than one," Sparkle added.

"Listen," he said. There was a humming all about. "It has. That's the House's entire substrate at work. Something's afoot."

"The lockwyrm..."

"Our body returns," he told her. "Our body."

"In *Princess Floofy*," Sparkle muttered. She got up from Pearl's embrace. "She's the coordinates." Sparkle stared at him. "Why would Hoidrac choose *Princess*-fucking-*Floofy*?"

Gibberish. What had the lockwyrm done to her?

CHAPTER EIGHT

S wirl followed Hargie and Kaysie up the coiling chromium stairs. She heard men talking above, smelled their tobacco smoke.

"Skip just neuraled," Hargie told them. "Vict wants to speak to me."

"Whatcha gonna say?" Kaysie asked.

"Won't know 'til it pours from my tongue, sis," he said.

"This is all," Swirl said, "encouraging."

"Got something better, do tell," Hargie said over his shoulder.

She didn't like the tone in his voice. Almost accusatory. Perhaps best to keep quiet while this thing played out. And it would. This Desic was her home now. She would prove it.

The door at the top of the stairs whirled open and the three of them stepped through. Desic control was like a circular lecture hall, concentric rings of terminals manned by scores of bubblemen staring into the air before them. Clearly, their neuralware was alive with breaking news and gleaned information: a world Swirl's leaf-augmented brain would never be privy to. At the centre of it stood Skip Darrow, stroking his long thin hair. He squinted at nothing, his tapered face--so uncharacteristic of his people--scowling.

"Skip," Hargie called, walking down a thoroughfare between the terminals. "We're all here."

Skip gave the slightest smile as they reached him. His smile wavered when he saw Swirl.

"She meant to stick at *Princess*," Skip told Hargie.

"Rules are recommendations to Sparkle," Hargie said.

"Mr Darrow," Swirl said, "I'd like my old pistol. The gun-taboo is past now."

Skip Darrow ignored her. "Vict's waiting," he told Hargie. "Patch you through?"

"Run it," Hargie said.

Hargie and his sister stared straight ahead, as did Skip.

"Could someone give me a screen?" Swirl asked. No one answered. "I'd like a screen, please."

Kaysie shrugged, blinked. A holo screen emerged above a nearby terminal.

"Thanks," Swirl said, but Kaysie was already staring ahead again.

"--had your chance," Nugo Vict was saying. He stood before a blank wall. Though Vict's face was freshly shaved, his eyes were red. "What I do, I do for all bubblemen."

"You take a census, Vict?" Hargie said beside her. "Or did you vox pop your own fat fuckin' ego?"

"History will see that statement as projection, Stukes," Vict said. "You gamble bubblefolk lives on a foreign witch, a worm slithering in our belly. You're bad news, same as your father. Mixing with Stats, drinking in their ways, thinking they could ever understand us. Us, who gave them star travel!" He shook his head. "No. Understanding *ruined* us."

"Ratshit," Kaysie blurted. "Y'shittin' on the Sisters, Vict."

Vict sighed. "Your dyke sister's here. Marvellous."

"My *pilot* dyke sister," Hargie said. "Better one than you."

171

"The Sisters--if they existed--were noble," Vict said on Swirl's screen. "But naïve. Empathic rationalism is for some better universe. Not ours. The Konsensus have thrived without it."

"Day we become those assholes," Hargie said, "is the day your pecker reaches an inch."

Vict growled. "Will you *please*, for once, just *once*, leave my penis out of this? I'm holding your friends at fucking gunpoint and *still* you fixate. My manhood's *pretty* far from significant here."

"Acceptance is the first step," Hargie said.

"Newsflash, Stukes: the Konsensus assure me it's a good size." Vict gave an angry smirk. "Case closed."

Everyone in the control room blinked.

"Whoa," Kaysie muttered. "They some *layers* to this conspiracy, man."

Swirl saw a figure over Kaysie's shoulder, beside the door they'd come through. Pink, entirely pink. But Kaysie moved her head, and when she moved back again, the figure was gone. Swirl returned to the holoscreen.

"Get the prisoner," Vict told someone off-screen.

The shorter Jaggard came into view, compaction rifle in hands. He prodded someone with it and they crawled into view. Old Durse: face bruised, beard matted with blood. Swirl bit her lip.

"Tell them what we're going to do," Vict told Durse.

"Fuck you," Durse said.

"Tell them, old man!"

The screen closed in on Durse.

"Harg', boy," he said. He gasped. "Your woman..."

Swirl tensed.

"She special," Durse continued. "Ask her. Me and the rest o' the Ring agree... don't give yourselves over. Don't." Jaggard grabbed him under his arms, dragged him out of shot. "Detach!" Durse shouted. "Blow the locks on us!" There was a punching sound and Durse was silent.

"Piece of shit," Hargie told Vict.

"Thirty minutes," Vict told him. "Then we shoot the ancient fart."

"Then we carry out his last wishes, Vict," Hargie said. "Blow your pod from the Desic." He muttered to Skip: "We can do that, right?"

Skip Darrow nodded.

"Ratshit," Vict told Hargie. "And kill the other hostages?"

"They sound prepared," Hargie said. "How about you, coward?"

Vict looked down, then back at the screen. "You've really no idea how committed I am. Thirty minutes." The screen dissolved.

"Now what?" Kaysie asked.

"Thirty minutes," Hargie said. "Nothing to it: we go in shooting."

"No way," Skip Darrow said. "Durse, man. The Ring."

"So find me a way in," Hargie said. He shook his head. "Air-con, whatever."

Skip Darrow looked at Swirl.

"No," Hargie said. "No."

"I'm not saying that, Harg'," Skip said. "Just, shit... shit, you asking me to trade friends for an innocent woman. No scene. This ain't no fuckin' scene."

"I'll do it," Swirl said. "Alone. I can take these fools."

"What?" Skip Darrow said. "You?"

"You don't understand," Swirl said, "I..."

The figure had re-materialised, like that, before the door. Sparkle. Swirl gazed at her own face gazing back at her, its expression blank. Scarlet-pink from head to toe.

"Sister..." Swirl whispered.

Hargie, Skip and Kaysie began arguing. They hadn't seen Sparkle, had thrown Swirl's suggestion to one side.

"Call Vict," Hargie was saying, "buy more time."

"For what?" Skip Darrow said. "They got us fixed."

Sparkle stared. She began to turn toward the door. What the hell was this? Leaf-hallucination, surely. Swirl was on a minimum these days, running out, but...

Everyone around her tensed. The whole of Control.

"What the fuck?" she heard Hargie say.

"Neural-wide," Skip Darrow said, staring into the air before him. "Whole Desic."

"Block it," Kaysie said.

Sparkle--the wraith of Sparkle--passed through the door.

"No," Hargie said. "Run it through a safe patch."

No one was looking at Swirl. She took the opportunity. She ran after Sparkle.

***

THE FICTY-SCREEN WAS A red blank. It must have been the same for everyone else's neuralware, everyone all over DesicWest. Hargie braced himself. No way any virus could cut through the safety patch they'd run it through. No way...

The red blank got supplanted with the face of a severe young man with a chin beard. Behind him loomed the unmistakable plated decor of all Konsensus installations.

"Greetings, DesicWest," the young man said with a surprisingly deep voice. "This is the Undercompany speaking. We ask for calm. Calm, because I'm informing you of your imminent deaths."

He paused, as if letting the panic set in.

"The arms of forty-three warships are aimed squarely at DesicWest," he continued. "Indeed, if the choice were mine alone, you would not even be receiving this message. The Undercompany, however, would rather avoid the sort of public attention only genocide can procure. Bear in mind this desire, much like yourselves, has only a lifespan of some thirty minutes.

174

If our request, which I will soon divulge, is not carried out by that time, then your aforementioned deaths are as guaranteed as they are horrific."

The young man's pupils looked as dark as the twin assholes of the Great Foozle. He didn't seem to blink. Hargie found himself missing Melid.

"Our request: kill the outsider Ms Sparkle Savard. She is a physically lethal individual, but imagination, a mob surge and thoughts of your children's deaths should prove an effective counter." The young man's face softened oh-so-very-slightly. "We wish you luck."

The message ended.

"Shit," Hargie said.

Kaysie sucked her teeth. "That boy a *monster...*"

Hargie turned to Sparkle. She wasn't there. She'd run. But she hadn't seen the message. How could she, with that fucked-up neural-less brain of hers?

"Cameras show her making for the docking ring," he heard Skip Darrow say. "Heading for *Princess.*"

Hargie looked at him. Skip had a pistol in his hand. Sparkle's pistol, muzzle aimed at Hargie's gut.

Hargie put his hands up. "Skip... how's this play?"

"You knows I respect you, respect your Pa," Skip said. "Respect got a limit."

Hargie nodded.

"One chance," Skip Darrow said. "We grab your woman and--if she ain't killed yet--we neural that Underking bastard, tell him to collect. Figure they still want that, given option, tune?"

"If not?" Kaysie said.

Skip Darrow shrugged. "Can't say it'll please me."

Hargie closed his eyes. "Do me one favour, Skip. Don't let her see. I'll hold her attention, and..."

"Sure." Skip nodded to another man nearby. The man pulled out another pistol and made his way over.

"Let's get this done," Hargie said. They ran for the door.

Finally. The single worst day of Hargie Stukes's life had a contender.

***

SWIRL HAD JUST SHOT A man through the leg. She hadn't wanted to.

He'd come at her with a wrench, but she couldn't stop and tangle with him. She'd had to keep moving. For Sparkle.

Swirl barrelled down an access tube that lead to the docking ring. She'd seen Sparkle heading up there, never running, always ahead.

And not some ghost. Really Sparkle, floating in the Geode's depths, surely, calling to Swirl. Sparkle needed her, that was all there was.

The door at the end of the tube whirled open, and Swirl powered through. The docking ring's tube lay empty, save for five men and two women standing in a huddle nearby. They saw her. They ran at her.

"I'll fire," she yelled. They kept running. One had a chain, another a table leg.

Swirl fired in the air and they faltered, yet didn't scatter.

"C'mon," one of the men told the others.

"Let me by," Swirl said. They didn't move. "I *belong* here. I'm one of you."

They relaxed. Odd.

Swirl spun around. A man with a rifle was coming down the access behind her. She lifted her pistol and the man wavered, more concerned with dodging his target's shot than taking his own. She fired and the man's barrel snapped, flew from his grip. The man screamed, fingers bleeding.

Swirl spun around again. The others were closer. She aimed and they faltered again. She'd never known civilians to be like this.

"I surrender," she lied, putting her pistol back in her pocket. She held her hands up.

They ran at her, swinging their weapons.

Swirl ran straight at the central assailant: short and stocky. Two strides from him, she leaped up. Her right heel landed square on the man's crown and Swirl used the footing to leap further, past the mob. She hit the ground and ran off towards *Princess*. She lost them soon enough.

Her hunch was rewarded. The Sparkle-wraith stood beside the hatch to the dockpod that housed *Princess Floofy*. Sparkle gazed back a moment, her face placid, and then passed through the hatch.

Swirl reached the hatch. She looked left and right: no one. She hit the button and the hatch whirled open. Blue light glowed beyond. Swirl girded herself. She stepped through.

Geode-light filled the dockpod's slim metallic space. *Princess's* hatch was open and her innards glowed half real, half not.

No sign of Sparkle.

Swirl's heart pumped in her ears. She closed the dockpod's hatch behind her. She stepped closer. She controlled her breath, as best she might.

Five feet away, she spied a silhouette inside *Princess*, at the end of the entry corridor.

"Sparkle?" she said. The word echoed in the strange light.

The silhouette turned to face her. Female, high hair. Too tall for Sparkle. Too thin.   Inhumanly thin. Horns.

Swirl stumbled back and fell on her haunches. She pulled out her gun and felt stupid for doing so.

Sparkle had been a lure, a light on an abyssal fish, luring victims to a colossal mouth. They had come for Swirl. Of course. Blasphemy must be paid for.

"Please..." She shook her head. "Let me stay."

For the first time the life inside Swirl, such as it was, became real to her. The most precious thing, no mere gambit. Her unborn child.

Swirl got up. Nothing was dragging her in, she realised. Not yet. The silhouette had vanished.

A hand shot through the hatchway. Swirl screamed.

A human hand. Male, smooth and young.

Corbie: the youth who'd tried to guard her. She could see the shadow of his head rising and lowering. Struggling.

Broken, assuredly. No. No point grabbing his arm, trying to save him. This struggle was only another lure of the Delighted Ones.

Swirl raised the pistol.

***

"OH, FUCK YOU, HARGIE STUKES."

She rather adored him. Simple as. She'd always been cursed with the ability to face ugly truths--when all other options became improbable, or when a trans-dimensional leviathan drew it out of her at least--and she... well, rather adored that feral loser, that primitive scumbag. It wasn't fair. It wasn't wanted. It didn't fit with her plans.

"Fuck you, Hargie Stukes." No, too strong a word, 'adored'. Too much.

Sparkle gazed at night's landscape, her hands resting upon a veranda wall she couldn't feel. The Daughter was a crescent in the sky. The lower half of it rippled blue, a reflection of Zahrir's wound beyond the equator. It dyed the snowy hills to the Trinity House's east, made of them vast and slumbering waves. She heard the wind's song coming over them. She couldn't feel it.

It was her newfound independence of mind, her new body, that made her realise she needed him. No, *required* him, merely required. Sparkle's old body, its hot, pulsing biological vitality, had lied to her, cajoled her that what began as lust had remained so, a bauble to be cast aside for any other. She had given her body to so many but never her, her... passion. *Affection*. She hadn't known how. Perhaps the very closeness of her siblings had atrophied such.

She watched a flight of corquills pass the crescent moon. *You always talk of this Hargie feral,* Pearl had said earlier, before the Womb. Pearl was about his business now, analysing. Oblivious to the seed he'd planted and the lockwyrm had fed. No shade in this desert, she thought, this wide plain of the soul her present condition brought. Everything that mattered now naked, exposed beneath a purest sun.

She had mended Hargie, and she had hurt Hargie, and she had thought nothing of either. *The difference between worlds is not so very great,* she'd said to him, back when they had first made... made... affection. Maybe so. But it was the differences, the distances, within herself that had proven insurmountable. And now she was all one. All broken.

"Look what you've wrought, Stukes," she said to the night. "I'm..." She smacked the wall with her talons. "...a moping... *wanker.*"

No. The change in body state, that was it. She'd have felt this for whomever she'd last screwed. A Harmonic citizen could never... fixate... upon a feral. Where was her pride?

"Did I just hear you slander the moon?" A male voice, behind her. The Envoy's.

Sparkle froze.

"Should hear what it said about *you*," she told him. Slowly, she turned around.

A two foot-high metal disc, a communic, floated toward her. The Envoy's face was rendered in its molten grey metal.

"Could I be so rude to ask you, Ashemi," it said with his cruel grin, "why the very foundations of the towers you languish in are currently saturated with lockwyrm energy? This Trinity House, after all, is now my property. All Zahrir too, come to mention it."

She had no answer. Or, at least, no lie.

"Ashemi business," she replied. "No Blessed of the Hoidrac should ever be accused of trespassing. I wouldn't have thought you so gauche as to insinuate so."

The communic stopped an arm's length from Sparkle.

"No, I would not, dear Midnight," the Envoy said. "And only a wretch, some feral lout, would go further and question your very identity. Such a clod might point out that Pearl, whom you liaise with and who currently appears to analyse said lockwyrm energies, is no true Ashemi, but a criminal. Why should you be any different? Where's proof of your authenticity?" The Envoy's face looked askance at her. "A bore might well ask."

"My body is my authenticity," Sparkle answered. "I could not inhabit it without the permission of one Hoidrac or another. The mortal Pearl is the exception proving the rule: he aids my inquiries."

"Depends upon the Hoidrac, though, does it not?" the Envoy asked. "Mine is in ascendancy. Zahrir's is a fading goddess. You could be a jape of the former or... more likely, a desperate bid of the latter." The communic tilted his face to a suitably leering angle. "And, if so, would she risk a true Ashemi? Or throw away some mortal patsy in Ashemi bones?"

"You're clearly very tired," Sparkle said. "And increasingly tiring."

"'Tiredness makes me annihilate buildings from orbit."

"You wouldn't be so crude." She tilted her marble head, mirroring the Envoy. "We've a game here, yes? To delight our masters? There's no wit to a sledgehammer."

"Depends how one swings," the Envoy said.

"If I were a counterfeit, your own world's patron would know, surely?" Sparkle pointed out. "Mohatoi would alert you in some leaf-dream, some vision."

It occurred to Sparkle that perhaps Mohatoi Embossed had done so. That right now the Envoy toyed with her.

"True," the liquid-metal face said. "Arguably. But one can equally argue my divine master hasn't warned me to leave you inviolate, either. I think that's revealing in itself."

"Do you, now?"

"Mm. Perhaps, like the bargain that used Pearl's misery, this too is a test set by both our patrons. Perhaps it merely falls upon me to call your bluff, eh, dear Midnight?"

"You embarrass yourself," Sparkle said.

"Oh, given a hundred megatons I can be an absolute arse." The Envoy paused, his metal face seemingly solid, a frieze. "Do you hear that, Midnight?"

By the Eye, she could. A humming, ever louder, coming from above.

"You wouldn't," Sparkle said.

"Give me reason not to," the Envoy said. "Own up or prove yourself."

Once again, she found herself glad of her lifeless and un-guessable face.

The Envoy's grin widened like a pulled wound. Sadism and exhibitionism were an alloy in him, mm-yes. Sparkle thought of the observatory ballroom, his plan to make the Zahriran guests strangle one another. To make them watch.

"Very well," she said, clothing her trepidation in a bored tone. "I know you didn't enact your quaint diversion."

"Eh?"

The humming was getting louder, vibrating her limbs.

"You didn't have your guests murder one another," she said. "You sent them home." She made a display of shrugging. "After insulting them, of course. At length."

"What of it?" asked the Envoy.

"Check your flight records," Sparkle said. "Pearl and I had already left."

"And?"

"And the ball was private, no? No transmissions in or out, to ensure a conscionable end to Zahrir and Culakwun's Pleasing War. So, ask yourself, how could I--a counterfeit, a phony--possibly know you'd been merciful? Why, I'd have to possess a direct link to our masters, would I not? I'd have to be a, what's the word?" She clicked her fingers, looked about. "Begins with..." She pointed at him. "Ass. Ashemi!"

The face on the floating disc became entirely still.

Had he slaughtered his guests? Her gambit depended on the negative, on his ego having been dented earlier, when Sparkle indicated such slaughter had been done before.

Yet the hum was a roar now. She wondered where she'd go once her marble body vaporised.

His grin returned. "Joke."

Lights shone behind her. She turned around, toward the landscape.

The hum had been that of a lifter-craft, not a falling warhead. The lifter's atmosphere-capable hull, long as a sports field, glistened in the moon's weird light. The vehicle settled just beyond the House's ancient walls.

"I'm speaking to you now from that very craft," the Envoy said, floating beside her. "Go on; give me a wave."

Sparkle rested her palms on the veranda wall. "Quite the jape, Envoy."

"I've decided to rule the Zahrir system from this very House," he told her. Sparkle wasn't certain she had convinced the Envoy with her gambit. More likely he knew she'd merely manipulated, then predicted, his actions. He'd have no wish to acknowledge the fact in words. "I've grown accustomed to this place. And your capital city's pretensions of refinement I find unctuous. I'd burn it to the ground and sow salt, etcetera, but I don't know..."

"Its existence is its own punishment?"

The face in the floating communic smiled. "I think I rather like you, Midnight. You're fun."

Sparkle didn't respond. Instead, she watched the lifter-craft unload its cargo. A strange consignment: ugly things, made by no sane Harmonic hand.

Crates. Feral-built shipping crates. She'd seen similar back on the Rig.

"What are those?" she asked him.

"You have your lockwyrm mystery," he said. "I have my mystery. Keeps things interesting."

Somewhere, Sparkle was sure, the Hoidrac watched, delighted.

***

HARGIE RAN ALONG THE DOCKING ring, Kaysie and the two armed bubblemen behind. In truth, he wouldn't blame Skip Darrow if the man shot him in the back of the skull any moment. Like his father. Be fitting.

They reached the hatch to the docking pod that housed *Princess Floofy*, skulls intact.

"Fifteen minutes," Skip Darrow said.

"Hope she here," Kaysie said.

Hargie hit the button and the hatch opened.

Shit. That Geode-light shit, pouring from his goddamn ship. He looked about for metal fish or the like. None such. On the floor lay two bodies, one of them Sparkle. He clambered through and heard the others follow.

Hargie ran over. The other body was the kid, Corbie. Maybe it was the light, but he seemed to glow of himself. Hargie shouldn't have left him here, should have told him to dust.

Sparkle looked up. She was breathing heavily.

"Saved him," she said.

He squeezed her shoulder. "My girl."

"What's all this shit?" he heard his sister say above him. "Serious."

183

"All like this where she's from," Hargie told the others. "I think." He looked down at Sparkle. "What is this?"

"Lockwyrm," Sparkle said. She got up. "Maybe. A gateway."

"Home?"

"Here's home," she said.

"Opinion's divided," Hargie replied.

Sparkle squinted at him. Then she saw Skip Darrow and the other man's pistols.

"That's my old gun," she said to Skip Darrow.

Hargie shoved his hand into her overall's pocket. He pulled out her pistol and stepped back. He was surprised she hadn't reacted, hadn't torn his arm from the socket.

"Whoa, whoa," Kaysie said.

Sparkle looked at Hargie, her face blank. Hargie couldn't point the gun at her. He let it hang from his hand.

"Harg'," Skip Darrow said. "I just neuraled Underking. No pickup." The look on his face said it all.

"Wait," Hargie told him.

"For what?" Sparkle asked Hargie. "What's happening, my love?"

She'd never called him that before. A ploy. A shitty hook.

"You gotta step on through," Hargie told her. "If you don't... everyone dies."

"We can handle Nugo Vict," she said.

"Vict ain't shit now." He pointed at Skip and his pal. "See these guys? They have to shoot you, tune? Konsensus gonna blow Desic, kill us all. Unless they shoot you."

"Twelve minutes," Skip Darrow said.

"Skip, man..." Hargie said. "We let her walk through there..." He pointed at *Princess'* hatchway. "She vanishes, tune? Fucking Foozle magic."

"No," Sparkle said.

"We can't know that," Skip Darrow said. "We can't know those bastards won't kill us all anyway."

Hargie shook his head. "They know she's gone from here. That's it. No point blowing their cover. You heard the asshole yourself, Skip. They all about cover."

Skip Darrow shrugged. "Worth a try."

"Best deal for all," Kaysie added. "Considerin'." She knelt down to check Corbie.

"Do I get a say in this?" Sparkle asked.

"Too many lives, Sparky," Hargie told her. "Too many."

Sparkle's face screwed up. She hugged her shoulders.

"They'll destroy me, Hargie," she said. "I denied them."

"You don't know that," Hargie said.

"Dead anyway," Skip Darrow said.

"Scum!" she shouted at Skip. "Feral scum!"

Fury rose in Hargie, a fury that had lurked since they'd been here. He lifted the pistol to her head.

"Fuck you," he said. "Fuck you, you selfish piece of shit."

"Hargie..."

"You ain't no bubblefolk," he said. "Bubblefolk'd throw themselves at that hatchway. For everyone. Now walk. They ain't gonna kill you. They'd have done that already."

"I *trusted* you, you little rat," Sparkle said.

He waited for her to make a move. Not a trace. The blue light glistened off the whites of her eyes, the gold of her piercings.

"You ain't the woman I loved," Hargie said. "Not no more."

She stared at him.

"You heard," he said. "You're so fucking cold now. Remember what you said? About the difference between us, between worlds?"

She just stared.

"Shit," he said. 'You don't, do you? You forgot. Just a lie. A lure." He shook the pistol. "Go."

She shook her head, looked ready to say something, but didn't. She rubbed her belly, stood around like a kid about to piss. Then she stumbled toward the hatch.

Skip Darrow lifted his pistol, but Hargie knocked his arm out of the way.

"Time," Hargie said. "Please."

"Six minutes," Skip told him. "Three more, I shoot."

Hargie didn't reply. He turned around and watched Sparkle climb through into the light. Her body seemed to warp in there. *Just the light rippling*, he told himself.

Fuck, but this was the right thing to do.

He remembered her coming to him. Kissing his brow that first time. Her body. How she used to be; laughter, brightness in her eyes and words.

What she could be again.

He offered his pistol to Skip.

"Swap," Hargie told him.

"What?"

Hargie eyed the pistol in Skip's hand. "It's her favourite."

Skip Darrow met his gaze. The man knew what Hargie was thinking.

"Dumb fuck," Skip said. He smiled, and they swapped.

Hargie looked down at his sister, kneeling beside Corbie. "Drag this boy through the hatch. Close it once you're all through."

"What?" he heard Kaysie say. She stood up. "Whatchu saying, bro-zo?"

Skip and the other guy lifted Corbie by the armpits, began dragging him out.

"Too good a thing, sis," Hargie told her. "Too good."

"Ratshit!" Already her eyes were wet. "Stay!"

"One day you'll tune," he said. "Find that someone, tune?"

186

"Fuck your sugar shit, asshole!" She grabbed his shoulders. "You ain't goin' in there. Love ya, bro-zo." She tried to drag him toward the docking ring hatch. "Stupid bastard... c'mon!"

Say it, Hargie thought.

He knocked her hands away.

"I did it," he said.

She squinted.

"Father," he told her. He lifted his pistol to the back of his head and mimed firing. "Me. I went back. Killed the men. He thanked me and I shot him." He could feel years dissolve. He mimed the shot again.

His sister's face looked a mask.

"What he did to me, I knew he was gonna do to you," Hargie said. "That was my limit." He looked her up and down. "But he'd already started, hadn't he?"

She wasn't even staring at him anymore. She stared at nothing, as if accessing her neuralware.

"I fuckin' love you, sis," he said.

She slapped him away. A sanity to it, slapping him away. He couldn't begrudge her.

"Fuck the past," he told her, his eyes watering. "Go be the best bubblepilot ever damn was."

He couldn't think of more. He turned and ran for *Princesses'* hatchway. No going back. No accommodating, no accepting, no coming to terms. Just movement, always movement. You stop: you crumble. You die.

Hargie Stukes leaped through the hatchway, into the weird. He barely knew where he ended and the air around him began. He wasn't inside *Princess,* but the idea of *Princess.* Shit, he wasn't a thinker. A mover, Hargie Stukes.

A shape approached him. He didn't fight. He felt a hand--the idea of a hand--shove fingers into his mouth. Sparkle.

The fingers pulled out. They'd left something: smooth, thin, pulsing with power. A leaf.

He swallowed.

***

NORTH, EVER NORTH, HIGH UP the galactic spire, into the Fugue itself. Desperate. Suicidal. Sick with hope.

Melid, suspended in a gel-sac like a foetus in its vat, had awoken for her three-day diagnostic, as had all the crew. She would sleep soon enough.

She didn't feel the gel around her limbs, nor gaze impotently at the inside of her bound eyelids. Melid was the craft itself: hull for flesh, sensors her senses. She felt the wash of the grav tunnel, its superluminal torus cradling the craft, compressing gravity before it and stretching it far, far behind.

Forty-eight craft out there, Hunter-Killers, travelling faster than any object in Konsensus history, faster than any hunter-killer should. Any human not inside their gel-sac would have been splattered against a bulwark. Speed was a necessity, the arbiter of success. More Hunter-Killers could have been found, plenty more, but the present konvergence would have been slowed in its mission. Every hour, every second might be the moment of perfected humanity's extinction.

Melid reached out to her crew, felt their pooled feeling. Relief, mainly, that their minds had awoken intact and functioning, not some kancerised soup. Below relief, a mannered terror that their neural genocide might still occur at any moment.

She felt no connection beyond the craft. The crew was a kollective in miniature, like back on Calran. Connection whilst engaging a torus drive was patchy at the best of times, but this was the Fugue, that far reach of the galaxy wherein kollective colonisation became unviable. Until recently they had thought it some weakness of kollectiveware, stretched to impotence by distance.

Not weakness, competition. The Fugue was rich with the Unreal, that strange energy of the Scalpels, the essence of the Harmonies and the monster Sparkle Savard. The deeper the craft went, the clearer that truth became. Their Hunter-Killer could no longer reach out, touch its comrades. She felt that, the craft's mute solitude.

They were the doomed. However events transpired, their craft aggregation--quickly named 'the Northern Konvergence'--would likely never return. They had used ancient astronavigation methods, predating the Kollective-at-Large, to deliver them to a distant star that, Silvercloud records and luck permitting, would transpire to be Zahrir. For all they knew, they might emerge inside a gas giant or, more fittingly, an asteroid. For all they knew, they would be detected and annihilated on arrival. For all they knew, their human target might not be there. Horrific odds, but they had been selected to save their very species. They knew no better way of dying.

It was possible Sung Eucharist had lied. Worlders did. But alien 'gods'? Who knew what they were capable of?

Their mission was plain: find and terminate Sparkle Savard. Remain undetected if such was still possible, destroy without restraint if not.

Melid smiled. A hunt, then. A hunt.

PART FOUR

LOCKWYRM

CHAPTER NINE

S wirl laughed. So many seahorses. Streams of them, bobbing and dipping through the air, silver-skinned, tumbling and righting themselves, passing her face.

Swirl had loved these beasts as a child. All Harmonic children did. Silver seahorses. A silver world here.

Swirl looked around: a room shaped like the innards of a spiralling shell, its surfaces square mirrors, each mirror a foot wide. Many mirrors were cracked or chipped at their edges, but none had lost their lustre. No dirt. Everything clean. Swirl liked order.

She wore a blue ball gown. Wide skirts, silver sequins. She'd worn a similar one as a child. She didn't dress in ball gowns anymore.

The seahorses--airhorses--had passed her by. She turned to see where they went. Her brother, Pearl, sat cross-legged at the far end of the shell, where it coiled to a cone. Dressed in white, skin pale, hair silver-blond, Pearl seemed born from the mirrored shell, an equation, a holograph. The airhorses shoaled around him.

She headed toward Pearl, careful where to tread at first, careful of her balance, yet neither mattered. Her soles floated a half-inch above the mirrored squares, never touching. She was an endless reflection: figures in mirrored squares passing figures in mirrored squares, shrinking to infinity.

Swirl stopped, inspected her image.

No, not Swirl. The woman in every mirror wore white silk, skin and hair white. She gazed back at Swirl, her eyes silver pearls. Pheoni. Pheoni the Appropriate.

The goddess' mouth stretched wide. She raised her palms. Swirl waited for her judgement.

None came. Swirl realised Pheoni's pose was her own. She lowered her hands and Pheoni did the same. Exactly the same.

"Swirl," Pearl called to her. "Don't dally."

She floated to him.

Pearl looked up at her: her own features, yet male and pallid. He smiled through the shoaling airhorses.

"Sit," he said.

He never smiled like he did now. His was usually a pinched expression. This new smile put her at ease. She sat cross-legged before him.

"I've missed you," Swirl said.

"She's always been with you, Swirl," Pearl replied.

Swirl spied Pearl's reflection in the collage of mirrors. Pheoni sat there, cross-legged in her white silks, talking to another Pheoni sitting before her.

"Brother..." Swirl said. "Are we just reflections?"

"Don't be scared," Pearl replied. "A mask wears its wearer."

Swirl didn't understand. "I'm a coward," she told him. "I betrayed the Hoidrac, betrayed their love."

"Why?"

"I'd never been alone before," she said.

Pearl laughed. "You are never alone."

The airhorses shoaled around Swirl. Their presence had warmth beyond warmth, their very skins a benediction. A forgiveness.

"She loves you, sister," Pearl said. "You were always her special one. But you needed time in the waste, to become strong."

So true, Swirl thought. Self-deception was dissolution of the self. And the recognition of truth brought a soul back together, for truth was the cement of identity. Swirl had needed the former to ascend to the latter. She moaned with pure being. Her body glowed.

"Return to Zahrir, Swirl. Enter the flames, for she is forever there. You will join the chosen."

"Ashemi," Swirl muttered, full with delicate ecstasy. To live with the Hoidrac, an Ashemi. *Forever.*

"Forever," Pearl said. "And never alone."

"Never alone," Swirl said, rippling with blue flames. She hugged her belly.

CHAPTER TEN

argie watched the shanties burn, their black smoke one cloud rising into the night. Dead forests beyond, stretching into the dark.

He stood on a veranda carved of some weird black stone. Part of a tower, maybe, a huge one. Like no architecture he'd ever known. It hadn't been on the horizon when he'd lived in the shanties. Hargie'd remember something like that.

:This is how it looked after you left,: a voice beside him said. The voice lay somewhere between a man's and a woman's. *:After you shot me, sweet-sweet-sweetest boy.:*

Hargie looked toward the voice. A man in silhouette, only the lower face, his grinning mouth, visible in the distant inferno's light. His hand, too, resting on the veranda's stone wall.

Hargie could hear the baying of jaqruzzils somewhere in the night. Their canine howls seemed frightened, broken.

"I had to," Hargie told him. "Ain't proud. But I ain't scared. Not no more." He spat over the veranda wall. "And you ain't my father, asshole."

:No.:

Hargie looked back at the burning houses.

"Stupid idea," Hargie said. "World for bubblefolk. We never tuned sky." He shook his head. "Got *you* tuned, y'son of a bitch. You ain't the Foozle, ain't even a nightmare. Just a vagrant holed up in my head."

:Soon to vacate,: the man said. *:Exeunt, stage transcendental.:*

"Good," Hargie said. "Get running. Just like me and the girls have to."

:'Girls'.: The voice chuckled. *:Here, sweet boy, truth glints like blades in an alley. Outside? You won't recall. You will need a fool's telling.:*

"What's your fucking use, then?" Hargie looked at the silhouette. "I never remember any of this out there, I don't remember you. Can't act on your ratshit even if I wanted."

:One more dumb cunt.: No anger, a statement. *:All dumb cunts, awake. Do as bidden, think it choice.:*

"Which girl's which? Which is the one--"

The hand on the veranda wall was no longer human. Taloned, light-green, and all but skeletal. A creature had landed beside it: like a bird. Winged, black feathers. It had spider eyes and four crooked legs.

"You ain't gonna tell me, are you?" Hargie asked.

:No.:

"I won't remember shit anyhow," Hargie said.

:No.:

"Trying to protect me, that it? Protect my feelings?"

For the first time, the mouth looked surprised, in a delighted sort of way.

:I wouldn't even know...: it muttered, *:...how to begin to care.:*

James Worrad

PART FIVE

ZAHRIR

James Worrad

CHAPTER ELEVEN

No one ever came to the Trinity House's crystal library anymore, and that was how Pearl Savard liked it. It housed eighty thousand data crystals--ancient, obsolete, carried on the original colony ship--stored in embarrassingly old-fashioned refrigeration banks. Almost all of the crystals were corrupted anyway, either through age or the machinations of the first colony generation, their rationale a mystery.

He hadn't come here when a student; this was more Sparkle's area. But the hum of the many banks--black steel boxes with flashing lights--relaxed Pearl. He had taken of late, as now, to sit cross-legged atop one at the centre of the circular library and meditate. It helped that the walls were soundproofed: the House had gone to chaos these last three weeks.

The facts themselves, he thought, *the facts...*

He and Sparkle had summoned the lockwyrm, the Trinity House's substrate had become an inferno of Geode-energy, rising to some mouth-watering crescendo, and then... nothing. It had just stopped. Pearl had suspected Culakwun forces had played some hand, but not so. At least *he* couldn't find hint of sabotage, so that was as good as proven. Pearl had been stripped of most his memory, true, but his technical skills were demonstrably intact.

No; whatever his previous self had intended for that surge had almost certainly occurred, beyond the sight and awareness of Pearl and his sister. He had to trust himself, the Pearl that existed before his memory had been stripped. No one would go to such draconian lengths without some serious planning. The problem was that that logic flowed both ways: the pre-wipe Pearl had clearly put great faith into the post-wipe Pearl, the shell he was now. Living up to oneself was the slipperiest hell: a Zahriran proverb. Pearl did so hate aphorisms becoming apt to one's life.

So what *had* occurred? A lockwyrm had but one function: to freight something from one part of space to another, practically instantaneously. He'd expected the first he'd heard of it would be the Grand Fleet of Culakwun being hammered by some materialised fleet, but no. And yet, it had to be *something*. He had--

There came a whirling sound: the sealed trapdoor, before and below him. He opened his eyes.

The trapdoor's adamantine lid slid to one side and Sparkle's upper torso clambered through, her cord hair--newly fitted after the Womb--rattling in the library's previous silence.

"Shitmonger," she said. "Consummate crap flask."

Bye-bye meditation, Pearl thought.

"To what do I owe these accolades?" he asked.

"Not you," Sparkle said, beating her talons against the library floor. "I'm giving a lively character sketch of our convivial psychopath the Envoy. He's elected to spray the Trinity House from top to bottom with pure gold, and has begun encrusting the roofs with diamonds."

"You're joking," Pearl said.

"Never been more serious." As she said this, a shoal of five airhorses floated up from the trapdoor hatch. They bumbled around Sparkle's pink stone chest awhile, before getting caught in the breeze of a refrigeration tank and dispersing across the library.

"The Envoy's doing, I take it?" Pearl said, gesturing at the hapless, genetically altered fish.

"Filled the halls with them," Sparkle said. "In fact, he's drowning every civic building in kitsch, a sort of... twee-pocalypse. His cronies find it just *hilarious*. Whatever happened to magnanimity in victory?"

"Hardly Culakwun's style," Pearl said. An airhorse tumbled past him. A hideous novelty throughout the Harmonies, airhorses, reserved for children's parties and adults' suicides. "I imagine he's doing it to draw Zahrir's rebels into the open. Exploit aesthetic outrage."

"Well then, it's a masterstroke, because I'm fucking apoplectic," Sparkle said. She climbed out of the hatchway with surprising speed and bared her rear to Pearl. "Witness his scorched earth policy."

There was a swirl pattern on each of her body's abstractly sculptured buttocks.

Pearl had to prevent his vocal unit from registering a guffaw. "That's, erm, avant-garde."

"Envoy's got a thousand Geode-beasts spraying everything," Sparkle said. "Apparently I 'stood in the way'. An 'accident'." She waved a claw in the air. "I want to murder him, brother, I want to murder him in the face." Then her shoulders slumped and her head dipped. "Gods, I miss my arse."

"Our arse," Pearl corrected her.

"For a start, it didn't scratch anything it sat upon. A quality we took for granted." She growled and turned around to face him. "Speaking of which... any clue as to our exquisite and lamented derriere's present coordinates?"

"Not yet." He made show of a shrug. "In time."

"The stress is unbearable," Sparkle said, "knowing each second our lives could snuff out through no fault of our own. Swirl can't be trusted to handle that body alone."

"She can finish a man with one blow."

"And she can get herself snuffed with one remark," Sparkle said. "Social moron."

"You just missed a humorous opportunity to mock Swirl's fellatio skills," Pearl said. "Quite unlike you."

"Yes," Sparkle said, "*that's* how stressed I am." She climbed onto the refrigerator bank beside Pearl's. "I never trusted her."

"Because you're too alike," Pearl said. "Look, if you want to feel useful, do some snooping, some casual conversation with our invaders. You're good at that. Superlative."

"Always depended on me for that, didn't you? Neither of you appreciate the energy it takes, smiling at fools and pleasing bores, expected to be witty every moment."

Pearl felt annoyance. It was no easy task mastering the Geode's powers or, like Swirl, training their shared body to near-physical perfection.

Instead, he said: "I suppose not. But I don't suppose I remember much of anything at all."

Sparkle placed a hand on his shoulder and, for a moment, it was like he could actually feel it.

"Have you remembered anything about Gleam?" she asked. "I'd have thought something might have risen up by now. It must have been a powerful love you and he had. Irrational. Intoxicating."

"No," he replied. "Not in the slightest. Why do you ask?"

"I don't know." She looked down, between her hanging knees. "Just good to share a problem."

"No problem to share."

"No," Sparkle said. "Guess not."

***

"HEY, BABY. HEY," HARGIE SAID, stroking the hull. "Welcome back."

He kept tears back. Not in front of the natives.

"A pleasing thing," the old woman said.

"Bet ya ball--" He stopped. "Absolutely."

He hadn't imagined the Harmonies' metal fish-things could heal. Silvercloud had taught him they could only harm. But heal they could, at least these smaller kinds. They swam about the blue-lit cavern, circling over and around *Princess Floofy*, firing beams of weirdest Geode-shit at her lumpy body. Hargie loved these fishes. Wouldn't hear a bad word about 'em.

A thought struck him. "It won't... I don't know how to put this, lady."

"In words fresh made," she told him.

"Alrighty. It won't make my ship, y'know... weird? Like all alien and shit?"

The old woman, dark-skinned, her hair in a topknot, smiled at him. The flesh of her eye sockets had been tattooed in a way that seemed to change pattern when she smiled.

"No, *Sem-hoish*," she said. "It is the Anointed's belief all things must be true to their way. We've no wish to soil her foul purity." She placed her hand on his shoulder. "And shit."

"Smoosh," Hargie said. "No offence."

"We are not offended," she said, "but fascinated. Your void-machine is as alien to us as we are to you. Its navigator is, after all, the cloned brain of a domestic cat. Your remarkable ancestors made remarkable technological choices."

"Hey, if it ain't broke, why fix it?"

She looked at him with admiration. Or through him. These Anointed heads always seemed to be staring through you. "Truest wisdom," she said.

The pair of them stared at *Princess Floofy*. Sweet baby.

They had awoken here after leaving DesicWest, after things had gotten weird and... Geodey. Leafy. He couldn't remember much of that; just Sparkle sticking a leaf in his mouth, then... here. A thought about his father, maybe. He wouldn't think about that. Nothing but fear there. He missed Kaysie.

They were under the Husks, apparently. Some mountain range on Sparkle's homeworld. Three weeks. Waiting here bothered Sparkle more than Hargie. But he could tune her frustration: all this travel and no chance to see the land of her birth. The Anointed said Zahrir had got itself conquered. Everyone who could had ducked below the Husks.

The Anointed hosted them. They'd lived under the Husks for some time. Sparkle said they had been the first humans to meet Hoidrac. The Hoidrac had made them their, well, foremen maybe, paying them in dreams. A different dream each night, sculpted for them alone, shared by legions. Talking about the latest dream was the only subject that seemed to excite the Anointed. They were sports fans about their dreams. Otherwise, they treated life like a movie on a neural screen.

The actual citizens of Zahrir? Sparkle's folk? Hargie hadn't met a single one.

"We could fit a weapon," the old woman said. Not decrepit old. If anything, she made Hargie feel decrepit.

"What?" Hargie said. "Shit, no. I mean thanks, but..."

"Dreams say a new epoch comes," she said. "Defence suits all."

"Movement's the only defence I know." He chuckled. "You should see me work that cockpit, Lady. *Peshoooo...*" He danced his hand about like a bubbleship pursued.

The old woman grinned. "We understand."

Understand. Something Hargie needed to get with.

"So what's the deal?" he asked her. "What's next for Sparkle?"

"She makes her case before Ninemind and its cabinet as we speak."

"Really?" Ninemind was the leader of Zahrir. Sparkle had waited weeks for an audience. "Great."

"Smoosh," the woman said. "As you say."

"Smoosh." But was it? "Sparkle says she has to walk into... flames or something. Meet her Hoidrac." He looked at *Princess*. "I don't know what any of that means. I don't know if she even comes back. She comes back, right?"

She looked at him then. Not through him, *at* him. Hargie knew that look; that she knew things. That he had been discussed and was now handled like a puppy.

"Whatever," he said. He pulled out a smoke and lit up. "I never made plans."

She put her hand on his shoulder once more.

"You will walk with her," she said. Not an order. Simple fact.

Shit. It was.

***

"IDIOTS, BLOODY-MINDED IDIOTS..."

Swirl, sitting on a sofa in the blue-lit corridor outside the parliament-in-exile's chamber, fumed. They had laughed at her, mocked. She was the instrument of Pheoni. She had told them of that vision, and they had laughed. *Every Harmonic citizen of every concept-world has dreamed of Hoidrac,* the Shadow Secretary had observed, *and the vast majority are mere fancy. Why favour one dream over billions?* Fool.

Idiots in their ditch, waiting to die. What had they to lose, letting Swirl fly a feral craft toward Zahrir's transcendental equator? Their disdain for ferals had played its part, of course. But more that that, they *feared* her. She was sure of it. She was a Triune stripped of all siblings, made a monomind. A fearful thing.

Still, one or two had spoken for her. The High Secretary, notably. Most importantly, Ninemind itself had expressed no bias. That quadruped statueform, its great head crest enclosing three linked Triune brains, would have the final say. The lifeblood in its ceramic veins was purest leaf juice.

A being with that much affinity for the Geode would recognise the truth of Swirl's words, the truth of her destiny.

The Ninety exited the chamber, a collage of chatter and official garb: scintillating velvets cut to the shape of the first colony's uniforms. Swirl sat up, unsure whom to speak to.

"I've bad news," came a familiar voice beside her: the High Secretary, a woman of middle years who wore her short dreads in a bejewelled side knot. "Ninemind has denied your request."

Swirl stood up. "What?"

"We can appeal," the High Secretary said. "I believe, given time, I shall be able to convince all."

"There's no time," Swirl said. "There--wait--is your sibling watching?"

"The Shadow Secretary is in our head-residence at present."

"I didn't appreciate her mockery." Swirl shook her head. "I don't understand this. What does parliament have to lose letting me venture out to the equator?"

"My sentiments exactly," the High Secretary said. "But you must understand that the present Ninemind has lost a great deal of face with the invasion. Another folly might bring a vote of no confidence, a change in its brains." She lifted an eyebrow. "You have to admit your tale is... singular. These ferals chasing you, these..."

"Konsensus," Swirl said.

"They seem a paranoid creation. I mean no insult, but the idea of any feral group threatening the Harmonies is default laughable. So too their invisibility from our masters."

"Then I'll ignore the Ninety," Swirl said. "Ignore Ninemind. The Anointed will help. *They* comprehend my purpose."

"Please, Swirl," the High Secretary said. "From what I gather, they were merely concerned with getting you here. They lose interest if asked further."

True enough. Swirl ran a hand through her hair, grumbled. "They're fixing my pilot's ship."

"A courtesy."

"Perhaps." Swirl looked at the High Secretary. Her eyes were bright things, hazel stars. "So why are you supporting me?"

"Frankly, you're the only game in town, my girl," she said. "Like you said, we're hiding under a mountain, sans palace, privilege or ideas. If you *are* deluded, well, we're all condemned to life down here. But, if you're right..."

"You're the hero of the hour," Swirl said.

The High Secretary smiled. "Besides, I've seen your psyche readings. I might not believe your story, but there's clearly a sliver of something-- whatever it is--inside your essence. And only the Hoidrac could have stripped you of your poor sister." She looked at Swirl's expression. "I like to think she waits for you beyond the flames."

"Thank you," Swirl said. It struck her then that the High Secretary *did* believe her, feared her, almost. It made sense to charm anyone who claimed imminent ascension to Ashemihood. They might put a good word in with the Hoidrac.

"I must leave you now," the High Secretary said. She made to turn away, but stopped herself. "Oh..."

Her bindi turned purple. Swirl hadn't not seen that before. The High Secretary's third sibling.

"I too support your cause," this other minister said, head bowing forward, eyes peering from beneath her brow. "But after this is over, your feral must be put down. The security risks..."

She turned and walked away.

Swirl sat back down.

***

SPARKLE STOOD STILL AS... WELL, a statue upon the stairwell. Similes be damned.

The gloom hid her. One could lurk there of a night, unseen, with a clear view of the long gallery with its chequered floor and slim, lily-shaped pillars. She and her siblings had learned as much when pupils of the House, sneaking out from the dormitories. Swirl had referred to the stairwell back then as 'the high ground'. Strange girl.

Sparkle had been watching a guard, one of those Phoskmuj bred for cruelty, wander up and down the gallery for some ten minutes or more. She had become infatuated with the new skill Pearl had taught her: the ability to listen in on anything she gazed at, no matter the distance. She could hear the creak and crank of the guard's armour, the rattle of his breath. Her ability complimented the fact he couldn't see her, not with all the infra-red and other life sign-detecting gadgets his suit no doubt featured. Hmm. Explained the apparent omniscience of Ashemi in all the folktales and histories she'd read.

The guard spun away from Sparkle's direction, his armour sighing. A woman wearing the robes of Culakwun's middle-breeds approached him: one of the Envoy's staff.

"The female Ashemi," she said to him. "Has she passed here?"

The guard shook his head.

"She's around," the woman said. "He would speak to her."

The guard nodded.

"At dawn," Sparkle said, amplifying her voice. She didn't know it could get so loud.

The woman gazed up at the stairwell, her far-off mouth a black hole, fists drawn to her chest. The guard lifted his gun. Sparkle realised they still couldn't see her. She turned and headed up the stairs, keeping to the shadows.

So the Envoy wished to speak with her. The first step was to deny him the immediacy he craved.

Sparkle loitered awhile in dark hallways. *He must be in the convivium,* she thought. The woman had come from that direction.

Sparkle made her way there, taking the smaller entrance. Now that he expected her at dawn, it was vital she deny him the wait. This was the game now: outthinking, outplaying. It required an odd sort of connection with one's opponent. A venomous empathy.

The lights were low in the silent convivium. She walked along the thoroughfare between the high marble wall and the fat pillars, their upturned whirlwind shapes casting shadows across her. Beyond the pillars lay the convivium proper: a lounge built to the scale of a great temple's sanctum. Old-fashioned braziers daubed the marble floor and opposing pillars with flickering illumination. The ceiling above was entirely dark, though Sparkle knew it to feature an incredible mural of Pheoni blessing Zahrir. She hoped the Envoy had let the mural be.

At the centre of the convivium lay a dais some forty feet in diameter, drenched with cushions, silks and slumbering bodies. The dais was a gently sloping cone, rising up to a glass bowl full of drug-eels.

Sparkle walked around the disc, treading softly as her stone feet might, studying the unconscious party guests. Beautiful bodies of every Harmonic gender, flawless as the breeding programmes and surgery of Culakwun could make them. Many were of the Ingresine class; their torsos with their stretched spines, rising over or dipping under those of their fellow guests, lent them the quality of serpents at rest.

She found him at the edge of the dais, at the lowest level, his body supine and his eyes closed. The Envoy wore only tights. A pipe rested upon his tanned chest, its lead trailing up to the eel bowl. Further up the dais lay the kohl-eyed woman, legs spread and makeup smeared, entirely naked save for a guest's head obscuring her crotch.

Such banality. In Sparkle's old body this would have been a voyeuristic, if guilty, delight. She tried to recall physical arousal: the giddiness, the feathery sensation below and to the sides of her belly. But, no: nothing. Mere theory. She saw too much in the bodies before her now: the greasy, mottled skin of cocks; the fat-sack reality of breasts; buttocks with their pitted pores. Perhaps, Sparkle wondered, sexual excitement hid detail more than drew attention to it.

"Hello, Midnight."

The Envoy was staring up at her.

"Good evening," Sparkle said.

"You said you'd come at dawn," the Envoy said.

She wondered whether he'd been awake this whole time, feigning slumber.

"The stars are limitless." She sat on the dais, before his chest, looking out and away from him. "Always dawn somewhere."

"A mawkish thought," he said. "You'll give me nightmares." He squinted at her. "I was sorry to hear about the accident with the paint and your body."

"You wished to see me." Sparkle had spent an hour between two mirrors getting that stuff off. She wasn't convinced she'd entirely succeeded.

"To thank you," he said. She could hear him move, his voice getting closer behind her head. "You make our time here so much more interesting, Midnight."

"The term you're looking for is 'Your Ashemi'," Sparkle said. Looking down, she noticed his thighs had curled around the side of her left hip and that his arms circled her inhumanly thin waist. His chin, she guessed (she had no wish to look), rested upon her right shoulder. The Envoy seemed poised to constrict.

"Ashemi..." he whispered. "Where I come from, the days are so dull. Nought but fashion and slander. No meaning. I yearn for meaning. You keep a blade sharp, 'Ashemi'."

"I can barely contain my indifference," she told him.

"If you *are* an Ashemi," he whispered, "you are no unbiased observer. You're the last playful bid of Pheoni, yes? Some gamble, like how that Pearl fool was for my own world's patron. How arduous for you, charged with turning the tide. A hopeless task. I'm sure you can feel it..."

"This body feels nothing," Sparkle said. "And currently I'm thankful."

"Mmm." His palms had risen up her chest. They fondled the abstract breasts that sat either side of her heart-furnace. "But your furnace, your essence feels it: Pheoni draining from Zahrir, her power pouring away as fast as my own god fills it. You won't win, Midnight. You could never delight the Hoidrac enough. No one could."

No coward, the Envoy. An Ashemi could happily kill him for pawing over her sacred body. Yet, if Sparkle did, what then? Likely she'd forfeit this game they played, whatever its exact rules were. She knew it, and so did he. His groping was no bout of agalmatophilia, no lust, but a taunt. A trap. Better she feigned an immortal's indifference.

"You could join us," the Envoy said. "Fall before Mohatoi, worship him. That might be his ultimate victory here, I fancy."

"You're really the most ill-informed creature." She put the slightest lilt of doubt in her words. His offer was absurd, of course, but it was healthy to throw his suspicions, to kindle false hopes. She looked away, as if lost in thought, and he kept silent.

Sparkle noticed one of the bodies along the dais had no eyes. Long-plucked. A youth, short-bodied, one of the low-breeds of Culakwun. There were burn marks on his pale chest, and gouges, slices, sex-stains on ruptured flesh.

Sparkle used the sight skill Pearl had taught her, the gaze that listened from a distance. She was relieved, and rather pleased, to discover she could hear the youth's heart pound within its ribcage. One could listen *within* a body then, not just to it. Useful, that. Mm-yes.

"I know about your fleet," the Envoy said.

"What?" She turned to look at him. His beautiful face rested upon her shoulder.

He grinned his beast's grin. "That tumult of lockwyrm energy you and Pearl generated in this very edifice, remember? I waited for a 'wyrm to disgorge its interstellar contents somewhere in this system, but none came. So *then* I thought your actions mere bluff."

"Think what you like," Sparkle said. "I give no reasons for mine and Pearl's actions."

"That does seem to be the tendency, eh?" the Envoy asked. "But a week past, I awoke from a fitful night's sleep."

"Diddums," Sparkle said.

"A fitful night's sleep that birthed a notion: scan this system, not for lockwyrm signal, but for any fluctuation in Geodic energy. We're drenched in Geode-energy, after all, what with Zahrir's wound. Know what I found?"

"Fashion sense?" Sparkle asked.

"A brief but profound absence," he said. "Three days ago. Like a hole in the solar system, soon mended. The fleet lord tells me he's never known the like. Nothing remains now, but... you know what I think? I think it some new form of lockwyrm, a stealth-wyrm, discharging an equally furtive fleet."

"Errant nonsense." Wasn't it? Was that what the 'wyrm had done: produced a fleet? She had to tell Pearl.

"But it's of no real use," the Envoy said, "because we've discovered this fleet's presence, if not its nature and location. This is a Pleasing War, recall?

Your fleet loses before it begins. My own fleet is ready for whatever jest it plans. That's why I asked you here." He raised a hand from one stone breast and used it to caress an equally cold cheek. Sparkle didn't respond. "To mock."

"I know of no fleet," she said. She really didn't, but she put the barest tremble in her voice, as if protesting too much.

"You know," he said, sliding an index finger into the hole of her voice-amp and moving it back and forth, "I've never fucked a statue."

"But you've bored every lover rigid." She brushed his hand away. Sparkle stood up and spun around. She looked down at him. "Doubtless."

"I love you, Midnight." He reached for the drug pipe beside himself and took a drag. The great bowl at the dais' peak rippled with electricity, and the eels danced to frenzy. "One day you'll love me. I guarantee."

"I am here in an observatory capacity," Sparkle told him, hands on hips. "How many times must I repeat myself?"

The Envoy blew out eel smoke. "I was wondering that myself."

"And I observe this: you do not control Zahrir. Not fully. And you never will. Zahrir's leaders, all your most adamant opponents, hide beneath the Husk Mountains, guests of the Anointed. No Harmonic citizen may assault Anointed, nor defy their wishes. No one ever has. It is blasphemy. To that extent, then, your dreams of total domination are--not to put too fine a point on it--fucked. They can live beneath the Husks for generations, plotting against you and whatever cretins are your antecedents. The hidden Triunes will venerate this world's true patron--Pheoni the Appropriate-- and nothing, *nothing* you do will change that."

The Envoy stared in fright. Then he chuckled.

He wouldn't stop chuckling. Others on the dais began to cackle also. Likely they'd been awake this whole time.

Sparkle turned and strutted off. Into the dark. Away from laughter.

***

NO SIGN OF SPARKLE SAVARD in system. Either she was obscured, the tracker inside her had been negated, or she wasn't present at all. Melid wouldn't countenance the last option. Sparkle would be here.

Melid, Doum, and Craft-Emissary Gei sat in the Hunter-Killer's social core, fixed to seat-pits beside one another along the core's hemisphere. Others from around the konvergence-fleet observed, though were not physically present. A core full of instrums was no longer a sign of moral strength, but a luxury their situation could ill afford.

"Nightmare," Gei said, studying their shared construct of Zahrir and its moon. "Nightmare world."

"Agreed," Melid said, exuding a stoic acceptance, a humble courage. The essence of this konvergence-fleet.

It seemed the Harmonies' alien despots had gone to vast lengths to taint this otherwise ordinary star system. It was saturated with Scalpel-energy at the quantum level, a baseline of unreal. Much of the taint came from the sun itself. Its poles had been, for lack of a proper term, tattooed with an unknown insignia: three interlocking rings. Sensors suggested these 'tattoos' were sunspots somehow coerced into a static shape. Scalpel energy billowed from them, thousands of miles in height. Its ceaseless flow had saturated local space with a background radiation.

These vast plumes rising from the star's poles were unreadable to Konsensus technology and Konsensite eye, being a flat, featureless grey. Solar winds dissipated the Scalpel-energy across the system, reducing it from an unseen phenomenon to a soup-like nuisance that reduced the range of all Konsensus sensors to often little more than a few miles.

The konvergence-fleet had jumped into this near-blindness. Upon materialising, each Hunter-Killer could only detect those nearest it, rendering the fleet's mental kollective a mosaic of semi-connected elements. Panic had set in.

A strange thing had occurred then. Melid had exuded for calm, and the individual crew-kollectives of nearby Hunter-Killers had grasped at it. They had grasped for Melid, the simple idea of her. The Melid who had killed her birth-asteroid to kill the kancer, who had remained pure, even when threatened with disconnection. The Melid who had long hunted their present quarry. Melid was uncomfortable with this phenomenon, even now, but it had averted disaster. Indeed, it sharpened the fleet, lent it a unique ethic.

The fleet soon adapted to its alien environs. Direct laser transmissions between craft had worked well enough at close range, and were evidently undetectable to the enemy as long as a beam wasn't physically intercepted. The last three days had been spent producing thousands of stealth probe-remotes from the fleet's hoxnite reserves. Launching them one by one, a comm/sensor nexus had been fashioned around Zahrir. It fluctuated, what with the environment, but it served.

The probe nexus offered a picture of unimaginable, alien horror. The planet Zahrir was infested with Scalpel-energy. The cities of both its continents glimmered and rippled with it, its skies scarred by trails of the stuff that issued from impractical and dreamlike vehicles. Their entire civilisation was maintained by an unreal potency.

Sickening, to see humans brought so low. Melid's sentiment passed through the rest of those present. The Worlders they'd become accustomed to--those of Calran, say, or Qur'bella or Luharna--were merely inferior to the Konsensus, a motley of scuffling fools, yet self-reliant. A nobility in that, one Melid hadn't recognised before. She'd assumed self-reliance axiomatic to humanity. But Harmonics? They had proffered up their dignity for convenience. For ease. Illik had once tried to explain a Worlder term: 'whore'. She hadn't really understood it then. She comprehended it now.

Melid brought Zahrir's equator into group focus. She felt Doum and Gei shudder, held back the urge herself.

An impossibility, a... half-world. Where was its other hemisphere? Removed? Destroyed? Hidden in that other plane, that 'Geode'? Unreality poured from its wound, a ceaseless grey blur to Konsensus eyes and sensors.

The others waited expectedly, feeling Melid's sentiments but hungry for her words. She didn't articulate them. She studied.

"Domov," she said.

The Domov materialised. Not Conybeare, but another: the collective product of the konvergence-fleet's minds alone. Female, this one, its face too similar to Melid's own for Melid's liking.

Egeria, it said, Konvergence composite.

"Enemy," Melid said. "Latest."

Egeria shifted everyone's focus toward the enemy fleet. The fleet shifted in and out of vision as banks of Scalpel-energy billowed over them. Four great-craft--nearly the size of Worlder fearzeros, and undoubtedly more advanced--kept a ring formation some hundred kilometres above the planet's atmosphere, their prows facing out into deep space. The four great-craft, vertically arrayed and towering, moved their ring formation like a wheel, completing a clockwise rotation every 38.7 minutes. An odd tactical choice, one Egeria could infer no reason for.

But if the great-crafts' behaviour were questionable, the mid-size crafts' were outright deranged. Some thirty in all, the midsizes preoccupied themselves with passing through the space between the greatships' formation ring, circling around and repeating the pattern. They did so in belts of ten, prow to stern, four belts weaving between the great-craft. Impressive piloting, Gei had pointed out, given the midsizes operated with limited room and narrowly avoided colliding with the upper atmosphere of Zahrir.

Yet tactically? Absurd. They rendered themselves predictable targets and--presumably--limited their ability to focus fire. Yet more disturbing than hilarious, ultimately. The Harmonics would not behave so without reason. Some factor the konvergence-fleet was entirely ignorant of.

"Surface," Craft-Emissary Gei said. "Below fixed point."

The Domov zoomed the construct to a closeup of the planet's surface directly below the Harmonic fleet. Perceptive, Gei. Melid emoted as much to him. The area was a plain some fifty kilometres in diameter, at its centre an installation obscured by its own Scalpel-energy. No, *Geode-energy*; the term was known now. The thing was churning the stuff out with remarkable vigour.

"Run back," Melid said.

The image of the installation rewound over twenty-four hours, the Geode-energy surrounding it undulating like tentacles.

"Stop," Melid said.

At minus 13.4 hours, something emerged from the grey haze. Towers, nine of them, emaciated in their architecture. Golden in colour.

"Closer."

The roofs of eight were of a likeness--conical, pointed--but one possessed a roof garden.

"Egeria," Melid said to the Domov, "if Sparkle there: tracker obscured? Possible?"

Certain, Egeria said. If there. Geode-energy substantial.

There were many installations on the planet generating just as much Geode-energy. Sparkle might be hiding in any of them. Was it coincidence the enemy fleet were in fixed orbit over this particular one?

"Tactical," Melid said. "Choices?"

"Assuming Sparkle manifest," Gei said.

"Assuming." Melid's own frustration embarrassed her. Gei emoted apology, that he hadn't taken offence. Melid reflected those same sentiments back.

Optimum tactic simulation, Egeria said. Prepare download.

A half-sphere appeared in Melid's mind: Zahrir, its surface exuding Geode-energy, the enemy fleet above it. The Konsensus fleet approached in three waves. The primary wave consisted of just two Hunter-Killers, their holds taken up with armed and ready cadres. It would be their function to make landfall and terminate Sparkle as discreetly as possible. The second wave numbered four Hunter-Killers. If the first wave should fail, it would be their function to release warhead-remotes and eradicate everything within a thirty-kilometre radius of the target. At that point, of course, all subtlety would be lost, but eradication of the first wave's landing parties would ensure the enemy couldn't ascertain the nature and identity of their attackers. The third wave, the rest of the Hunter-Killers, were an insurance against the first two waves being detected. Hiding would be redundant then, and the third wave would commit itself to attacking the enemy fleet. That, hopefully, would permit the second wave to complete its mission.

The simulation ran a scenario of Sparkle appearing on Zahrir's moon instead, and the tactic was essentially the same. The moon's stratosphere was swarming with packs of those tiny ships of the enemy, that the Konsensus fleet had termed 'fighters'. They were something of a mystery. By Konsensus, or indeed, Worlder standards, they should be useless: too small to carry effective ranged weaponry, too large to avoid targeting. Probes, perhaps.

Which would be worse. The entire tactic counted on avoiding detection, keeping to the long unbroken history of the Great Hiding.

"Detection chances?" Melid asked Egeria.

Dependent: approach, velocity, skill, chance, the Domov said. Avoid Geode-energy densities. Best simulation: nine percent chance.

Gei and the others issued satisfaction at that. No doubt the sentiment would repeat throughout the fleet as and when it reached them.

Melid could not share it. "Estimated completion time?"

Three point nine hours, Egeria said.

"No," Melid said, slapping her knees with her hands. "No. Three hour? Sparkle could gone." She looked at Egeria. "Faster?"

Detection chance increase, Egeria said. Exponential. Time: one point thirty hours. Detection: forty-eight percent.

"No," Melid said and this time she felt Gei agree. "Both unacceptable."

"Then what?" Gei asked, frustration uncoiling within.

"Sparkle appears: end Great Hiding." She took a breath. "Direct assault."

A shiver passed through the local kollective. Even Doum was startled.

"Never..." Gei didn't complete the sentence. His emotic told all: bemusement, incredulity. Melid could understand. Gei was a seasoned Craft-Emissary, obfuscation and stealth his very blood. Melid? A Field-Emissary, young, no training in star tactics. Suggesting they should discard the Konsensus's one rule, their policy for thousands of years.

She reached out a hand, held Gei's chin ever-so-gently, radiated respect blended with sobriety.

"All things changed now," she said. "Hoidrac..."--she sneered the word--"...know Konsensus exist. We succeed: they still know. We fail..." She looked down. She let go of his chin.

"Kancerisation," Gei said. "All Konsensus." The logic clawed at him, but a fear also, to be the one to break the Great Hiding...

Gei looked at Melid. "Plan?" he said to her.

"Like fist," she said. "Tight. As one." She punched the air. "One strike." She indicated the simulations they'd just watched. "Three waves: too complex. Communication limited. So go simple. All warhead, no landing party."

"Outnumbered," Gei said.

"Shock, surprise." Melid emoted a keen certainty. "Enough."

"Shell attack," Gei said.

Melid frowned, emoted for meaning.

"Hypothetical tactic," Gei said. "Untried."

Melid reached out to the kollective, downloaded the simulation. She smiled.

"Shell attack," she said. "Alter, amend... but good."

Gei laughed, radiated incredulity. "Future they call this Melid gambit."

"Not Gei gambit?"

"You keep, Melid." He chuckled. "You keep."

Egeria's eyes lit pure white. She spoke: Attention. Fleet hailed. Konsensus craft in system.

The crew ceased chuckling.

***

ARMS AND LEGS ALL A-tangled on the bed, cooling skin. His lips beside the heat of her cheekbone.

She'd come in and fucked him. No words. Three times, every coo-coo way and still no words. Hadn't even met his eyes. And now silence in this little room, this chamber with its low lights and sculpted walls and fountain that was meant to be relaxing, but just made Hargie want to piss.

"You good?" he whispered.

He felt her nod affirmatively.

He drifted his fingers back and forth over her smooth shoulder blade.

"Love your shoulders," he said.

She didn't reply.

"They turned you down, right?" he asked.

"Yes," Sparkle said.

That pleased him, though he didn't show it. Funny; a few months back Sparkle would have picked up on that, would have been leaping out of bed and throwing shoes at him. He would have mattered enough back then. Save for his ability to fly her or not, Hargie was a sideshow.

"Something'll turn up," he whispered. "Your gods have got your back."

"I... keep failing them," she whispered back.

He said nothing, ran his hand through her dreads. She was letting herself go in here. No movement, no sky. She'd stopped exercising like she used to, her body softer. Going right to her stomach. He could feel it pressing against his.

"No one'll tell me what'll happen," he said. "When you walk into the flames. If I'm gonna lose you..." He took a deep breath. "Not sure I can fly you."

She tensed. She pulled her face away and met his eyes. "Of course I'll return," she said. "The Hoidrac wouldn't harm me, would they?"

They kissed.

"Sorry," he said. "I'm kinda unstuck, you tune? No memestream out here, can't pick up shit on my neuralware 'cept *Princess*."

"I'm sorry," she said.

"I kinda like it," Hargie said. "The peace. Makes me feel... human." Fuck it, he'd say it. "So I've been reading. They got Anglurati books around here." He chuckled. An act. "You Harmonic girls, you got storage, right? Six little stores downtown."

She studied him. "Seed palette," she said eventually.

"If we make it through this"--fuck it--"I wanna do a better job than my fuckin' father. I don't even want to *be* a father. I just wanna..."

"What?" she asked.

"Be there. Shit, I dunno." He looked up at the light above: a pattern in the rock itself. "I know you can't have mine. I'm a mutt around here. Probably got princes and lords in your, er, palette already. And I don't mind. You ever want a kid, I just wanna be there, whoever's it is. Be responsible for once. With you."

"Oh, Hargopal..." She lifted herself up onto her elbow, gazed down, and stroked his face. The scent of sweat mixed with that perfume she emitted naturally. "I've *already* stored you. Just, you know, in case anything happened."

He smiled. "Mighta told me, Sparks."

"You'd think me broody." She kissed his forehead. "And males don't really get a say anyhow."

"I see the logic," he said.

"We come through this and I promise you: you, me, a quiet little planet."

"No," Hargie said. "No sky."

"A star-barque, then," Swirl said. "You should see them: miles long and cast from glassteel, full of gardens and lakes. And we'll have babies, you and I, because it'll be safe to do so then, with my eyes and your crazy, stupid, wonderful hair. And... I know I've been dour and scowling for so long, but I'll be funny again. Like I used to be, remember? Like... I know you've missed."

He grasped her hip. "And pink hair? You rocked the shit outta that look."

"Yes." She took a deep breath. "Anything you want. I love you, Hargie Stukes. Utterly."

She clambered back on top of him and he felt her tongue inside his mouth. This was good. Things could be good. He'd felt like an actor in the wrong role, ever since they'd got out of Silvercloud. But he'd fly her now. All the way.

***

PEARL FOUND SPARKLE ON THE veranda of the forty-eighth floor of the western tower again, an hour before dawn. Sparkle was leant on the wall, her sleek form a ghost in the Daughter's blue light.

"I've made a discovery," he said, strutting toward her. "Or tripped over a hunch, at least."

"Summer," she said, never looking over her shoulder. "It'll be a wonderful summer's day."

"Listen."

She turned around, stretched her arms wide, rested her palms flat upon the wall behind her. She said nothing, a caryatid, a gauche relief rising from the architecture.

"I decided to think outside my obsessions for once," Pearl told her. "Discarded the Geode and inspected Zahrir, the very ground beneath us. Sparkle, there were earth tremors, low yet consistent, for a two-hour period after we..." He checked himself. The Trinity House might be drenched in recording devices. "...performed our duty."

"Between 0.6 and 1.8 Richter?" Sparkle asked.

"0.87," Pearl said.

"Consistent with this locality," she said. "Probably coincidence."

"How is it you always--"

"My mind's like a home for injured cats," Sparkle said. "You took all the useful stuff, brother." She paused. "I'd better explain I'm smiling in a friendly way right now."

"Noted," Pearl said. "What if I told you the epicentre lay beneath the Husks?"

"I'd be less flippant." She paused. "I'm staring at you with a pinched look of focus."

"Appreciated," Pearl said. "It's my hypothesis that..."

He stopped. He began to tap out a message on his chest, the finger-talk of the Triunes: **Anointed received Lockwyrm.**

225

Subterfuge comes late, Sparkle signalled. **According to Envoy, he's detected secret stealth fleet. Now lost. But here. There's our Lockwyrm.**

He may lie, Pearl signalled.

He may, she tapped. **But suspect not.**

Pearl had to trust Sparkle's judgement in that area. His own record in handling the Envoy was far from impeccable. He tapped on his chest again: **We must make contact: Anointed. If I'm wrong: eliminates. If right...**

Sparkle nodded. **Whichever,** she tapped, **visit to Husks serve to fuck Envoy's mind.**

Make him second guess?

Yes, Sparkle tapped. **But mainly fuck mind.**

"Time to visit the Husks, Pearl," Sparkle said. "One cannot deny an Anointed request."

"Yes, Midnight," he replied.

"I imagine the... 'subject'... must have absorbed the wave-chrysalis. It shall need its advocates."

What? Pearl tapped.

Sorry, Sparkle tapped. **Picturing that Envoy prick's face when he listens to this.**

CHAPTER TWELVE

No vehicle on Zahrir would go near the blockade, so Sparkle and her brother had had to walk the last five miles. No strain, that, not to their manner of limbs. A dislocation from things wasn't always so bad.

"I've been thinking," Sparkle said as they both clambered up the grassy rise. The snow had mostly vanished. Patches of it shone beneath the morning sun. "What if we're both right?"

"How so?" Pearl said, never looking at her, his glass eyes fixed upon the mountain range beyond the foothill's rise.

"That your wyrm-gate below the Husks hunch is correct *and* the Envoy's telling the truth about a mysterious fleet."

"Not a cloud in the sky," Pearl muttered.

"Pearl," Sparkle said.

"Then we've double the reason for hope, eh?" he said. "Allies below and above."

"And if they're not allies?" Sparkle asked. "I got the sense the Envoy's fleet detection had occurred days, maybe hours before he told me." She paused, strutted over a rock that jutted from the grass. "Weeks after our wyrm-bothering. What if this fleet of his has nothing to do with our recent escapade?"

"What if our Envoy is seeing patterns where there are none?" Pearl said. "You've done a fine job of stirring his paranoia all this time, after all."

"The Konsensus' ships were invisible," Sparkle noted.

"You don't say," Pearl said.

"You still think I'm making them up, don't you?"

Pearl stopped. "No. I think you overestimate them. Years spent in feral space have warped your judgement."

Sparkle stopped and looked back at him. "Wonder who I should thank for that.'

"I've no doubt this Konsensus is foremost among ferals," Pearl said. "But that's like being queen among corquill birds. Savages cannot compete with our empire, much less threaten."

"Pearl, do you ever listen to a word I say? The Hoidrac can't *see* them, not truly. Damn it, that's the whole reason we're on the course we're on. Swirl said as much."

"Then Swirl misinterpreted," Pearl said. "History is full of such. As long as we're moved by Hoidrac hand, it doesn't matter what we believe. Indeed, it often *helps* if we're mistaken. Plainly, our mission lies in freeing Zahrir from Culakwun. How can you even entertain the idea that might be secondary to, to... furtive primitives?"

"Listen--"

"You listen," Pearl said. "What feral nation would ever be insane enough to violate Harmonic space? All right, let's imagine the Hoidrac can't perceive them. How is that possibly going to hold out in Harmonic space? We're drenched in Geode-energy: it permeates everything. Their very non-presence would act as a presence; they would be holes in the fabric of--"

"Which is exactly what happened, dickhead, that's why--"

Humming ahead, over the rise.

"Well," Pearl said. "They certainly took their time."

Two Selachia swam over the rise of the hill toward them, three feet above the grass, the sun above reflecting off their silver hides.

"I hate Selachia," Sparkle said.

"They're as domesticated as any Geode-fauna," Pearl said, "even with their weapons."

The two armoured Geode-beasts circled around them, finned tails beating, closing in. They stopped an arm's length behind Pearl and Sparkle.

"Guess that's an invite to walk on," Sparkle said.

At the top of the hill floated a most direful sight: a chariot-skiff of pure gold, the sort of tasteless audacity only Culakwun believed it could get away with. Steedless. A woman standing on its decking.

The two Selachia swam toward the chariot. They took their positions before the thing, becoming its draught animals. The woman beckoned Sparkle and her brother.

"Oh, fuck this," Sparkle muttered.

"What?" Pearl said.

"Her, acting all mystical," Sparkle said. "Peerless wanker. And the whole visual. It's like... like a feral's idea of how we all look, something they'd get inked on their hairy man-boob before passing out and vomiting."

"It's just a ride, sister," Pearl said.

"Very well," Sparkle said. "But remember this sacrifice. Remember."

They strode over to the thing. Sparkle recognised the woman: the middle-breed from the night before, who'd questioned the guard as to Sparkle's whereabouts.

"The Envoy sent me," the woman said. "We saw you leave, your Ashemis. You'll need help crossing the blockade. We wouldn't want any misunderstandings."

"This the Envoy's plan?" Sparkle asked the woman. "Record us riding this thing and blackmail us?"

"It's a customary transport of the high-breeds," the woman explained. She shrugged, smiled. "Sort of an ironic statement."

"How am I not surprised," Sparkle muttered.

They climbed aboard. The two Selachia, harnessed by unseen fields, dashed their tails against the air and the chariot floated forward. Soon they saw the valley below: Culakwun weapon emplacements; squat barracks; scarab-shaped hover-artillery. Sparkle was no tactician, no Swirl, but even she could see this wasn't a force bracing for attack, nor expecting to receive one. A mere reminder to any Zahrirans inside the Husks as to who ran their world now.

The Husks lay beyond. No sky traffic swarmed around them now.

"Midnight," Pearl said, using Sparkle's pseudonym.

She looked at him, and he indicated something behind one of the barracks. A crate, like those that littered the outskirts of the Trinity House. Rectangular and ribbed, menacing in its utilitarian aspect. Nothing Culakwun would ever make.

"What is that?" Sparkle asked the woman. "Looks feral in design."

"Fusion generator," the woman said, never taking her eyes off the path they travelled along. "A non-Geodic energy akin to stars--"

"I know what fusion is," Sparkle said. "Why?"

"A backup," she said. "We plan for everything."

"Not another ironic fucking statement, then?"

For the briefest moment, a look crossed the woman's face that made Sparkle almost pity her.

"I wish," she said.

Having passed through the blockade, the chariot floated over a ditch and came to rest on the other side. Three corpses lay in the ditch, their skins and clothes burnt equally black, one of them a child. Perhaps a boy. Another frightened boy.

"Such is war," the woman said.

"A sensible attitude," Sparkle replied. "Cures the discomforts of empathy." She looked at the woman. "You must be dreadfully comfortable."

The woman said nothing. Sparkle and Pearl stepped off the execrable vehicle, and it turned back.

"You've been quiet," Sparkle said to Pearl.

"I've been observant," Pearl said. "She lied earlier. Whatever those crates are, they're not generators."

"How do you know?"

"I listened to her heartbeat as you spoke," Pearl said. "It sped up when you asked your questions."

"Impressive," Sparkle said.

Pearl looked over his shoulder toward the Husks. "I also listened into the crate. Nothing save the mildest, indecipherable hum. Soundproofed, I suspect. Telling in itself."

"Come on," Sparkle said.

They made their way up the other side of the valley. The grass gave way to rock, Husk rock, like aged skin. Her feet scratched and rattled against stone.

"Would you happen to know if this entry point is obvious?" Pearl asked after some time. "A carved threshold or somesuch?"

"I've really no idea," Sparkle said. Things were getting steeper now. "Local legend claims one here."

"How reassuring," Pearl said.

"You forget our cottage's relative proximity. Said local legend was preserved by our very ancestors, Pearl. That's a guarantee of truth, albeit decorated." She leaped over a fissure of amethyst. "We used to play at being Anointed."

"Yes," Pearl said, clambering behind her. "I recall that."

"You're remembering more, then?" Sparkle asked.

"Like ice crystals on a window pane," he said. "Reaching out, joining together. But most of the window's still bare."

"Any memories of you and Gleam?" she asked him. "When you were in our body, I mean."

"Why do you keep asking?"

"I don't know." She did. "Gleam had love enough to sacrifice everything for you, and you for him. Now nothing. Not even Swirl nor I recalled him. You wiped us well."

"If you felt guilt over feeling no guilt, sister," Pearl said, "you wouldn't be so quick to remind others. I choose to look forward. To when we possess our own body once more. To being reunited."

Sparkle said nothing. She had to use her hands now, such was the incline.

"Sparkle?" she heard Pearl say from behind her. "You do want to be reunited, don't you?"

She stopped and turned to face him. He was using all fours too. He stopped, satchel swinging from his shoulders, gazing at her like a wrought-iron pup.

"You're talking as if there's a choice," Sparkle said. "We either die in these senseless, sexless shells or we get back to before. I'm drunk on individualism right now, I admit, but I hunger for touch, for the sanctuary of flesh."

"And if you could have both?" Pearl asked. "A body without me? Without Swirl?"

"Pearl."

"Answer."

Reunification was everything to Pearl. How had she missed that? He was a threadbare thing, mm-yes, deracinated and hollow. He'd barely remember what sharing their body was even like.

"As with all of life's desires," Sparkle answered, "it's entirely beside the fucking point."

"Our furnaces need fuel," Pearl said. He sat down and opened his satchel.

Sparkle thought of Hargie, and immediately hated the ratty little shithead for it. Incongruous. Tacky. "Pearl, I--"

They were surrounded. Figures in grey, rising from the rocks, from the cracks in the rock's skin. Hooded. A score of them.

"Peace, Anointed," Sparkle said aloud. She made the Loican sign with her marble fingers. "We kneel in the light of the Delighted, penitent before you."

"Please, Ashemis," a familiar woman's voice said. The closest figure.

An armoured hand reached up and pulled down the hood. Her head was shaved, save for a side-knot, and the flesh around her eyes was tattooed in traditional Anointed patterns where once blue kohl had been.

"You used to call me Ovia," the old woman said.

***

"OVIA SAID *PRINCESS* IS NEAR-ready to go," Hargie shouted, drying his hair with the weird heated glove thing he'd only just learned to use.

"Great," Sparkle called from the other side of the bathroom door. She'd dropped half a leaf two hours past--her use was rising again--but she was conversational. She'd visited her parents earlier. They were safe in the Husks. Hargie would have liked to meet them. But Sparkle didn't even want to talk about them.

He removed the glove and gazed in the bathroom's long mirror. His hair had fluffed up stupidly. His naked body looked like an overweight earbud stick. Rich food here, nowhere to exercise far as he knew. Ah, *Princess* would see him right.

"Thought we'd take a look at her today," he said aloud.

"I'd like that," came Sparkle's voice.

"I should warn you, the Anointed are acting all bat-ladder, tune? Some dream o' theirs. Like kids before... whatever holiday you have around here." He decided he'd put his old pilot clothes on, none of those coo-coo robes the locals had thrown him. "Maybe it's the food around here, maybe they're hypoglyseemol." The door melted and he walked into their bedroom. "Heck, it ain't doing my--"

Some woman sat on the chair that faced their bed, a man flanking her either side. The men, pale-skinned and high-collared, had ornate-looking wrist-blades. The woman, dark-skinned, braids up in a side-knot, had a proud way about her. She was old enough to be, if not Sparkle's mother, then Sparkle's mother if she'd lived on Calran or DesicWest. Her clothes were too classy for both those joints. And Hargie had no clothes at all.

Sparkle sat up on the bed, threw him his hat. Hargie caught it and covered up Tiny H and the H-Band.

"*Eild*," Sparkle said to the woman, "*Sem-hoish Aul dan kolo Issaressi.*"

The woman half-smiled, looking at Sparkle. "*Issaressi? Na Aul?*"

"*Dreeca var,*" Sparkle replied, her face blank.

The woman made a sound like she'd been shown a nasty graze.

"*Cujarj,*" she said to Sparkle. She looked up at Hargie and nodded.

"Hey," Hargie said, nodding. He kept both hands on his hat. No one seemed phased at his nudity. He said to Sparkle: "What you talking about?"

"This is the High Secretary," she said. "I was telling her we've settled in fine."

"Smoosh." That didn't check with Hargie. Sparkle had said her own name in her own language: Issaressi. Why? She'd already met the Secretary, she'd told Hargie as much. Heck, why was the Secretary saying Sparkle's name like a question? And '*Sem-hoish*': that's what the Anointed called him. Sure, leave Hargie out the loop. Knock yourselves out, girls.

"*Dula,*" the Secretary said to Sparkle. "*Dula ti var. Mattan... Ashemi.*"

Hargie got none of that, but Sparkle sure-as-shit did. She got up from the bed, made a sound like she'd been slapped around the back of her neck.

"What?" Hargie asked Sparkle. He smiled, looked down at himself. "How much she offer?"

"Ashemi have arrived," she said. "They want to meet us."

"Ash-who?"

"Blessed of the Hoidrac," Sparkle said.

"Anointed?"

"Decidedly more so," Sparkle said.

"A big deal," the High Secretary said, her demeanour suddenly slumped and frumpish, no longer proud.

"You speak Anglurati?" Hargie asked.

"Yes," she said, standing up. "You possess a most charming penis." She turned to Sparkle and gave her a look. "For a feral."

With that, she and her cronies strutted out.

"Ignore her insult," Sparkle said.

He put his hat on. "That was an insult?"

"About me," she said. "The insult to me." She slapped her collarbone, her eyes wide.

"Right." He said nothing. Best not to. Between her parents and these Ashemi, this clearly wasn't Sparkle's day.

***

MELID WATCHED VICT DRY his hair. He wore a gown woven from silkform.

"I've lightened the gravity in here," he said, a man proud of a ship he'd never earned. "Did you notice?"

"Gravity's gravity," Melid said. She sat next to Doum, the pair of them at a round table in the hybrid craft's meeting room. She couldn't believe the updates Vict's ship had brought, the farce at DesicWest. She couldn't

235

believe the Instrum had permitted Vict to live. Then again, the Instrum wasted nothing.

Vict stopped towelling his hair and looked at her. "Small steps. I'm attempting to adapt." He sat down on a chair across the table from them.

"To our life?" Melid asked. "You'd die in months."

Vict smiled. "Not if we succeed. Your people's harnessing of the genome is unmatched. You've upgrades that allow you to thrive on a planet's surface, this very room, without the need of suits. Do you think that irreversible?"

"You want to live among us?" Melid said. The dead skin and hair that would float off of him alone...

"I want to *become* you," Vict said. He smiled defiantly at Melid and Doum's shared confusion. "I've had to time to think. Much time. I've lost a fortune, my culture, my old ships. Oh, and respect, that greatest of follies. All stripped away, leaving just a man." He looked at his upturned hands.

Melid checked the kollective. What information there was, at least what was permitted, suggested that a Worlder joining the kollective neural program was theoretically possible.

"I'm tired, Emissary," he said. "Tired of what you'd call the Worlder life. Always misjudging, being misjudged. The fear. You'll never comprehend the fear, my friends. Constant in the waking hours and saturating every dream. Fear of never really knowing what even those closest to you feel. I want the Eden you people have. I'm told if we win here, I can have that." He stroked down his chin beard. "But there remains a final weakness I must expunge: revenge. With Hargie Stukes' death, I shall be a blank screen." He looked at Melid. "Wiped. Ready to connect."

Melid laughed. Dead thing. Cold hand reaching for life.

"You're beautiful when you laugh, Emissary," Vict said.

Doum growled. His and Melid's revulsions were identical.

"I'm sorry," Vict said. "I thought you people were open."

"It's clearly been a long journey for you," Melid said, "Worlder. But an extra craft is an extra craft. This mission makes the best use of you and your hybrid."

"You want to catch Sparkle Savard?" he asked. "You need my ship. Relocate over here."

She frowned. "You'll never achieve coitus with me, Nugo Vict. Cease your devices."

Vict shook his head. "I've been studying your Hunter-Killers," he told her. "The largest jump-capable craft available to humanity. Twice the mass of any bubbleship. Impressive."

"Their efficiency satisfies," Melid said.

"But your H-Ks lack precision," Vict said. "They can jump kilometres off target. A bubbleship? Jumps within *metres*. An H-K can manage two jumps before recharging, a bubbleship skips as much as its pilot can handle his jumpjunk. Superior acceleration, if not top speed. Of course, a B-ship hasn't the luxury of your remarkable stealth fields, but..." He made a face, as if struck by some notion. "Hang on a moment." He gestured at the room around him. "Best of both worlds. And likely a challenge for these Harmonics."

"Firepower," Melid said. "You've one *tiny* gun."

"To kill one tiny person."

Vict had a point. Several. More significantly, a bubbleship could jump deeper within a gravity well, not that Melid would tell Vict that. Room for a cadre in his craft too, should an interdiction be necessary...

"Very well," Melid said.

Vict smiled.

"They have told you we're all to die here, Vict?" she asked.

His smile vanished. Doum chuckled.

"That's the 'deal', as you Worlders would say," Melid continued. "Our 'Eden' you speak of?" She leaned forward. "It's all sacrifice. Each of us understands we are wholly expendable, utterly insignificant before the Konsensus as a whole." That truth was starker than ever, of course. The Konsensus faced a humiliating extinction, not that anyone had told Vict as much. "I don't think you've the cultural background to accept such a reality."

"I have it," Vict said, but he didn't sound confident.

"Whether you do or don't is irrelevant," Melid said. "You've still that coronary patch under your skin, the one Blas administered. I have use of it now." She took a moment to watch him draw pale. "But I likely won't. Betray us, and I'd much rather Doum here eviscerated you slowly."

"Slowwwly," Doum said.

"And we'll be able to do that," Melid said, "because we'll be here. Right next to you, Nugo Vict. Skin-tight." She stood up. "As per your suggestion."

Melid and Doum made their way toward the hatchway.

"Emissary," Vict called to her. "You'll think differently of me when I'm in the Kollective. You'll know me for what I am."

She stopped, looked at him.

"So will you," she said. "My condolences."

***

STRANGE, TO FEEL SUCH NERVES and have no belly to feel them in. No muscles to shudder.

Pearl stood on the flat level, wide as a fencing court and possessing no walls. He'd glanced over the edge when Ovia first brought them here, and found an aged stairway cut into the mountain's rippled skin. The stairs were too large for any human, or even an Ashemi statue, and they ceased abruptly halfway down. The ways of the Anointed were famously inscrutable.

At the bottom of the mountain lay a dry stream bed with no sign of vegetation or trackway, merely rock and melting snow. Beyond lay more mountains, slumbering under late afternoon's sky. He should have tasted the cool air, felt the warmth of the sun. In truth he couldn't recall what any of that had ever felt like.

"If we look through here," Sparkle said somewhere behind him, the breeze vying against her words, "I don't think they'll spot us." She paused. "Vital we see them first. And listen."

He turned to look at her. She had her back to him, gazing though one of the many crescent-shaped holes that lined the rock wall in an interconnecting pattern. To her left was the carved archway from which they had emerged. The Anointed had led them through their subterranean home to here, the other side of the mountain. Their home was a dreamlike place of winding tunnels, blue light and curling mists that rose from nowhere, like folklore described.

Pearl walked over to her, looked through a half-moon hole to the great hall within. The floor lay someway below, wide with great tiles of Husk rock and amethyst laid out in a chequered pattern. Save for Ovia--no servant of the Trinity House, but an Anointed--the floor lay deserted. A stone staircase wound its way up from the floor, along the far wall of the hall, opening itself out onto the level where Pearl and his sister now waited. The hall's ceiling, high above, was utterly obscured by a bluish cloud of glittering mist. Up there, as Pearl understood it, bushes of leaf would manifest, growing from out of the Geode cell by cell, ready for harvesting when Zahrir's moon, the Daughter, eclipsed the sun.

"If we touch her," Sparkle said, "will we be reunified, do you think?"

"No," Pearl said. "We'd need some very advanced technology for that. More likely we'll reunite when we walk into the Wound's fire."

"Question is," Sparkle said, "will we walk out?"

"Have courage. We will. Pheoni will see to it." It seemed the likeliest result.

"Shh..."

Down on the chequered floor, Ovia raised her arms in greeting to someone.

Swirl! And another, a short male in barbaric clothing. They walked toward Ovia, arm in arm.

"Is that Hargie?" Pearl asked Sparkle.

She didn't reply. Her marble face held still, glass eyes locked on Swirl and her companion.

Something was wrong with Swirl's face. It glinted.

"She has piercings," Pearl said. "She's made our face a pincushion."

Sparkle said nothing, never moved. Pearl focussed on Swirl and the other two, used his body's listening-sight.

"*Benchoda* cloud for a ceiling," the feral man said in Anglurati, looking up. Pearl's Anglurati wasn't brilliant.

"We have many," Ovia said in the same language.

"What's the latest, *Ledi*?" he asked her. "With *Rajakun*?"

"Your ship can fly tonight," Ovia said.

"*Chodi' A!*" The man grinned like a child, but stopped when he looked at Swirl.

Swirl was straight-backed yet pensive, her fists clenched, as any Harmonic citizen summoned by Ashemi might be, if they possessed granite resolve. Seeing Swirl's bravery, her fatalism, he desired to know her again. To know both his sisters. To cease being an amputated shade.

"I'm ready, your Anointed," Swirl said to Ovia.

"I'll check *Rajakun*," Hargie said. "Give you space."

Swirl turned to him. "Wait here. Please, Hargie." She kissed him upon the lips. Kissed a *feral*.

"Sure," he said. He looked up at the ceiling. "Shoulda packed an umbrella."

The two women walked away from him, toward the stairs. Pearl tracked them with his listen-sight.

"--arker purpose," Swirl was saying in Tu'la'lec as they ascended. "These are Pheoni's Ashemi, I take it?"

"Perhaps," Ovia replied. "It is never for us to ask." She laughed. "A beautiful dream last night. That is all we know. A beautiful dream from the Delighted Ones."

"May I ask what?"

"We cannot divulge," Ovia said.

"Anointed," Swirl said, "I've a request."

They passed beyond the edge of Pearl's view through the hole. They would be here in moments.

"Come on, Sparkle," he told her. "Let's stand away from here. Sparkle?"

He had to pull her away from the wall. They walked some distance away, to the centre of the carved rock level.

"Pearl," Sparkle said, gripping him as if suddenly awake, "did you listen?"

"Of course," Pearl said.

"Not the words," Sparkle said. "Her heartbeat."

"No."

"Two, Pearl." Sparkle raised her talons before her face, never looking at him. "She's pregnant."

***

SWIRL STOPPED ON THE STAIRS. Ovia, seeing her, did likewise. She looked at Swirl with kind, ink-rimmed eyes.

"Tell me your request," Ovia said.

"The Ninety say Hargie cannot leave and cannot stay," Swirl replied.

"I'm certain they will be kind in their killing," Ovia said.

"I will be an Ashemi soon: Pheoni told me in a dream." Swirl shrugged. She still had trouble accepting it. "Or I will be dead."

"Yes, yes." Ovia bowed. "A holy thing."

"Promise me he'll live," Swirl said. "That you'll see him safe from here when all this is done. He doesn't know about Triunes and he's... sort of an idiot. He's harmless."

"He means much to you," the Anointed said.

"I suppose he does."

Ovia smiled. "We shall do as you ask."

They continued up the stairs. The archway ahead was a rectangle of daylight, causing Swirl's eyes to squint and water. Her instincts kicked in: she would be exposed up there, in the open. But who would ever attack the Anointed? No, this fear of open spaces was really a fear of accounting for herself. To these... arbiters. She hoped the Ashemi carried some message from Pheoni the Appropriate.

Before her eyes adjusted, she felt the sun of home on her skin and the breeze that tempered it. For years she had wondered if she would ever know this moment.

"Swirl." A male voice to her left, Zahriran accent synthesised cold.

Her eyes adjusted and she looked toward the voice: a wrought-iron figure framed by the distant mountains, its face callous alabaster. It stood eight feet tall, nine if she counted the plume of corquill feathers that rose from its cranium. Its eyes were of blue glass: aniridic, unreadable.

"Your Ashemi," Swirl said.

"Call me Pearl."

Her vision and vitality blurred, as when a heatwave overcomes. But it wasn't the sun above. *His* voice. Pearl's voice. Her legs wanted to buckle.

She staggered. Too scared to call him liar, too wise to call him true. Too proud.

The Ashemi pointed. Not at Swirl, but behind her.

"Sparkle," he said.

Swirl spun around. Another. How had she forgot there would be another? A statueform of pink marble, its face white stone, its hair cords and rubies. Silent. Towering.

The solitude consumed Swirl, like when she'd first known solitude. She fell on all fours and retched. Her old inner life dissected and bared, subject to a strange cartography: Swirl centre, Pearl west, Sparkle east. The cut rock they stood upon, their shared skull. She tried to vomit. She couldn't.

She stared at the stone floor. "What is this?" she muttered through spit.

Pearl's voice began to explain. Between laboured breaths, Swirl scavenged pieces of it. His lack of recollection, a parody of an investigation, Sparkle manifesting and something about the Culakwun Envoy. An invasion...

"Your face?" Pearl said. For she knew it was he, she *knew*.

Swirl drew a finger across her wet lips, felt the cold metal against her knuckles.

"I ran from the light," she said. "Into the wastes. These rings are my reminder."

"It wasn't your body to abuse," Pearl said. "Not the rings, not..." He paused. "Not alone."

"But I *was* alone." She glowered at his wrought-iron bones. "*You* left us alone." Her anger passed. She looked to her right, to Sparkle. Swirl smiled. "And I thought you destroyed, Sparkle. I thought Mohatoi Embossed had..."

Sparkle hadn't moved, hadn't spoken.

"Sparkle?"

She studied the pink statue. Was this a joke? Sparkle would have been the first to speak. She always spoke. No: a statue, simple as. Pearl's next senseless torture.

Swirl looked up at him. "Why? Why any of this?"

"I... don't know," Pearl said.

She glared at him again. She had wanted to hug that statue of Sparkle, wrap her arms around its coldness, even if Sparkle couldn't feel her from inside that thing. But it wasn't Sparkle. Sparkle was dead.

"You bastard," Swirl said to Pearl. "You piece of shit."

"You never swear," his synthesised voice said. "Not ever."

She gestured at him. "Congratulations." She gestured at herself, her face pierced, fighting back puke, panting upon her knees. "Your masterpiece."

"Yet alive," Pearl said. "Alive. We're proud of you, sister."

Swirl opened her mouth to spit fury. She heard noise to her right, like a horse charging over stone. The Sparkle statue running at her.

Swirl tried to get up but the weakness in her, the surprise. She fell on her back.

The statueform stopped, towered over her, its legs wide. It leant forward, its hair swinging like fifty nooses. It blocked the sun, its glass eyes two malevolent stars within a silhouette.

"Pervert," it said.

Swirl felt cold in its shade. She drew her hands to her face.

"Deviant," it said. Sparkle's voice.

"Sparkle?" Pearl's voice. "What is this?"

The Sparkle-statue never took its eyes off Swirl.

"Oh, didn't you know?" she said. "Swirly-girl here has committed the most degenerate, most *pathetic* crime our people know." Its face tilted an inch left, and the bejewelled braids clattered against one another. "Sexual molestation. Persona fraud."

Swirl drew her legs up toward her body. She looked at the statue's--at Sparkle's--right leg. As a child she'd made another girl cry, a monomind girl, had reminded her her pet dog had died in much pain. Swirl remembered standing in front of her own family, all of them wondering how Swirl could say such nasty things. Swirl had cried worse than the girl over her dog. The exposure, the adult incredulity--partly feigned, but so real to a child--at who Swirly-girl really was.

She dreaded hearing Pearl's voice, and when it came, she flinched.

"I don't understand," he said. Naivety, soon to surrender to disgust.

"We travelled under my name," Sparkle said. "That man in there thinks she's me. She is *fucking* him while he screams *my* name."

"Swirl," Pearl said. "That's..."

"He loves me," Swirl blurted. Defiant. She wouldn't be treated like filth. She wasn't filth. *Far from it, sister.* She looked Sparkle in her dead eyes. "He said so." Never said as much to Sparkle, Swirl bet.

Sparkle's carved face revealed nothing, of course. But Swirl wanted something from Sparkle: for her to curse like she always used to. For her to hit Swirl. Anything.

Instead she said: "Do you love him?"

Swirl worked her expression into something resembling calm, a hint of a smile.

"Yes," she said.

"Liar," Sparkle said.

Swirl widened her smile. "No, sister."

"Actually you are," Pearl's voice said. "We can both read your nervous system."

Ashemi. They could read lies.

Swirl slapped the stones with the back of her fists. She grunted. They had her.

"All right, then," Swirl said. "All right. He's a toy, as he was a toy to you, Sparkle. We've both used him. He's *there* to be used. It's not the same as, as deluding one of *us*." She pointed up at Sparkle. "We needed his ship, girl. You recognised that well enough and you were *quite* happy to use these enchanting eyes," she blinked them, "and these staggering breasts," she shook them, "to drag that *reeking* piece of junk light years!" She took a deep

245

breath. She was shouting. She had to remain calm. "You're not offended, Spar-ki-dar. You just never liked me taking your things. Even that which you threw away."

Go on, Swirl thought, *say something. Let's see clever words defeat truth.*

Sparkle leaned in closer. "Is it his?"

They knew. They could read her, bone and brain.

Swirl gave a half-smile.

"Yes or no." Pearl's voice.

Swirl growled, rolled over, crawled from out of Sparkle's shadow and stood up. She backed away some three steps. The nausea had vanished.

"No," she told them both. "He's ours." Swirl shrugged. "Like Mother, Father. A clone."

"Why?" Sparkle said. She stood erect now.

"I was *lonely*," Swirl said. "Insane. Stripped of you both."

"Get rid of it," Sparkle said.

"No," Swirl said. "Don't want to. My flesh. You're just... *objets d'art*."

Sparkle took a step forward.

"What?" Swirl said. "What are you going to do? Hmm? Hurt me? Kill me?" She looked at them both. "So high on your statueform powers you forget yourselves. I've the high ground here. This body dies, you both cease."

Their faces might have been lifeless, but the slump of their limbs said all.

"Can I tell you two standing lamps something?" Swirl said, getting things in order. Matters would need to be ordered. "I conceived in maddest desperation. To please some old feral intent on throwing me from an airlock. I probably *would* have terminated this future child. But it's not going to be a child." She shook her head. "It will be an Ashorus."

The two statues looked at one another. She let the word sink in.

"A little demigod to cradle in divine arms." Swirl took a deep breath of the fresh mountain air. "You're scanning me now, aren't you? You can see I don't lie. You're behind the news, my siblings. We're not returning from those flames, nor returning to what we are. We are chosen, chosen above billions to idle in the lap of the Hoidrac, to be immortal by their side. A Triune Ashemi." She tapped her belly. "With divine offspring."

"How do you know this?" Pearl asked.

"Pheoni said," Swirl replied. She nodded with aggression. "Pheoni. She came to me inside the lockwyrm. To our body. Our heart. If--when--we fulfil her wishes, nothing shall be denied us." She pointed at Pearl. "Imagine: your memories back. And the key to all Geode, brother."

"The very depths..." His synthesised voice hit a tremolo. He gathered himself. "You could be insane," he said.

"No," Sparkle said. "Worse." She looked at Swirl. "A prophet."

"Yes," Swirl said. "I didn't ask for it. None of us did." She bared her palms to Sparkle. "I'm sorry for all that's happened. But all this will be less than dust when our apotheosis comes. We three: immortal." She laughed.

"Sparkle doesn't want that," Pearl said. "She likes solitude now. Independence."

"What?" Swirl said. Independence was hell. It had only ever broken Swirl.

Sparkle said nothing.

"Tell her, Sparkle," Pearl said. Swirl sensed ire in that metal-cold voice.

The pink statue's head tilted down. "I can't go back. I can't. Not now. I'm not the same, I..." She fell silent.

They were all silent. This was a detail, Swirl told herself. A detail.

"Fine," she said. "Fine. We respect your wishes, Sparkle, as typically eccentric as they are." She laughed, but no one joined her. She sniffed, returned to her serious demeanour. "Fine. Well, you'll have independence beyond anything this present universe can offer. In the realm of the

Delighted, whatever you want shall be. Think of it, Sparkle: all that knowledge for your ravenous mind. The countless unknown dimensions. The life of--"

"An immortal mind," Sparkle said to the granite floor. Oh yes. Swirl had her now.

"Are you seriously telling me Hargie Stukes compares to that?" Swirl asked. "Hmm? You're no idiot. He's a mortal toy you became a little over-affectionate for. But we must put away mortal things. Silly things."

Sparkle nodded. "Silly."

Swirl turned to Pearl. "And, brother: *we* can be a trio again. We can fill the hole Sparkle leaves with a psychic clone: the Ashorus. Our child, Pearl."

"Our child," Pearl said.

"And soon to be our new sibling," Swirl said. "To teach, to love beyond love. And should Sparkle ever tire of being alone," and she gave Pearl a look as if to say *when she tires*, "what's to stop us being a quartet? Impossible for a biological mind, but..."

"A quadrune" Pearl said, as if studying an uncanny object.

Swirl looked from statue to statue. "Are we agreed, then?" She already knew they were, for this was destiny. Destiny.

"Agreed," Pearl said.

Sparkle looked over her shoulder at the mountain behind them.

"Agreed," she said. "But bring Hargie up here. I want to speak with him."

"Sparkle," Pearl said, "you can't tell him who you are."

"I know," Sparkle said. "I just want to see him. Alone."

"He'll be fine," Swirl said, "I've assured his safety. You'll speak to him anyway when we--"

"Swirl," Sparkle snapped, "you've won. You've fucking beaten me, okay? Checkmate. I won't throw away godhood..." She put her silver clawed hand over her face. "I want to see him. Can't you at least allow me that?"

"Let's show we can trust her, Swirl," Pearl said.

"Fine," Swirl said. She nodded, smiled. "All right, Spar-ki-dar."

***

THERE WERE OTHER ANOINTED IN the great hall now, in the shadows, watching Hargie. He hadn't seen them arrive.

Ovia stood beside him. She had a funny smile, a funny glint in those tattooed eyes of hers. Last time he'd seen a look like that was his Mom, when she was alive and he was five.

"What?" Hargie said.

"A most beautiful dream last night," she said. "Very humorous." She chuckled.

"Right," Hargie said, adjusting his hat. "You all... have the same dream of a night, right?"

He looked around the wide and gloomy hall. Maybe twenty Anointed, twenty pairs of ink-framed eyes studying him. Twenty smiles keeping a joke.

A hand stroked his cheek.

"Easy, Ovie," Hargie said, stepping back from the weird old woman.

"This dream is given unto us by the Delighted," she said.

The Hoidrac. Delighted was a name for them.

"What..." He wasn't sure he should ask. "What was it about?"

"It is not given for us to say," Ovia told him. "But we can advise you this much..." She leaned in. "Catch!"

Hargie looked around, palms ready. When no one threw anything, he looked up to the indoor cloud above. He waited. Nothing fell from its cumulo-strangeness.

The Anointed laughed. All of 'em. Real back-slap stuff. Ovia had to cover her mouth.

"Right, I tune," Hargie said to them all. "Hilarious."

Simple pleasures, these cave-dwelling freaks. He couldn't get angry with them. They were kids. He made show of laughing along. Why not? Give baby its bottle.

"Remember," Ovia said. Then she indicated the stairs.

Sparkle descended, a sliver of blue. Blue robes, blue hair.

He didn't see the figure behind her, at first. Partly because it was almost all black, but also because of its size. Too big, too towering, its limbs and body too thin in relation to its height.

The Anointed had ceased laughing. Only a rattling sound in the hall. The thing's 'hair'.

"An Ashemi," Ovia whispered to Hargie. "Did Sparkle not tell you their nature?"

"Yeah, but..." He didn't finish. He'd have said something about thinking it ratshit. Dumb of him. The Harmonies could jimmy up floating silver sharks already. Why not this?

Sparkle and her friend stopped before Hargie and Ovia. Ovia and her colleagues all bowed. Hargie cricked his neck to look up. The iron Ashemi stood more than a foot taller than Sparkle, who in herself was tall. Its face was carved from some shiny white stone. Severe, with blue crystal for eyes. Hargie had never felt so far from anything resembling home.

"Her Ashemi would speak with you," Sparkle said.

Hargie pointed at himself, mouthed *me?* He looked at the Ashemi.

"Not me," the Ashemi said, its voice cold, reverb heavy. It pointed toward the stairs it had come down. "Her name, Midnight. Mine, Noon."

Up there? Hargie mouthed the words again.

"Up there," Sparkle told him.

Hargie eyed the silver claws on Noon's hands.

"Smoosh," he said. He couldn't stop a gulp.

***

SPARKLE WAITED FOR OVIA TO bring Hargie. She looked away from the archway he would come from, down into the mountain valley with its dry stream bed.

There was a tale about the valley below--well, more of a historical footnote, the useless sort Sparkle's brain absorbed. In the near-death age, before the Anointed had arrived, before Zahriran minds were altered, a great blizzard had come, like nothing before or since. It took out whatever communications they'd had back then and a scientist--Laura--became trapped in the valley below. Her lover, Azami, went into the blizzard to find her, against all advice and sense. The two women's corpses were discovered by the Anointed a century later. They were but a quarter mile apart, had never seen each other.

Morons. And yet, poor wretches. Azami was always played up as the tragic hero in the telling, but it was Laura's story that always haunted Sparkle. She'd died alone, never knowing someone risked everything to save her.

A Sethwen interceptor flew high over: Culakwun. They couldn't see her, of course, couldn't even detect the level she stood on. Deceptor-fields cloaked this place.

Sparkle heard footsteps behind her: two people. She didn't turn around. Midnight the Ashemi would not turn around. She had to keep her part.

"Ashemi," she heard Ovia say. "The feral."

Sparkle nodded.

She saw his shadow first; the sun was now above them. Taller than him, stretched, but she recognised that stupid hat with the flaps.

She turned her head and gazed down upon him. Hargie. His eyes were wide. His mouth was an open smile. For a moment she half-believed he recognised her, but he only stared in wonder, spellbound by this carved and animated figure, this body she was not.

"Hey there," he said. *He doesn't look all that,* she thought. She'd built him up in her memory. Perhaps being underwhelmed was for the best.

"You are Hargie Stukes? The... Outworlder?"

"I'm comfortable with 'feral'," he said. "Really."

"I am Midnight," she said.

"Honoured. You... work for those Hoidrac? I got that right?"

"In essence," she said. "I can't say more." She looked away from him, to the blank rock of the far mountain. "It is essential I know more about you. You will play a vital part in matters of consequence."

"I understand," he said.

She hated his deference. She wanted him casual, swearing, the Hargie who annoyed her, who lay on a bed and watched movies. A crumb of that, one last time. But how could he be those things now, standing before Midnight, this sculpture, this high fetish of an alien culture? She was cold marble.

"Why?" she asked. "Why choose to help us?"

"I figure you people are the only ones who can stop this." He paused. Sparkle knew he would have said "and shit" or "tune?", but had stopped himself. "My people can't do it. None of 'em. Not bubblefolk, not Calran, not none of the, er, Feral Worlds. Konsensus'll just roll us. Konsensus don't think anyone but themselves human. I've seen their monsters, heard 'em tell me stuff they did. Kill children." He clicked his fingers. "Nothing. You guys are the only pair of fists around. Least I can do is point you toward those bastards' teeth."

Her voice box emitted a chuckle. She hadn't meant to. "Noble," she said. "But why you, Hargie Stukes?"

"No one else is gonna get past that fleet," he said, "deliver Sparkle where she's gotta be. Bubbleship don't run on the same energies as Harmony ships. Assholes won't be expecting." He stopped, embarrassed by his language. "And I'm the best living B-pilot."

"You're a braggart, Hargie Stukes."

"A realist," he answered. "Journey here made me that."

"They say you once took out a Falcatta with just a chuck charge," Sparkle said.

"You know that?"

"Word travels."

He grinned. "Word right."

"Perhaps I'm not being specific," Sparkle said. Here it came. "Why follow Sparkle Savard? It is... important I--*we*--understand what it is between you."

"She's everything that's left of me," he said. "Everything good. Heck, I feel like a sap saying it but..." He coughed. "Mind if I smoke?" He didn't wait for a reply; he never did. "And I still don't know her, tune? That's the magic. When this is over... I wanna spend the rest of my days learning about my Issaressi."

Issaressi. Sparkle's name in Tu'la'lec. He had learnt that from her, back on Silvercloud, the hellhole where she'd discarded him. And he didn't even know.

"So you'll live here?" she said. An impossibility. Swirl had lied to him.

"Not here," Hargie said. "Big glass ship in space. Settle down, see what happens."

Fuck all, that's what'd happen. Sparkle wanted to rage. She didn't believe Swirl's talk of protecting him after all this. *And can't you see--*

"She'll never be yours," Sparkle said. "We're not possessive here, not like your kind."

"I know," he said. "Doesn't faze me."

"She may choose to become male," Sparkle said, out of ideas. "It's easy here. Takes days."

"That... I didn't know."

His archaic heterosexuality might actually save him. Delighted be praised.

"Wait..." he said. "That mean I could zap into a chi--, I mean, woman? Because I could learn to be smoosh with that, if she were a man. What the hell's it matter what we're packing either way?"

"Oh yes!" She couldn't stop herself. "Hargie Stukes: interstellar pansexual legend! Don't kid yourself, feral. She doesn't need you. We can do this without your kind." Her voicebox fed back, a high whine. "Walk away."

He stepped back from her, eyeing those silver claws.

"I don't know what hot shit you are 'round here," Hargie said, panting, meeting her dead eyes. He was terrified of her. "But you can't tell me to leave Sparkle."

She lifted a talon up, slowly, beneath his chin. Lowered her face to his.

"Why?" she asked.

"...Cuz."

"Why?"

"Cuz..." He looked out to the mountains. "She made a stupid face." He seemed pained, embarrassed. "A face..."

"I don't understand," Sparkle said.

"We'd touched down in Calran," he said. "That's a world. I'd crashed out. I mean the jumpjunk we bubblemen do, we crash. She came in my room. Tried to make me smile." He looked into Sparkle's eyes again. "What you call where I come from? Feral space? Well, I got my own brand of that. All around me. Always have, and its cold and its jaws are forever wide."

"Isolation," she said. "Hell."

"Worse than hell, because I didn't mind it at all." He remembered his cigarette, took a puff and threw it away. "But she strolled in and cut straight through it, tune? Messed with my hair and bugged me and made a stupid face because she wanted me to laugh. I couldn't, but... she was there. She got it. There she was. A better human than she'd ever think herself to be. And after that... I did mind. I did mind being alone."

She moved her stone face closer to his flesh. "Ever have that moment again?"

"I leave her, I sure won't." He shrugged. "That I know."

"Me," her voice box said.

"What?"

"You've... convinced me." She rose up. "You pass the test. You'll fly."

"Huh."

Sparkle gazed down at the valley where Laura and Azami had died, a metaphor ungainly and crude.

She would be a god of the Geode soon, she told herself. An individual. None of this would matter. There were things that mattered even more than her and her siblings' immortality. Billions of lives, Harmonic and, yes, feral too. Hargie was right: the Konsensus saw nothing human in this galaxy save themselves. They were wicked, and they had to be fought. Funny: Swirl and Pearl hadn't mentioned any of that earlier. In their heads, they were already cradled by Hoidrac. But this reality still counted. The suffering counted. It still did.

"Beautiful world," Hargie said.

"Indeed." That was entirely the problem.

Sparkle and Hargie: a detail, a speck. Fleets prowled, empires flexed. What did it matter if Sparkle...

Well, she didn't, did she? Mere fascination. Passion, tops. Not... well, not *that*. She'd never really been *that* with anyone. Sparkle was melodrama's fool, whatever her body.

Wings fluttered to her right. A corquill had landed on the ledge near Hargie. The bird righted itself on its four hairy legs, tested the air with its blue-black tongue.

"What is that?" Hargie asked. Its six red bead eyes studied him.

"Quite harmless," Sparkle said. "Native creature. A corquill."

Hargie seemed transfixed by it.

"Are you all right?" Sparkle asked.

"Musta... seen it on a nature show. Familiar."

"Trust not the corquill's song," Sparkle recited. "Trust only her cold and piercing eye. Trust her disdain."

Hargie stared at Sparkle as if she'd exploded. "What?"

"Ancient poem."

He looked at the bird again, then his own feet. He rubbed his right eye.

"This fresh air... getting to me." Hargie turned around and shuffled back toward the archway and the hall beyond.

It wasn't possible Hargie had ever seen a corquill on a neural show. Zahrir was designated a *sub rosa* world, a Harmonic secret, due to its Triune program.

She looked at the corquill, now tonguing the ledge for mites. *Princess Floofy* had been the target of the lockwyrm. Might the ship's owner also be targeted? The Hoidrac picking out a feral for their game, pulling his subconscious? Would they stoop so low?

Absurd. She shooed the bird away.

***

ONLINE, HARGIE'S NEURALWARE TOLD HIM. He hooted. His hoot filled their small quarters.

"Everything all right?" came Sparkle's voice from the bathroom.

"Smooshy, darlin'," he said. "*Princess Floofy* is back online!" Hargie stretched his arms wide, fell back on the bed. The ceiling above, a whirlpool of carved stone, was beautiful. He'd noticed before now, but he'd never really *noticed*. Artists, these Anointed, not just some goofy fucks.

Tension he hadn't noticed left his bones. He was ready, had his old pilot clothes on, his lucky hat. Today he had to be the best bub-jockey humanity

had ever birthed. Right now it felt like a cinch. He'd walked into the Nukes'
lair and come out laughing, natch Silvercloud, dodged every Freightways
man from here to Eucrow. A flight to the hemisphere? Nothing! A damn
pizza delivery!

The bathroom door melted open and Sparkle stepped through. Hargie
stood up, so as to take her in.

She wore the armour of the Anointed. Boy, did she. Metallic blue, but
when a detail caught the light, swirling patterns glinted red. Plate where it
mattered, ribbed where she curved, all of it one tight whole. For the life of
him Hargie couldn't figure how she got in and out of the thing, but he'd
gladly spend the rest of it trying to find out. Vict's old pistol hung from
her hips.

"Don't look like that," Sparkle told him. "It's practical."

"Intensely," Hargie agreed. "Nice colour scheme. Goes with your hair."

"Yes," Sparkle said. "That's the reason I picked it, idiot."

"C'mere."

He walked over and put his arms around her waist, looked into her
brown eyes. She knelt her head a few inches and kissed him, her armour
squeaking. He had gloved hands on his ass.

"Not too late to get you armour," she said.

"My armour's sitting in the bay."

Sparkle closed her eyes. "I'll miss this."

"Don't be like that," he said. "We'll be this again."

She opened her eyes and smiled.

"Yes," she whispered. "You're right."

"This last run," he said. "Gonna be like that first time we made love."

"Magical?" She squeezed his ass.

"No: over before you know it," he said. "Remember?"

She chuckled with surprise. "I'd, er, forgotten about that."

"Shit," he said. She'd forgot? "Wish I hadn'ta mentioned it now."

"Come on," Sparkle said. "Let's go, eh?"

In the big hall with a cloud for a ceiling, the two Ashemi were waiting, that whacko Midnight and the other one, Noon. He still couldn't adjust to their animatronic asses, suspected a theme park somewhere missed two mascots. There was that officious woman too, the High Secretary.

No Ovia, though. Hargie had hoped she'd be here. He liked that old freak.

The High Secretary nodded to Hargie, then exchanged a few words in Tu'la'lec with Sparkle. The two Ashemi towered silent.

Sparkle didn't nod to them, just to the Secretary, which was the kind of thing that made Hargie uncomfortable in any social scene.

"Hey, Midnight," he said, then looked at the male statue. "Hey, Noon."

Noon nodded back at Hargie.

"You guys riding with us, right?" Hargie asked them both.

Sparkle nudged him. "Ashemi," she muttered.

"Apologies," Hargie said to the statues. "Ashemi."

"Indeed," Midnight replied. "We're your guys."

Hargie smiled. He couldn't figure Midnight out. Maybe several people controlled that statue remotely at different times. Maybe that was the deal. Hargie was sure as shit he wasn't getting the full low-down. Dumb outsider. Well, let 'em think that.

"So," Hargie said. "You two..." He struggled for words. "Help with this ritual, right?"

Sparkle said something in Tu'la'lec to the High Secretary, cutting Hargie off.

The High Secretary took on that happy-proud look she had. She spoke in response to Sparkle, but in Anglurati.

"Well," she said, "with the arrival of Pheoni's hand..." She indicated the Ashemis, and bowed. "There remained no more argument. I, personally, have no doubt it will succeed." She looked at Hargie, something in her expression shifting. "However, there's a half-hour delay yet. Cloud cover and such." She shrugged. "Have to take every advantage, I suppose."

Hargie nodded. He felt the tension from earlier return. Planet-bound Hargie, groping for the cockpit chair. "Sure."

Her smile returned. "Come, let us take the mountain air while we wait, eh? The veranda." She indicated the winding stairs that led up and outside. She said the same in Tu'la'lec to the others, or so he assumed.

"Why not?" Hargie said to her. Get him outside, at least, thirty feet closer to the deep black. "You've a pretty planet." Well, she'd called his dick charming. Only fair to return the compliment.

They climbed the stairs up to the great ledge over the mountain valley, where he'd had his bat-ladder chat with Midnight. He got that naked feeling, that sudden coldness in the belly and bones. He'd let a stranger-- made of marble, no less--open him up. Had everyone here discussed that? Even Sparkle? He wanted this over.

Out on the ledge, night was drawing in. Hargie stared at the moon.

Never seen the like before. Shit, its crescent rippled and shivered, blue and lilac and silver. It made Hargie think of that stone, what was it? Amethyst.

"It's reflecting the flames," the High Secretary told him. The others were talking to each other in their language, gathered in a circle. "The Wound's flames, where Zahrir's hemisphere enters the Geode. Where you're headed."

"That so?" Hargie said. "These flames, they mess with a ship's flight?"

"Not ours," she replied. "I wouldn't know about yours." She sighed, looked at the moon as if it were a window in her vision, her neuralware. "Excuse me a moment."

She took something from her pocket and slapped it on her forehead: a dark metallic cross. The High Secretary shivered, looked ready to topple backward, but soon recovered.

She smiled. "My medication," she explained. "Mister Stukes, I'll draw your attention to our moon the Daughter once more. Look at the very centre of its crescent."

Hargie squinted. "What am I looking for?"

"A black dot," she said, and there it was.

"Hey," Hargie said. "Am I crazy, or is it getting bigger?"

"You're not crazy." She put a hand on his shoulder. "But it's no product of the moon. It's something within our own atmosphere, and it's getting closer."

Sure was. It filled the centre of the moon, orb-shaped.

"That's a vehicle," Hargie said. "Coming right at us."

The Secretary seized his mouth. She leered at him.

"Brace yourself, scum," she said.

A humming sound. Hargie looked over at the others. He saw Noon turn to face the noise.

A second of pure white and everyone dropped, even the High Secretary. Hargie felt no pain. He couldn't feel the floor beneath him. He stared at the stars.

Shots rang out. Compaction rounds: the guns of home, not the Harmonies. Boots hitting the floor. Plenty of them. More shots, closer this time.

Then silence.

Hargie tried to move, but his body didn't respond, felt like one big batch of pins and needles. He could move his eyes. His mind boiled with terror.

A silhouette looked down upon him. Bulky, heavy breaths. It moved, and the light from the great hall illuminated its face. Its mask.

Hargie couldn't believe what he saw. A battle suit: no Harmony suaveness, but the ugly practicality of a trooper from home. From feral space.

The plated gas-mask of a Freightways corporation soldier.

CHAPTER THIRTEEN

*H*ugo Vict had been cleaning his teeth when Doum had wrenched the bathroom door open and carried him off under his armpit.

"What is this?" Vict demanded. No answer, not from that ogre. With each step Doum's bicep squeezed Vict's stomach, urging him to vomit. How had things come to this?

The cockpit hatch whirled open and the two of them passed through, Vict's night-gown flapping over his thighs.

The 'pit was full of people. Vict had time to see maybe six troopers-- Instrums, was that their name?--loading guns and sealing their masks.

"The chair, Vict." Melid's voice.

Doum threw Vict at the cockpit chair. He hit the floor. Vict scrambled up, climbed in.

"Of course, of course," Vict muttered, knee aching. He wouldn't ask questions. He'd know soon enough. He'd show them, show her. Show them all he could be.

The needles drove into his neck studs, callipers pinched his legs. Information poured in via his neuralware, a familiar veneer above the kollective's processing depths below. Unknowable, the kollective. For now.

The tracker. Hell, they'd located Sparkle Savard. Vict was presented with a vision of Zahrir's southern continent, a tracker mark racing across it. Data: tracker emerged from unpopulated mountain range, travelling 310 kph. On course for a towered installation, 132 km ahead. Said installation lay directly below the enemy fleet's fixed orbit.

"Wake up," Melid said. "Move this ship."

"Of course," Vict said.

Vict reached out to the rest of the konvergence fleet. A red marker delineated *Snowy*'s position: dead centre, centre of a fleet pattern spherical in shape. He accelerated to keep *Snowy*'s place within it. Wake, Vict, wake.

His orders came, not in words but in a kind of instinct. Incredible: it seemed they'd already fitted him with at least some kollectiveware, without him knowing.

They had chosen the shell attack pattern, then. Melid and Gei had explained at least some of that to Vict. Tight formation, a single punch through the enemy. Untried. The Konsensus had never had reason to fight a pitched battle. Assassins playing at prize fighters.

Oh, Vict was awake now, fear was seeing to that. He'd never had reason for a pitched battle either. What was it his mother used to say?

Oh, that was a bad sign: mother. Classically so, almost clichéd. He stopped thinking of her. Tried to stop thinking of himself. Konsensites didn't think of themselves. He focussed on the fleet, its pattern. Beyond the formation-sphere of Hunter-Killers lay larger concentric spheres. Shells.

They were a fleet within a shell within a shell within a shell. Three layers of drones--remotes, they were called, Vict had to remember that-- surrounding them in all directions. The outermost shell of remotes was there as sensors, he knew that much, providing the fleet with a far greater vision than they had enjoyed thus far. The other two remote shells below that one? He'd no clue. Dammit, no one had told him. He couldn't access that data, he couldn't...

He had to remain calm. He had a talent for calm. Calm was the decider in a battle, in a full-scale battle with all its destruction and pain and decompression at any moment. He had to...

He was hyperventilating. He couldn't do that, not with Melid watching. He took deep breaths, focussed on *Snowy*'s place within the fleet. Deep inside. Safe. He was a taxi here, ushering Melid about so she might control the fight. Others would do the dying.

He concentrated on the target, a marker on his neuralware's schematic. Sparkle Savard, racing toward some installation. He took a closer look at the vehicle.

"Erm, is anyone else seeing this?" he asked the cockpit. "The vehicle she's in, it's not Harmonic."

Silence.

"You can see it?" Melid asked.

"Yes," he said. "Somewhat." Yes. All that Scalpel-energy--or whatever it was called--churning over the world's surface, was a thick soup to the Konsensus. But Vict could see, or at least saw more. He was vital here. Needed.

"Worlder built, I think," he told Melid. He felt a surge, sheer excitement. Was that *Princess Floofy* down there? Had it revived? They were capable of much, these Harmonics.

No. Not *Princess*.

"Armoured carrier," he reported, deflated. "Used by corporate military."

"Freightways," Melid hissed. "Then it's true." She said something in her own language. Vict could have sworn he heard "Eucharist".

"Why would they be here?" he asked.

She didn't answer.

Seconds passed. He hated those seconds, vast wastes in which to think. To fear.

Melid leaned in behind him. He could smell her clean skin, the material of her suit. "Focus on the tracker," she said. "Whatever occurs, focus only on that. We are the hunters here."

"Understood," he said.

No taxi, then. Hunters.

He thought of his mother again.

***

SWIRL OPENED HER EYES. SHE was on her back, gazing up at the leaves of a palm tree. Night sky between those leaves, pure black, its stars extinguished by artificial lighting nearby. The floor beneath her was smooth stone. She could hear chatter.

"She's awake," a woman's voice said.

A face came into view: the High Secretary gazing down at her, smiling. Proud: definitely her, not her headsiblings. A drink in either hand.

"Care for one?" the High Secretary offered. Ice rattled against glass.

Swirl waved in the negative. What had happened? The High Secretary's forehead had a dark metal cross upon it: an inhibitor. Psychiatrists used them to suppress minds that might be a danger to themselves or their headsiblings.

Swirl got to her feet. Her legs shook, but she remained standing. She massaged her right temple. Her vision was blurred. Movement ahead, people. All she could discern.

"What happened?" she asked the High Secretary.

"Keep calm," she replied. "Do what's asked. You'll see this through, my girl."

"Why the cross?" Swirl nodded at the Secretary's forehead.

The woman sniggered. "We're the same now, you and me. Ex-Triunes, nascent monominds. Peculiar sensation, isn't it? Only difference is, I can feel my siblings scratching at the walls, so to speak." She took a sip from her drink and sighed. "Still, they'll come around. Compromise: that's the watchword here." She waved her drink at Swirl. "Remember that."

Swirl couldn't take her words in. She looked over the woman's shoulder.

They were on a roof, a roof garden. Wide. Plants from many worlds, gilded floor tiles. Humid. She hadn't noticed that, which was proof her armour still functioned. Her body felt cool, if not her face.

Swirl reached for her pistol. Gone. Belt and holster, too. She stepped back from the High Secretary and raised her armoured fists.

Two men with guns stood just beyond the High Secretary. Masks. Feral armour. Feral rifles. One of them lifted the barrel at her and lowered it, a nonchalant display.

"Traitor," she said to the High Secretary.

"My, you're quick," the High Secretary replied.

"Where is this?"

"Trinity House. Our alma mater, eh? Perhaps we should sing the school song: 'together we prevail'." The High Secretary's expression changed to one of kindness. "If history calls me traitor, so be it." She leaned in. "I preserve what can be preserved. Help our world, girl. Do his bidding." With that, she turned and walked away.

Across the tiled floor lay Pearl and Sparkle, their statueforms inert, their furnaces dead. Swirl's fists unclenched, became palms against her face.

"Oh, they're fine," a male voice said. "Still embers burning in their hearts. Still time."

Swirl looked toward the voice. It came from the pouting mouth of the most beautiful man she'd ever seen. An Ingresine of Culakwun, with the trademark stretched torso. His coiffured hair was kept in place with a golden tiara that rose into two slim horns. He sat in a sapphire-encrusted chair, his silver-grey suit immaculate, without crease from high collar to flared ends. A woman pouted beside him in an identical chair, her dress cut from identical material: an Ingresine too, and almost as beautiful. Kohl smeared her eyelids in a deliberately carefree style. Her black hair writhed like a pit of snakes, the jewellery sparkling within it pre-programmed floatstones. Around her waist was Swirl's gun belt. Swirl's gun.

The High Secretary stood beside the man. She passed one of her drinks to him. He nodded his appreciation.

Swirl opened her mouth to speak, but the man placed a ringed finger to his own lips and hushed her. Without looking, he gestured to someone in the shadows behind him.

A trudge of boots and five Phoskmuj warriors, the psychobreed of Culakwun, emerged into the light, three of them with scythe guns, two with the most brutal axes. Behind them strode a supple youth, perhaps a middle-breed, carrying a brass jar.

"Welcome home, Swirl Savard," the man said. He smiled, then, turning to the two feral troopers, said: "As I mentioned earlier..." He said it in Anglurati, a crude language from such a glazed mouth.

The two Phoskmuj threw their axes at the feral troopers' boots. The troopers waited a moment, uncertain, and then they picked up the axes, their rifles swinging from their shoulders.

They strode over to Pearl and Sparkle's bodies. Swirl tensed to move, but noticed the scythe guns pointing at her.

The man hushed her again. "A mere prophylactic," he said in Tu'la'lec.

The two troopers set about hacking off the Ashemis' legs. Sacrilege. Everyone here: blasphemers. The Hoidrac would have their justice, surely.

The garden reverberated with the sound of torn metal and powdered stone. Swirl covered her ears and used the current distraction to look behind her. She found another feral trooper some feet away, female, her rifle pointing at Swirl's stomach. Far off behind the trooper rose the central tower of the House, piercing the night. Someone had seen fit to paint it gold and encrust diamonds upon its roofs. A Culakwun atrocity, unquestionably. To its right hung the Daughter, its silver crescent dancing with amethyst fire.

"Enough," the man said.

The two feral troopers ceased their sacrilege and stepped away, back to where they'd once stood. They dropped the axes and lifted their rifles again.

The youth stepped forward, cantering over the detritus of Pearl and Sparkle's legs. He bent over, opened Pearl's heart-furnace, and poured leaf into it from the jar he carried. He repeated the action with Sparkle and then stepped away.

Blue flames glowed from between their ribs, then settled. The youth closed their heart-furnace doors and retreated backwards, bowing with each step.

The two statues began to move. First their heads scratched and rattled against the tiles as they turned them side-to-side, trying to take in new surroundings.

"Pearl," the man in the chair said. "Midnight."

Swirl's two siblings jolted at the man's voice. They scrambled to rise, found they had no legs. There was no shock on their faces, naturally. Swirl envied them.

Sparkle rolled on her side, then her front, used her palms and talons to leverage herself upright, her two arms bearing her own weight. Turning her head, she saw Swirl, and they held each other's gaze. Swirl nodded.

Sparkle looked about the roof garden, searching for something. Not seeing it, she used her talons to drag herself around, her hips a pinion, until she faced the man and woman in their chairs.

She was looking for Hargie. Swirl hadn't even thought of him until that moment.

"War," the man said, "with armour wise, conquers worlds." He sipped his drink. "Desire, a poisoned wine, holds them."

"The Nine Conceits," Sparkle said. "Book five, poem six. Opaque Savard."

"Observant, your ancestor." The man raised his glass to Sparkle, then to Swirl, lastly to Pearl, currently going through the same process as Sparkle had, scraping the floor as he righted and turned himself to face the conversation. "If derivative."

"They're not my relations," Swirl said to the man. "They're Ashemi."

The man shook his head. "You really aren't the adroit one of the set, are you?" He pointed at the High Secretary stood beside him. "Our mutual friend here informs me you are a soul deracinated of both your brother and sister. Interesting, that. Pearl, of course, has been both my toy and my key to conquering your world--you can thank him later--but that leaves Sparkle. Or should I say, Midnight."

Swirl feigned a sigh. "She's not Sparkle."

"Oh, I think so," the man said. "My Freightways associates tell me you--well, your body at least--travelled through feral space under the name Sparkle. Now you're Swirl. High Secretary here informs me you told her Sparkle was snatched from you, drawn out of your body by Hoidrac unknown while you were gallivanting about some feral dump. Apparently it occurred around about the time darling Midnight here made herself known to me." He looked at Sparkle. "You were fun, my dear, but you got arrogant, that most comely of failings. Should have realised I've friends everywhere. I'm famously ebullient like that."

The kohl-eyed woman beside him tittered.

"Sorry to disappoint you, Envoy," Sparkle said. She seemed distracted. Still looking.   "Don't put yourself down," he said. "It was hilarious while it lasted. And the fun's not over yet."

"Heretic," Swirl said. "Desecrating Ashemi bodies? Assaulting the Anointed? No one has ever dared that, not in the history of our civilisation.

You violate the honour of all Hoidrac. Nothing I or anyone can do will be a thousandth of the tortures they'll bring upon you and Culakwun entire."

"I haven't," the Envoy said, his dark lashes fluttering. "Nor has any subject under Hoidrac guidance. Why, that would be unprecedented sacrilege."

"Freightways," Sparkle said.

"Frightfully clever, don't you think?" he asked her. "Not a Harmonic hand laid in blasphemy. Not one. My world has an understanding with Freightways; we aid their enterprise in a manner I cannot divulge. Thus they are happy to lend me a legion or two, slumbering in those ugly boxes you saw when you approached the Husk mountains. As you can see, they're awake. And not only did they prize you from Anointed clutches, they besiege the last refuge of Zahrir's former government. Plus, I might add, almost every Triune alive. With them extinguished, our..." He sighed, shook his head. "Please forgive the cliché. Our triumph will be complete. And your patroness, Pheoni, will lose all purchase of Zahrir. Mohatoi Embossed arises."

"A dicey gambit," Sparkle said. "You still direct them."

"Absolutely," the Envoy said. "That's the point, dear. It's absurdly, ridiculously, flamboyantly dangerous. An unprecedented outrage. I risk everything. Recall the game we've been playing, you and I? To delight the Delighted Ones? Well, I won. My audacity won. I held to the rules and broke them, and the paradox shakes the Geode's very depths with mirth."

The kohl-eyed woman clapped her fingers and smiled. "Thank you," the Envoy said to her.

"Idiots," Swirl said to them both. When no one shot her, she continued: "You presume the Hoidracs' intent?"

"Still here, aren't we?" the Envoy said. "Still gutting your world at leisure. The fact I still live painlessly we can take as a standing ovation from our masters. I suspect even your Pheoni has to admit its brilliance. Rather an objective fact, don't you think?" He turned to Sparkle. "Swirl always this slow?"

"Where's our feral?" Sparkle snapped at him.

"The one with the cute eyes and the hat? Him?"

Sparkle just stared.

"Castrated," the Envoy said. "Flayed, thrown from the tower."

No.

Swirl felt her own legs move. The two feral guards aimed their rifles at her. She stopped. She could hear Sparkle scrape the tiles with her talons, trying to drag herself toward the bastard.

"Joke," the Envoy said in a high-pitched voice. "We were prudent to slice your legs off, I see."

The kohl-eyed woman spoke to Sparkle as if addressing a baby: "Must be vewy attached to dat ickle animal. Ahh..."

"He's property," Sparkle said. "You shouldn't mess with what isn't yours. Bring him here."

"In time," the Envoy said.

"A thought strikes me," Sparkle said. She said it in Anglurati, the trade language of feral space. "You'll have to kill all these Freightways soldiers, won't you? And ritually destroy their bodies."

"Yes," Swirl said in Anglurati, eyeing the feral soldiers. "Otherwise you'll be impure."

The feral troopers didn't move. Their guns kept trained on Swirl.

"Unfortunately for you," the Envoy said, "these troopers are no cold murderers. They're family men and women. I keep their children and promise not to throw them to our psychobreeds, if only they perform their tasks and accept their fate thereafter." He wagged his finger at the sisters. "Nice try, though."

"Enough," Pearl said. He'd been silent all this time. "What do you want, you absurd monster?"

The Envoy grinned, put his drink down and stood up. His long coat swung to the undulation of his serpentine torso. "I want you," he said. "All three of you. I've been promised you all my life."

***

PEARL KEPT HIS PALMS FLAT to the ground; otherwise he'd topple. A neat little torture, this, he had to admit. One could either keep in the conversation or scythe one's claws about with face to the floor.

"A Triune," the Envoy explained. "One carrying a... sliver of something within their psyche. One they must take physically into the flames of their world, to be rewarded with immortality." He sniffed. "That's the tragedy of our great culture, is it not? Ferals imagine afterlives for all, other ferals wax brave and lyrical about death being all that waits. But they don't *know*. We know. We see the psyches of the dying dissipate, see them dissolve into the Geode's penumbra, strands of them eaten by Geode-beasts, the rest dispersing to nothing. All one has to do is take leaf, comadose, and one can witness oblivion's very clockwork."

"You're scared of death?" Swirl asked.

"You aren't? You know, I suppose that's why we Harmonics, whatever our world's aesthetic, seize at life. We've a mannered desperation, well hidden, that no other humans possess. Don't you think?"

"You've long struck me as desperate," Sparkle said.

"Mohatoi Embossed," the Envoy said, "has promised me one thing throughout my life, throughout my dreams: if I walk hand-in-hand with you siblings into Zahrir's flames, I will never die. My proximity ensures the sliver inside you will fall into Mohatoi's claws and not Pheoni's. Rules of the game." He sighed, shook his head. "Must be awfully important, this sliver."

"Don't look at me," Swirl said to him. "If anything, I was hoping *you* could tell *us*."

If Swirl was trying to hide the fact she *did* know that the sliver had some connection to the feral race Sparkle had talked about, it worked. The Envoy probably wouldn't have believed her anyway.

The Envoy picked up his drink for the chair arm, sipped and stared at the Daughter, its ocean-silver wreathed with cloud.

"It's not *all* about immortality, you know," he said. "I don't imagine non-existence is that bad once the formality of dying is complete. But you've been promised me, all of you. That's my chief drive." He looked at them, his expression tender in a way Pearl had thought the beast incapable of. "Empathy has always been something others do. I want to know what it is. I'm bored of all else. In dreams they offer me glimpses of an empathy with you."

"Could you sign for a delivery, please?" Sparkle asked. "It's nine metric tonnes of *fuck that.*"

"I'll say," Swirl added. "We didn't cross light years for this."

"It doesn't matter what you think," the Envoy said. "Once we're through the flames, nothing now will matter. We're like spermatozoa arguing about the people we'll become. As Ashemi in the Geode's depths, we'll be beyond the shackles of this reality, from our tawdry senses and listless flesh. Love is a colourless thing, made so by the veil of our own perceptions. No one really knows anyone, that's the problem. Maggots, blind all, hooked and writhing upon each other's lies."

Pearl had had quite enough of this.

"You'll forgive me," he told the Envoy, "but I think I know you well enough already. You tortured me."

"None of that will matter," the Envoy said. "Are you even listening?"

"Yes it will," Swirl said. "Of course it will. You're a monster. That's clear enough. One cannot give devotion to one so, so--"

The Envoy threw his glass across the floor. It smashed upon gilded tiles.

"Oh, get over yourselves," he said. "You're the most self-absorbed trio this side of Andromeda. Your homeworld's crushed and you stare at your own bellies. Your parents--their minds broken--sit inside the Husks as they're shelled, and you've not said a word. I've just declared I've hundreds of children enchained--whom I'll throw to perverts and killers as and when the mood takes me--and it's barely bothered any of you. And you know why? Because it isn't *you*. None of those horrors compliments the solipsistic drama of your interior lives. You've gone through existence stepping on everyone's heads, only in your darkest moments wondering whether your morality is genuine or mythical. And it's the latter, trust me. You're all as incapable of empathy as me." A cold assurance tightened his face. "But we *will* know. Ours shall be an empathy beyond anything this universe can offer. I would commit a thousand genocides to have it. You hear?" His lips curled to a snarl, teeth bared. An animal. "I want to *care*."

The roof garden fell silent. No breeze, force fields forever denying them. Pearl looked at Sparkle. Her marble face studied the floor.

"Enough," the Envoy said. "I hate bragging like this. I want this to be over." He looked over to his Phoskmuj guards. "Bring it. And bring the feral."

The feral, Hargie Stukes, came up the stairs at the far end of the roof garden, a guard on either side of him. His wrists were bound together in front of him, and something silver encircled his neck. A constrictor: a breed of Geode-beast. Likely, Hargie already understood struggling only made things worse.

Two low-breeds came forth, bearing a palanquin. The palanquin was small, as if fashioned for some midget khan. Upon its cushion sat a dark brown egg. No: the opal. The opal Pearl had been lied to about by Gleam and the rest. The alleged prison of the criminal Pearl Savard.

"I don't know what you hope to achieve with that," Pearl told the Envoy. "It's a prop. None of us were ever inside it."

"Pearl," the Envoy said, "you're as much a dolt now as you were back when I toyed with you. I'm chief architect of the practical joke you suffered, recall? I think I know the efficacy of the props I use."

The two low-breeds rested the palanquin on the floor just before Pearl and Sparkle. The opal, with its galaxy-like sliver of metallic green inside, was an arm's reach away.

"What was torn can be re-stitched," the Envoy said as the two lowbreeds walked away, leaving the head-sized opal. "Touch the opal together and you'll all be back in your body. Like old times."

"Liar," Swirl said.

He raised an eyebrow at her. "I can hardly hold all your hands when we walk through the flames." He pointed at Pearl and Sparkle. "These two can't even fucking walk."

"Bring the feral closer," Sparkle said. "I want to see he's undamaged."

The Envoy looked down on her.

"Playing for time, eh, Sparkle?" He gestured at the High Secretary to walk Hargie Stukes over. "Won't work. I know your secret fleet approaches. They haven't a chance."

***

A STRANGE MIX, THIS SHELL formation: vulnerable yet empowering. Melid had had time to consider the experience, as had everyone.

Vulnerable, yes: being packed so close together your neighbouring craft glinted on the edge of human sight was unnerving. But there was strength in such a ludicrous formation. The morass of Geode-energy all around couldn't erode communication. The Domov Egeria functioned at full capacity, allowing it to direct all craft, a fleet commander built from its subordinates.

Empowering. She closed her eyes, dipped her mind into the fleet's kollective. Just like the Kollective-at-Large, though far smaller. The same love. Galvanised by their cause, the survival instinct of humanity perfected.

To succeed. All else was unthinkable, a betrayal not just of the Konsensus but of all the upward struggles of the species' genome, from Earth's most primeval ancestor. Worlder humanity couldn't be trusted to survive the eons. Too infantile, too selfish. Harmonic humanity was beyond corrupt. No, there was the Konsensus or there was a void. Nothing else. The cold universe could not be allowed to win. Not so soon. Not without a fight.

The fleet picked up on her sentiments. They had waited for it. Uncomfortable, to be monitored by so many, but if it steeled them, so be it. Melid was but an instrument.

She opened her eyes.

"I've visual," Vict told her. "Ships." He paused. "So damn many."

Good. She'd doubted placing herself within a Worlder ship with a Worlder pilot. But she'd been right: Vict could *see*. See with his primitive neuralware, his nervous system unsullied by the kollective. Curious, how a being so base might ensure her people's survival.

Moments passed. Then the outer shell of the formation--a great sphere of remotes configured as sensor drones--made contact. What had been mere impressions within the sensor nexus they had built now became fully realised images. Melid ran her vision through the sensor shells, focussed in on the enemy fleet's core. Four towering horrors, forty times the mass of a Hunter-Killer. The Geode-energy poured from their cracks and orifices, but their hulls were as human-built as the bubbleship Melid rode in. Perhaps more remarkable, but as much a victim to a warhead.

She was thankful there were no Scalpels here. She'd feared that.

The Harmonic fleet kept to their indecipherable formation: fixed orbit, smaller ships darting between the ring pattern of the four giants. Good. It implied the konvergence fleet remained undetected.

"Vict," she said, her vision still locked into that of the sensor shell. "Can you see Sparkle yet?" They had lost her tracker in the thick mists of the towered installation.

"No," she heard Vict say. "A little closer, maybe. That'd help."

"We'll get you closer, bubbleman," she said. "Rely on it."

"Yes, commander."

She almost laughed at Vict's--

Alarm raced through the fleet: Harmonic ships surging with Geode-energy. Weapon ports readying, Egeria surmised.

Harmonic fleet still outside the shells. No hope.

Outranged, thought Melid. *We're outra--*

***

THE HIGH SECRETARY HELPED HARGIE forward, but it was Swirl Hargie stumbled toward. Sparkle ignored the unconscious snub. He had a bruise along his cheekbone.

"Are you fine?" Swirl asked him in Anglurati.

"Aside from this shit round my neck?" Hargie said. "Peachy keen."

He was talking, aware. All Sparkle needed to know.

She looked up at the Envoy. "How did you detect our fleet?" In truth, she was trying to find out who this fleet even were. Feign a little power. Feigning power was akin to owning it.

"A ravishing talent for invisibility, your friends," the Envoy said. "Never witnessed the like. But their invisibility leaves a void amid the thick energies that swirl around this planet. One just has to know what to look for." He shook his head. "Almost feel sorry for them."

Invisibility. The Konsensus, come all this way. She couldn't think. Couldn't see the game moves, the branching variations.

"Their one advantage they've frittered away," the Envoy said. "The Grand Fleet of Culakwun is the greatest in all the Harmonies, the most hardened at Pleasing War. Whichever of Zahrir's allies you might name are outclassed by us, both in number and skill. Torochoi? Kal-Mirrach? What can any of their tawdry fleets offer? What drive-dance? What display of light, particle and colour? No one can challenge Culakwun, no one surpass our fleet's gilt beauty or exceed its aesthetic delight."

Sparkle was glad of her immobile face. She would have let a smile slip otherwise. "Well," she said, "when you put it like *that*..."

***

THE POWER SURGED HER SENSES: sight, touch, taste. Everything white.

The fleet's kollective wailed, a lamentation of some five hundred nervous systems. Melid felt her hands clutch her face. She braced, like all the fleet, for the whiteout to turn into oblivion.

Failure, Melid thought. *All lost.*

The whiteout faded. The fleet was alive, unharmed.

Space had become a pattern, a complex of lines melting to fractals that dispersed into ambient energy at every known frequency. It emanated from every craft in the enemy's fleet, a hundred coronae knotting into one.

The pattern transfixed Melid, transfixed everyone. The... intricacy... singularity... no emotic term for such. A complexity *from* simplicity. To think such a vision could reside inside the universe...

Melid shook it off. The pattern had no utility. It did nothing. The essence of uselessness was in its dismissal.

Melid's sentiment passed through the fleet, became dominant. The Hunter-Killers set about their purpose.

The formation's second shell was in range of the enemy. Composed of autonomous dazzle-remotes, the frontal hemisphere accelerated from the fleet, a wall of some three hundred missiles.

Each picked a target. Not one of the enemy's ships went un-catered for, and none of them threw up any form of defence. Perhaps they were surprised, perhaps they'd no answer. It didn't matter. The remotes detonated.

Each Harmonic vessel became engulfed with electromagnetic energy. Just as their blasts began to fade, the shell's rear hemisphere of dazzle-remotes flew into the formation, re-igniting that volume of space with EMP.

Enough EMP to blind the sensors of a thousand Worlder craft. Providence allowing it would do the same to these deviants.

The next shell. The final shell.

The final shell's entire frontal hemisphere targeted the four large craft, twenty warhead-remotes apiece. The towering monstrosities evaporated, became a particle mist with the heat of a hundred stars.

The rear hemisphere targeted the smaller craft that had danced around the larger. A few vaporised, though most were merely disabled, left broken and smouldering, emptying their guts into the void.

Wild adulation passed through the kollective. Joy in the veins. Melid heard herself laugh, heard Vict whoop. The greatest assault ever executed by the Konsensus, perhaps the greatest action in the galaxy's history, and the Konsensus had won it.

Or seemed to. Waves of the tiny vessels, the fighters, were heading toward them from the moon, racing in on a tide of Geode-energy, of unreal.

Ahead lay two medium craft, one only partly injured, the other wholly intact. It seemed they had been at the rear, had overcome the sensory overload and had used some form of area weapon to deny their warheads. Engines down, though, drifting.

The Konsensus fleet had no more warhead-remotes, save a handful for use against the installation on Zahrir's surface. Close quarters, then, cutter beams. So be it.

"You become legend, Emissary," Vict told her.

She felt a sentiment pass through the Instrums beside her. They agreed with Nugo Vict.

"One citizen," she said, as much to herself as anyone. "One citizen."

***

THE ENVOY STOOD FROZEN, STARING into the scry-jewel bound to the back of his right hand with ornate chains. His face was still, and might have convinced, if not for the kohl-eyed woman staring into her own scry. Her eyes and mouth were circles framed with paint and her dancing hair, a sartorial triumph before, had become a cartoonish frame to her obvious shock.

Whatever happened next, Sparkle made sure to drink this moment in.

The Envoy looked at her. He said nothing.

"Fleet not so grand?" Sparkle asked.

And there it was: the veneer cracking, the beast scratching behind his eyes. The monster.

"You want to say it, don't you?" Sparkle continued. "That it's cheating? That it's not fair? But you're bright, you know you'd be a hypocrite. Because it's no different than you using Freightways against the Anointed. But you hadn't the imagination to jape big enough." She leaned her weight on one palm and lifted her left arm into the air, pointing upwards. "And now, here's the punch line."

"Who?" the Envoy asked. "Who are they?"

"Not bullies, not like you lot," she said. "No swagger into defenceless systems, all bravura and display. No 'Pleasing War' rules. No mockery. They just... *do*."

The Envoy turned away. No wish to look in Sparkle's eyes. Mm-yes.

"Call the teardrop," he said to a servant. "Now."

"What's happening?" the High Secretary asked him.

The Envoy didn't reply. He was checking the scry diadem on his hand again.

"What *is* happening?" Pearl said to Sparkle.

My imaginary ferals are wrenching the tits off his fleet, she tapped out on the patio tiles with her right hand, leaning her weight on her left. **To think you doubted their existence, brother.**

Swirl was watching them both, studying her sister's finger-talk. Strange, to watch Swirl's mannerisms from outside. Swirl could keep a very calm face in such times, more than she likely believed.

The Envoy turned to face them, his expression blank. He grabbed Hargie by the shoulder and marched him toward the opal on its palanquin. Hargie looked tiny next to the Envoy's lithe body, like a puppet. The Envoy shoved him down on his knees before the opal. The constrictor lay still around Hargie's neck, its long body running down the front of his chest with its tail around his wrists.

A teardrop landed on the patio at the far end of the roof garden, the Envoy's getaway vehicle. Its metallic green hide split into four sides that opened out like petals. Room for four. But which four?

Hargie looked at Sparkle and seemed ready to speak. Instead, he choked. The constrictor tightened its silver coils around his throat.

"Get over here," the Envoy told Swirl. "All three of you. Put your palms on the opal or the feral dies."

"Fine," Swirl said, walking over. "There's no need to hurt him. We *want* to be reunited." She removed a glove, leaned over, and placed her left palm on the oval. The little galaxy within the opal shivered, taking on a bluish sheen.

Pearl leant his weight on his left arm and, with his right, placed a wrought-iron palm upon the opal's surface. The galaxy shuddered, glinted green.

Sparkle didn't want to go back. Couldn't.

"Sparkle," Swirl said. Her face--their shared face--was a picture of offence. "Do it."

She couldn't look at Swirl. She found herself looking at Hargie instead. His eyes wide, tongue pushing its way out, his wrists shaking against the crushing beast. No idea. The man had no idea why he was dying under an alien sky, as all skies were alien to him, strangers discussing him in a language he'd never know.

But she didn't want to be a Triune.

"Sparkle," Swirl said. "I know what he means to you. I always have. Please. For Hargie."

Sparkle couldn't. She was weak, she couldn't.

She saw Swirl grab her marble, silver-gilded hand. She let Swirl perform the action for her. The surface of the opal tingled. For the first time in this body, she felt something. Her world filled with pink light. Pain followed.

***

THE FORMATION BROKE. HUNTER-KILLER packs chose their prey.

Destabilising, Egeria's voice said in Melid's skull. Becoming unviable.

"Domov relieved," Melid said. The warmth of Egeria's control vanished. Just pack-sized kollectives now, in Melid's case her immediate crew and the five Hunter-Killers escorting *Snowy*, Vict's bubbleship. One warhead to each, the last five in the Konsensus fleet. All other H-Ks were down to cutters.

Another pack of five raced past Melid's own, aiming to sweep away the two Harmonic craft ahead. The other thirty-one, Melid assumed, must have broken off to meet the oncoming fighter swarm.

Melid focused her fleet-vision, watched the five other H-Ks charge the two remaining craft. With luck their weapons wou--

Three of them exploded from within, popped in a blast of grey, featureless Scalpel-energy.

"Fuck!" Vict said.

Without looking, Melid pulled out her pistol and pressed it to the Worlder's skull. "Hold course," she said.

She watched the two remaining Hunter-Killers dive at the injured Harmonic ship. The top of its glittering hull plumed with white-hot shrapnel and exploding oxygen. Fine cutter work. The two H-Ks spun starboard and rushed the healthy ship.

Pop, pop, and they were gone, became dual clouds of Geode-energy.

Harmonic ship: intact, weaponised. Sat between Melid's pack and Zahrir's surface. Guarding the target.

Melid ordered the two outmost Hunter-Killers to launch warheads. Risky, but three to spare.

The two H-Ks released, accelerated, and followed their warheads. The Harmonic ship released something: a ball, a crystal. It shattered, spread wide, a blast of shards that shredded the two warheads.

"Aww fuck," she heard Vict say and, as if to accentuate the statement, the two launching Hunter-Killers popped into hot dust. Their crew's minds vanished.

"Forward," she snapped at Vict, emoted as much to the rest of the pack. The pack's kollective steeled itself, their fear of these Harmonic weapons compressing to a thoughtless will. They would drive under the ship, race past, race for Zahrir. Whatever cost.

The pack's kollective thickened: another H-K in range, its crew's minds joining.

Gei, above the Harmonic ship, hurtling prow-first toward his prey. Melid watched the Hunter-Killer she'd spent the last year within discharge the entirety of its cutter's energy banks into one vast X-ray. The roof of the Harmonic ship spurted a geyser of Geode-energy as the cutter beam drove through.

Gei and his crew emoted one thought: *Konsensus*. Melid's pack saluted them. Gei followed the beam down, down into the enemy ship's alien core. Their minds vanished from the kollective. The Harmonic erupted in two.

The way lay clear. *Prepare warheads*, Melid emoted. The H-K pack would enter the planet's atmosphere, direct strike. Sight and confirm. Only way to be certain.

A grey patch came into existence at the top of the atmosphere, directly above the installation. It spread, a rupture between reality and the Geode. It began to dissipate immediately, but none of the H-Ks could target through it. Remotes would lose their way in such a penumbra.

Melid growled. At least Sparkle's tracker hadn't vanished. *Pull up*, she sentimented. They would circle around, come back round without losing velocity. Try again.

"Commander," Vict said.

Melid harrumphed. "Yes?"

"You see that?"

"What?" Frustrating to be at the mercy of this animal's sight.

"Object came out," Vict said. "Inert. Falling toward the planet."

Melid emoted to the pack: *fast, faster, turn and try again!*

They flew up, away from Zahrir, into a melee of H-K and enemy fighters.

***

THE CHOKING STOPPED. HARGIE TOOK in a breath like when the midwife slaps your ass. He didn't cry like a newborn. Then again, his eyes were wet and he hadn't understood anything anyone was doing or saying. He couldn't make out a thing, save the silver blur of that goddamned moon. He dropped on his side, rolled onto his back. The thing around his neck and wrists still held him, but it had laid off with the mean-squeeze.

Boots shuffled nearby, things being moved.

A silhouette crossed his watery vision, blocking the light from the moon.

"Can you hear me, feral?" a voice said. It was that tall asshole with the tiara. He spoke in Anglurati. About fucking time.

"What..." Hargie had to cough, clean out his throat. "What is this shit, man?"

"I did not understand that last part," the tall man said.

"What's. Going. On?" Hargie took another deep breath. "Shithead."

"I understood that." The silhouette came closer, stooping right over Hargie. "Now understand this: we're leaving. And you're dying. Slowly."

"What I do to you?" Hargie asked.

"Nothing." The tall man smelled of, well, beautiful stuff. Some flower Hargie would never see. "But you mean a great deal to my fondest enemy. I wish to hurt her a little bit more before we come to adore one another." He snorted. "Don't ask. You wouldn't comprehend."

"My default setting, truth be--" The metal thing tightened, more slowly this time. Just a threat to his breathing, so far, but not for long.

"It'll strangle you in exactly ten minutes," the tall man said. Hargie could see his face now, a face that'd make any man think about jumping the wall. Beautiful. The most beautiful sick fuck creation ever shat. "I want you to know something." He reached a manicured hand out and held Hargie's chin. "Two things actually, feral. Firstly: no life after death. Geode science can see personalities dissipate with their body's death, so trust me when I tell you these really are the last minutes before your non-existence. It's important to me you comprehend that." He tapped Hargie's nose. "Secondly..." The tall man made a whistling sound as if he'd seen a nasty wound. "That journey you've been on? The woman you helped and, I can't help but infer, fucked? It was never one woman. Two. Two sisters, one head." He looked around. "Using you. Lying to you. Making you a fool."

The fuck? The collar was tightening. Soft fingers ran down his collarbone. Way to bail out: caressed by a bilingual loon.

A window came up in the top right corner of Hargie's vision. His neuralware. The window was a proximity alert. Connection request. He wanted to hit it but kept his cool, ran a location check instead.

"What's that?" the tall man was saying. "Don't believe me? You will before you die; you've seen how she's behaved. Switching on you. Confusing you. That's what they've always done here on Zahrir. People with many minds abusing those with one. Their whole culture, each of them trained from birth. Don't even think of you or me as human."

Ratshit. Talking ratshit. Fuck him. Location check told Hargie the neuralware request was, was... half a mile above.

"Enjoy asphyxiating," the tall man said. He squeezed Hargie's cheeks, then stood up.

Hargie laughed. Agony. Spit ran down his chin.

"Cuthh," he said.

The man looked at him, sighed.

"I know that word too." He walked out of view, muttering something in his own tongue.

Hargie couldn't say the word, but he knew it; and it wasn't what that asshole thought.

The word was 'catch!'

He accepted the request, and *Princess Floofy* came online.

"Envoy," a voice called: the High Secretary's. "Please, after you."

Not easy at the best of times, driving *Princess* from outside her cockpit seat. But the collar around his throat, closing, closing. And that tiara asshole's words. Two minds? Two...

He blanked it out, concentrated. Called up a visual, window filling his vision: he saw through *Princess'* eyes. Night sky, lights below, tower roof a growing dot, a halo.

He kicked the antigrav in, retros too. Slowed the fall, injected it with purpose. Aimed for the lights of the roof garden.

He heard people shout. Someone screamed. He began to corkscrew his ship, buy some room to slow gently. He saw the roof garden through *Princess*: tile patterns, a canopy of palms. People moving.

By the time Hargie heard shots in his ears, *Princess Floofy* was already hovering at roof garden height, ten feet out from the edge.

Neck tighter, Hargie thought the tall man had tuned his trick. But no, just fear. Just harder to breathe now...

He saw with *Princess'* nose cone. Could see the tall man ducking, his woman prostrate, hands to head. Shit, Hargie could see himself on his back, middle of the roof's patio, feigning shock. Pretty convincing. Then muzzle flare: two from the Freightways boys behind a raised flower bed, another from inside the little palm jungle behind them.

Hyperventilating now. Needing a plan.

He saw two of the local thugs--evil armour, inhuman--carrying an inert Sparkle between them, axes in their spare hands. Trying to run. Couldn't run *Princess* at them; would kill Sparkle.

Their getaway. The whatisit, 'teardrop'. He panned *Princess* hard left, across the roof's outer edge. Heard a collision in his ears, a shatter like glass, saw scraps of teardrop spin past *Princess'* vision, left to right. Heard something big dragging against stone, followed by a shower of glass and metal. The teardrop wreck, its topple and fall. *Bye-bye escape plan, dicks.*

An iron ring inside his neck. Eyesight vibrating. He could feel his knees rising up, legs drawing in. Fists tight. Slow and nasty this, slow.

He growled. Focussed. Rounds bounced off *Princess*, each one blurring her vision every second. The two local guards just stood there, each with an arm under Sparkle's armpits, uncertain what to do.

The sides of their helmets exploded, the sides facing away from Sparkle's own head. The guards dropped, and the three of them were a heap on the tiles.

The fuck? Who'd shot 'em? Hargie shrunk his *Princess*-sight window from full vision down into bottom left corner. He looked with his own eyes toward his ship and saw two Anointed leaning out the side hatch, firing their native guns, their mercy scythes. Smooshy-A.

He dragged *Princess'* window back into full vision. Pushed *Princess* left. She was snared: the teardrop wreckage beneath her ass. Hargie applied lift'n'thrust, and *Princess* came free. He pushed left again, circling the circumference of the roof. Plants tore and sculptures powdered. The two Anointed fired on the Freightways troopers hiding behind the raised bed, hit stone and soil, then armour and flesh as *Princess* circled around their cover. Hargie saw the High Secretary stand to run, saw her head crush like a can inside a fist then nova from the hemisphere, a blue flash dyed red.

Shots against the hull from the left, from the trees, but *Princess* crashed into the palms and came to rest on the flattened trunks. The firing stopped. Silence.

Pain. He wanted to grab the thing around his neck, knew that would only make it worse. He closed ship-vision, looked up at stars, sky. He pushed his head back, floor tiles hard through the cloth of his hat. He could see *Princess Floofy* upside down. No; his own eyes were upside down to *Princess*. The Anointed were leaping down from her hatch. One of them waved. Ovia.

"Catch!" she said, seeing Hargie look at her. She laughed. "Catch!"

Hargie raised a thumb to show he got the joke now. Then he pointed at the tightening coil around his throat.

***

SWIRL OPENED HER EYES TO a corpse on either side. Armoured, fresh wounds: mercy scythe damage. The Envoy's guards.

"It's him," she heard the kohl-eyed woman hiss. "The feral's directing it!"

:Get the Envoy: a voice said, warm in her skull. Sparkle.

Swirl leaped to her feet, saw the Envoy ahead clambering onto his own. His back to her, stooped, catching breath. He was reaching for the scry jewel on the back of his hand.

Swirl jumped over the guard's corpse and ran at him.

The Envoy spun to face her. Quick, this one, the quickest. He pulled some trinket from his hair. Gold. A blade.

Swirl drove her fist into his blade-fist. His blade-fist flew into his own face. Warmth freckled Swirl's nose, and the Envoy dropped on his back. She stooped over him, prized the blade's length out of his nose and lips and the handle out of his fingers. She threw it into some flowers. The Envoy was conscious but stupefied, his good looks bisected. She seized his right hand and tore off the scry, its dainty gold chains snapping and tinkling. She held it with her gloveless hand, visualised a coil unwinding, tightness softening.

Swirl got up from the Envoy, walked toward Hargie's supine body. Swirl realised it wasn't herself controlling her legs.

She took control of her left arm and gestured back at the Envoy and the kohl-eyed woman.

"Cover them," she said to the Anointed. They did so.

"Nuh," she heard the Envoy splutter behind her, likely to his crony, words from swollen and quartered lips. "Nuh mirruh. Doh'n show meh."

Swirl's legs came to a stop just beside Hargie.

He already had his wrists free and was pulling the constrictor from off his neck. No real marks. Hadn't been so bad.

"Good plan," Swirl told him. Her mouth froze and then moved without her direction. "But you're still not wearing socks in bed," it said.

Hargie stared up at her, like he was assessing her.

She tried to speak, but so did Sparkle, and out came a gurgling sound. They fell silent.

:*Pearl,*: Sparkle sent. :*You there?*:

Both sisters waited. No answer.

Swirl looked over to Pearl's Ashemi body. It lay on the tiles, pieces of its head all around. Only a mouth remained attached to the neck.

"Pearl," Sparkle said, using their mouth without permission.

***

OH SHIT, SHIT.

Shit. Nugo Vict slowed his breathing. Maybe they wouldn't shoot him. *Snowy* hadn't fired a shot, so maybe they wouldn't shoot him. Not before everyone else.

They'd looped. Back up into the black deep, into the fire-fight. Konsensus killing native killing Konsensus up there. Freewheeling duels, gang-ups, hull ruptures. Was this how the galaxy would be now? Fights like this? Only reason *Snowy* lived was because everyone was too busy killing one another.

He'd peed himself. Fuck. Maybe when he was Konsensus he wouldn't pee himself. Their hive mind wouldn't allow that.

They fell toward Zahrir's atmosphere: *Snowy*, the two Hunter-Killers. Black flashed gold, then became blue. They pulled up. Clouds below, sea. Target two K ahead.

Two blips. Behind, catching up. Fucking fighters. At least these fighters' weapons were outranged by the Konsensus's cutter beams.

The Hunter-Killers fired their rear beams. The fighters danced, spun, jinked. They were hard enough to shoot already with all that mist they produced; just Vict's luck they'd have smart pilots too.

Two could play that game. He wanted to bubblejump, but that was impossible in a gravity well. He moved *Snowy* on her axis, dip-up-dip.

He felt her pistol push against his skull. "You flee, you die," Melid said.

"Jinking, dammit," he said.

"What?"

"Evasive action." Fuck these stealth-dependent dipshits. "Try it sometime."

Port-side Hunter-Killer took out a fighter. Fighter took H-K's engine out in the exchange. It fell from the pack, hit the ocean with a flash. Gone.

"Get us between the fighter and the other craft," Melid said.

"*What?*"

"We're expendable," Melid said. "Craft has our last warhead."

Hard to argue with a pistol. Theatre, that pistol. She could burst his heart with a thought.

Vict squeezed throttle, pulled back behind the remaining Hunter-K. Jumpjuice rushed through his arteries. He kept jinking, best he could without exposing the H-K. Suicide. Fucki--

Snowy shuddered. Warning and noises in Victs eyes and ears, neuralware freaking out. He felt the pistol fall from his skull.

Side hit, minor breach. *Snowy* released cannisters of hoxnites, fixed the hole.

"Flesh wound," he told Melid. No reply. He kept jinking. *Fire that warhead, dammit.*

A window came up in his right eye. He'd never seen it before. Target in range. *Snowy*'s gun! He'd forgotten about that. Target... fire!

Fighter didn't expect it. Shot its vertical wing off. Smoke, cartwheeling, falling.

Vict whooped. No bubbleman compared. *None.*

The Hunter-Killer launched its warhead.

"Let's go," Vict said.

"We follow it in," Melid said.

"Sure." Whatever. Vict was unstoppable. A force of fucking nature.

***

"HERE," PEARL SAID, HIS VOICE oddly warped.

Blackness. His head must have been shot off. Only hearing left. Speaking.

Still inside a statue, then. One couldn't live biologically without a head. Obviously.

"I'm here," he called out.

Footsteps approached.

"Brother." Swirl's voice. It had the severity, if somewhat slurred. "We're going to get you aboard Hargie's ship."

"Didn't work. Not meant to, Hoidrac intended." Yes. Yes, of course. "Pheoni. Go."

"Nuah." Swirl uttered. Sparkle taking control; Pearl knew her tone. "No. *Please.*"

More footsteps. He wished he could see. His blindness was a maelstrom, an assault of nothing.

"What?" Swirl's voice this time. Not to Pearl, to someone else.

No talking for a span. He concentrated on his inner state. Yes: a geyser in him, a vent in the abyss of his consciousness, fountaining memory and command. Hoidrac command.

Why no talking?

"Am I alone?" he asked.

"Hargie had to gesture," Swirl told him. "Ship's sensed incoming. Anointed just confirmed. Three minutes. Come on." He had to wonder whether she was trying to lift his iron body. Very Swirl, that.

He almost moved his arm, but stopped himself. Either it was broken, or it might hurt someone.

"Listen," he said. "Things come to me. I meet you at the flames, the Mendicant Isle. I stand within the flames and help you through. It's how this works. Go."

"Purrr..." Sparkle, struggling for their shared mouth.

"Take her, Swirl," Pearl said. "Now."

Boots stumbling away. The feral ship began to hum.

"What of these two?" Ovia shouted. "The scythe's mercy?"

"No." His sisters' voice, some distance now. He wasn't sure which one spoke. "Leave them here. Maybe he'll finally grasp empathy." She paused. "You'll find it cruel, Envoy."

He thought he heard her shout farewell, but the feral ship's engines kicked in. A dual roar, then a lessening whine. Sounds of torn plants and broken masonry collapsing, settling. Then silence.

Completion. Or near enough, one could never be sure. His childhood was full in him now, not the false memory of running through flowers--a placating ghost, that, designed to be so--but rich memories of snow, the cottage, the Trinity House. A life shared with sisters. Never alone.

He could see the clockwork of their shared existence too, their half-blind movements within Pheoni the Appropriate's plan. Pearl saw it all, or as much as human consciousness might. Saw its merciless necessity, its offer of hope. The Hoidrac loved their servants.

Love. Gleam had loved Pearl without question. Each suppressed memory of his lover unravelled itself, connected with the rest. Too much. Too fast. But Gleam's sacrifice, here on this same roof, made painful, sweetest sense. Utterly irrefutable. Pearl had been needed. Pearl had been loved. The facts themselves.

He thought he heard himself weep, but that was impossible. It was the woman, the Envoy's accomplice.

"You'd said I'd rule Zahrir!" she shouted. "We're going to die!"

Silence.

"Loser!" she screamed. "Look at you! You ugly, ruined f--"

A cracking sound and she gurgled, hissed. A dull thud against tiles.

"Puhh..." The Envoy's voice, inches close. Pearl hadn't heard him approach. "Speah t'meh..."

"Yes?" Pearl said.

He heard the Envoy spit out the liquid contents of his mouth. Unpleasant.

"Who ah theh?" he said. "Who attahin' uh?"

"Who's attacking you?" Pearl asked. "The fleet, you mean?"

"Noh lohn nah," the Envoy said. "Teh meh."

"Not long for you, maybe." He wished he could see the Envoy's face. Noise far above. A falling howl.

"Teh me!" Pearl could hear wrought iron on stone: his ribcage being shaken. "Teh mehhh!"

"Trust me," Pearl said. "It's funnier if you never know."

***

GOLDEN. MELID HAD NEVER SEEN a warhead-remote detonate beneath a world's sky. A ball of white gold some hundred kilometres wide, wreathed in dying Geode-energy.

Sparkle's tracker reappeared in Melid's fleet-vision, like a punch to her gut. Everyone felt the same. She covered her mouth.

"How?" Melid muttered.

"Bubbleship..." she heard Vict whisper.

Sparkle's tracker was moving away from the detonation at increasing speed.

"*Princess Floofy!*" Vict shouted. He could see it. He slapped the arm of his chair.

"Pursue," Melid said. "Now."

"Don't sweat," he said. "I've got this bitch nailed."

Snowy accelerated.

***

HARGIE FLEW TIGHT AND LOW over the continent. Pretty, Zahrir. He wished he'd seen more of it. Where they'd left was now a tiny sun. He'd be happier to see less of that.

Good to be in the chair, the junk rush. Despite everything.

"Hey, Ovia," he said. He couldn't see anyone else in the cockpit, his neuralware filling his vision. "Quite a trick you pulled."

"Hargie, could we have visual?" Sparkle's voice. Or someone.

"How'd you know I'd tune you, Ovia?" Hargie asked, lifting and dipping over mountains. "How'd you know I wouldn't be dead? Shit, you let yourself fall from the sky."

"You did," Ovia said. "And you weren't. The dream told us." She chuckled. "Catch!"

He heard all the Anointed--eight in all--laugh.

"Only gets funnier," Hargie muttered.

"Hargie," the Sparkle-woman said, "could we have the walls vis--"

"Listen up, folks," Hargie said, cutting Sparkle off. "Strap yourselves into the wall huggies." He neuraled and the walls hissed. "They'll form around you. We may lose dampeners in this. Wouldn't want you painting the walls, tune? Ovia?"

"Yes?"

"Make sure your pals don't touch anything." Hargie shrank ship vision to the right top corner, looked at Sparkle. "And you... just... talk amongst yourself."

Sparkle stared at him. She tried to speak, but only slurred.

"Tuned your ratshit game, girls." Hargie looked away from her. Strange light on the horizon. Shimmering. "Planet schizo welcomes careful drivers."

Sparkle ran out of the cockpit.

Hargie adjusted his hat, spat, made the cockpit's wrap-around come on. He'd need all the information he could get. No more blindness.

***

SWIRL KICKED THE BUTTON, AND the door to her old quarters whirled open. Easy enough; Sparkle had just given up any hold on their body.

Nothing had changed in there. Their bag on the floor, even the bedclothes left as they were. The quarters smelled off. A mouldy cake sat on the side.

"Here somewhere," Swirl said. She couldn't remember where she'd hidden it. "We're going to get through this, Sparkle," she said, glancing around. "We're going to exist forever."

Sparkle said nothing.

Swirl checked under the mattress. Not there. She lifted the bed on its side and found the sachet of leaf pressed beneath one of the bed's legs.

Swirl smiled. She felt her mouth say: "He hates me."

"Sparkle, we haven't time for 'he hates me because of you, Swirl'."

Swirl slapped her mouth. They'd both spoken: Swirl the beginning, Sparkle the end. No control anymore, no driving seat. No rules.

Swirl was thrown up on to her feet. She turned around and tumbled toward the sideboard, her leaf-free palm crushing the mouldy cake. The cake-smeared hand struck out and grabbed one of the cosmetics in the mug they'd used to contain such. The dye stick.

The hand flew up and started jabbing the roots of her dreads where they parted.

"Sick of blue," her mouth said. "Sick of you. My body's rancid. Violated."

"Give it a rest," Swirl said and, with her left hand, tried to stop the right. She couldn't control the right, Sparkle putting all her focus there. "This is destiny, Spar-ki-dar."

She wrestled the dye stick away and threw it from them. She looked in the mirror: six, no, eight dreads now pink, all on the right side. Her eyes were red-veined, eyeliner all smeared. Quite mad.

Sparkle was about to say something, but Swirl took control of the mouth. Tensed it tight and a whistling slur came out.

:*Why'd you make him hate me?*: Sparkle sent. :*Why do you always shit on everything?*:

:*Sparkle, it won't matter soon. We'll be Ashemi. Deities.*:

:*And these things are mutually bloody exclusive?*: Sparkle sent.: *They have to be?*:

Swirl looked straight in the mirror at those mad eyes. "You love him, then?" she asked Sparkle.

:*Fuck off. Fuck you.*:

Swirl grinned. "Thought not."

***

HE HEARD HER COME BACK in. He didn't look. *Princess* was racing into daylight, crossing a meridian. Below, land had given way to ocean, blue and cold and empty.

"What's going on?" she asked.

"False alarm," he said. Had to stop thinking 'she'. *Them.*

"You brought up the visual," they--shit--*she* said, referring to the dawn sky all around.

"Not for you," Hargie said. But he kinda had, now he thought about it.

He heard her walk to the wall behind and grab the fold-out chair.

"No," Hargie told her. "Get in one of the huggies."

She ignored him, opened the chair and plonked it down beside his. She sat down. Goddammit.

"Update," she said. Like that. Update.

"Flying headlong toward my given coordinates," Hargie said, tight-lipped. "Fast as atmosphere allows. Everyone fighting above seems too busy to notice us."

"Fine," she said. Like that: fine.

"These coordinates?" he asked, eyes ahead, never looking. "What's there?"

"An island right on the equator," she said. "The Mendicant Isle. Half in this world, half in the Geode."

"Understood," he said. The cockpit fell silent awhile. "So which of you's fucking me?"

"Hargie!"

He turned to look at her, the callipers holding the needles in his neck twisting to compensate. He thought he'd outstare her, but she was ten times crazier-looking, her makeup smeared. She'd dyed the dreads on her right side pink.

"I really don't know what you mean," she replied, pink and blue dreads shaking. She seemed to be trying to control her own lips. "The Envoy, yes? He lied. He wanted to... hurt you. And he has."

He kept his eyes on hers. "Ovia?"

"Sem-hoish?" the old woman answered.

"Bodies got more than one mind on Zahrir?" Hargie asked her. "That's the deal, right?"

"That," Ovia said calmly, "or their minds are broken early. Only the Delighted truly know."

"See?" Hargie said to, to... her. Them. "I suspected something back on Silvercloud, but Eucharist, oh... he ratshitted me. Why not just tell me you'd a split personality?"

"Split?" Sparkle's lips twitched. "We're two people, feral. Individuals. Respect that."

"Respect?" he said. "Five seconds ago you were lying to me. Said that Envoy butthole was lying."

"Wasn't me who said that, was it?" she replied. "My sister."

"Yeah, but *you* just called me feral." Hargie sucked his teeth. "Shit. 'Business mood', 'funny-crazy'. Fucked up. Pair of fucking liars."

She gulped. Her right eye watered.

"Hargie, we..." She slapped herself. "Straighten up, girl."

Weirder than a silo full of dicks.

"Was it you fucking me, Slappy?" Hargie said. "You, Weepy? See, I thought it was Weepy, but now I think you took turns. The other watch? Get off on it? Me not knowing?" He grinned angrily. "Which of you begged me to do that, that *thing* that one time?"

Her brows creased, suspicious. "What thing?"

Hargie nearly said it aloud, but he remembered the Anointed. He made the gesture. "You know."

Her face went rigid. "*Eww...*" She stopped, slurred and spoke again. "He's lying, Sparkle."

"I loved you," he said like a fucking sap. "But that was just a buffet. Took whatever my vanity wanted, best of both whackos. Ignored the rest." He sniffed. "*My* Sparkle? She never even existed."

She looked set to say something, but she froze. Her head shook. She grabbed her own head and bent forward in her chair, warring in that evil skull of hers, a madwoman or a pair of sick liars. Hargie Stukes could sure pick 'em.

Warning blips. Shit. Two craft in pursuit, low to the ground, leaving the coast. *Princess* hadn't picked 'em up before, what with the warhead blast.

One a goddamn bubbleship. No: hybrid. Nugo-frigging-Vict.

Hargie kicked *Princess* into life.

***

NUGO VICT GRINNED. THE JUMPJUNK and everything was right. This was him, everything he was or ever would be, stripped down. Pure.

"Can you see them, Vict?" Melid's voice. She had a nice voice.

He could detect *Princess*, a distant buzz in the far-fore, in the crazy alienness of this world, in the swirling mist of it all. He shot more junk in his neck. Ooh yeah. Swirling mist. His battlefield. His hunting ground.

***

SPARKLE WATCHED THE WALLS. THE sky and sea were the same, divided only by a line in the far horizon, a curved line of stranger blue. The equator, the flames of Zahrir's wound.

Hargie's woman had never existed? How could he say that? Sparkle was the personality, a star. If Hargie insisted he'd loved what he saw, he had Sparkle to thank for that. Swirl was the drag factor.

:*Not long, sister,*: Swirl sent. :*None of the pain will matter.*:

:*Tell Hargie,*: Sparkle sent.

Swirl didn't reply.

Sparkle felt Swirl try to take control of their body. Sparkle jammed her.

"What are you doing?" she asked Swirl.

"Seeing if anyone's chasing *Princess*," Swirl said.

"Don't bother. They wouldn't appear on the visual. Too far away." *Idiot*, Sparkle thought.

"Fine." Swirl paused. :*Sparkle, we're talking out loud.*:

Sparkle looked around. No one was staring, at least.

:*So we are,*: Sparkle sent. :*Better watch for that.*:

:*What's wrong with us?*: Swirl sent. :*We must have... realigned improperly. The opal must have had some dysfunction.*:

:*The dysfunction's us,*: Swirl sent. :*We don't fit our own skull anymore.*:

:*The time alone changed us?*:

:*Seems time alone can do nothing else.*:

Their shared body sighed, Swirl causing it to do so. Sparkle knew that was the sort of thought Swirl would rather block out than ever face up to.

:*I'm going to look behind us,*: Swirl sent.

:*There's really no--*:

299

Swirl looked over their right shoulder at the wall behind them. Two little red lights hurtling over the ocean, *Princess'* highlighted markers of the vehicles in pursuit.

***

BLUE FLAMES AHEAD. A WALL to the sky from east to west, like a static tidal wave. The walls of Zahrir's burning wound.

Princess was warning him to slow down. Not for fear of the wall itself, that was too far away. But something was thickening the air outside.

Banks of mist barely visible in the flames' light. Like smoke, rising from the flames and filling the atmosphere. Question was, were the Spindlies behind him feeling it too?

Hargie descended, found it wasn't so bad down there. At forty feet above sea level, he could maintain top planetary speed. But it fixed him in place, a meal on a plate. Those pursuing assholes had no missiles left. Hargie'd be dead now if they did. Still beams, though: not as powerful or ranged as in a vacuum, but lethal with proximity. And they were gaining, both the hybrid (who had to be Vict, bet your ball-sack, Jack) and its Spindly pal.

Hargie needed ideas. Fast. He--

Shit, this wasn't as fun as it used to be. The jumpjunk and the jinking weren't the same, now she had his mind all schtooked. No fun left.

Just survival.

***

"YOU CAN CATCH HIM?" MELID ASKED.

"I keep telling you," Vict said.

Melid needed to believe him. All her kind did. The horizon nothing but flat grey. Incapable of being processed by kollective perception, anathema. How would it be, closer to that grey? Would all their minds... well, short out?

Vict's talents's permitting, there should be no reason to find out.

300

***

VICT FLEW LOW. HE HADN'T tuned why Hargie had done that. Now he knew. All that weird alien ether ahead fattened the upper air, a feeling in his neuralware like swimming through treacle.

Fine. It kept Hargie low, out of options. A pursuer's game now. Always was.

"Approaching range," Melid said.

Nowhere near, but of course she meant the Hunter-Killer beside them: bigger beams, longer. Not at Vict's command.

Damn, he had to fight an urge not to shoot that H-K. Be easy from here.

Jumpjunk kicking in him, a racing fire, vengeance in the veins. Bad mix. Let them shoot. Get this over.

Princess stretched and warped, the horizon around her likewise. A gravity wall.

The Hunter-Killer pulled up, into the slowing thickness above.

"Brace," Melid said.

"Ratshit," Vict said and he giggled. "Just a chuck charge."

Vict wouldn't buy Hargie's lies, his ratshit bragger's rep. No chuck barrel could take out a ship. *Snowy* wasn't a rinky-dink ickle missile. *Snowy* was the greatest bubbleship that ever rolled. Vict's ship. Ask around.

Wouldn't lie: a moment there, as the grav wave passed over *Snowy*, Vict almost bought Hargie's chicanery. But no. Chuck wave didn't do shit. Of course not. *Snowy* shook, but sailed through.

"Told you," Vict said to the cockpit.

He neuraled *Princess*.

"That your best game, Stukes?" he said into his comm. "That all?"

No reply, but Hargie must have picked that up.

"Stop communicating," he heard Melid say.

Vict ignored her. "Stukes," he said into the comm, "you weren't even a contender."

He shut the comm off. Hargie Stukes cringing in his chair now, Vict thought. Trapped rat, a mongrel. Still, he'd have thought Hargie would have a comeback. Something.

Vict sharpened up for the kill.

***

SEA SPRAYED ON THE VR walls of *Princess'* cockpit, rolling down in blurred droplets. Swirl was no pilot, but... they were inches above the waves. That couldn't be good.

"Can't we go higher?" she asked him.

He said nothing, his eyes staring at nothing, at all the calculations and radiuses and who-knew-what of his trade. She had to believe in him. To think: she and her siblings' destinies, the Hoidracs' plans, all in the hands of this little rat and his junk-heap.

:Don't distract him,: Sparkle sent.

"Trust in our destiny," Swirl said.

:I'll trust in Hargie,: Sparkle sent.

They lowered, slowed. The sisters hugged themselves.

Princess Floofy hit the water.

***

"HE'S GONE UNDER," MELID SAID.

Vict ignored her. A distraction.

"Tracker still operating," Melid said. "Still moving under there. Still alive."

"Shut up," Vict told her. Of course they were alive. "I'm going under. Tell your H-K to stay above. Shoot Hargie if he breeches."

Vict slowed a little; then his world turned blue. He felt the cold tickle of the ocean against the hull, his skin. He pumped more jumpjunk. Yes,

302

yes. He had Hargie. No moves from that fuck-stick, out of ideas now he'd used up his only lie.

Hargie was buying time. Beams shorter ranged under here, under the waves, but still lethal. The seabed was rising ahead, soon to be shore. Either Hargie would pull some turn in the water (dead), pop up (dead), or hit the shore (all kind of dead!). Checkmate. Victory. Vict free. Then join the Konsensus. He needed that. But only after Hargie Stukes died. Only then.

Snowy's cutter had adjusted to the new medium. *Princess* was rising to avoid the seabed. Slowing. *Snowy* gaining on *Princess*. Hundred meters to range...

The depths warped ahead. *Princess* had detonated another chuck charge. Ha! No fucking--

Water. New medium. A gravity wall in an ocean...

Vict pulled up. No. No!

The grav wall hit. He felt pain compress his heart's chambers, his muscles. Heard the roar of impact, the twist of metal deep in his ship. In his head.

Water turned to sky. Up, up.

Alarms, the bubblecoil buckling. Ready to blow. He--

Vict neuraled, and the cockpit ejected from the hull. He watched the hull fly away, upwards. It collided with a black shadow, swift and diamond-shaped. The Hunter-Killer.

He closed his eyes, could hear shouting all around, more alarms.

So a chuck charge really *could* take out a ship.

Make that two.

***

MELID WATCHED ZAHRIR SPIN AROUND: sea, coast, sky, sea, coast, sky. She saw shadows and flame above the ocean, and on the next revolution realised it was the Hunter-Killer exploding. She felt the last of its crew scream, then vanish.

Standing beside the cockpit's chair, she gazed down upon Nugo Vict. She wanted to demand what was happening, but he seemed focussed on his work, utterly consumed.

Something else out there...

Something happening in the flat grey wall; she could see movement in its nothing. The cockpit revolved and she gazed down at the floor, now facing the flat grey horizon. There. Tall and thin and massive. A shape.

A Scalpel.

She spun to follow it as the ship revolved. Against the back wall of the cockpit now: a great Scalpel, type 2(1a), gliding forward. Toward them.

Time slowed. She studied its armour. That was the only part of a Scalpel a Konsensite could ever really see, the armour's origins being of this universe, protection from this universe for whatever it truly held. But now she saw the armour had never been fully apparent to her, until now. Its surfaces seethed with pattern, perhaps even meaning, something Melid could sense but never grasp.

She had to turn again to keep her eyes upon it, to face Zahrir's equatorial wall as the cockpit spun and people screamed. Such armour. Lost in that armour, she realised she had missed a greater revelation. The Geode-energy rising between the armour's cracks was no longer the same flat grey. It flickered, modulating between grey and a blue beyond blue, of a kind Melid had never imagined.

Was this what the Worlders could see? How could she see now? What was happening? Was the kollective program adjusting? Or the Scalpel?

Vict had righted his craft, was heading for the bare and rocky coast.

The Scalpel--tall as a tower--began to rise. In seconds it was tiny, piercing the atmosphere. Then a memory, one Melid couldn't fully remember, even so soon.

Her enemy. In no particular hurry to annihilate the Konsensus fleet above Zahrir.

And more beautiful than she'd thought anything could be.

CHAPTER FOURTEEN

"Can't take her any further," Hargie said. "I'm landing."

His head was all full of warning signs, little windows popping up and glowing at him. His muscles ached. His veins glowed with junk.

He set *Princess* down in a diamond-shaped space between four stone outcrops that looked like melted glass. Green glass.

"This as far as you can go?" Sparkle asked.

"What I just say?" He didn't look at her. "Closer I get to the flames, the lower I have to fly. *Princess* been hugging the rocks for the last ten-mo. Fly any further, I'll have to stick a drill on her nose."

He blinked and the needles pulled from his neck. The callipers came off his legs. His body sighed. There was a brief silence, and he listened to the hum of *Princess'* grav plates cooling.

"How far to the flames?" she asked.

"About a kilometre," Hargie said. "More."

"But the Konsensus are still..." She stopped speaking, her eyes darting about. She was listening to someone. It occurred to Hargie that she'd always had that look, that he'd never noticed. "Fine. Let's go."

She was the first to step out, followed by the eight Anointed, followed by Hargie.

The warm winds smothered Hargie's face like a drunk man's hands: each and every direction, no sense to it. It made no sound. How'd it make no sound?

Nothing had ever spooked him out as this place, not even Silvercloud. The spires of rock all around made no sense. They looked ready to pour down, drown him in their green translucence. Nothing about the rock's skin seemed fixed. The surface had those shapes you saw in clouds or nebulas, suggestions of things your brain's pattern recognition threw up. He could see planets in the rock, or machine parts, or animals, or things half-animal and man. It changed constantly. He'd look at a fixed point again and some other image would present itself. No sounds. No life.

He lit a cigarette, looked down. His boots were wavering, like in a heat shimmer No heat, though. The rock below his wavering boots began to do its little eye trick. Eyes were pop-popping into existence like bubbles on water. Like there was some beast under the surface of the ground, ready to snatch him under.

"*Sem-hoish*," Ovia called to him. He stood in the dip alone. Everyone else was clambering up a ridge between the spires, Sparkle already stood at the top. Beyond her, the sky was crystalline and blue. Alive with Geode-energy, Geode mists. To Hargie, skies had always been too thin, too open to the void beyond. Not this sky. This sky was suffocating.

He clambered up the crystal ridge, his hands heat-wavering against the rock. No smells here, though he had a taste like kissing a battery on his tongue.

"Keep close, *Sem-hoish*," Ovia said as he reached the top. "The land can occlude the solitary."

"That's as scary as its gibberish, O-girl," he said. "You're getting me all tuned out."

"Not as much as the land may," she replied. "You could become a melody different from ours."

Demanding clarity would be a truck-stop on the road to madness. Speaking of which, Hargie looked at the way ahead. More spires of rock, more ridges. A silent land, its surfaces eyes and patterns and faces, and then gone, becoming something else. He took an up-patch from his pocket and slapped it on his neck, to stop the junk comedown before it happened.

They reached the summit of the ridge and gazed at the far flames, the wall between worlds.

The flames themselves were fairly obscured by the mess they made. 'Smoke' didn't really cut it as a description of that mess. It looked like bleach when poured in water, rolling liquid cloud columns, pillars of milk melting kilometres high into the sky. Shit, he hadn't the words. It was a wall from one end of the horizon to the other; at its base, deep within its rolling misty belly, blue light smouldered. The flames themselves.

"Hargie." Sparkle's voice.

He looked over at her and she was staring at him, her eyes frightened and kind. She opened her mouth to speak.

The sky screamed, and then it rumbled. Everyone ducked. Somewhere a ship had crashed. Where was anyone's guess. The sound bounced off every spire in the landscape.

"Let's move," Sparkle said. Her expression had changed. She'd changed.

"Probably all dead," Hargie told her, reassuring himself more than anyone listening. Nugo Vict was a better pilot than he'd like to admit.

Sparkle turned and made her way down the other side of the rise. The Anointed followed.

They'd both spoken just now, both sisters. He knew them both: one a world of crazy, one all solidity, a bedrock. At least he thought. The first he sorely wanted, the second he likely needed. He needed to talk and...

Shit. Thousands dying, galaxy in the balance, and here he was making this all about him. He took one last look at *Princess,* then caught up with the others. Quickly, before he might vanish into the land.

***

THE INTERIOR GRAVITY HAD GONE. The cockpit floor was at an angle. Melid reached her mind out. One of the Assaults, Kolg, was no longer within the kollective. Everyone else was alive and conscious, a better result than Melid had right to expect.

She opened her eyes and stared at the plated ceiling above. She was on her back, relatively unharmed.

"Stukes," Vict was saying. She could see the back of his head, his long hair dangling, stroking the floor.

The floor had buckled beneath him, had torn the pilot chair from its fittings. The pilot chair hung on its side at a right angle, the back of its seat facing Melid. Two feet--Kolg's--stuck out from underneath it.

Vict hadn't noticed. He was pulling off the callipers around his thighs. Melid watched him struggle. Vict stopped, reached for his neck. He pulled out a needle, still embedded in his neck-stud, that had broken off from the chair's headrest. He winced, threw the needle away.

"Come on!" he shouted. "Still time!"

Melid shot him in the skull. Vict's brow flew across the cockpit. It rattled off a bulkhead.

She felt the cadre's surprise. "Would slow us," she said, less like an explanation and more an affirmation of their intent. She felt them all take succour from it.

Melid got up, careful not to slip and roll down the angled, buckled floor. Gravity... "Lifters," she said.

The cadre opened up the storage unit on the rear wall and extracted the lifters. Doum passed one to Melid. The lifter was like a black ribcage. Melid opened it at the sternum, put the lifter on, and locked it over her chest.

Everyone activated their lifter and made their way up the slanted floor toward the hatchway. The lifters weren't exactly like zero-g, but they did make any planet a saner prospect. Life at a sixth of the gravity of this world was acceptable enough.

The hatch out of *Snowy* was jammed, and they lost time blowing it open. A strange and dreadful light poured in. Blue-beyond-blue, the light of the Geode, of Scalpels. Melid missed the flat grey she used to experience. What had occurred that they could all now see it? Their kollectiveware had finally adapted to the Geode-energy's presence. At least, better to think that than that the Scalpel had induced the phenomenon. More comforting.

Two Assaults--brave, a testament to their role--exited first, drifting down onto the surface of the terror-world. Melid followed, her lifter slowing her fall. She had time to look at the ground as she hit it. Green stone, infected by the Geode-energy, saturated by it over centuries. She knew this because patches of the ground kept flashing grey and flat, her kollectiveware still not capable of full comprehension. A moment of irrationality before she touched down: that she might fall through the blighted surface, fall through this earth forever.

The others followed her out. Melid looked around.

They had crashed in a long thin valley of glass-like rock, green like the ground, with its high crags polished to diamond by the winds. Silent winds. She felt their warmth blowing at her face, but not their whistle in her ears. She could hear nothing save the scuffling of her comrades' boots upon rock. Impossible. Impossible place.

Her vision was grainy, flecks of grey in the air and the land where her sight couldn't process the unreal medium all around. She thought of the Scalpel again. She couldn't be rid of the notion. Everything had changed in that moment.

No point getting lost in that thinking. It didn't help the mission. It didn't help survival. She reached out. She could feel the cadre: Doum, nine

Assaults. All solid. Their shared mood was inspiring. Faced with certain death, with species extinction, they ignored their higher minds, thought with their nerves. The mission alone.

She couldn't reach out further. Not to the fleet. Perhaps the Geode-energy here prevented it. No matter. Just these eleven, the Konsensus squeezed to a threadbare purity.

Melid closed her eyes. Yes. The tracker was out there, broadcasting from Sparkle Savard's body, its crystals in her bones. Melid had no map inside her skull now, no detailed coordinates of that monster's location. The tracker merely exerted a pull like an animal's sense of magnetic north, an instinct of where Melid must be.

The cadre made their way around the naked cockpit's wreck and gazed at the landscape beyond, spires and ridges warped by things stranger than time. She looked up, into the dizziness and insanity of the sky. Beyond the rocks hung a mist-like shroud from one end of the horizon to the other, like a mushroom cloud stretched wide and suspended in time. Where the Scalpel had risen. A shudder passed through the cadre. Another reality's violation of the universe, a tear in the now, unknown filth spewing out.

Sparkle's tracker shambled toward it. But there was time, time enough.

Melid made no speech, issued no sentiment. She leapt forward and the lifter carried her six meters in the air. She landed forty feet ahead, never kicking up dust in this world of silence. She leapt again, and the others followed.

***

SPARKLE LET SWIRL DO THE walking and climbing. Her sister liked all that stuff, after all. But it was strange, the way no driving seat existed within them anymore. Sparkle could simply take control of some part of their body if she desired, if Swirl was unprepared. Their body was a disputed land. Neither sister had the will to test ownership, to see who could win a fight for control, but it must have occurred to Swirl as much as it had to Sparkle.

Ovia's armoured arse was a foot away from Sparkle's face, the old woman leading the way up the steep ridge. She watched Swirl grip their body's gloved fingers against rock. Sparkle got that cliff-edge tingle: if she were to seize their body's limbs now they would freeze and fall, knock everyone behind them off and over the edge. Broken bodies, moans, blood. Mm-yes. A peculiar end to a peculiar quest. A farce at the gates of forever.

"Wait up," Hargie called from behind.

Swirl didn't stop. Sparkle wanted to look back, almost did.

Swirl made it to the top, stood straight. A downhill stretch awaited, flat rock carved with scores of man-deep and interconnecting gullies, a trench-land bathed in blue light and rolling mist. Each and every trench ran slowly and eccentrically toward the feet of the mist-obscured flames.

Sparkle had expected more heat, certainly more than the warm breezes that tousled her hair. The silence too was eerily incongruous. The flames, hidden among their deluge of mists, could only be--what--a quarter of a mile away? Perhaps this universe and the Geode acted as opposing magnets to one another, repelling the greater deluge of either, despite this hole between realms. Somehow, the reasons had escaped Sparkle's preternatural curiosity. *If Pearl were here*, Sparkle thought, *he would know*.

Sparkle watched the horizon while Swirl breathed. To think it ran the entire equator. The clouds obscuring the flames were pure leaf-mist, unimaginable quantities of the stuff.

:Swirl,: Sparkle sent, *:let's have some leaf.:*

Swirl said nothing. She pulled out the pack from the pocket on their holster and placed half a leaf upon their tongue. It tingled even more than usual. She heard some of the Anointed reach for their own leaf supply.

Swirl closed her eyes. *:Sparkle, can you feel that?:* Swirl sent.

Sparkle could. Her whole skin felt caressed, encouraged, a tactile sensation that, when she focussed upon it, rendered the winds about her mere detail.

She opened her eyes. She could see Pheoni in the milky blue horizon, the pale lady dancing slowly, eyes closed, mouth a smile. A pattern made of the mists, yes, but real. Intended to be seen.

She felt her sister taken by the moment, their body's breathing deep and slow, their muscles shuddering. Sparkle watched her left hand rise toward the mist-images and the flames they shrouded. Her palm opened.

"Swirl?" Sparkle said.

"She bids us on, sister," she heard her lips say. "There's cure for your lack of belief, eh?"

:Yes,: Sparkle sent. The brute reality of it. It chilled her, as did Swirl.

Pheoni vanished, blended to nothing in the swirling distance.

"Wait up," Hargie said. He'd made it to the top of the ridge. "Shit."

"Come on," Swirl told him.

"Need a smoke." He lay against a rock.

"Idiot," Swirl said. "Come on."

"Smoke." He gazed at her, pulled out his cigarettes and lit one. The anger coming off of him was tenfold; Sparkle wasn't sure if the leaf and its insight were wholly responsible. She hadn't taken a whole lot, but the smallest dose had power here.

"I need you, Hargie," Sparkle said before Swirl could stop her.

"Need me?" Hargie said. He hadn't taken his eyes off her. "'Need' ended with my ship back there. Tired of following. Tired of not knowing what I'm following."

"Life was better when you'd nothing to follow?" For a second she thought Swirl said that. But no. "You were a nothing, Hargie. You'd made yourself nothing. Until me."

"And who you?" He pointed his cigarette at the right side of her head. "Pinky?" He pointed at the left. "Blue?"

:He's right,: Swirl sent to Sparkle. *:We don't need him now.:* She turned their body away from the bubbleman.

"Blue, right?" Hargie said. "That's you walking away?" He laughed. "Help me out here: you walking because you're throwing me away, or because it hurts too much? Who are you, Blue? Look at me, dammit."

:Walk,: Sparkle sent to Swirl. *:I can't handle this.:* Another quarter mile to be free of this. Human pain, human farce. An end to looking in his eyes.

Swirl stepped along the downward pathway, toward the waiting Anointed nearby.

Boots on stone behind her.

"Come here." He grabbed her right wrist.

Swirl spun and shoved the pistol in his face. Sparkle felt their shared finger pull, and Sparkle jolted their arm up and the shot went off, off over his hat. Hargie staggered back. He froze.

The gun pointed at his face. Sparkle had control of the arm, but it felt paralysed. She couldn't lower it. Swirl had control too, a growing pressure. Sparkle could hear the Anointed behind her, stepping closer.

:Fuck,: she sent to Swirl, *:you would have shot him.:*

:I'll shoot him now,: Swirl sent back. *:Don't you get it? Guilt won't matter once we transcend. For either of us. Why can't you grasp that?:*

Sparkle went to speak, but Swirl mentally seized the lips too, and they pursed into a tight silence.

:Who's the stronger here?: Swirl sent. *:Think you can stay my hand forever?:*

Sparkle had to put more focus into the arm. Swirl really *would* pull the trigger.

:No.: It was all Sparkle could send. With her own independent vision she looked at the gun, but she and her sister's shared pupils burnt through Hargie's own. Swirl had control of the face. She made it an animal's scowl.

:I won't entertain this anymore,: Swirl sent. *:We could die out here, a thousand feet from life ever after. I will not let my baby die for your toy.:*

Of course. How'd Sparkle been so blind? A mother's brutality.

:Tell him to go,: Swirl sent.

:You tell him,: Sparkle replied.

:You.:

Swirl applied pressure to their gun arm, reserves of pressure. Sparkle couldn't hold out.

:Tell him,: Swirl sent. She relinquished control of their lips.

"Fuck off!" Sparkle yelled. "Stinking-feral-fuck-off!"

Hargie gazed at her. Terrified, hurt. Like that boy in Silvercloud.

"We *used* you, animal!" Sparkle said, the trigger-finger ever-tightening. "All lies! Everything! Go!"

His face quivered. He turned, started clambering down the cliff. A tawdry little nothing, Hargie, in a universe full of nothings. Yet beside all these gods and empires, Hargie's little nothing seemed...

:I'm proud of you,: Swirl sent. She lowered the gun. *:Best this way.:* She paused, then said: "We're saving the galaxy here, sister."

Sparkle sent nothing. She started to sob.

***

SWIRL WIPED HER EYES. SHE needed them dry. Sparkle's tears. It had been the right thing to do.

Swirl led the Anointed down toward a thin stone-carved gully, one of many in the interconnecting mess that lay before the flames. It might have been quicker to risk the hard ground above the gulleys, to run over the wrinkled plain, but even with the leaf mists it was open ground, an invite to any loitering Konsensite. Better these trenches, though in truth a single grenade might kill them all.

For elite warriors, Swirl thought, the Anointed showed little care for any of that. Leastways, they said nothing.

They turned a corner. A mist filled the entire trench ahead from top to bottom.

"We'll get lost," Swirl said.

"Head toward where the mists roll from," Ovia said. "That is the road."

"But if we're drenched in mist--"

A figure ahead. Swirl ducked, lifted her gun, braced for a fire fight that never came.

Hargie. She recognised the hat's silhouette. He'd got ahead of them.

"Hargie," she said. She stepped closer, pistol still raised. She felt Sparkle inside her, rising to readiness.

The mists thinned. Not Hargie. A *guji* stick, a carved fetish of a Hoidrac head, decorated with a copper crown that had seemed like Hargie's wretched hat. A torn leather cape hanging from the stick's length gave an impression of body whenever the noiseless breeze got behind it. Swirl stepped closer.

:Why Hargie?: Sparkle sent.

"Are there many of these?" Swirl asked Ovia, ignoring Sparkle.

Ovia chuckled. "Of course."

:Why'd you see Hargie, Swirl?: Sparkle sent.

Swirl ignored her again. "Ovia, who placed them here?"

"The Anointed will," Ovia said. "One day."

:Guilt, Swirl? That it?: Sparkle sent. *:Twitching conscience there?:*

She could still hurt, Sparkle, even now, minutes from apotheosis. The Hargie silhouette had been in that pose back on Desic, seconds from him holding her, from making love, of a sort. From Swirl fooling him.

"Shut up," Swirl said.

:I'm sorry,: Sparkle sent. *:But you should suffer a little in this life before the next absolves you.:*

The *guji* carving was beautiful, something in its varnished dragon face welcoming, nurturing. Her leaf-vision imbued it with a nameless potential.

"This life?" she said to Sparkle. "This is no life. A copy of a copy. Meaningless." She reached out and caressed the *guji* carving's snout, felt the energy pour from it down through her veins, felt the essence of Pheoni the Appropriate, the essence of preceding visions. "*This*. This is life. You're scared, sister. I understand. But I'll carry you. Because I love you."

"Blessed," Ovia said to Swirl. "We shall wait here, guard your ascension."

Swirl turned and nodded. It made sense: the trenches, the mists. No threat of aerial attack, if *Princess Floofy's* plight was anything to go by. A solid defence.

"They are coming," Ovia told her. "The *guji* tells us. We will fight."

Swirl made the Loican sign.

"An honour to have you guide us." She looked around at all the Anointed. "All of you. I thank you."

"Do not thank us, Blessed One," Ovia said. "This story proceeds no other way."

Swirl nodded. She turned and began to jog along the trench, boots careful over uneven ground. She could see images as she ran, patterns in the stone walls that her eyes lent purpose and movement. A common property of Geode-saturated rock, given brighter life by the leaf she had taken. Hands, elegant and clawed, beckoned from beneath the glassy surfaces of each contour; cracks became full lips, weather marks swaying figures.

The truth in all things: that was the Hoidrac's gift. The rocks, the drugs, these were just intimations, hints.

Life, not just faith. Swirl fought for *life*. Did she not carry a child? Did she not carry her sister, sullen and babelike? Who better to preserve this galaxy? Who better to save it than those destined to transcend its horrors?

Swirl laughed as she jogged. She shared in a laughter everywhere and hidden. Finally, she was becoming herself.

***

THE CADRE HAD SPOTTED MOVEMENT in the gullies ahead, a shadow in the mists that rolled over the open ground and filled its many ditches. A logical place for their adversaries to mount a defence.

The eleven-strong cadre were lined out along the ridge over a distance of some hundred feet. The ridge gave a good view of the trench plain below, at least when one of them risked looking over their cover. No satellite images here, no wealth of intelligence. Just happenstance, wits. A thoughtless cadre could easily have crossed the ridge thinking it higher ground, safe. A thoughtless cadre would be dead.

In the sloping ground between the ridge and the trenches, any cadre would be dead. These Harmonics knew that, perhaps even wished the cadre to know that they waited, guns ready. All these Harmonics--six or eight in number, Melid had found boot prints in dust--had to do was wait, and in that they defined the rules.

Sparkle's tracker was reaching the other side of the trench plain, into whatever ground existed beneath the tumbling mists the great flames spewed. Melid had no idea where the flames exactly began and reality ended, where Sparkle Savard's mission would terminate. Minutes, that much was clear. They had minutes.

The cadre waited upon Melid's order. The most important order any Field-Emissary would ever give.

The problem was this: their stealth suits were useless here. They'd noticed earlier, as they bounced across the miserable land. The suits couldn't replicate the mists, rendered the wearer a grey blob. Perhaps these Harmonics already knew that, depended on it. This was their ground, after all. Perhaps...

They waited: Doum, the entire cadre. The last move. She couldn't just send them out to death. To failure. She...

Why hadn't the tracker decayed? The mists, the presence of the flames, all these things impaired the kollective, mired its ware. Why not the tracker? Were they being allowed to see the tracker? Could it...

She took a deep breath. Only then did Melid realise that the rest of the cadre had encouraged her to do so. They were soothing her. If hope remained, they emoted, it lay in Melid of Silvercloud.

They had their rifles. They had their lifters. Melid emoted her pride, her humility, to serve with such Instrums. She showed them her plan.

***

HARGIE STUKES WAS A FUCKING idiot. He should hide in his ship, wait things out. Duck, dive, run like a rat. Never failed him before.

Instead, he'd scurried into a... a ditch, a trench carved by those motherfucking winds, snaking downhill and crisscrossing with other motherfucker ditches. He kept his head low.

Fucking mist. Fucking everywhere. He kept seeing shapes. Memories in the mist, the rocks. He scrambled over a rise and rolled down into the next carved stone motherfucking ditch. No one killed him. So far so good. Keep it up, Hargie.

He was tailing her. Them. Whatever.

He was tailing because he had a theory, because he was stupid and because of her motherfucking eyes. His theory was this: what if one sister dominated the other? Kidnap her in her own body, bat-ladder as that sounded. They couldn't work that body simultaneously, surely? Simpler to take turns, and maybe one of them was gaming that system. Hargie had to be sure things were smoosh with her. Them. He had to be sure. Evade-automatic-weaponry sure.

Which was the stupid part, or a great chunk of same. Stupid also covered his use of his people's old philosophy, empathic rationalism, which had, by this point, clearly become as useful as a water-resistant teabag. The whole 'What would I do if I were them?' schtick only worked if there was one personality to consider. It got real hazy after that. Whose actions were whose? Which girl pointed the gun? Fired over his head? Told him to dust outta there like he wasn't even shit?

At a guess, there seemed to be one sister who was a little crazy, the one who'd argue with him, rip him up. She seemed capable of shooting him, admittedly. But, well, maybe she was worth getting shot about.

The other sister? If Hargie were a betting man, and he was, he'd say Girl B had either connived or been left with all the Hargie-time during Desic. Serious, devout, dependable. He'd *needed* that security for decades. Desic had been all that. But he couldn't love anyone dependable. He hadn't loved Girl B. Girl B had just been coasting off Girl A. Unless he had it wrong...

He couldn't see ahead of himself. So much of that weird, dancing mist. But he was following the gentle slope down. Down led to those hidden flames.

Her eyes. Yeah. That was a factor too, the reason he was dangling his balls in a vice right now.

The girl who'd pinned the gun on him just before, who'd scowled, who'd yelled at him to fuck off? She wasn't the same as the girl staring out of those eyes. Couldn't be. Hargie knew those eyes. If nothing else, he knew *them*. Same eyes as back on the Rig, as back by the river and before the first kiss. A stare right through him, right through the heart.

Theory: one sister kidnapping the other. If crazy-funny Girl A was the victim, and serious-dependable Girl B had gone mission nuts, there was no question but to try and save Girl A. Girl A was his world. Probably. And if Girl B? Well, if he didn't love her, he at least owed her. She'd fucking tried. No one ever fucking tried.

The other option was that both sisters were likeminded in their will to blow his head off. Objectively and shit... that seemed likelier. But there was a woman in his head and, even if she was ratshit, a lie, a collage of two liars, *that* woman was worth trying to save. Not that Hargie had a gun, or a plan. But *someone* in this mess was worth dying for, even if they'd never existed. Bet your ball-sack, Jack.

Father. He saw his father, further up the ditch. Kneeling, back to Hargie, tied to the grave. Hargie stumbled, fell against the ditch's stone wall.

Shit. A silhouette. Memory in the mist. The mist cleared a little, and Hargie could see the thing wasn't Father, just an outcrop in the middle of the trench's path. The top of the outcropping was missing. Shorn off.

Hargie got to his feet and shambled over to the thing. Rock. Weird rock. He was careful not to stare at any part of it for too long.

But something *was* there: a chain, delicate and gold, wrapped around the outcropping. Hargie stepped around the rock. On the other side, something was hanging from the chain. Wooden, carved. Painted in bright colours.

A mouth, fanged and grinning. Something about that scared the shit out of him, a fear pouring out of his brain like a snail's head from a shell.

A flash to his right, deep in the mist. Then a rumble.

An explosion.

***

MELID ARCED THROUGH THE AIR, watching her and her cadre's grenades detonate above the trenches. Forty feet above and descending gently; the ridge had lent their lifter jumps extra length and height. Blue mists covered the trenches, but now and then those mists blazed white with fusion detonations.

The assault's shock didn't last long. Muzzle flashes of black light danced in the fog below. Melid felt one of the cadre--Toli--vanish from the kollective. Solid, these Harmonics, whoever they were.

Eight of the cadre remained. The idea was not to break the defenders, nor surround them, but to punch through. It only required one to punch through, to leap past the trenches and zone in on Sparkle. With luck, the Harmonics hadn't thought to defend in depth.

The ground drifted toward her, wreathed in its strange fog. Melid darted her pistol downwards, left and right. No one.

She missed the wall of a trench by inches, slid down. The walls had pockmarks, portions freshly melted. She'd landed in the detonation zone of her grenade. Her suit protected her from residual heat. She leaped again.

At her leap's apogee, she dropped her remaining grenade forward and left, careful not to hit her comrades. White flashed in the mist and an enemy weapon ceased firing.

This time she hit the wall of a trench with her hips and she fell backwards. The pain wasn't as bad as she'd expected. She heard shuffling, got up to see a deformed beast charging her. She fired, took its left leg out. Only when the beast dropped did Melid realise it was human, one burnt to a crisp by someone's grenade, skin charcoal, nose melting. Its strange armour completed the horror.

The Harmonic wasn't dead. It lifted some wrist weapon. Before it could fire, Doum landed upon it and shot its baked head off.

Melid emoted thanks.

Both Konsensites looked at one another. They were the only two to have full connection. Others in the cadre were still out there, but the connection was patchy, intermittent. Hopefully the others had a better konnection to one another. The alternative would be agonising. Something about the mist or the increasing proximity of the flames was interfering with their kollective, much as it had around Zahrir's orbit.

Zo and Doum shared a resolve. Drive for the flames, for Sparkle.

They leapt in the air, and their lifters carried them high. With any luck the others would hold--

Melid's world turned white and silent.

***

SPARKLE STOOD ON THE BEACH and waited.

Everything was wrong. The tides were higher than the sand, for a start. She studied the glitch: a black void underneath the sea's surface. Indeed, the sea was nothing *but* surface. One would need a stepladder to get up from the beach and into the sea.

The villa itself had also... well, *crashed*, to use the ancient term. Its many purple roofs were currently curling up into the sky, then uncurling again, never making contact with the rest of the building. As for the walls, they waltzed between one another, sometimes passing through each other's bulk. Sparkle saw her bedroom gobble up then excrete the upstairs library, which seemed quite unharmed by the experience.

Syncopation breakdown, mm-yes. No different to their body's current lack of a control, of a 'driving seat'. Sparkle and her sister's psyches were no longer complimentary. Time and experience away from each other had seen to that. People changed; a lesson Triunes were probably slower than monominds to learn.

The sky had kept dependable, though. Right now it flashed with an aurora borealis of adrenalin and fear. Swirl was surviving out there, doing what she did best.

Damn it, she was Sparkle's sister. Damn it. They would be gods together soon, or they would die together. You couldn't pick your destiny or who you shared it with. Sparkle was a coward, waiting here. Hargie wouldn't matter soon. He didn't matter. Not to the fate of billions, not to--

Sand flew up on her face. She coughed, blinked.

Confused, heart pounding, Sparkle looked at the small and freshly formed crater. It lay exactly where she'd been staring.

Fascinating. Had she done that? Her suppressed anger? This cognitive crash had peculiar qualities.

Oh. She wished it hadn't ended like that. With Hargie. Telling him to fuck off...

Sparkle shook it off. Dust, detail, pedantry. It was humanity that mattered now. No individual, but all of it. If nothing else, her time running through feral space had taught her that. Sparkle ascended.

The ascension was peculiar this time around. No blink-and-shift to the outer world of her physical senses. There was a moment, perhaps some eight seconds, where she was a stream, a river to the sky, her awareness loading into her body.

And her body was running, ducking, hyper-aware. Swirl was coming to the end of her particular trench, its length rising up into an eroded stone plain.

Billowing mists all about, thin shadows. Ahead lay the interstitial, the place between here and the Geode.

:Run,: Sparkle sent. :I'm with you.:

***

FUCK THIS IN THE TOES. Only reason Hargie hadn't given up was because all hell was behind him, and getting closer. He could hear compaction rounds behind, that weird Harmonic gunfire all around. Grenades, too, fucking fusion. White light, crazy heat, even from a distance. He kept low, ran low, his head well beneath the trench's lips.

A male Anointed stepped out ahead, raised his gun. Hargie froze. He fired over

Hargie's head.

Hargie felt a boot in the back of his neck. He dropped, palms hitting the stone floor. Looking up, he saw a headless body in a Spindly suit glide down to the trench floor. The body's boots touched the ground just before the Anointed and then, in sick slow motion, it began to pitch forward.

The Anointed looked at Hargie and smiled. The man stepped to one side and indicated for Hargie to pass on by.

Hargie got up. He tipped his hat at the Anointed. He walked by the headless Spindly, still falling in slow-mo, its neck pouring out blood like a gravy boat, and walked by the Anointed, still smiling at Hargie like the friendly uncle he'd never had.

Hargie ran. Best to leave this weird scene behind. Only be others ahead, anyhow.

***

MELID AWOKE TO AGONY. HER fingers. Three on her right jutted out in directions they were never intended to, two on her left. Both trigger fingers broken.

She looked around, still feeling the hum, the warmth of kollective connection, but a connection trying to recalibrate itself. She'd reached the end of the trenches. Flat plain shrouded in the fog, the great flame wall rising to the sky, becoming sky. Impossible to judge the distance. She felt dizzy.

Her left eye stung, blood running in from her scalp. She ordered her suit to recede its mask, and then she rubbed her eye with her wrist. Her fingers stung and she winced, suppressed a yelp.

A round fired behind. Konsensus, not Harmonic. She turned to see Doum aiming his rifle into one of the trenches. Doum emoted to Melid that he'd taken out their immediate attacker. There was still gunfire amid the trenches, but less of it, whatever that meant. Only Doum. She could only feel Doum now. The mists, the proximity to the flames, all cutting down the range of the local kollective. There were still others in the cadre out there; she could hear their fire.

Doum came over, feeling the same isolation. Strange, like they were the only two Konsensites in existence. Doum was frightened.

"Can't shoot," Melid said to him. "Fingers."

He picked up her pistol from nearby and gestured for her hand. She held out her left, usually her inferior hand, now superior for its functioning digits. Doum, more delicately than his form would ever suggest, placed the trigger guard over her middle finger, the index and ring quite smashed. Melid held back the pain, turned her wrist so her palm was horizontal. The weight of the pistol seemed tenfold. Hateful gravity.

Melid looked out into the mist. She sensed the tracker ahead. Sixty metres, slowing.

"Split," she told Doum. "Maybe fifteen metre distant. Kollective degrade, get closer me."

"Split?" Doum said.

"Split," Melid said. "Surround. You killer. Me eyes, support." She indicated her pistol. "Either us see, both shoot." She sighed. "No use lifter. Disconnection risk."

"Emissary," Doum said. His eyes were wet. They were alone, Doum and Melid. Alone. The feeling saturated them.

"Melid now," she told him. "Proud, Doum." She embraced him, felt tears in her own eyes, mingling with blood. "Brave now." Melid radiated love, all the love she'd ever been capable of. Love of her people, her life. All on Doum.

She let go. "Now."

Doum nodded. They ran into the mists. Seconds later she lost visual of him, but not connection. Not that.

***

SWIRL HAD STOPPED RUNNING. IT had gone out of her. Wonder had saturated fear.

Everywhere, *guji* sticks. Lines of them, ranks and files, ten feet apart, their poles driven into the green rock. Silhouettes all around. Occasionally a lick of mist would part and reveal more *guji* sticks, and more thin silhouettes beyond them. Had she stumbled on a patch by luck? By divine direction? Or could this army of carved dragonheads stretch across the entire edge of the lost isle?

With her free hand, she made the Loican sign. Divine wonder. The gates of apotheosis, Delighted be praised.

:Here we are then,: Sparkle sent.

What a tawdry thing to say. Still tawdry, Sparkle, still lost in the detritus of a paler reality. Mundane. Swirl and Pearl and the baby would be a superior Ashemi without her.

But Swirl was beyond hate. She gazed at the carved and painted head on the *guji* stick beside her. White and blue: Pheoni the Appropriate. Swirl smiled back at it.

:Can you hear that?: Sparkle sent.

Swirl raised her gun, listened.

"What?"

:Firing's stopped,: Sparkle sent.

She was right. Silence, the most profound she'd ever known. In the distance, deep, deep in the penumbra, blue Geode-light brooded. She walked toward it.

:You hear that?: Sparkle sent.

Idiot. *"What?"*

:Listen,: Sparkle sent.

A voice. Sometimes ahead, near the Geode-lights. Sometimes far to the left. Now right.

"Hello?" Swirl called.

:Pearl's voice,: Sparkle sent.

"Pearl!" Swirl shouted.

"Sisters!" Pearl's voice. "Come on!" It faded off at the end. It seemed to bounce off the rocks, the *gujis*.

She kept walking toward the flames, which seemed forever away, even now. Perhaps one entered them before one knew it. They passed carved snouts and horns, images of Pheoni, Shavisku, Menkharna, Mohatoi Embossed. She knew them all, all the gods.

"The sliver!" Pearl cried, ahead now. "I can see it inside you!"

The voice came a little to the left. Swirl was going off course. She righted herself. Kept going, a trot now.

"What is it?" she heard her voice call. Felt her lips move. Sparkle. "What's it do?"

:Sparkle!: Swirl sent, careful not to confuse their vocalisation. *:It doesn't matter.:*

"What's it do, Pearl?" Sparkle called again, ignoring Swirl. "What's in me?"

:Idiot,: Swirl sent. *:Your stupid curiosity.:*

"I want to know now," Sparkle muttered. "While I'm still me."

Swirl had lost her way. Too much mist. She stopped. She had to get her bearings.

"Pearl?" Sparkle called. *Idiot.*

"Salvation!" Pearl shouted. "For the galaxy!" He sounded closer now. Then silence.

"And?" Sparkle called. *By the Delighted...*

"No more Konsensus!" Pearl shouted. "An inoculation! Their very own essence!" Silence again.

"Kill them?" Sparkle shouted.

"Yes!" Pearl's voice. "Salvation! Now come!"

Swirl was surprised by joy. She was thankful Sparkle had asked now. No war. No billions dead. The galaxy cleansed of abomination.

"Come on, sister," Swirl said, unable to contain the joy within. "The Hoidrac were with us all along. They love us, *love* us!"

Heat tore her right calf and she hit the floor. Gunfire.

***

MELID HATED HERSELF. SHE'D FIRED at a stick. A stick with a head. A Scalpel head. So many heads on sticks.

Her fingers raged with pain. Mistake. Surprise gone.

She'd felt the tracker just ahead, seen a silhouette, fired. The tracker was imprecise this close. It wasn't a thing of local precision. She'd assumed so, but...

Doum. Still Doum, racing forward, into a volume of the hateful mist. Sparkle wouldn't know he was coming. Sparkle wouldn't return fire, either. She'd give herself away. Clever, Sparkle, she'd know not to run, to keep low. She'd be watching in the direction the round had come from.

She wouldn't see Doum coming.

Melid ducked, braced herself for the pain, and fired more shots in the direction of Sparkle's tracker. Suppression: Melid's role here. This would work.

***

SHOTS AHEAD. HARGIE PRESSED ON, out of the trenches, head bowed. He wasn't thinking any more. Hadn't for a while.

Someone ran in front of him. Big Spindly suit. Doum.

Asshole hadn't seen Hargie. Damn lucky. Asshole had a big gun.

Hargie followed him, unsure what else to do. He'd no idea where Sparkle was. Doum seemed to be going somewhere, seemed to know what he was doing. Leastways, Hargie wasn't gonna argue with him.

Hargie saw a nice fist-sized rock. He picked it up and kept moving.

***

SWIRL CRAWLED TOWARD HER PISTOL.

Suppressive fire above. Intermittent, aimless. The firer wanted Swirl to retaliate, give her position away. Someone else would be coming for the kill.

But which direction?

She kept crawling.

***

HARGIE FOLLOWED DOUM THROUGH THE mists. Creepy fucking Hoidrac faces everywhere, painted and carved. People needed better hobbies around here.

He had his rock. He could run up and brain Doum, but Hargie was scared of that ogre. And Doum might not have a brain to brain. Hargie felt like a damn rat, which was all he'd ever been.

Doum would shoot Sparkle. He'd shoot her if he saw her. Hargie had to do this, had to try. Tap, back of the skull. He stepped faster, readied the rock in his palm. Heavy, sharp at one end. Two steps from Doum. He'd have to jump to hit the guy's head. Do it. Do--

Shots. Hargie flinched. Doum stumbled.

The ground to Doum's left was washed red. Doum had been shot through the belly, maybe spine. Doum staggered, fell forward.

Harmonic shot. Hargie looked right. He saw an Anointed, Ovia maybe. They'd already turned, looking for some target not Doum.

Doum: still alive. His gun under him. Man was unkillable.

Hargie, stepping forward, hunched up, lifted his stone. Doum was getting up, but not getting up, trapped like a man tied to a grave. What was it like for Doum, Hargie wondered, life pouring out, agony upon the stones? Knowing his chips were cleared...

Doum groaned, and Hargie loitered above his groaning like a rat, scared the dying man might get it together to shoot him.

Like a rat.

***

MELID FELT DOUM CALLING OUT, but still alive. Suit fixing him. It was enough. She had his connection.

She traced from where the shot had hit Doum, saw a shadow in the fog, fired her pistol, pain in her fingers. The shadow went down, a piece of it flying off.

She emoted calm to Doum. *Keep alive, keep alive.*

She ran at the tracker signal, firing shot after shot after shot, fingers throwing each shot, smashing stone and ripping carved alien grimaces, turning monsters to splinters. Shots everywhere. She aimed low and mid and high, running, running. Rattle of compaction, triumph of Konsensus or last scream. Die, Sparkle, die. Die, die, die, die, die!

Mist parted. She saw Doum on all fours to her left.

She saw a body hunched over him.

Hargie Stukes. No gun.

Their eyes met, and for a moment she felt she truly knew him.

She aimed.

***

HARGIE DROVE THE ROCK INTO Doum's skull.

He closed his eyes and waited to be wrong.

***

SWIRL GRABBED HER PISTOL AND leapt up. Her right leg gave up on her and she tumbled to one side. Pain kicked. She kept her pistol up, ready.

The firing had stopped. Silence of the flames, their blue and distant glow.

Fine, it was fine.

She could move on her leg. Flesh wound. She staggered toward where the blizzard of shots had come from. Swirl had a hunch she was in no danger, despite the recent fire. A desperate move, that; no one suppressing would just go quiet. But she kept ready. She always had, her whole life.

Splintered *guji* sticks everywhere. She couldn't help but tread on them. Pheoni forgive.

Body on the floor ahead, legs splayed, head propped up by a leaning *guji* stick. Spindly suit.

Melid. Alive, shaking. Face bare to the world. Swirl pointed her gun at the woman. At the abomination.

Swirl stood over her. White foam poured from Melid's mouth, ran down her cheeks and into her short black hair. Her eyes were wide. She stared into nothing. Swirl watched the abomination's limbs twitch.

Of course. All her cronies dead. No more kollective, not locally. The *Kharmund* must have wiped the Konsensus fleet away, as gods were wont to do.

Victory. Evil vanquished. Ha. Could it have been any other way?

Swirl fired twice, reduced scythe-shot in either thigh. Melid's legs shuddered, then returned to twitching. Swirl reached down and pulled the primitive pistol from Melid's broken fingers and threw it across the ground.

"Look at you," she said to the twitching thing. "You failed."

Melid dribbled.

"You killed thousands," Swirl said. "No mercy, no feeling." Rage built in her, a year's worth. "Oh, you can *live* awhile. Watch me ascend. You hear me, cunt? You can feel all your kind *die*."

Swirl turned around. The flames called her, sacred and forgiving...

Swirl's legs froze. Her arms seized up.

"Sparrkur!" she tried to say, but her mouth had seized up too.

***

HARGIE COULDN'T BELIEVE HE WASN'T riddled with rounds and bleeding out, couldn't believe his hunch had worked. But there Melid was, or had been before another wave of mist blew in: staring up at the sky and dribbling. A baby.

He'd seen Melid freeze, stagger, fall down. Stood to reason: you couldn't have a kollective of one. She'd inherited the mind-life of Hargie and everyone else, and Hargie could understand her response. Many were the times he'd wanted to lie on his back and shake, shit himself at the loneliness of it all. Hadn't everyone?

Sparkle seemed smoosh enough, or leastways she wasn't bleeding out all over. He watched her, half-submerged in the fog, the two minds apparently fighting over who was in charge of what.

Melid, Sparkle. These women in Hargie Stukes' life, man. These women.

Ovia. He made his way over to where she'd fallen, past ghastly wooden monsters on sticks. He found her, face up in a corona of blood, her right shoulder missing. Eyes open, smiling, as if thinking 'just so'.

He felt as if he should say something.

He said, "Catch."

All he could think. He knelt down and closed her eyes, dyed her eyelids red with Doum's drying blood. He smiled back at her.

Better see to Sparkle. He headed back the way he'd come, using the sticks' ugly faces to guide him. He passed Doum's body but didn't look. Hargie had whatever life remained to think on Doum.

"Stopeh," came a voice in the mist. "Idyuh..."

"Sparkle?" Hargie said.

***

IDIOT. WHAT WAS SHE DOING?

But Swirl was getting the hang of dominating, slowly. She stood, willing their body still. Sparkle could do little to challenge that. Swirl felt her try, felt their limbs shiver, but she couldn't beat Swirl. Clearly, Sparkle was panicking once more. Swirl closed their eyes, took deep breaths. Still Sparkle struggled.

:*Stop panicking,*: Swirl sent.

:*Never so composed in my life,*: Sparkle sent back. :*We're going back, Swirl. We're getting in* Princess *and we're running back to feral space.*:

:*What?*:

:*You heard.*: Sparkle tried to seize their limbs again. Swirl held her off. :*We're getting in that tin can, flying off and keeping our head down the rest of our lives.*:

:*You're insane,*: Swirl sent. :*Ashemi, Sparks. We're to be immortal...*:

:*At whose expense?*: Sparkle sent.

Oh no. :*You can't possibly mean this. You can't.*:

:*Trillions, Swirl. Trillions. Children. Babies. People happy inside their shitty rocks until we got ideas.*:

Swirl raged, got full grip on their upper half. The legs were another story. Rigid, pinned to the rock below.

"They're monsters!" Swirl shouted. "Monsters!"

"It's smoosh, Sparky," she heard someone say behind her. Hargie.

Sparkle tried to seize their mouth. Swirl held it rigid, a pout leaking spittle and sound. The mouth was vital; Hargie might help Swirl's idiot sister. Oh, that feral would drag them over half a world for Sparkle.

:*If our immortality rides on the back of a single corpse,*: Sparkle sent, struggling to seize the mouth, : *then we deserve oblivion. Remember the boy? The Silvercloud boy? You want to kill him?*:

:*War's coming,*: Swirl sent. :*We can stop it.*:

:*Nothing's decided,*: Sparkle sent. :*Not ever.*:

:*The Hoidrac tell us.*:

:*Fuck the Hoidrac,*: Sparkle sent.

:*Blasphemy!*:

:*This is a human problem. For humans to solve. Human understanding.*:

:*You monster,*: Swirl sent. :*We've lost you, Sparkle.*:

:*Never fucking had me.*:

Sparkle struggled again, but Swirl was stronger. Her muscle memory, her physical intelligence, was a hundredfold to Sparkle's cake-eating sloth. Swirl began to move her legs. Not far now. She'd crawl inch-by-inch if need be.

:*Hey,*: Sparkle sent. :*Reckon they'll let us in if we've shat ourself?*:

Swirl froze, tensed their shared bowels.

"Hargiehelp!" Sparkle shouted before Swirl seized their mouth.

Swirl cursed her own stupidity. She felt hands upon her shoulders.

"I got you," Hargie was saying. "Fight her. Fight her. Come on, you can do this."

Hargie was right.

Swirl growled, snorted, beseeched the Hoidrac. Tightened her body until she hurt.

Sparkle flew out, down, down into their villa.

Swirl ruled here. That runt of the litter would know her place.

"You smoosh, girl?" Hargie, still gripping her shoulders.

"Fine," Swirl replied. She didn't look at him. Couldn't risk Sparkle coming back and speaking. She took the safety off her pistol and--

Fell on her rear. Pain shot up her spine. Both her legs had high-kicked. Sparkle.

Swirl got on all fours. Her arms shot out in crucifix pose and she fell on her chin.

Sparkle again. Crazy bitch. Swirl took control once more.

Her mouth blurted, and she only just stopped it in time. Then nothing.

Her body rolled over as if kicked in the stomach. Swirl stared at the mists above.

Sparkle had switched tactics. She couldn't hope to dominate Swirl, so now she was taking a hit-and-run approach, flying in and out of their villa, flailing a limb here and a limb there before Swirl might predict.

Crafty. But delaying the inevitable.

"C'mon, Sparkle," Hargie said.

Swirl got up on her feet and nearly fell again, her knees giving way, but Hargie held on, kept her upright.

"I've got this," Swirl managed to tell him.

She would have to negate her sister. Swirl shifted down, into the villa.

***

SHOULD DO THE TRICK. SPARKLE knew Swirl well enough, despite not knowing her at all now. She would come here for a… a decisive strike. Or some term like that.

Sparkle stood in the music room and waited. She watched the glasshouse and its garden pass through the far end of the room like a silent train. Each glass panel, transom and palm plant shivered, then granulated as it passed through the wall, presumably reconstituting on the other side. The villa couldn't function any more. Nothing inside this shared mind-world really could. If it ever had.

Another running attack on Swirl? Had Sparkle done enough? She--

She had. She could feel Swirl descending, something in the atmosphere around her warping. The time signature between here and the outside world was off; a psyche had to wait to load. The fear rose in Sparkle, memories of the beating received from Swirl, of all those more subtle and unconscious dominance displays throughout their conjoined inner life. For the first time, Sparkle was pleased Pearl wasn't there.

The ceiling began to flicker, appearing and disappearing, a blinking sky above. Sunshine, then gloom.

Swirl appeared at the end of the music room beside the wide haspichol, in the flickering light. She saw Sparkle and began to step toward her, a predator caught in low resolution, a flickering animation. Swirl had been possessed of an unknown Hoidrac in this music room. Sparkle, watching Swirl's leer, wondered if it had ever really left her.

"Sister," Swirl said. "Don't make me do this."

A blade materialised in her left hand.

***

SPARKLE HAD GONE WHITE-EYED, unconscious in Hargie's arms. He held her weight, a woman taller than himself. Her head fell back. He was staring at her neck. He'd always loved her neck, one of her best features. He smelled that old perfume on her.

"Sparkle?"

You're not the dying kind. You're not dying.

"Fight," he told her. *Whoever you are.* "*Fight.*"

***

SPARKLE TOOK A STEP BACK.

"I can't kill you here," Swirl said. "But I can take your limbs. I can make you a living head." The blade flashed silver each time the ceiling gave way to sky. She was eight strides away. Her expression softened. "Please, Sparkle. Do nothing. I'll walk us both to destiny."

Sparkle stepped back another step. She could do what Swirl asked. Easy. The smart choice.

"No, Swirl. No." Her voice squeaked, but she held her nerve. "I can't allow you to kill so many. *Please.* Think about it."

"They're not human," Swirl said. "They lost that long ago when their technology occluded them from the Geode. Be logical, Sparkle. Be sensible."

"Bit late in the game." All she could think to say. Sparkle stepped back further, around and behind the wide springed instrument.

"I'll maim you, sister," Swirl said. "I'll slice you up and none of this will matter, because moments from now the pain will be gone."

"I know," Sparkle said. She looked at the brass springs of the instrument before her, pointing up at different lengths. She concentrated on the largest.

"In moments, you won't care for those beasts," Swirl said. "You'll be an Ashemi, you'll be above the tangible world. Better than it."

"I know."

The large spring flew from its wooden holster and drove into Swirl's stomach. She yelled and stumbled back. Sparkle compelled the second largest forward, straight for Swirl's head, but Swirl dodged.

"Think I'm weak, don't you?" Sparkle said. "Outside, maybe. Not here. This is the mind. You can't rule me here!" She concentrated, fired off the remaining springs like ammo.

Swirl knocked the first away with her blade, second, third, fourth, the rest. The room echoed with the springs' reverberation.

Swirl glared at her, her face vanishing and appearing as the ceiling above flickered in and out of existence. One second the mirror of Sparkle's face torn by a grin, the next just a white grin and her eyes, a demon in the dark. Swirl reached down, twisted and pulled the spring from her belly, its brass dappled with gore. She threw it aside, breathed deep. The wound healed.

"Me and my body are one, Spar-ki-dar," Swirl said. "In here..." She stepped closer, glacier-slow. "I can fix myself in seconds. You can't. You're terrified by pain. For me it's all there is."

Sparkle compelled the springed instrument's mahogany weight toward Swirl. It collapsed on top of her.

"Sure looks it," Sparkle said.

For a moment Sparkle believed it finished. But when the smashed instrument began to move, Sparkle knew she'd been deluding herself.

She ran out of the music room, no plan left.

***

SWIRL PUSHED THE WOODEN WEIGHT to one side, got up. She tightened her fists and concentrated. Her ribs popped back into shape. She'd long practised fixing her wounds inside the villa, had expected something like this one day. She remembered the first time: looking in the mirror, an hour after her... experiment with Pearl in his bed while Sparkle toiled outside, sitting some exam. Swirl's torso slick with blood, the same blade as now in her hand. She'd stood there, forced the self-made wounds to vanish, and with them the shame. How had she let him? Whose idea had it even been? She didn't want to remember.

She shook herself down, took a breath. It seemed Sparkle had been planning for something like this too. Swirl was proud of her, shifting objects with her mind like that. Obvious, really.

But useless. Swirl couldn't be harmed. Neither could her child: it hadn't the awareness to comprehend this villa and its violence. She ran out of the room, into the corridor.

The corridor kept rippling, its walls and fittings like an inch-deep stream. Place was falling apart. Didn't matter. She would say goodbye to all of it. Accursed place.

Swirl heard footsteps. Sparkle's? The shadow-memory of Pearl?

"You can't win!" Swirl shouted, walking, blade ready. "You hear?" No reply. "Pheoni showed me the galaxy aflame, Sparkle! Worlds on fire! You want that?"

More footsteps. Swirl couldn't locate them. Sometimes above, sometimes either side of the corridor. Footsteps through shifting rooms. No stability.

She reached the foot of the stairs and leapt onto them before they moved out of view. Sparkle's bedroom lay at the top. Sort of place she'd hide. Whimper.

"Nice try with the telekinesis, Spar-ki-dar," Swirl called up the stairs. It was better to talk than be silent. The talk was breaking Sparkle. She knew her sister. "But you've lost the surprise. I'm a *killer*, my girl. Best in the galaxy. Feral space threw what it had at me. *And* your beloved Konsensus. Crushed them all. And you?" Swirl was three stairs away from the landing, away from Sparkle's bedroom door. The door stood ajar. "You had a breakdown, Spar-ki-dar, over mere exams. We had to look after you, remember? Me and Pearl, help you get better." No response. "Sparkle... you couldn't even get past those statues on the jetty. Remember that? When Pheoni visited? I could walk by them. You couldn't. Caught in their beauty. So weak."

She'd reached the door. Put her palm against it. No more chances. She lifted the blade.

"Maybe..." she heard Sparkle mutter, "...maybe that's why *you're* weak."

Swirl kicked the door open and the room exploded with feathers.

The mattress. Three swings and the blade covered the room. No one could have avoided it. But Sparkle wasn't there. The window lay open.

Swirl looked out the window, checked for traps. She saw Sparkle running faster than she'd ever seen her, halfway down the beach. Heading for the jetty.

The jetty startled Swirl. It lay between a void below it and the surface of the sea twenty feet above. The sea's depth had vanished entirely. The jetty itself had warped, twisting anti-clockwise on itself, a corkscrew.

Sparkle was heading for it, probably hoping to use her one remaining statue there as a weapon. Then no more ideas.

Swirl leapt from the villa window out onto the beach. Sand flew up and remained in the air. She burst through it and ran after Sparkle.

***

SPARKLE WATCHED HER SISTER RUN towards her across the beach. Swirl was horizontal to her, Sparkle horizontal to her sister, the jetty's stone length twisted to a slant. Divine killer, Swirl. Blade of the Delighted.

Sparkle was afraid. Afraid of Swirl. Afraid to be this. Protector of a people who would never thank her, who couldn't understand her or she them. Defying every god's will.

She looked at the statue before her. The boy's face, the boy she'd terrified in Silvercloud. She thought of Hargie's eyes by the river. Foreign creatures both. But the difference, oh, the difference between worlds wasn't so great. It wasn't. And that closeness, no matter how small, had to be fought for. *Someone* had to. Mm-yes.

Swirl ran at her. Sparkle focused.

***

SWIRL RAN DOWN THE JETTY, Sparkle and her statue righting to her point of reference the closer she got. No sister here, no mercy. Destiny greater than both. Swirl had to save the very galaxy.

"Make your play, Spar-ki-dar!" Swirl yelled. Throw that statue? Swirl would dodge it. Throw Swirl off the jetty? Swirl would get back, re-emerge, slice, slice and serve the Delighted. "Make your play!"

The statue--a statue of a boy--slid mere feet toward her. Too heavy. Sparkle couldn't move it.

Swirl laughed.

Sparkle met her gaze. She seemed to gaze through her. Past her.

An explosion behind, back on the beach. Swirl ducked and spun around.

The glasshouse. Sparkle had detonated the glasshouse. A blizzard of shards, steel, splinters, branches, dirt and sand raced toward them.

"Idiot." All Swirl could think to say. "Id--"

***

SPARKLE CLOSED HER EYES AND covered her ears, but she knew she'd be fine. She directed all this. The villa, the mind-place, all hers.

The sand and detritus cleared. Sparkle stepped over to the statue. She hadn't long.

She found her sister on the other side of the statue, body impaled by a thousand stakes: steel, glass, wood. Through her eyes, mouth, nose: her head a bloodied pulp of skin and bone and hair. Sparkle heard breathing.

"I love you, sister," Sparkle said. "But you leave me no choice."

The red pulp shuddered and moaned. The stakes began to push out.

No time. Sparkle ascended.

A slow ascent, seconds to load her psyche to the outside.

She felt a force behind her, racing, chasing her to their shared body.

:Please!: it sent :My baby! Pleeeaaa...:

Sparkle didn't reply.

***

"C'MON, GIRL," HARGIE SAID. "C'MON..."

Maybe he should get her medical attention. Shout for an Anointed, or...

Her pupils shook alive, darted about. Hargie couldn't help but laugh. She felt lighter in his arms. "Sparkle..."

She seemed to recognise him. She smiled. That look. Straight to his heart.

"I love you, Hargie Stukes," she said.

Hargie felt movement between their chests. A pistol slid in her mouth and fired.

CHAPTER FIFTEEN

*H*argie stood in the mist. She lay on the ground. She was like a painting, an icon. Some shit. Back of her head gone, hair gone. Her face pure, a mask. The gun had slid out when she. He had her gun in his hand now, she. He wasn't sure, couldn't remember. And a halo, red and bitty. Around her head. Sun streaks. Like. Like.

Must be hours. Hours all like this. Hargie. Hours.

"Who were you, girl?" he heard his voice say. "Who *were* you?"

Eyes were just another meat when they were dead. Nothing. Another meat.

Hours. Her face was turning water. World a pool, rippling. Hargie had to. Maybe. Could.

:*A curious sport.*:

Female voice. Tinkling. Behind.

Hargie turned. Shape before him but wet, blurred. Wiped eyes. Wipe.

Face on a stick. Carved, painted, looking at him. Pale white and horns and dragon face. Lady. Silver eyes.

:*Curious,*: it said. :*When severed.*:

The voice sounded far away. Sounded like a recording on a solid object, a disc or a cylinder, cut into some surface long, long ago. Delicate tinkle, a tinkle under voice.

:*Delighting*,: another voice said, male-female, but same sound beneath, same tinkle. Hargie recognised that voice.

Hargie looked toward it, saw another carved face on a stick. All of it blacked out, scratched. Except for a mouth. A grinning mouth.

:*Delighting*,: Female said.

Hargie turned back to look at her.

"But..." A million years since Hargie spoke. "She didn't cross your flames. Lost. Lost your... sliver."

:*No sliver*,: the carved female head said. :*Never was. And no rivalries. All of us... one.*:

Then why? He couldn't mouth the words.

:*Tease them out*,: said the male-female mouth. :*Watch them dance.*:

"Spindlies," Hargie muttered. Yeah. Feed 'em ratshit. Make 'em dance, give themselves away. No sliver. Never was. Not really. A lure. These guys... Hoidrac... sacrifice fleets for that. A world. What was a world for an edge, an edge over their hidden enemy, to draw them out?

What was a woman?

Hargie could feel blood in his mouth. He wasn't sure from where.

"She have to..." He couldn't say it. "That the plan?"

:*No*,: female said. Tinkle tinkle. :*Bu--*:

:*War coming*,: Mouth said, cutting into the female's moment. :*A nec--*:

The mouth-carving, the male-female, shattered, caught fire. Stopped talking.

:*No*,: the female said, shard of anger in it. :*No. Just broken little Triune. Sullied.*:

"What?" Hargie asked.

:*Useless*,: female stick said. :*But, ultimately, you, the dance...*: The face paused, as if savouring Hargie. "*Her. Her. Her. All delighting all. Entertained us.*"

"Fuh..."

:Entertaining. Entertaining.: More voices, other faces on sticks joined her. Tinkle-tinkle. *:Entertaining. Entertaining. ENTERTAINING. ENTERTAINING. ENTERTAINING. ENTERTAINING. ENTERTAINING. ENTERTAINING. ENTERTAINING. ENTERTAINING. ENTERTAINING. ENTERTAINING. ENTERTAINING. ENTERTAINING--:*

Hargie lifted the gun and fired, blew the wooden bitch's head away. Still she wouldn't stop. None of them stopped.

:ENTERTAINING. ENTERTAINING. ENTERTAINING. ENTERTAINING. ENTERTAINING. ENTERTAINING. ENTERTAINING. ENTERTAINING. ENTERTAINING.:

Hargie fired again and again, blowing heads off sticks.

"Jokers, huh?" he said between shots. *Boom, boom.*

:ENTERTAINING. ENTERTAINING. ENTERTAINING. ENTERTAINING.:

Boom, another head, *boom.* Then he fired again, again toward the distant flames, that motherfucking ratshit Geode.

"Think you can joke forever?" *Boom, boom.* "Huh?" *Boom.* "Think you can joke forever?"

The ammo ran out and the pistol whirred. Nothing but whirr. The heads had stopped speaking.

Hargie let go of the trigger.

He could hear laughter again. Different: human. Slow claps, off in the mist.

***

FUNNY. MELID HAD TO HAND it to them. Funny little heads.

Had to hand it to them. *Played us,* she thought. *Had us thinking extinction. Made us dance.* Had to hand it to them.

She kept clapping. Fingers at angles, but no pain. Her suit medicating, fixing all wounds but inside. Inside the head.

Melid. Melidy, Melidy, Melidy... the thought echoed. The world a hole. An absence, this universe. Melidy Melidy falling forever through it. But had to laugh. Laugh, Melid, laugh. Feel laughter disperse, touching nothing.

No kollective. Melid wasn't kollective. Kollective needed two, minimum, not one. What was one? Nothing. One was corpse person, puppet-man. Melid was corpse, nothing, puppet, falling in nothing, carrion, stretching out to nothing, foetus in endless wombmachine alone, baby drifting, drifting nowhere. Joke. Melid laughed.

A shadow passed over her. A face. Mister Hargie Stukes.

Silly. Face screwed and wet. That meant pain. Silly.

You've no one, puppet-man, she thought. *Corpse man. Your female died with a head-pop. Pop! Corpses and carrion eaters, us. Corpses.*

She laughed and felt face run wet. Felt wet warmth in suit. Silly animal, Stukes.

He ducked from view. She heard ammo barrel, the *click-clack.*

Hargie Stukes came into view again. His face still, unwrinkled. Dry. His dead eyes met Melid's.

Melid giggled. He pointed a pistol at her and she laughed.

Do it. Konsensus safe. Nothing mattered. *Do it.*

The gun shivered, but Mister Hargie Stukes was still as rock.

Her laugh dropped to a smile. She gave her mind up to the greater hum, the...

But of course it wasn't there, the hum. Just hollow, thoughts falling through nothing. No hum. Smile flicker like dying light. She forced the smile back to her face, offered its obscenity. *I like that your Sparkle died,* she offered in the smile, *I like your pain, do you see, Mister Hargie Stukes? Do you see that?*

His face didn't change. She couldn't read that, why it would do that?

She wanted the hum. Anything. Hum of Konsensus. The feel of anyone.

What did his face mean? What thoughts? Just pull the...

Her smile had gone. Couldn't hold. Didn't think she'd still be here, looking at that face.

Alone. Alone and... No one should die alone. No. Wrong, that. No.

His face gave nothing, and she heard whimpering. She didn't want to whimper. Kend had whimpered. When Melid had... Melid must have seemed like Hargie Stukes to Kend. Unreadable. Corpse. She must have felt...

Body squirmed. Limbs shifting. Couldn't get up.

Make a face, Mister Hargie Stukes. Give me a face.

His face blurred. But not enough, it wouldn't go. Her eyes stung, and warm lines rolled over her cheeks. Dripped. High whine from throat and when her lips closed made it worse. She didn't...

Not this, not alone. Not alone, falling and nothing after. No thoughts, no Melid. This wasn't meant to happen alone. To die. She'd never expected...

She tried to sentiment, to emote herself. Nothing. Stunted things, Melid and Stukes.

His face. Dead as universe. Dead.

"Please," she heard a female say. Jiang. Naked Jiang, no emotic. "Please..."

His face. Nothing. Blank.

"Please..."

She didn't want it like this. She couldn't. Not to die. Please. *Please.*

"*Pleassse...*"

She didn't want--

PART SIX

DEEP SPACE

James Worrad

CHAPTER SIXTEEN

"What's with the beast?" Aewyn Nuke asked.

Hargie looked up at the stuffed animal over the bar, the one between the snacks and the contraceptive serums.

"Native to here," Hargie said. He poured Aewyn's shot and passed it over the bar to him. "Sorta."

"And?"

"You really wanna know?" Hargie asked.

Aewyn seemed to think about this. "Do I, fuck." He took a sip of the whiskey and winced. "'Nough beasts in life as is."

"Can't choose your family," Hargie said. He picked up a cloth and wiped the bar's surface.

"Me aunty Horthie," Aewyn said. "She's a right fucking animal. 'Specially in her day."

Hargie smelled a story coming. Good stories, Aewyn. But Hargie felt outta sorts. Like he was expecting something his brain knew would never happen. Not ever. Just one of those weird feelings you get, time to time.

"That so?" Hargie said. He glanced away from Aewyn a mo-mo, over to the man drinking at the far end, next to the toilets. He wore a black pinstripe onesuit, a wide-brimmed hat that obscured his face. One of Hargie's totalist staff had served him earlier. Hargie hadn't seen the guy's face. Off-worlder. You had to keep an eye on off-worlders.

"Oh fuckin' 'ell," Aewyn said. "Booze, cock and gamblin': that's aunty's particular hamster wheel."

"Real can-do spirit." Hargie poured a shot for himself. "Inspiring."

"She's the change she wants to see in the world, aunty." Aewyn took another sip. "So there's these two corporate types, right, off-world, not Freightways but the same kinda shit. Executive couple. Executive One: he wants a fucking kid, isn't it? A baby. And Executive Two, well, he just wants Executive One happy. Happens, that: people reach a certain age and think liquid shit and screaming's the answer."

"Tune," agreed Hargie.

Aewyn clinked his glass against Hargie's. "Tune. Anyways, they knows aunty Horthie, see? See she's got a certain Calranese vitality, strong hips and that. More to the point, nova-sized debts to pay."

"Wait," Hargie said. "How these execudicks know your aunty?"

"Dunno," Aewyn said. "Brain laundering, probs. Pa had got her to run that end of the biz. Ew move in a lot of high circles with that lark."

"Figures," Hargie said. He took a sip of his shot and, though he knew it should have burnt, it didn't.

Aewyn continued. "'All your debts, love, paid off', Executive One tells her. 'Lease us your womb'. Or words to that effect. So she looks 'em up and down, aunty, spies their muscles and their perfect cheekbones-- remember they're rich bastards born of rich bastards, gen-fixed and sculpted and shit--and says 'I'll knock you down a third if you knock me up old school.' Executive One don't like minge but he wants a baby, see, and Executive Two goes on about, sure, this is like handmade artisanal baby-making, but secretly he probably swings and is a tight cunt with his rupees."

"Don't get that rich throwing lakh around," Hargie said.

"Tell me about it." Aewyn sighed, shook his head. He waved his glass at Hargie, and Hargie poured him another. "Long story short, aunty's got these two tanned off-world Adonises spit-roasting her on command. Executive One in the front door, Executive Two in the tradesman's."

"Ratshit," Hargie said.

"Swear. She's convinced Two it's symbolic on his part, which convinces One who, let's be fair now, probably needs Two there to maintain rigidity. Suitably gangbanged, aunty takes her money and heads down the bookies. Every Wednesday for five-fucking-months."

"Fairytale romance." Hargie took another sip. No burn.

"Not over, Harg-o," Aewyn said. "Uncle Myfwyn hears about it, see. Aunty's been mouthing off to everyone in the bookies who'll listen. Well, you would, you fucking knows you would. So uncle pays the execs a little visit..."

"He tear 'em new a-holes?" Hargie asked.

"He's hardly gonna pin medals on their chests, is he? Fucking his missus, man. So he kicks the door down at their fucking boardroom, front of their boss--"

"Wait," Hargie said. "He just walks into a interstellar corp board room?"

"No," Aewyn said, "like I say, he *kicks* the door down and--"

"They got sensors, guards." Hargie looked over at the man at the end of the bar. The guy was still looking at his drink, hat's brim still obscuring his face. "Ratshit."

"S'how I was tolds it," Aewyn said. "Shit, man, I was barely a glint in the pool cleaner's eye when it happened. Story doesn't have to be *true* to be true, bubbletit. Not hundred percent, anyways..."

Hargie looked at Aewyn. He seemed a little hurt. They'd both had it rough of late, though Hargie couldn't remember why.

"Sorry, man," Hargie told his friend. "Continue."

351

"Appreciated. Well, Uncle Myfwyn wants answers, answers that the two Execs can't get out their dental-worked mouths fast enough. No harm meant, they say. Baby, they say. *Money.* Shit, they say, didn't she *tell* you?"

Aewyn shook his head. He continued:

"'No', says Uncle Myfwyn. Then he laughs. 'What?' Executives say. 'Joke's on you two pricks,' Uncle tells 'em. 'She had her tubes snipped ten years ago!'"

Hargie laughed, kinda. But not. That was the way with most laughter.

"What happened to Aunty Horthie?" he asked Aewyn.

"Two years locked in the Wash. Pa had to do something, way the executives' boss were going on."

"Tough gig," Hargie said.

"Ah, I dunno. She was a sex offender, when you think about it." Aewyn shrugged, sipped.

Hargie looked over at the man along the bar, then back to Aewyn again.

"So what's the lesson?" Hargie asked.

"What?" Aewyn said.

"There a moral?"

"Not in me Aunty Horthie's vicinity," Aewyn said.

Hargie's face must have been sad, because Aewyn clearly noticed.

"Harg', man," he said. "Always felching for meaning, you are. Like every fucker, thinking it's reality's job to dish it out. Nothing--shit, man---no *one*, exists to dish it out. Gotta snatch whatever crumbs from the buffet yourself." He lifted his glass and inspected the gold nectar therein. "When you have it, enjoy it. And when it's gone..." He downed the shot, slammed the empty glass on the table. "Remember you had it. Because you *had* it. And that's how it is."

The man in the pinstripe onesuit thumbed the tip-ball on the bar. He got up from his stool and headed for the door. On his way out, in one fluid motion, he turned his head toward Hargie and made a 'shush' gesture.

Hargie never saw his eyes, nor most of his face, but he saw a grinning mouth, shiny-fanged. And across it, vertical and centre, a taloned green finger.

Shush. Keep it under your hat, Hargie Stukes. That's what the man meant.

Hargie looked back at him. A look that said *Good day, safe journey, but don't be coming back in here. Keep your secret, whatever it is. This here's my bar.*

"Another?" Hargie said to Aewyn.

"Best not," his old friend said, grinning. "Have you heard the way I'm chompsing on here? Shit, man..."

***

HARGIE HAD FALLEN ASLEEP IN his clothes. He couldn't remember when he'd changed them last. His crotch felt sore at the joints, elastic of his underwear like bandsaws. He'd left his hat somewhere, he wasn't sure.

He was staring at the ceiling of his quarters. Where else?

Hargie got up from the dirty sheets and sat on the edge of his bed, sat a long while. He'd had some dream. His chin shook and he started to weep. His body, with all its old scars and new bruises, shook too. He wept long.

"What's the fucking lesson?" he said to no one.

The gun was on the soap dish above his sink. Nine shots left. He hadn't thought to get rid of it. He looked at the barrel's business end, wondered how cold it must have felt on her lips.

He cried a little more, then he picked it up. He'd need it soon. He saw a man's face in the mirror. Red eyes. Eyes he didn't know.

He made his way to the cargo hold. The door whirled open and Hargie stepped through.

She looked at him, her head the only part of her sticking out of the translucent chrysalis or whatever the heck it was. Fixed bones and flesh, the Anointed had told him. None of that weird Geode shit, though. Just basic, this chrysalis. Human-made.

"Looking better," he told her.

Melid said nothing. Looked away, acted disinterested, as if looking at Hargie was embarrassing.

"Have you outta there," Hargie said. "Couple days."

Nothing. But Hargie knew she was no vegetable. She was aware, aware as anyone.

"Well," Hargie said. "Thought I'd tell you." Yesterday he'd told her they'd come out the lockwyrm, were back home, and she hadn't said shit.

Bored, he turned to walk away.

"I can't feel them," Melid said. "I should feel them by now. Out here."

He turned back to look at her. "They don't want you."

"...I know."

One long journey, Hargie thought, *and for what?* Two broken lumps of flesh.

"Remember that system with the rig you wiped?" Hargie said. "The thousands you killed?"

She made a face like he'd said something stupid. "Here it comes. 'Justice'."

"There's a world nearby," he said, "town where everyone's neuralware's linked up. Totalists. Do nothing but watch each other shit all day. You'd love it."

"You've a gun in your hand," Melid said.

"Mercy? That it?"

"My people cannot abide waste."

"Been preparing your speech there," Hargie said.

"I'm *waste*, Hargie Stukes. Beyond--"

"I saw your eyes!" Hargie yelled. "You wanted to live! Stop acting like it don't mean shit! You and all your rock assholes! Stop acting like it don't mean shit!"

His shouting echoed, metallic, off the walls of the empty hold. He felt stupid. He looked at her, but she didn't look at him.

"C'mon," he said. "Two weeks. Two weeks with the Totals and if you're still bawling, I'll shoot you myself." He put the gun in his jacket pocket. No danger here. "All I ask."

Melid said nothing, an example Hargie followed. He headed for the hatch.

"Mr Stukes," she called out. "Mr Stukes..."

He looked across the hold at her.

"Why?" she said.

A face framed in a translucent machine. Her eyes were too distant to get any measure of. His must have been, too.

"I'm bubblefolk," he said. "Figure it out."

***

THE WALLS OF HIS COCKPIT were bare and metallic. How he liked them. He didn't need a visual, had it all in his neural: stellar position, speed, grav-field. All he needed. Visuals were for passengers, tourists.

His head felt weird. A little dizzy, an odd warmth rising. Dehydration, surely. He got in his seat and readied to jump. Alnar system first. He was a wanted man now. Alnar was a dandy hole for wanted men.

Fuck it. One look wouldn't hurt. He blinked and the walls turned to deep space, a sun not so far away. He pictured a beautiful woman in a shirt, standing in the cockpit, waltzing barelegged between stars. Gazing in wonder. Smiling her smile.

He didn't suppose he'd smile again.

Shit. Lotta stars out here. Stupid, but the thought cracked him hard. And when you multiplied for planets...

People. Countless people, all inside their own heads, as far from another's as a star from a star. There was the problem, right there. Bet your ball-sack, Jack.

Or maybe, Hargie Stukes, maybe there was beauty.

He shook it off. Dumb. Ratshit. Just this damn headache or whatever it was. He brought up a window in the top left corner of his eye, set coordinates and--

:Erm... hello?:

ABOUT THE AUTHOR

JAMES LIVES IN LEICESTER, ENGLAND, and has for almost all his life. Currently he shares a house with a cat and another writer. He works for a well-known brand of hotel, an occupation that never leaves him short of writing material.

He has a degree in classical studies from Lampeter University, Wales. He has found this invaluable to his growth as a science fiction and fantasy writer in that he soon discovered how varied and peculiar human cultures can be.

In 2011 James attended Clarion, the prestigious six-week SF workshop held at the University of California, San Diego. There, he studied under some of the genre's leading professionals and also got to see a lot of wild hummingbirds.

He's had short stories published by Daily Science Fiction, Flurb, Newcon Press and Obverse Books. He also writes screen plays for short films, one of which- Flawless- won the Seven/Five Film Festival Award and was selected for both the Cannes and NYC Independent film festivals. (It was also screened at CERN, home of the Large Hadron Collider).

He's a regular face on the science fiction convention scene. Should you see him at one feel free to say hello.

BOOKS BY JAMES WORRAD

CONNECT WITH THE AUTHOR

Find James here:
http://www.castrumpress.com/james-worrad/

James Worrad

CASTRUM PRESS PRESENTS

FUTURE DAYS

A Science Fiction Short Story Collction

Hitch a thrilling ride into the future days of humanity.

Featuring:
USA TODAY bestselling author Christopher Nuttall
Amazon #1 bestselling author Rick Partlow
Amazon #1 bestselling author PP Corcoran
Irish Writers' Centre Novel Fair Award Winner R. B. Kelly

Visit: www.castrumpress.com/SciFi-Fantasy-books/Future-Days-Anthology

Made in the USA
Las Vegas, NV
17 August 2021